# THE DROWNED HORSE CHRONICLE VOLUME ONE

## THE FORREST YEARS

DAVID BOOP

WOLFPACK
PUBLISHING
— EST 2013 —

**The Drowned Horse Chronicle Volume One: The Forrest Years**
Paperback Edition
Copyright © 2022 David Boop

Wolfpack Publishing
5130 S. Fort Apache Rd. 215-380
Las Vegas, NV 89148

wolfpackpublishing.com

Paperback ISBN 978-1-63977-505-7
eBook ISBN 978-1-63977-418-0
LCCN 2022943766

"The Metal Skins" originally published in *Six Guns Straight from Hell 3* by SFT Publishing, 2020. Edited by David B Riley and J.A. Campbell.

"Where Justice Ends, Vengeance Begins" originally published in *Menagerie de Mystique* by Fantasia Divinity Magazine, 2018. Edited by Amber M. Simpson and Madeline L. Stout.

"Kit Carson Vs the Toad Men of the Rio Gila" originally published in *Gears and Levers 3* by Sky Warrior Book Publishing, 2013. Edited by Phyllis Irene Radford.

"The Dragon and the Shark" originally published in *The Old Weird South* by QW Publishers, 2013. Edited by Tim Westover.

"Love...in the Age of the Weird West" originally published in *Science Fiction Trails Magazine Issue #14.* by Science Fiction Trails Press, 2019. Edited by David B Riley.

"Unlocking the Gates of Fear" originally published in *Particular*

*Passages* by Knight Writing Press, March, 2021. Edited by Sam Knight.

"Sinking to the Level of Demons" originally published in *Penny Dread Tales 4: Perfidious and Paranormal Punkery of Steam* by RuneWright Publishing, May, 2014. Edited by Christopher Ficco.

"Dragon Draw" originally published in *Science Fiction Trails Magazine Issue #11* by Science Fiction Trails Press, 2014. Edited by David B. Riley.

# THE DROWNED HORSE CHRONICLE VOLUME ONE

# THE DROWNED HORSE CHRONICLE
## A PRIMER

You hold in your hands my 1/3rd life's work. It's not a full-life's work or even half. I'm 53-years-old, and it's currently 2022 as I type. The Drowned Horse Chronicle started in 2007 with the publication of "The Rag Doll Kid" in *Tales of the Talisman* magazine. For those of you not expecting a math test, that means this train left the station in Colorado and traveled fifteen years, or 3.5333% of my time on Earth.

"Well," you might ask, "if it's taken up that much of your life, what exactly am I about to read?"

Good question.

As you may know, Bob, [or insert name of choice here], a chronicle is a record of events, often factual, and presented in a linear order. In that regard, this is indeed a chronicle. It's the tale of the fictional (and cursed) town of Drowned Horse in the Arizona Territory, which may or may not resemble a town where I once resided [for which the name has been changed to protect the not-so innocent—me. I won't go on record that the town I lived in was also cursed, but after twenty-five years+ there, I can't rightly say that it wasn't, neither]. Chronicles, by their nature lend to a particular writing style that we hadn't seen so much of in decades past, but has grown more popular due to digital books, push technology, collaborative storytelling, and Tik Tokin': and that is the mosaic novel.

According to Wikipedia, mosaic novels are a "novel in which individual chapters or short stories share a common setting or set of characters with the aim of telling a linear story from beginning to end, with the individual chapters, however, refracting a plurality of viewpoints and styles." Author Jo Walton described the mosaic novel on Tor.com in this way: "[It] builds up a picture of a world and a story obliquely, so that the whole is more than the sum of the parts." I like this definition better. Classic examples of this type of storytelling include *As I Lay Dying*, by William Faulkner, *Wild Cards* written and edited by George R.R. Martin, and *Thieves' World* written and edited by Robert Lynn Asprin.

So yes, this chronicle is also a mosaic novel built on individual stories that I've blended into a single narrative. The stories are [mostly] linear and focused on the lives of people living in a cursed Arizona town between the years of 1865 and 1871. Those were the early years for the territory; recently separated from New Mexico and given a chance to create its own identity. As mentioned, I wrote the first DHC story in 2006 for the Tony Hillerman Mystery Short Story Contest. In it, an outlaw wakes up dead and his ghost has to solve his own murder. Even though it didn't win, I sold the story shortly afterward to editor David Lee Summers. He enlightened me to the notion I'd written a weird Western—a genre he loved and often published.

"What's a 'weird Western'?" I'd asked.

He explained that any Western crossed with another genre, usually horror, but sometimes science fiction or fantasy could be considered a weird western.

That summed up what I'd written quite nicely. After the story hit the pages of his magazine, *Tales of the Talisman*, I received an email from another editor, David B. Riley [R.I.P.] who said he liked my weird western very much and would I write him a science fiction-themed story for his *Science Fiction Trails* magazine?

Heck, yeah, I would.

I hadn't named the town my first story took place in but for the next story, I decided on "Drowned Horse" after Dead Horse State Park in Cottonwood, AZ. I added to the mythology, creating a sheriff for the town. This time my lawman would face off against aliens looking for the fastest gun on Earth in "Grismal Guffeyfeld's Quickdrawatorium."

Riley was so happy, he asked me if I'd be in his first horror western anthology *Six-Guns Straight from Hell*. "Bleeding the Bank Dry" would be told from the POV of a vampire which ended with a very nice twist thanks to co-editor Laura Givens.

[Just in case you're wondering, those three stories will be in DHC – Volumes 2 & 3 respectively.]

I now had three published Drowned Horse stories and yet, the first didn't fit neatly with the second two, who featured the same lawman. I needed to build a timeline and place these stories on it because—before I knew it—I'd received more requests to write weird westerns, and steampunk tales, and holiday-themed vignettes, all that I could set in Drowned Horse. I created reoccurring characters, wrote in multiple genres, and devised the origin of the curse. This wouldn't be a natural curse, of course, just some sort of residue off a spiritual land. No, it had to have been placed by someone...which meant that it could also be removed someday.

I also stopped using generic terms for things like Indians, guns, horses, etc. I wanted to bring a deeper level of realism to my world. I delved into research on Arizona, finding more prompts for stories. As of 2021, I had written about thirty stories of which twenty found professional publication.

My timeline turned into three distinct eras:

"The Forrest Years," the volume you hold in your hands;

"The Lawless Years," when chaos runs rampant in the Verde Valley;

And "The Last Stand of Drowned Horse," the penultimate arc before I'd wrap up everything in a full-length novel.

I also wrote side story novels, flash fictions, and occasional weird westerns that had nothing to do with Drowned Horse because I couldn't make the theme fit into my narrative.

Real personages from history would pass through and intermingle with my fictional characters. Those characters would change along the way. Some transformations were subtle, others more dramatic. Their goal was always removing the curse, but not all would see that dream a reality. If you accompany me on this trail to the end, you'll experience loss of characters I hope you've grown to love as much as I have, and I apologize ahead for the tears you might shed. I guarantee you weren't alone.

Overall, I could see the whole arc, knew the stories I'd need to write still, and had my vision of a final battle. I grew restless to sell the series to someone willing to ride with me through the Arizona desert.

At the 2021 Western Writers of America conference in Loveland, CO, I met Jake Bray of Wolfpack Publishing, who patiently listened as I laid out my world and my plans. Jake got onboard with my plan and agreed on a mosaic novel approach, as opposed to turning the stories into "chapters," and thus removing the dime novel feel. He, like me, wanted a novel that read like a great season of T.V. After we struck a deal, I went to work finishing this first part of my opus.

Then things got real.

I had, at best, a short story collection, not a mosaic novel. The stories weren't cohesive yet, and large gaps existed in the narrative. Some were intentional, as I hope someday to do a shared-world anthology with other popular weird Western writers exploring the "Lost Tales of Drowned Horse," but others were accidental. For this novel, I'd have to write ten new stories, add new characters, and introduce the curse in a way that felt natural and real. I spent months tying in all the previously written shorts with the new ones. When story chronology changed, events from the "real world" needed to be altered alongside them. I walked a tightrope between reality and fantasy, but it was worth it. For after all the years of stress, tears, prayer, and hope, I'm finally able to present to you, for your reading pleasure, the first act in my Drowned Horse Chronicle.

Enjoy.

D.B.
06/30/22

# ALLEGRO
## NOQOÌLPI THE GAMBLER

Some time before, there had descended among the Pueblos, from the heavens, a divine gambler or gambling-god, named *Noqoìlpi*, or He-who-wins-men (at play); his talisman was a great piece of turquoise. When he came, he challenged the people to all sorts of games and contests, and in all of these he was successful. He won from them, first their property, then their women and children, and finally some of the men themselves. Then he told them he would give them part of their property back in payment if they would build a great house; so when the Navajos came, the Pueblos were busy building in order that they might release their enthralled relatives and their property. They were also busy making a race-track, and preparing for all kinds of games of chance and skill.

When all was ready, and four days' notice had been given, twelve men came from the neighboring pueblo of *Kinçolíj*, or Blue-house, to compete with the great gambler. They bet their own persons, and after a brief contest they lost themselves to *Noqoìlpi*. Again a notice of four days was given, and again twelve men of *Kinçolíj*—relatives of the former twelve—came to play, and these also lost themselves. For the third time an announcement, four days in advance of a game, was given; this time some women were among the twelve contestants, and they, too, lost themselves. All were put to work on the building of *Kintyèl* as soon as they forfeited their liberty. At the end of another four days the children of these men and women came to try to win back their parents, but they succeeded only in adding themselves to the number of the gambler's slaves. On a fifth trial, after four days' warning, twelve leading men of Blue-house were lost, among them the chief of the pueblo. On a sixth duly announced gambling-day twelve more men, all important persons, staked their liberty and lost it. Up to this time the Navajos had kept count of the winnings of *Noqoìlpi*, but afterwards people from other pueblos came in such numbers to play and lose that they could keep count no longer. In addition to their own persons the later victims brought in beads, shells, turquoise, and all sorts of valuables, and gambled them away. With the labor of all these slaves it was not long until the great *Kintyèl* was finished.

But all this time the Navajos had been merely spectators, and had taken no part in the games. One day the voice of the beneficent god *Qastcèyalçi* was heard faintly in the distance crying his usual call "hu`hu`hu`hu`."

His voice was heard, as it is always heard, four times, each time nearer and nearer, and immediately after the last call, which was loud and clear, *Qastcèyalçi* appeared at the door of a hut where dwelt a young couple who had no children, and with them he communicated by means of signs. He told them that the people of *Kinçolíj* had lost at game with *Noqoìlpi* two great shells, the greatest treasures of the pueblo; that the Sun had coveted these shells, and had begged them from the gambler; that the latter had refused the request of the Sun and the Sun was angry. In consequence of all this, as *Qastcèyalçi* related, in twelve days from his visit certain divine personages would meet in the mountains, in a place which he designated, to hold a great ceremony. He invited the young man to be present at the ceremony, and disappeared.

The Navajo kept count of the passing days; on the

twelfth day he repaired to the appointed place, and there he found a great assemblage of the *Yei*. There were *Qastcèyalçi*, *Qastcèqogan* and his son, *Níltci*, the Wind, *Tcalyèl*, the Darkness, *Tcàapani*, the Bat, *Klictsò*, the Great Snake, *Tsilkàli*, *Nasísi*, the Gopher, and many others. Beside these, there were present a number of pets or domesticated animals belonging to the gambler, who were dissatisfied with their lot, were anxious to be free, and would gladly obtain their share of the spoils in case their master was ruined. *Níltci*, the Wind, had spoken to them, and they had come to enter into the plot against *Noqoìlpi*. All night the gods danced and sang, and performed their mystic rites, for the purpose of giving to the son of *Qastcèqogan* powers as a gambler equal to those of *Noqoìlpi*. When the morning came they washed the young neophyte all over, dried him with [corn] meal, dressed him in clothes exactly like those the gambler wore, and in every way made him look as much like the gambler as possible, and then they counseled as to what other means they should take to outwit *Noqoìlpi*.

In the first place, they desired to find out how he felt about having refused to his father, the Sun, the two great shells.

"I will do this," said *Níltci*, the Wind, "for I can penetrate everywhere, and no one can see me;" but the others said, "No, you can go everywhere, but you cannot travel without making a noise and disturbing people. Let *Tcalyèl*, the Darkness, go on this errand, for he also goes wherever he wills, yet he makes no noise."

So *Tcalyèl* went to the gambler's house, entered his room, went all through his body while he slept, and searched well his mind, and he came back saying, "*Noqoìlpi* is sorry for what he has done."

*Níltci*, however, did not believe this; so, although his services had been before refused, he repaired to the chamber where the gambler slept, and went all through his body and searched well his mind; but he, too, came back saying *Noqoìlpi* was sorry that he had refused to give the great shells to his father.

One of the games they proposed to play is called *çàka-çqadsàç*, or the thirteen chips; it is played with thirteen thin flat pieces of wood, which are colored red on one side and left white or uncolored on the other side. Success depends on the number of chips, which, being thrown upward, fall with their white sides up.

"Leave the game to me," said the Bat; "I have made thirteen chips that are white on both sides. I will hide myself in the ceiling, and when our champion throws up his chips I will grasp them and throw down my chips instead."

Another game they were to play is called *nanjoj*; it is played with two long sticks or poles, of peculiar shape and construction with one marked with red and the other with black, and a single hoop. A long many-tailed string, called the "turkey-claw," is secured to the center of each pole.

"Leave *nanjoj* to me," said the Great Snake. "I will hide myself in the hoop and make it fall where I please."

Another game was one called *tsínbetsil*, or push-on-the-wood; in this the contestants push against a tree until it is torn from its roots and falls.

"I will see that this game is won," said *Nasísi*, the Gopher; "I will gnaw the roots of the tree, so that he who shoves it may easily make it fall."

In the game of *tcol*, or ball, the object was to hit the ball so that it would fall beyond a certain line.

"I will win this game for you," said the little bird, *Tsilkàli*, "for I will hide within the ball, and fly with it wherever I want to go. Do not hit the ball hard; give it only a light tap, and depend on me to carry it."

The pets of the gambler begged the Wind to blow hard, so that they might have an excuse to give their master for not keeping due watch when he was in danger, and in the morning the Wind blew for them a strong gale. At dawn the whole party of conspirators left the mountain, and came down to the brow of the *cañon* to watch until sunrise.

*Noqoìlpi* had two wives, who were the prettiest women in the whole land. Wherever she went, each carried in her hand a stick with something tied on the end of it, as a sign that she was the wife of the great gambler.

It was their custom for one of them to go every morning at sunrise to a neighboring spring to get water. So at sunrise the watchers on the brow of the cliff saw one of the wives coming out of the gambler's house with a water jar on her head, whereupon the son of *Qastcèqogan* descended into the *cañon*, and followed her to the spring. She was not aware of his presence until she had filled her water-jar; then she supposed it to be her own husband, whom the youth was dressed and adorned to represent, and she allowed him to approach her. She soon discovered her error, however, but deeming it prudent to say nothing, she suffered him to follow her into the house. As he entered, he observed that many of the slaves had already assembled; perhaps they were aware that some trouble was in store for their master. The latter looked up with an angry face; he felt jealous when he saw the stranger entering immediately after his wife. He said nothing of this, however, but asked at once the important question, "Have you come to gamble with me?" This he repeated four times, and each time the young *Qastcèqogan* said "No." Thinking the stranger feared to play with him, *Noqoìlpi* went on challenging him recklessly.

"I'll bet myself against yourself;"

"I'll bet my feet against your feet;"

"I'll bet my legs against your legs;"

and so on he offered to bet every and any part of his body against the same part of his adversary, ending by mentioning his hair.

In the meantime the party of divine ones, who had been watching from above, came down, and people from the neighboring pueblos came in, and among these were two boys, who were dressed in costumes similar to those worn by the wives of the gambler. The young *Qastcèqogan* pointed to these and said, "I will bet my wives against your wives."

The great gambler accepted the wager, and the four persons, two women and two mock women, were placed sitting in a row near the wall. First they played the game of thirteen chips. The Bat assisted, as he had promised the son of *Qastcèqogan*, and the latter soon won the game, and with it the wives of *Noqoìlpi*.

This was the only game played inside the house; then all went out of doors, and games of various kinds were played. First they tried *nanjoj*. The track already prepared lay east and west, but, prompted by the wind god, the stranger insisted on having a track made from north to south, and again, at the bidding of the Wind, he chose the red stick. The son of *Qastcèqogan* threw the wheel: at first it seemed about to fall on the gambler's pole, in the "turkey-claw" of which it was entangled, but to the great surprise of the gambler it extricated itself, rolled farther on, and fell on the pole of his opponent. The latter ran to pick up the ring, lest *Noqoìlpi* in doing so might hurt the Snake inside, but the gambler was so angry that he threw his stick away and gave up the game, hoping to do better in the next contest, which was that of pushing down trees.

For this the great gambler pointed out two small trees, but his opponent insisted that larger trees must be found. After some search they agreed upon two of good size, which grew close together, and of these the wind-god told the youth which one he must select. The gambler strained with all his might at his tree, but could not move it, while his opponent, when his turn came, shoved the other tree prostrate with little effort, for its roots had all been severed by the Gopher.

Then followed a variety of games, on which *Noqoìlpi* staked his wealth in shells and precious stones, his houses, and many of his slaves, and lost all.

The last game was that of the ball. On the line over which the ball was to be knocked all the people were assembled: on one side were those who still remained slaves; on the other side were the freedmen and those who had come to wager themselves, hoping to rescue their kinsmen. *Noqoìlpi* bet on this game the last of his slaves and his own person. The gambler struck his ball a heavy blow, but it did not reach the line; the stranger gave his but a light tap, and the bird within it flew with it far beyond the line, where at the released captives jumped over the line and joined their people.

The victor ordered all the shell beads and precious stones and the great shells to be brought forth. He gave the beads and shells to *Qastcèyalçi*, that they might be distributed among the gods; the two great shells were given to the Sun.

In the meantime, *Noqoìlpi* sat to one side saying bitter things, bemoaning his fate, and cursing and threatening his enemies:

"I will kill you all with the lightning. I will send war and disease among you. May the cold freeze you! May the fire burn you! May the waters drown you!" he cried.

"He has cursed enough," whispered *Níltci* to the son of *Qastcèqogan*. "Put an end to his angry words." So the young victor called *Noqoìlpi* to him, and said, "You have bet yourself and have lost; you are now my slave and must do my bidding. You are not a god, for my power has prevailed against yours."

The victor had a bow of magic power named *Eçin C-ilyil*, or the Bow of Darkness: he bent this upwards, and placing the string on the ground, he bade his illustrious slave stand on the string; then he shot *Noqoìlpi* up into the sky as if he had been an arrow. Up and up he went, growing smaller and smaller to the sight till he faded to a mere speck, and finally disappeared altogether. As he flew upwards he was heard to mutter in the angry tones of abuse and imprecation, until he was too far away to be heard, but no one could distinguish anything he said as he ascended.

He flew up in the sky until he came to the home of *Bekot-cic-e*, the god who carries the moon, and who is supposed by the Navajos to be identical with the god of the Americans.

He is very old, and dwells in a long row of stone houses. When *Noqoìlpi* arrived at the house of *Bekotcic-e*, he related to the latter all his misadventures in the lower world and said, "Now I am poor, and this is why I have come to see you."

"You need be poor no longer," said *Bekotcic-e*. "I will provide for you."

So he made for the gambler pets or domestic animals of new kinds, different to those which he had in the Chaco valley. He made for him sheep, asses, horses, swine, goats, and fowls. He also gave him *bayeta*, and other cloths of bright colors, more beautiful than those woven by his slaves at *Kintyèl*. He made, too, a new people, the Mexicans, for the gambler to rule over, and then he sent him back to this world again, but he descended far to the south of his former abode, and reached the earth in old Mexico.

*Noqoìlpi's* people increased greatly in Mexico, and after a while they moved toward the north, and built towns along the Rio Grande. *Noqoìlpi* came with them until they arrived at a place north of Santa Fé. There they ceased building, and he returned to old Mexico, where he still lives, and where he is now the *Nakài C-igíni*, or God of the Mexicans.

—*Journal of American Folklore*, Vol II, No. V, April-June, 1889.

However, the Navajo storytellers did not tell Dr. Matthews the whole truth, because the tale of *Noqoìlpi's* revenge is not for those without a willingness to believe the improbable, see the impossible, and face the unimaginable.

*This* is the chronicle of a curse.

A town.

And of a people who would defy a god.

# ACT ONE

## ORIGINS AND PORTENTS

# ONE
# "KIIYÍI"

Arizona Territory
February, 1865

IN FEBRUARY OF THE YEAR 1865, NINETEEN ABLE-
bodied men headed east from Prescott—the largest settlement in the Arizona Territory and home of Fort Whipple—
to the Verde Valley, a lush oasis formed by runoff from the
Four Peaks mountain range, or *Gah-jess-ah* in the Yavapai
tongue, if you'd prefer.

Their plan was to establish a farming community in the
middle of, what was then, Apache country. Called "impracti-
cal" and "insane" by their friends and family, these determined visionaries were predicted to be dead by April.

One month later, a single man returned, speaking
nonsense to all who would listen. A doctor checked him
over to determine if the man's mind had not been broken by
the horrors he must've been witness to.

For, he said that when the expedition had arrived in the
Verde Valley, somebody had already started a town, against
all odds, with a single building.

A saloon, to be exact.

Called "The Sagebrush" by the man who only identified himself as "Owner." He cordially offered everyone their first drink for free.

Perplexed, the settlers asked if there was anyone else in the area or even in the bar. The place sat in the heart of Indian farming land, and certainly he couldn't have built the saloon all by himself.

"Nope, no one else is here...yet," Owner said. "Been waiting for someone to arrive."

The men asked how long he'd been there and who did he wait for?

To which the bald man shrugged and replied, "Awhile. And don't know who. Maybe one of you."

They asked him about the land, and if it was good for the type of crops they wished to plant.

"Well," Owner admitted, "every spring there's a terrible rage of water that comes down the wash from the mountain and floods the area. It catches a lot of people and wild animals unawares, seeing as it's unpredictable and all."

That didn't seem so much a problem, they suggested. Just learn where the flood plane was, and they wouldn't plant near there. Or maybe dam up the wash.

Owner shook his head. "No, that's not it. The locals— the Apache, and the Wiipukepaya tribes—have taken to raising horses up on top a plateau to the north and, every spring, I've gotta haul dead horses from the creek, lest they poison the water here."

That *was* a problem, they admitted, but said they would help remove the carcasses come spring, once they got themselves established.

"I thank you for that, but before you agree to settle here," Owner continued, "you should be aware that the land has been cursed for many a year. You won't have to just deal with floods and droughts, or the Indians raiders." The bald man continued pouring drinks. "Nope, you'll also have to contend with ghosts, demons, and monsters from your worst nightmares."

They all laughed, save for one man.

Levi Forrest, only nineteen, stared into his whiskey as if were a window to the past.

"Cursed, you say?" he asked in the midst of his partners' revelry.

Owner nodded.

The other men stared at Levi strangely. He had only recently arrived in Prescott, and none knew him too well. The settlers then mocked him, calling him superstitious and saying that if he was so afraid of the dark, he should go back to the Fort.

Undeterred, Forrest said, "They can be killed, though? These monsters?"

The barkeep shrugged. "That's the thing about the curse. It isn't, you know, like clockwork or anything. Save for me, most who have taken on the evil directly have ended up as dead as those drowned horses. The locals have made peace with the reality that on any given day, one of their own might just up and vanish."

"And that's what'll happen to us if these men set up shop here, you're sayin'," Levi continued. "And any of their families that they bring down?"

With a slight nod and a discerning glare, Owner swore everything he'd said was true.

Forrest finally downed his drink. "Well, then, someone's gonna to have to make sure that doesn't happen, right?"

Owner smiled a very knowing smile and reached under his counter. He pulled from it a slightly tarnished metal star with the word "Sheriff" engraved on it.

"It's 'bout time you got here."

---

June

I sat in the back of the Sagebrush that morning, like I had almost every morning, listening to the hammering of nails into wood. Of the original nineteen of us to arrive in Drowned Horse, only twelve remained, but then nine more showed up once word of us survivin' got out. The livery was the first thing they built, to protect the horses from thieves, followed by my soon-to-be-finished jail. Can't rightly arrest someone for stealin' horses if I don't have someplace to put them.

After that would come a mercantile, a church, and a doctor's office. The town would be quite legitimate by the time the snows hit the region mid-November. Owner says it can get right frigid, but not like Prescott or further north. The mountains shielded the valley from the worst of the weather. Didn't mean that we shouldn't buckle down for an extended period of cold nights.

"Lost a friend one time when the river froze over," Owner told me once time, his voice tinged with the sound of grief past. "He died saving a local girl. Part of the reason they cut me slack around here."

"So, there have been others *here*, in your one saloon town?"

Owner smirked. "From time to time," and he shared no more, nor did I ask.

I hadn't had much to do in the last three months. I settled a couple disputes regarding property lines, and I headed off a couple confrontations with the natives. The natives were not at all happy about a town suddenly showing up on what was prime grazing land for them. Despite the Government's assurances that this territory would only be partially occupied by settlers, the Indians were suspicious of those promises, especially after we'd gone and broke every one we've ever made with them. Strange that they wouldn't trust our word.

I didn't give them false promises when I dealt with them. When I could find one who spoke English, I explained that killin' us would just bring more of the *higow'ah*—"blue eyes," that's what they called us—to the area and lots more of their people would die, and there'd still be a town here afterwards. Some of the more reasonable tribes, like the Wiipukepaya, heard the logic in my words and stayed away from us. The Apache, however, always itched for a fight. They burnt our crops and then we lost a man to altercation with one of their warriors, who also died from his wounds. I convinced all parties that it was an even swap and stayed any escalation.

The citizens of Drowned Horse trusted me well enough. They didn't know much about my past coming into this, so I'm usually seen as a neutral party. They talked behind my back, though—the crazy man who believes in ghost stories. I would've laughed along with them, to ease their minds, right up until the day James Polk ran down the street one morning a yellin', "Enos Barnett got carried off by a giant bat last night!"

And me, right in the middle of my eggs.

I checked with Owner, who raised an eyebrow.

"Had to happen eventually, Sheriff."

I sighed. He was right, of course. I'd believed him when he told us about curses, and monsters, and things like that. I had up-close and personal knowledge of them. Owner never asked me for more, nor did I share. We had an under-standing.

"It was a good run," I said as I slid back from the table.

"A fine run. Three months."

"Three *quiet* months," I agreed.

Owner asked, "Know what you're up against?"

"Nope. Does it matter?"

"Not really. Mostly, these things die like we do. Some take a little…creativity."

I went to my room to get prepared. My first trip back to Prescott as Sheriff of Drowned Horse afforded me some pull with the army. After negotiating a less-than-fair price to me, the Fort's commander let me have my pick from their seized guns and such. I left with an old Colt rifle I liked 'cause it could use anything from .34 to .44 rounds in it, a Sharps carbine, and one 4-bore powder loader some fool brought back from elephant hunting in Africa and promptly lost in a card game. Luckily, one of the things my father taught me was how to make my own bullets. I also grabbed a knife, a bow, and a quiver that I'd been told was recovered from a Tolkapaya camp the Army had encountered north some time back. Something about that weapon spoke to me. The engraving on the wood of the bow and etching in the quiver indicated power. Maybe even dark magic.

Everyone has demons. Some travel with them as luggage.

I stepped out of the saloon and into the crowd of men that'd gathered in the middle of what would someday be the main road into town. A few had brought wives with them. Mostly, those ladies came from hard stock and, as much as *we* had faith that we would make good in the Verde Valley, no sense riskin' the gentle women with the tribes so close.

Polk regaled the people with his story as I arrived.

"As I said, we was sittin' by the fire, havin' a smoke before turnin' in for the night. Enos had just stood up when this thing just swooped down and locked its claws around his shoulders. They dug right in. Enos screamed like no man I'd ever heard before! I'll never forget the sound long as I live."

Those that believed in such things crossed themselves. The rest held their hats in reverence.

Polk continued. "It appeared so quickly, and then took off just as quick with Enos in tow. It flapped these giant demon wings like it was Satan's offspring." Polk was the storyteller amongst our group, though his many exploits bordered just this side of believable.

While I didn't entirely doubt the veracity of his story, I'd need to know more.

"Excuse me, Jim, but exactly how tall was the creature?"

Everyone turned to me, noticing me really for the first time.

"Sheriff!" Polk exclaimed. "I was comin' to see you next. You think this is the type of thing Owner was talkin' about?"

"No idea. Certainly has the sound of one. How big? Like taller than Enos? And the wingspan? Wider than a horse and wagon?"

Polk thought a moment. "It was dark, and I only had the campfire light to see it by, but I'd say easily bigger than Enos; maybe twice as so. And the wings? From tip to tip, probably a full team and stagecoach."

Yeah, that definitely put it in the category of a monster. Something of that size would've made an explorer's journal by now. Lewis and Clarke didn't write about it, so I s'posed it could be supernatural.

"Did you see its face?" I asked.

Polk shook his head. "Only it's eyes. They glowed yella in the firelight. Oval and full of evil, they was."

"Full of evil. I'll make note of that."

The others barraged me with questions:

"Whatcha going to do, Sheriff?"

"Are we safe?"

"Think Enos is still alive?"

"Or was he fed to its young?"

I blinked and held up my hands in surrender. "No, hold on a moment, will ya? How do I even know it has young? I haven't seen it yet. Give me a chance to track it down. This is what you pay me for."

For the record, I hadn't been paid anythin' since no one had made any money yet. The office would be my recompense, and I guessed it was time to earn it.

———

POLK AND BARNETT'S PLOT WAS A GOOD HOUR RIDE by horse and, seeing as Polk hadn't ridden into town, he must've run all night. The partners had served in the war together and, upon making it out of that nightmare alive, decided on a fresh start far away from bad memories. I didn't expect to find Enos alive. Helluva thing to make it through war only to get killed randomly by some bird looking for a worm. Nor did I suspect him being the first to be carried off.

From their camp, I pointed myself west toward the mountains. The Black Hills were riddled with caves big enough to hold something of the size Polk described. But then the thought of exploring caves without knowin' what I hunted made me decide to sidetrack a bit toward the north.

Most of the travelers through the region will tell you that one Indian is the same as the next, and the only good one is a dead one. While I don't like to voice my opinion in those circumstances, I did feel for the locals. My own people had a history of persecution and bein' driven out of places, so I could empathize. Now that the war between the states was over, more and more people would come to the territories. Most were on their way to places like California, Oregon, or Utah, while others planted roots in the territories before they became states. That upset a lot of tribes who were told these lands would still be their own...this time.

I might've been a little overly cautious when dealing with the locals back then. I didn't have a lot of information to do my job and—you might not know this—but an angry Indian is not a helpful one. Seein' though they'd been here, and dealt with the curse longer than anyone else, I sought them out often for information and tried not to take it personally when they tried to kill me first.

A Wiipukepaya camp nearest to our town would be the best first stop. Hopefully, the only stop, as I didn't have all day to make a tour of the area. As I forded the creek, I counted a dozen or so dwellings ahead. A flurry of activity had already begun. I hated to cause a ruckus and all, so I had raised my hands, letting my horse, Roland, do all the work. Hear tell from Owner, the tribe had previously been run by a committee. There was a leader, or sorts, but he was just the strongest in their settlement. As more settlers and more Army moved in, the need for wiser leaders became evident. Hard to fight someone for the best land, as they had previously done with other tribes, when your opponent had a gun and you just had your fists. Chiefs were elected not for being the strongest, but the smartest.

Still, a *Paya* chief might speak only for their tribe, and not for the Yavapai as a whole, which numbered over six thousand in the Verde Valley, spread out over hundreds of miles. I had to pick a camp that already knew me, and hopefully knew I meant no harm.

As I approached the one I felt safest talking to, already Chief Long Tooth and five of his fittest young men waited for me by the entrance.

"Chief." I nodded.

I spoke no *Paya* yet, nor did he speak English. One of his warriors did, though. I believe his name was Waning Moon. He gave me a crossways glare, and I couldn't help but notice the rifles slung over each of the warriors' backs. They really shouldn't have those, since that would just bring them more trouble, but I wasn't there to quibble.

"What pain have you brought us today?" Waning Moon asked.

Right to the point, that one.

"One my people mighta been carried off by some flyin' creature last night."

"Not our problem."

The chief strained to figure out what we were saying, his eyes shifting back and forth between us.

"Not saying it is, but you've been in this area a long time. Ever heard of a creature picking off grown-sized men in the middle of the night?" I recounted the description Polk had given me. I even included some pantomime with me circling and flapping my arms like wings.

Long Tooth gave me an uncomfortable glare. The chief pulled on Moon's elbow and indicated he wanted my words translated. Reluctantly, Moon did so. The chief swayed as if his knees had become water. His face contorted in grief; broken eyes that told me all the story I needed to know.

Still, Moon explained.

"The creature you speak of took the Chief's young son, Fox Tail. They were night hunting together, and Fox Tail ran after a rabbit, getting too far ahead of his father. As he called after him, a dark shape flew down and grabbed the boy. It came out of the night sky faster than Long Tooth could react. It was not as big as you describe now, but that was many years ago."

Moon went on to tell me how the Chief formed a hunting party to find the beast, but they searched the *Gah-jess-ah* for weeks and never found its cave or any sign of the boy's body. I asked Moon to give my condolences to the chief and then asked a few more questions about which areas they searched. If *they* couldn't find it, it wasn't there.

That left me wondering where else a giant bat-like thing might hide. While I considered myself well read, I certainly wasn't no scientist. Nor did I know of one in the region, but I did hear about some trappers who worked the area, though. Trappers, you see, are like wise men of the territories. If they didn't know it, it hadn't been.

---

IT WAS COMING ON NIGHT WHEN I HEARD THE tell-tale laughter of men taken to drink. I found the shack—it really wasn't more than a pile of logs tied together, but that's all most of these mountain men needed—at the base of the foothills. There hadn't been much of a path through the thick woods, but their hootenanny led me to them.

"Hello, the shack," I called out, as to not surprise them.

The laughter stopped, and it was a moment or two before someone called out, "Who's thar?"

I identified myself.

"Why a drowned herse need a shariff? Was it merdered?"

That started the laughter again.

I groaned.

"We're a new settlement down near the Sagebrush."

The door to the shack did not open so much as fall over. The man standing in the doorway looked more like the animals he preyed on than a human. I could see two more shapes behind him.

"Owner's finally gat sum company, eh? Well, come on closer."

As I drew up, I tied my horse loosely nearby. On the branches around the shack hung a selection of everything that could be caught in those woods, from squirrel to stag. The smell wasn't great, but I'd smelled worse.

They offered me a swig of something from a jug as I sat down, but I declined.

"What bring ye up har?" asked my host.

I could see now where the skins he wore ended and he began. He was of thick Nordic stock—dirty blond hair poked out from a coonskin cap.

"I'm tracking something, and you fellas know more about this region than I do."

"Sí, you came to the right place," a lanky Mexican said. "We've covered this whole valley over the years. Good hunting up here, señor."

"Whatcha after, Sheriff?" The third man was a light-skinned negro. Like the rest, he was filthy to the point he could've passed for an unkempt white man unless you looked closely. An interestin' trio, to be sure.

"A man-eating bat," I said straight-faced. I expected them to break out laughing, but the air grew dark, and their tone shifted.

"The camazotz," the Mexican said, and then crossed himself.

I wiggled my finger in my ear. "Come again? The cama what?"

"The camazotz," he repeated. "Is a legend from my home. Bad creature. Bites the head off of you."

The way he told it, the camazotz were demons that

worked for older, more powerful gods. They often brought sacrifices to their dark lords, usually just the head, in exchange for treasure or power. They were very strong and very fast, but easily distracted by their love of jewelry.

I was sure then, and I still am as I'm telling you this, some of the creatures plaguing the Verde Valley weren't native to these United States. In fact, I'd lay odds they were imported as settlers moved west. I'm certain that the Spanish and Mexicans brought their share up north, as well. The camazotz was evidence of that.

"If one listens closely, *señor*, you'll hear the tinkle of its many necklaces or earrings just before it strikes."

"Any idea where it calls home?"

The negro swore. "Sheet, mister. If we knew that, we'd stay as far away from that place as we could."

"It can't be keeled," my host agreed. "Ain't no gun beeg 'nuff to put a hole in et."

I turned back to the Mexican. "In the legends, how did a person kill one of these things?"

He took a swig from the jug and swished it around his mouth as he thought. "As I said, they love jewelry, but only silver jewelry. Other metals burn them. Probably, gold would do them harm."

Silver was a moon metal, whereas gold was the metal of the sun. The creature hunted at night, so that made sense.

I thanked them and departed.

Where was I going to get enough gold to fashion into a weapon? And when I did, how did I find the beast?

I headed back down to town before I lost my head next.

---

OWNER HAD NO GOOD SUGGESTIONS THE NEXT morning.

"Rob a bank? Or maybe a gold train?"

That wouldn't look good for our new town's reputation

if its first sheriff got caught doing exactly the opposite of his job.

"I don't have time to go panning for it, either."

The answer came from a most surprisin' arrival. Chief Long Tooth walked into Sagebrush. He gawked at the place. The saloon didn't have much in the way of decorations: a few trophy heads, a painting of a nude lady along the staircase to the second floor, where Owner hoped to have actual ladies someday. On the main floor, an array of empty tables waited in front of a stage where Owner hoped to have actual performers someday. Finally, a faro table sat empty to a corner where Owner hoped...you get it.

Long Tooth stared at everything all at once and thus was startled when I laid a hand on his shoulder.

"Can I help you, Chief?"

He nodded and spoke quickly. Owner, who slid up next to us, tried to translate.

"Slow down, Chief. What's this about a vision?"

The chief took a measured breath and stared over, slower.

"He says that he had a vision last night after you left," Owner relayed. "His son came to him and told him that he needed vengeance."

"I'd love to give the boy that, but I'm at a loss as to how."

Owner translated.

The chief titled his head oddly, as if I questioned his vision. Then he made a decision.

"He says," Owner continued, "that Fox Tail guided him to a certain spot in the creek and to pull up three handfuls of the dirt. In the third, there was this." Chief Long Tooth pulled out a lump of metal I couldn't help but think looked a lot like gold. "Fox Tail told him then to bring it to you."

"You did say ghosts worked this region, didn't you?" I asked Owner.

"Not the first one, hear tell. But there's your answer."

The nugget was big enough to make a bullet or six from.

The chief spoke urgently again.

"He says he wants to go with you. His son's spirit won't rest until he sees the creature dead."

I re-worked the plan in my mind.

Five bullets *and* an arrowhead. That would cover our bases.

---

IT TOOK US BETTER PART OF A DAY TO PREP FOR our hunt. Chief Long Tooth remained patient though he jumped often when spoken to, his hand nervously hovering near the knife strapped to his hip. Owner offered him food and drink, which he declined. The man had a mission, and he would only interact with us as much as necessary.

I did catch him glancing to my badge from time to time. Owner noticed it, too. Finally, Long Tooth asked Owner what it was.

"He wants to know why you wear a metal star on your chest, and asks if you believe you are a god descended from the sun."

I chuckled. "No, I am no God." I tried my best to explain. "I protect the people of the town we're buildin' here."

When Owner translated, Long Tooth furrowed his brow suspiciously.

"He says you don't look like a chief or a warrior."

I had to agree. "No, sir. I am neither, but I'll do what I must to keep my men safe, from any threat. And failin' that, seek justice for the dead."

Our eyes locked, and it was understood that I meant from *any* threat, including from his people. But he understood justice. Justice ranked high in their honor code. Chief Long Tooth nodded, and an unspoken agreement had been reached. He would do the same for his people, and that it was likely we wouldn't always be on the same side.

That day, however, we were brothers born out of a need to hunt.

Changing topics, I tried to get more from the chief on where this camazotz might build a lair.

"Maybe we're thinking this wrong," I said to him through Owner. "Maybe we shouldn't think of this thing as a bat, if it's some sort of henchman for its gods. Where are some of the holy places around here?"

The chief squirmed. His hesitancy at revealing place sacred to his people was respectable, so I rephrased the question.

"If this thing wanted to make a sacrifice to its gods, where might be a special place be for it do that?"

"*MaɖhyIvah*," he said. "*Wii'h whaa`ɖah. Wii'h whaa`ɖah.*"

The chief told us that, to the north, past the red rock mountains, there was a place that reeked of dark magic. A place even the *Dilzhe'e*—or Apache—wouldn't go.

You could see some of those formations from Drowned Horse, but there were hundreds if not thousands of them. Then it came to me. I asked Owner for a piece of flint and told Long Tooth to draw us a picture of the rock he was talking about.

The chief drew a mountain shaped like a large cathedral I'd seen when my family's caravan stopped in Louisiana. I agreed it had to be the place. Chief Long Tooth said it would take us until the following night to get there, if we left right then. I nodded and Owner got us provisions.

---

THE CLEAR SKY ALLOWED THE FULL MOON FREE access to the world below. I considered it a bad omen, since we were huntin' a night creature. I'd not traveled this part of the valley before. Lots of good ambush places, day or night. A reddish hue from the massive stone monoliths, even only moon-lit, cast an eerie glow over the area.

As a boy, my parents' caravan had traveled up and down

the east coast, making a far stretch into the south, but they didn't live long enough to come west. They'd been brought to America when their parents had escaped the *Heidenjachten* in Europe. For work, they traveled from town to town doing odd jobs or entertaining, as needed.

Until...

The chief got my attention, wrenchin' me from the past. I welcomed the distraction. Thoughts of that sort were like taking on wounds right before you started the battle.

He directed us to move closer to the rocks, and indicated he'd heard something in the wind.

"*Gŕen buñ gŕah*," he whispered, then waved his hands by the side of his head.

*Bat.* I really needed to learn the local languages if I was going to hunt monsters in their world.

As we hunkered down for a moment, quietly listening, my ear caught what he'd already heard.

The jingling of metal jewelry. Then flapping. Once. Twice.

We strained to see the sky above us, knowing as prey, we might not see the camazotz until too late. Fortune was with us, for as it passed overhead, the moonlight briefly illuminated it. Easily as big as Polk had estimated and faster than I feared. It didn't hunt us, though.

It already had someone in its talons.

---

WE PUSHED OUR HORSES THROUGH THE DAY, ONCE we had enough light to do so safely. We'd arrive before sundown and still have time to stake out the area. Whoever that was in the camazotz's clutches, would be sacrificed that night. The way the Mexican trapper told it, the camazotz needed this whole ceremony before the servant could present its gifts to the master. It meant that whoever the victim was might still be alive.

We were slowed down, but gratefully so, by having to

ford Oak Creek. Chief Long Tooth stripped down to his breechcloth holding his clothes in one hand, the reins in the other.

I wasn't comfortable getting *that* friendly with the natives, yet. I rode my horse, Roland, across, leaning back in the saddle, feet up on either side of his neck.

Long Tooth laughed at me, and said some words that I assumed were some sort of taunt about blue-eyes being lazy, or proud, or whatever. I could see now where he got his name. One of his bottom teeth was much longer than all the others. I'm surprised he hadn't been named after a beaver or something.

I smiled down at him as I passed and tipped my hat.

He shook his head and sighed.

Dressed and dried out, we continued through the range until the chief pointed to a distant shape.

Now, mind you, there are many such rock formations in the Verde Valley. Some as red as a sunset, others more yellow or gray. But none looked like this one. It had to be the largest one I'd seen in my time here.

The chief hadn't done it justice in his drawing. The cathedral wasn't made from just one formation, but several. A large wide rock formed the front face, while behind it, several tall but thinner spires spread out creating an open mall in the center. This new information made it clear why a creature like the camazotz chose to perform rituals there. The plaza made a perfectly level plateau to hold sacrifices in.

The sun readied to call it a day, and we quickly ran out of ground on which to ride our horses over. The angle grew steeper the closer we got. Finally, when Roland took a misstep that nearly brought us both down, I dismounted. The chief did the same. We left them tied to a stump and continued on by foot.

The climb would be rugged, so I carried only what was necessary: the Colt rifle with the golden bullets, my side-iron, and my knife. Chief Long Tooth pulled his bow from his saddle, but I told him to wait and called him over. I pulled from a cloth the bow I'd gotten up in Prescott at the Fort.

Long Tooth's eyes widened, and he spoke quickly.

"Now, now, Chief. I can't say anythin' more about it, nor would you understand if I did. I just think it might help. Will it?"

I offered it to him, and the chief took it very carefully from my hands. He studied it reverently before stringing it. He strummed it, listening to the thrum closely with his ear. He gauged me, in a different way than the day before.

"*Kiiyíi,*" he said and then grasped my forearm. "Friend," he said again in English.

I knew he must have heard that word a million times from blue-eyes like me, few men having meant it. I wondered if it was the first time he'd ever spoken it back to one. I'd given him a gift that signified something greater than just our mutual goal. What significance the bow had to his people I'd never know. It did strike me odd that in just a day, a man who'd just as likely killed me as call me friend had just done so.

What exactly was that bow?

"*Kiiyíi,*" I replied, out of respect. I liked him, but I knew I'd end up in odds with the Paya as long as I stayed a lawman in Drowned Horse. Regardless, it felt like a beginning. If we killed this monster, then maybe we'd take the next step to creating a longer peace.

---

As we climbed, I worried that our weapons still wouldn't be up to the task. We only had the hearsay of a drunk trapper and the dreams of a grieving father to go on. Owner said most of the monsters the curse brought to the area could be killed like any animal or man. This'd be the test of that.

The rocks slowly became cast in shadows as the sun went down behind the mountains. While speed was necessary, so was stealth. The Chief's foot pushed on a rock that slid out from under him like a slingshot. I grabbed it out of the air with one hand, nearly losin' my grip with the other, but the stone was big enough that it would've made an awful racket on the way down.

Lights appeared above us, flickering and waving like torches. We reached the plateau and slid carefully around the front face, hugging it tight. When we rounded a corner, a smell caught my nostrils, and I nearly vomited. The chief smelled it, too. He pointed to a cave about ten feet from us, but across the open space. He indicated we should look inside. I wasn't sure that was a good idea. I'd seen the aftermath of a slaughter and recognized the stench of death.

Chief Long Tooth wasn't to be dissuaded, and I conceded it might give us an idea of what we were up against. We quietly crept from one large rock formation to the other, getting our first full look into the center of the camazotz's "church."

Two large posts had been driven into the ground, each with a manacle hanging from it. No one occupied them yet, so we'd made it in time.

The cave wasn't deep, but it went back far enough that I had to light a match to see what I already knew was there.

Bodies. Lots of them.

Men. Women. Children.

Some more recent, flesh still rotting off their corpses. Others, no more than clothes and bones. I saw one that could have easily been Enos Barrent's body. The boots looked about right, and he was pretty fresh. Not a day or two dead. I couldn't be sure, though, as there was no head. Not a single head to be found on any of them.

Chief Long Tooth pulled bodies off a pile, and I knew who he search for.

"Not now," I said in a loud whisper. "We can do it later."

Again, the chief had his mind set on the task.

A few feet in, he paused, dropping to his knees. I didn't need to look over his shoulder to know what he had found. He wept silently, and I gave him his privacy. I peeked out of the cave just as a large, dark shape moved in the center of the formation, carrying something over its shoulder.

The camazotz had more humanistic features than I expected. It walked upright on thick, muscular legs. At the end of its "wings" were hands that carried its would-be victim and placed him into the manacles. The body slumped forward, held up only by the chains. In the torch light, I recognized it as Waning Moon, the warrior from the Wiipukepaya camp.

"Why in the ever lovin' hell is he here?"

A noise behind me had me turning around, pistol in hand.

Chief Long Tooth stood with a small bundle wrapped in scraps of clothing from various other bodies. I knew a funeral shroud when I saw one. He set it down, saying words I didn't understand.

He pointed to my tinderbox, and then to the remains. He did this several times until I understood. He wanted me to make a pier after we finished, for his son, to put him to rest.

I nodded, and then added, "When we *both* make it out of here alive."

When Chief Long Tooth peered out of the cave and saw Waning Moon strung up, he leapt forward, but I grabbed him quickly and pulled him back to the shadows.

"Not so fast," I whispered urgently. "I don't see the camazotz." I made the same flapping sign he'd made earlier. "Slowly. Stick to the sides." I slid my palm against the stone to hopefully get the point home. I motioned for Long Tooth to go back to the place we'd crossed, and then stay parallel with me as we moved forward. I had no idea how much he understood, but it seemed to be enough, as he left the cave the way we'd come in, and then crossed over quietly. With no sounds of alarm, we stayed close to the rock formations, slidin' forward at the same time.

Sooner than I woulda liked, we reached an impasse

where we had to act or wait. I wanted to draw the bat creature out, but wasn't sure how.

Then I remembered about the creature's love of jewelry.
None of the bodies in the cave had any left on them that I
could recall, but I had some items that would suffice.

In addition to my golden bullets, I'd brought several
regular ones. I found a few coins in my pockets that Owner
had given me for services rendered, as well. I signed for the
chief to wait. I slid back to the cave quickly and pulled a
coin purse from Enos's body.

"Sorry. I need to borrow this," I told his headless body. I
don't know why. Just seemed the neighborly thing to do. He
had a lot of coins which made me wonder if he'd been slipping up to Prescott to gamble after a run of bad luck at the
Sagebrush. Putting everything all together, the full purse
jingled and jangled enough that it could sound like jewelry.

Once again, in the closest position I could reach without
exposure, I flung the coin purse to the far side of the
plateau. It hit a loose boulder, split open and sent coins and
bullets cascading down in a very loud manner.

When the camazotz's screech hit us, we had to cover our
ears. From a perch above the center ring, the camazotz flew
down at the place with the purse landed.

Chief Long Tooth and I quick-stepped it to toward center
where Moon hung. The chief had his arrow strung, and I
had rifle up and scanned the spaces between the massive
rocks for movement.

The damn creature must've had excellent hearing 'cause
it turned and saw us before we made it half-way cross the
plateau. Screeching again, it flapped its massive arms and
took off into the night sky.

Outside the torches, any light from the moon and stars
were blocked by the height of the formations. The chief and
I moved back to back, keeping our eyes up to the sky, just
waiting for the camazotz to attack.

Which is what the sneaky beast counted on.

It came at us flying fast and low, only a couple feet off

the ground. It hit our legs, tossing us up and spinning us around. We landed hard. Gun and bow knocked from our hands, we scrambled back to the rock walls as best we could. It disappeared into the darkness on the opposite side of the plaza.

I rubbed my stinging leg. I'd been stepped on by a horse in my wilder youth, but this was even worse. The bone wasn't broken, but I wouldn't be running away anytime soon. Sliding my back up against the rock, I got to standing. The chief did much the same.

We could see our weapons out in the open. It didn't take a genius to realize the camazotz waited for us to make a run at them. It wouldn't fall for thrown coins twice.

Chief Long Tooth motioned to me. He suggested he work his way around and that we come at our weapons from different angles, in hopes one of us would make it. A damn fool idea, but I had nothing better.

The chief drew his knife, and something seemed odd about it in the torchlight.

As if it had been dipped in gold.

I thought back to when I was making the bullets and the arrowhead. Had I left Long Tooth alone by the smelting pot? Could he have had time to quickly dip the knife in?

And did he really mean for us both to reach our weapons?

With a cry, Chief Long Tooth leapt from the shadows, screaming curses at the monster. He didn't make it far before the camazotz dropped down at him faster than a hawk on a field mouse. It grabbed his shoulders, and bent over, maw gapping, preparing, I guessed, to bite the chief's head off.

Long Tooth had a different idea.

He stabbed his knife into the leg of the camazotz. The effect was immediate. The wound sizzled and burned as if someone had poured lye into it. The screeching took on a new tone, higher pitched, desperate.

Pushing off the chief, the bat creature flew unsteadily in a circle over the plateau.

I ran from cover to the chief. Massive holes in his back and shoulders poured blood. I reached to help him up, but he waved me away. He pointed at Waning Moon, and said, in his own way, that I had to go rescue him. He'd take care of the demon.

I scooped up my gun as I raced to the warrior. He, too, had gashes in his shoulders where the monster had grabbed him. He woke as I worked his manacles open.

"What?"

"That's what I want to know. Or more to the point, how?"

Waning Moon shook his head to get it clear.

"I didn't want my chief to give his life for some *higow'ah*. I was going to kill the monster and put the past to rest. Only..."

I got the first manacle off.

"Only, the thing is smarter and faster than you'd figured? Yeah. We noticed that, too."

The screeching came again as the camazotz swooped down at Chief Long Tooth, getting a slice across its belly as the chief dove underneath it as it passed.

By the time I got Moon free, the tally was three hits for Chief Long Tooth, and two for the monster. Neither fighter looked good.

Long Tooth locked eyes with Waning Moon, then put his fist to his chest, a signal his tribesman clearly understood.

"*Alyka'émk!* Don't be a fool!" Moon yelled, stumbling forward.

I didn't need to speak Paya to know what the old man had in mind.

When the camazotz swung in for another pass, the chief just stood there waiting. He grabbed the creature around the neck, plunging the knife into its back. The camazotz, barely able to get more the fifteen feet off the ground, hovered there. It bit down into Chief Long Tooth's shoulder, blood gushing over both their heads. The chief turned his face toward us and smiled resignedly.

Waning Moon took up the bow and, with great effort considering his wounds, pulled back the string. When he released it, the golden arrow glowed brightly in the torchlight as it pierced Long Tooth's back and passed through to the creature. I'd never seen an arrow do that before, and neither had Waning Moon who glared at the bow.

I made sure to place a golden bullet or three in the camazotz's head, to be safe, and when the monster and chief hit the ground, I walked up and put my remaining two in its black heart, guaranteeing that it would never hunt again.

Blood spewed from Long Tooth's mouth in ragged coughs. His brethren knelt beside him, tears flowing down face unashamedly. I can't say truthfully, he was alone.

The chief raised a hand to me, which I took.

"*Kii...yii...*" he managed to say.

"*Kiiyíi,*" I agreed.

Long Tooth closed his eyes and joined his son on the great hunt in the sky.

Waning Moon approached and placed a hand on my shoulder. "Where did you get this bow?"

I told him.

"I have only seen these markings near the well to the first and second worlds."

He meant Montezuma's well, near where the Army decided to build Camp Lincoln. Named by Conquistadors, the very deep lake had nothing to do with Montezuma and everything to do with the Yavapai's creation myth.

"It's yours," I told him. "You downed the creature with it."

He motioned his thanks, but I noticed he did not call *me* Kiiyíi.

MOON AND I SPENT THE BETTER PART OF THE night bringing all the bodies to the center of the plateau and burning them. With each, I could sense a soul getting to finally go home. Wherever you think that might be.

We placed Chief Long Tooth and his son on the pier last. That being done, Moon and I headed home ourselves.

If y'all are thinking Chief Waning Moon and I became best friends after that, well, real stories don't end like they do in the books. He and I had many run-ins as he defended his tribe, and I defended mine. Moon was killed a year later by the Apache in a raid.

Drowned Horse grew under the watchful eye of the locals, the Army, and the evil spirits that infused the land we chose to call home. Much as Owner had warned me at the beginning, there weren't many days of peace.

But then, I was never much for the quiet.

# TWO
# "THE METAL SKINS"

Arizona Territory
August, 1865

MOTHA SNUCK AWAY FROM HIS FATHER'S TENT just as the moon started its slow decent behind the mountains. He should not be doing that, but no one would listen, and he would keep his tribe, the Wiipukepaya, from being blamed for something they had not done. Yes, his family had attacked the *higow'ah*—the blue-eyes—before, but that was because since they arrived, the invaders took and gave nothing back to his people. That, Motha knew, was a betrayal of the tribe's code.

But there had been new attacks on blue-eyes wagons, and those were *not* his family's doing. Motha would find someone to believe him or the *sultá*, men-wearing-blue would come again. They would bring their horses and their guns and may never leave.

The young man had barely left the camp when a hand reached out from behind a tall rock and grabbed him by the shoulder. Motha drew his knife and bared his teeth.

"Whoa, there, Charlie! It's Aloysius Johns. Al. You know me. *Hŏmgah!* Hello!"

Johns, the one that most of the elders didn't trust because no matter what he promised, the men-in-blue would do something different. That meant Johns's words were weak.

Still, Motha liked short man. The "negotiator" had been always nice to everyone, though it was clear that Motha's father, their tribe's leader, would rather see him dead. Johns knew this, too, and yet helped the tribe where and when he could. Johns even tried learning Motha's language.

"Lucky I just happened to be leaving a meeting with a cactus when I saw you. Where are you off to, Charlie?"

Motha cocked his head to the side, confused.

Johns asked again, "Where're going? *Myámah Nú?*"

Motha let the dam break, the worries cascading from him like a child, not the future warrior he hoped to be. It embarrassed him, but what else could he do?

"The metal skins are hunting your people, not us. We have not killed any blue eyes in months. The metal skins walk as if spirits took control of kachina dolls, like the one you gave my sister. Please believe me!"

"Slow down there, Charlie." Motha hated that Johns called him Charlie, but he gave up correcting him. "I know only few of your words. Again. Slowly."

Motha pointed at the bullets on the belt Johns wore. He spoke slowly, as he would with his little sister. He flicked the metal casing. "There are men made of this. They look like us, but are not us. They are metal dolls. Living dolls. They are killing the blue-eyes. Not us."

Johns scratched his chin. "Men shoot bullets, kill settlers, but aren't your people? And they are talking dolls?"

Motha shook his head violently. He decided to speak using Johns' words, but he hated to sound as silly as Johns did when he tried to speak his tongue. "Metal skins. Kill whites. Blame us."

"I'm lost on 'metal skins,' Charlie. They're in suits of armor, like knights?" Johns had shown him books of legends from his people with men in armor and giant lizards called dragons.

But Motha did not have time for stories. He turned to leave, but once more, Johns reached out a hand.

"*Wíwo*? Show me?"

---

IT TOOK THEM BETTER PART OF TWO HOURS before they reached the ridge where Motha first saw the metal skins. Johns did well to follow in the half-light, only occasionally stepping on a cactus. The problem was Motha could not get the negotiator to stop talking. Johns said several times that they should turn around, that Motha must be mistaken. He swore he would speak on behalf of the tribe, which is what he always said, but never actually did. Finally, Motha shut him up by pinching the man's lips together and motioning for him to duck down.

Together, they crawled to the lip of a ravine. Light, like a fire, illuminated the inhabitants below, but no fire had been built. Instead, giant globes glowed like small suns that cast a circle of daylight all around their camp.

"*Kwehv'igk*," Motha told him, but Johns furrowed his brow. "Below,' Motha repeated in John's tongue.

From afar, the young man could see how the blue-eyes might mistake these creatures for Wiipukepaya. They wore the *bah-yuu-thii* of his tribe, only these fake warriors were much too large up close even dressed in such clothes. His uncle, who could eat a whole *m'thinn*, horns and all, was not *that* big.

To Motha, the metal skins moved as if in a trance. He had seen his father and uncles stumble around that way after a fire dance, but that was not the cause here. These fake men could not mimic the walk of real men, not exactly. They paused between steps a little too long, and their feet landed a little too hard. From the distance, though, they might be mistaken for real men.

Motha nudged Johns as the metal skins began the ritual that had first revealed their true nature to him when he had first sought them out.

"*Hū! Hū!*"

"Head? What are you..." The negotiator's jaw dropped when one of metal men took off the head of another. It held it up to the light and adjusted something inside of the neck. After a few moments of work, the fake man placed the head back on the repaired warrior. That one smiled a little bit more realistically than Motha had seen them do before. That meant they were becoming more convincing each day.

He heard Johns swallow hard. "I...I can't say that I've ever seen anything like that. And you're saying that these things down there have been the ones attacking the caravans and blaming your people for it?"

Motha did not understand all the words, but he nodded.

Suddenly, a noise erupted from below. Several of the metal skins rotated their heads to where Motha and Johns lay. Bullets rang out and hit rocks near the duo causing sparks. How did they know they were there? Motha would not wait around to find out. He ran with Johns close behind him.

As they escaped, Johns spoke between breaths.

"We have...to get...to Drowned Horse. Only one person...can help."

"*P'ká?*" Motha asked. "Who fights such evil?"

"Levi...Forrest. He does...this sort...of thing."

Motha wondered, *What kind of warrior lived in the trees and fought metal men?*

––––––––––

"DESPITE THE NEWLY CHRISTENED ARIZONA Territory having been open for expansion a year now, it hasn't produced many settlements so far," I said to no one.

"The town of Drowned Horse is one of the few; a lone oasis in the dusty red earth of the Lord's beautiful land."

Owner, the owner of the Sagebrush, Drowned Horse's only saloon, chose that moment to walk through the door to my office. He scanned the room, seeing no one else but me seated behind my desk, feet propped up, and hands behind my head. I tiled my hat back until our eyes met.

"Sheriff. May I inquire as to who you are talking to?"

I grinned. "I'm just testin' out an idea. I'm considering writing an article about the wonders of Drowned Horse. Maybe get some of that East Coast money comin' this way so I can hire a deputy."

Owner made a sound from his gut that clearly told me what he thought of the idea. "Levi. You know that isn't a good idea. This town, well...it's special. We really can't risk new blood being spilled around here. Place is troublesome enough as it is."

"Darn it, Owner. We need new blood. Every woman who comes to town arrives as someone's wife or daughter. We need a school marm or somethin'." I let my feet drop and sat up straight. "And before you go offerin' one of your girls, they're nice and all, but I'm lookin' for a lady who is a little more..."

"Wholesome?" Owner smirked.

"Demure. Your ladies can cuss, drink, shoot, and fight better than any man I know. Heck, I've considered bringin' *them* on as deputies."

"You should."

I imagined it for a second, and then waved it away. "Nah. Tough as they are, they aren't really up for the stuff I have to deal with. If this was a normal job..."

Owner pulled my only other chair away from in front of my desk and sat in it. "And this was a normal town..."

"Then I'd risk a lady deputy. But not yet. Not until the curse is lifted." Seeing that Owner sat down, I sat back in my chair and sighed. "Who knows what thing's gonna to slither up from the ground next? And since no one knows how to break the curse, I have the notion I ain't gonna leave this town alive. That gets a guy to thinkin', y'know? How he might not want to be alone at the end."

Owner smoothed the black vest he wore over his white shirt. The man's head had been shaved clean as long as I've known him and only his bushy, brown eyebrows indicated what it might have once looked like.

"Levi. So, what you're saying is, you want to make a widow of some poor soul?"

I hated it when he cut right to the truth like that. It's why I didn't drink at the Sagebrush. Too much truth ruined the taste of the whisky.

Footfalls hit the planks outside in rapid succession. Somebody—no, two somebodies—ran like they raced death himself. I unhitched my sidearm, and Owner swiveled his chair laying his own piece on his lap, so we could greet our newcomers.

I recognized Al Johns, the liaison of sorts between the military and Wiipukepaya out in the valley.

"Sheriff...need help!" Al could barely get the words out through his dry throat.

Owner got up for the pitcher of water I kept by the cells. "You know them, Levi?"

"Owner, meet Aloysius Johns, Indian Agent. A former mountain man who'd made enough deals with the Yavapai, the Apache—and the mixed tribes thereof—that when the government set up Fort Whipple in Prescott, they brought Al here in to negotiate treaties and sooth the savages, as it were. All he seems to do, though, is tell the locals what they want to hear, knowing that the government won't actually do a damn thing about it. Ain't that right, Al?"

Al nodded sheepishly as he accepted the water and drank hardily.

"Half my job is keepin' the delicate peace intact without starting another Indian war. Neither Al nor I are able to do enough to make anything better."

Owner handed Al's young companion a glass as well.

Al, finally able to better enunciate his words, spilled out, "Metal skins...can take their heads off...disguised as Indians...killing travelers."

"And there's the other half of your job." Owner guffawed.

I didn't like the smug way he said that. Damned if he wasn't right, though.

The boy standing behind Al had long black hair and a small mole near his left cheek. He didn't breathe nearly as hard, but his nervous eyes darted around my office. Twice they settled on the jail, and I could tell he was afraid of me. He waited patiently as Al told us *most* of their story, but I had a notion the kid knew more than the negotiator did.

"Why don't you both grab a seat," I suggested, "and explain to me what I have to go kill."

---

MOTHA SAT IN THE ROOM WITH TOO MANY *HIGOW'AH*. It made him uncomfortable, especially since it was their town. He could just vanish, and nobody would ever tell his family the truth of what happened to him. Motha knew such things occurred, but this new threat to his family was too big for him not to seek help.

The men talked rapidly to each other, and Motha could not keep up. He heard words he recognized, like "Charlie," and "metal men," and "heads," but unless they chose to slow down, or at least talked directly to him, Motha would wait.

So much of his family's future depended on people like Johns. Of the others in the room, the bald one's clothes smelled of the drink that made people do stupid things.

And then there was the man in the hat. Motha recognized him and the symbol of the sun he wore on his shirt. It meant he had permission to kill people, even his own kind, and no one would question it. He wore a gun like the *sultá* did, but had on different, normal clothes and often rode alone when he came to visit the camp. He took away members of Motha's tribe for doing things the *higow'ah* considered bad. Those men never returned. He must have killed them.

The man-with-the-sun-symbol would cast a glance at him from time to time as Johns talked. Finally, he held up a hand and walked over to Motha. He smiled and spoke slowly.

"How long you first see metal men?" he asked in imperfect Yuman.

"Three days," Motha answered.

"Know where they from?"

A wave of relief washed over him. This *mastava* would listen. Motha would send an evil warrior to fight a greater evil.

"Come! I will show you."

———

I GOT MY HORSE, ROLAND, FROM THE LIVERY IN town. Owner had asked to come along, which surprised me. Al, too, which annoyed me. Owner knew of the strange happenings that occurred in Drowned Horse, of course. He was the first settler here, after all. Built his bar while other folk still worked their way west. Now when travelers stopped for a drink, they'd want to stay and set up shop. Before we knew it, we had a town sitting on a cursed land. Oh, sure, we warned them, but Drowned Horse often drew bull-headed people to it.

I guess that included me. I had a particular set of skills that the future citizens of Drowned Horse needed. They felt safe so long as I stayed there.

Al, though, was different. He'd been drafted, not drawn. And while he'd done his fair share of hunting in the mountains above Prescott, he'd never admitted to seeing the type of stuff I had. I wasn't too sure how he'd be in a fight against monsters or whatever particular flavor these metal men actually were.

I packed heavy, just in case. I brought a variety of different weapons, not knowing what'd work on metal men. I threw a few sticks of TNT in my pack to be safe. Big blasts tended to fix most evil things, especially the larger ones. Everyone, save for the kid, brought enough ammunition to take down a charging rhino.

Or so I've been led to believe. Never shot a rhino.

Shot a sasquatch that was eating prospectors. Figured had to be about the same.

Motha—I preferred his real name to Charlie—indicated that we should dismount and go the rest of the way by foot. We crept up slowly to the place Al said they'd been in the wee hours of the morning. We peered over the ledge into the ravine below only to find it empty.

I asked Motha. "Any idea where they went?"

His smile told me he knew. I liked the boy. He wasn't *too* afraid of me, but showed a healthy respect. He might just be cautious enough to keep us alive. I wanted to meet more Indians like him; someone you could reason with. 'Course, those in charge of the 8th Cavalry out of Fort Whipple weren't the most reasonable type to deal with either, so I guess it's probably a wash.

Motha led us down into the gulch, and then tracked the metal skins. Something didn't ring true to me—the story these two told. Why would metal skins pose as Indians and go kill settlers? What was the goal? To start a war? To drive settlers away? I needed to know more.

The ravine curved to the left, and Motha held up a hand. He heard the noises before we did. Sharp ears, that kid.

I peeked around the corner. A huge cave held a dozen men inside—not metal ones, but the flesh and blood type— milling around a whole bunch of Motha's "metal skins." They fussed over them as if they were dressing them for Sunday church.

They were just a might too big to be taken for human up

close, but if they were shooting up caravans from a ways off, like up on a ridge, they'd be hard to tell the difference from any of the local tribes. I didn't see any horses, so they were probably too heavy to mount up. Had to be some sort of genius who made them, though.

The leader—See, I could tell he was the leader because he was louder and fatter than the rest, which meant he had more money and more food than his men—barked orders.

"We need to get this war party going. Who knows who that was up on the ridge? If it was a couple of reds, then we're okay. Ain't nobody going to believe them anyhow. But if it was the Army, then we gots to be ready, boys. No time for making theses tin-can injuns look any more real. Mount up!"

From the cave, little men came out by the handful. Not dwarves, nor midgets. I've seen dwarves and midgets. These, well, these looked like normal men, just tinier. Maybe like pixies or elves from a fairy tale. I shivered. I couldn't help wondering if they could fix my worn boots. I hear tell elves good at that sort of thing.

Each of them stood next to a metal Indian and unlatched the chest. An attendant would then help a pixie into the suit, guiding his arms and legs into stirrups. The stirrups, it seemed, allowed the rider to move the suit's arms and legs. Using pulleys attached to their fingers, the tiny man could control the expressions on the face of the fake Indian.

It was quite a contraption and like nothing I'd seen around these parts.

Owner and Johns also stared blank-faced at the operation below us. Motha, said "*Chaneque*," and spat on the ground, as if that should explain everything.

"Once word of our war party sweeps through the region, the 8th Cavalry will storm down Grief Hill and eradicate all the savages in the area, allowing me to buy up land on the cheap." He ran a caring hand over one of the metal men. "It'll make my investment in these beauties worth it.

Drowned Horse won't be the only town in the Verde Valley for long."

I stepped back and addressed my posse.

"Okay, I'm going to deputize the lot of you. We don't have much time, so subtlety's out of the question."

Then I asked Motha, "How's your throwing arm?"

---

MAYBE HE WAS TOO QUICK TO JUDGE THIS MAN AS evil, Motha thought. He was a *bamulva*—a warrior who leads, not like Johns and his lies. The Sheriff promised he'd find the people behind the attacks on blue-eyes and clear his family of any accusations. Motha wished he met more blue-eyes like Sheriff Forrest.

Motha waited behind the rocks as Sheriff Forrest had directed him to. He understood now that he was the "forest" Johns referred to. Not a tree, but as almost solid as one.

Forrest, Johns, and the one-whose-clothes-smelled-like-liquor, rode down the ravine quickly, guns firing up in the air, causing a panic around the camp. The metal warriors that already contained small men then fired back, but the three *higow'ah* darted around too rapidly to target. Forrest's bullets bounced off the metal skins' hides, so he put his gun away and drew out a long-handled ax from beside his saddle. He twirled it over his head, like Motha had seen Apaches do, and then rode forward swinging it low at the metal skins' legs. One by one, Forrest felled many of the fake men. The *chaneque* inside climbed out of the metal skins and scampered quickly up the sides of the ravine for safety.

It made sense the bad men used *chaneque* in their evil plan. The little demons had no honor either.

The rest of the bad men fled into the cave, taking a stand there. A terrible noise erupted from within, like a hot spring geyser, followed by a chugging sound. Lights burst on—the giant globes he and Johns had seen last night—blinding

Forrest and his warriors even in the daylight. Their horses reeled back, and Johns was thrown from his.

Suddenly, hundreds of bullets came in rapid succession from behind the lights, tearing up the ground all around them. The large gun seemed made of many guns, and Motha recalled a story his Uncle told him once of such evil being mounted on the *sultá* fortresses. It fired like a thousand men all at the same time.

The liquor man's horse collapsed, just as he jumped free.

Forrest dismounted, slapped his horse's rear, and ran for cover.

He yelled to Motha.

"Now!"

Motha lit the end of the stick, as Forrest had shown him and, taking careful aim, threw the stick in a high arc until it landed on top of the cave. He lit a second and a third, tossing them at both the positions Forrest had pointed out to him earlier.

When the sticks exploded, the front of the cave came down like the flap of a tent. Rocks trapped the men inside. Once all the firing had stopped, Forrest stood up and checked on his men. Everyone was still alive.

Motha ran down to join them.

"Wasn't expecting the auto-cannon," Sheriff Forrest said.

Johns, perplexed, asked, "You were expecting the rest?"

Forrest shrugged. "That should hold them until I can get the Army here to show them what's really going on." He rubbed the top of Motha's head. "See? We aren't *all* so bad."

Motha knew he had made the right choice.

But like Johns's promises, Forrest's words were lies, as well.

When Motha returned to his family's camp, twelve warriors lay dead on the ground, including Motha's father and two of his uncles. The rest of his family had been surrounded by twenty Mexican *sultá* astride their horses. Motha's people held their hands up in surrender.

Forrest grabbed one of the men, probably their leader, and dragged him from his mount to the ground.

"What did you do here? What did YOU DO?"

The commander stood, dusting himself off. "What I'm commissioned to do, by Special Order Twenty-21. I'm 1st Lieutenant Antonio Abeytia, and this is Company K from Fort Whipple. We've just arrived here after five days of hard travel to keep the Clear Creek settlers safe." He looked at Forrest's badge. "Just like *you're* supposed to."

Forrest kicked the *sultá's* legs out from under him, sending him back down. "Me? I was out there taking care of the real culprits attacking the settlers and blaming it on these folks. *You* slaughtered innocent men!"

Several of the *sultá* grabbed Forrest and held him. Their leader got up and dusted himself off again. He drew his gun and pointed it at Forrest's head.

Motha couldn't move. Would they kill him, too?

"We got word of these *indio sucio* attacking settlers. When we arrived here to question them, they defied us." He looked down at the dead, and spit. "They're soulless savages."

Johns moved in to stand in front of Forrest. "And it's because of that attitude, men like the ones we captured today continue to thrive in the territories, *Lieutenant* Abeytia. Take your men out of here so these people can grieve their dead. I'll lead you to where you can find the real killers. Hanging them won't make these people feel better, but it will make me."

Motha was sure Abeytia would shoot both Johns and Forrest, but then he caught the eye of the bald liquor man who slowly, subtly shook his head "no." Something in that man's expression told the leader he better put his gun down. Reluctantly, the *sultá* put it away and told his people to let Forrest go. They rode in sets of two out of the camp.

Johns apologized to Motha's mother for not being there to stop the killing. She turned from him, not listening, not caring. Johns bowed and raced to catch up to the horses.

Forrest grabbed a shovel from his pack and asked if he could help dig graves.

Motha cried next to his father's body, letting the grief wash out of him. When he was finished, he walked over to Forrest's horse while the man was distracted and took one of the sticks that explode from it. Motha hid it in his shirt, thinking that, someday, he might need to fight a big evil with an even bigger one, once again.

# THREE
# "PARADOXES AND A PAIR OF SIX-GUNS"

Arizona Territory
February 13th, 1866
6:57 A.M.

THE BULLETS HIT THE FRONT SIDE OF A BOULDER
that the man and a baby he held hid behind. Shards of rock
rained down on them, and Sheriff Levi Forrest leaned
forward, protecting the infant boy from the debris. Forest
pulled back the swaddling to check that the infant was okay.
The little one smiled, wide-eyed and bald as bean.

He waved his kerchief over the rock the top of the boulder, hoping the ones firing at them would see it. "Y'know, I
got here a baby here!" he shouted. "Don't seem right to
involve him. Bad enough ya killed his whole family, but
there's no reason to add him to that number."

Or the sheriff, for that matter.

In answer, more bullets and arrows showered them.

"I guess they ain't the forgiving types, huh?" he said to
the babe.

Daylight had broken only moments before, and Forrest
reckoned the attack on the Apaches would start soon. E

Company out of Camp Lincoln, led by Lieutenant Manuel Gallegos, had informed him of their plans while seeking volunteers at the Sagebrush Saloon.

The town still had that fresh lumber smell to it. Maybe three-hundred now called the area home, building business around the saloon. Company E couldn't draft any of the locals though, as none wanted more trouble.

Drowned Horse had plenty already.

The soldiers left angry. Apache raids had them overwhelmed and under fed, and there's nothing worse than a hungry man with a gun.

Of course, the same could be said of the *Diné*, who were also hungry, due to the Verde Valley's new settlers claiming farmlands that had once been theirs. In retaliation, they raided a wagon train heading to Utah, which left a young mother near death's door by the time Forrest arrived. With a thick Russian accent, she mumbled about a baby right before she stepped through the veil.

Forrest vowed to get the young'n back. Though sneaking into an Apache encampment—nestled securely cliffside—at night turned out to be a bad idea in hindsight. A single baby giggle was all it took to alert the sentries. His run from the cave was less than dignified, but he hadn't wanted to risk the child by returning fire.

Beaver Creek, swollen from Oak Creek Canyon's runoff, rolled just over the embankment from where they'd hunkered down. If they could get to it, without taking a bullet in the back, they'd be in the clear.

The baby cooed, oblivious to the maelstrom. The gunfire abruptly stopped when a bugle echoed in the distance. The cavalry's approach was none-too-subtle, hoping to scare the Apaches into surrendering.

They rarely did.

Seizing the opportunity, Forrest slipped down to the water's edge.

A boat waited there.

Convenient, as he left his horse Roland, tied a good distance away.

Forrest let the current take them away from the chaos, until after finally feeling safe, he relaxed and dozed just a bit...

---

Arizona Territory
February 13th, 1866
6:57 A.M.

THE BULLETS HITTING THE FRONT SIDE OF THE boulder rained shards of rock down on the man and child hiding behind it.

Sheriff Levi Forrest leaned forward, keeping the boy clear of the flying debris.

"What in the hell?"

His charge seemed heavier than a moment before. Forest pulled back the edge of the swaddling to find that he no longer held a months old baby. Instead, a one-year-old, if Forrest guessed right, smiled up at him. Still wide-eyed. Still bald.

"Dadad," the child spoke.

"Um, no. Just the guy trying to save you."

The child squiggled free of his grasp and made a break for it. Forrest gathered him up just as the sound of a bugle came across the canyon. Feeling he'd somehow done this all before, Forrest made a break for the creek and found a boat waiting there, just as he knew it would be.

He reasoned it away.

"Okay, so maybe déjà vu?"

He climbed in, and they bobbed down the stream. *And maybe I hadn't really been paying to close attention to the child's age.*

Not wanting to miss what he figured was about to

happen, Forrest did his best not to even blink, until he finally had to.

———————

Arizona Territory
February 13th, 1866
6:57 A.M.

BULLETS  HITTING  THE  FRONT  SIDE  OF  THE boulder rained shards of rock down on the man and toddler hiding behind it. Sheriff Levi Forrest hovered over the boy, who piled stones playfully in front of him. The bald child gave a frustrated grunt as the rocks fell over.

"Definitely, not déjà vu."

The sheriff decided to wait it out. E Company would be on site soon, and then he could retrieve Roland. Yes, he would retrieve Roland, and they'd ride to town, no boats needed.

Only, at that moment...

A Tonto warrior who had followed Forrest out of the cave chose to attack right then. He leapt onto of the boulder the lawman used for cover and screamed his intentions to kill the *higow'ah*. Hatchet held high, he leapt at Forrest, who instead of falling backwards, jumped up and caught the warrior in a bear hug so tight, he couldn't use the weapon.

They wrestled and fell over the embankment. Crashing into the frigid creek, Forrest let go. The warrior scrambled for the bank, but Forrest made it there first. As Tonto stood, Forrest drew and shot him.

The dead man fell into the boat.

Forrest kicked it free and climbed up the embankment to check on the boy, who seemed oblivious to everything, including the three Apaches who pointed their rifles at Forrest.

"Damn." Bullets struck Forrest in the chest, sending him sprawling back into the river.

---

Arizona Territory
February 13th, 1866
6:57 A.M.

BULLETS. ROCK. YEAR OLDER CHILD. STILL BALD.

"Okay. New plan."

Everyone from those parts knew the land around the town of Drowned Horse was cursed. That was a given. Ever since Forrest arrived and took on the role of protector, he'd seen all sorts of things that defied logic and reason, but this time-loop thing just pissed him off.

In the boat, Forrest didn't follow the current, choosing instead to paddle hard to the opposite shore. He knew the way to town from that side, though they'd have to ford the river again downstream.

Only...

---

Arizona Territory
February 13th, 1866
6:57 A.M.

"BLACK BEAR? REALLY?"

Prepared, Forrest shot the bear, shot the Apache who jumped into the stream after them, dodged the friendly fire from E company, and finally, got free from the area long enough to begin the long trek back to Drowned Horse.

But Forrest and his charge walked and walked and never seemed to get closer to town. No Roland where he was sure he'd left him tied up. While the red rock caves they'd just left were a distant dot on the horizon. None of the landmarks Forrest should've seen by then had shown up. The river was now out of sight, and yet they continued to march in the dry cold of an Arizona winter day.

The boy alternated riding on Forrest's back, walking, and riding again. Each time he got down, the boy looked older. He didn't speak much, save to say he was hungry. Forrest killed a rabbit and started a fire with his tinderbox. When night came, they hunkered inside a grouping of boulders. As the boy lay against the lawman's chest, Forrest wrapped his coat around them best he could.

His lawman job left him with little desire to raise a tot by himself, so he'd have to find a couple who'd lost a child to the cough or something and were willing to take him on.

Worried that in the morning they'd be back at the cave, Forrest tried keeping watch through the night, but he ultimately succumbed to the black.

When Forrest woke, the sun shone brightly, and he was still leaning against the boulders from the night before, but the boy no longer slept at his side.

Rising quickly, Forrest sought his bearings.

A child's laugh, followed by chicken squawking, drew the sheriff around to the backside of their lodgings. The boy, now around age seven, chased a chicken, nearly catching her, but the hen seemed to always dodge right at the last moment.

"That's quite a chicken run."

An old woman sat on a rock watching the show.

"No chicken puns! And you sleep too soundly for a lawman. That boy's been chasing my hen for an hour."

Age had bent the crone's back into a hump, and something wasn't right with her nose, but her eyes twinkled like a grandmother's. Her words were thick Slavic, much as the boy's dead mother spoke, and Forrest guessed Ukrainian or there 'bouts.

"I made him eggs. You could use some, too, I bet. Hope you like eggs." She grabbed the chicken remarkably fast as it ran by. The pair shuffled off around the corner.

Forrest tipped his hat. "That would be right kind of you." He called for the boy to follow, however, his nerves remained on high alert. The territories brought all types of people seeking opportunity. Yet, Forrest couldn't help but think it a bit too coincidental that the old woman and the boy might be from the same region of the world.

Coincidences, in Forrest's experience, rarely were the product of chance and often were the tools of gods playing with humans' lives.

When Forrest and the boy rounded the large red rocks, both woman and chicken had disappeared. The boy tugged on Forrest's coat and pointed at a space between the rocks. That he hadn't seen the archway immediately, or even last night, bothered him. It smelled of magic.

He hated magic.

After passing through the opening, his concern grew stronger. The passage opened to an impossibly large cavern with a grassy yard, thick vegetation, and a pond filled with fat goldfish. A thatched-roof hut, laced with chicken feathers, capped the far end of the cave. The lawman had no desire to find out what waited in there.

Forrest turned the boy around to exit, only to find the archway had vanished, leaving only smooth rock.

"You're in no danger. Not yet."

The old woman placed the chicken in a bamboo cage before walking around to a throne made of human bones. Her illusion faded revealing her real face. Her nose hung down over her mouth, flat and rotting with circling flies crawling into her nostrils, only to burst out of puss bubbles. Nothing kind existed in those eyes anymore.

Forrest pushed the boy behind him.

"What are you?"

"I am Baba Yuveleva, the youngest of the Babas, and I claim that child."

Forrest drew his six-guns only to discover chicken feathers in his grasp instead.

"It's useless to fight fate, Lawman. We can have a nice breakfast, and then you go, leaving him behind."

"Or?"

"Or I kill you and have something other than eggs for lunch."

That didn't sound like much of a choice to him.

"If I leave, where...and when...will I be?"

Baba Yuveleva raised a finger to her cheek and tapped it in time with her...chicken feet? From under her dress, a taloned foot poked out, echoing her contemplative rhythm.

"Hmmm. Good question. Not sure. Maybe right where you left off. Maybe in the future. Who knows? So much magic under the red sands, my head swims. That's why I came here from Russia. For magic. For power." She cackled, before extending her hand outward, urging Forrest to decide. "Come, come. You've a whole town to protect. Forget the boy."

"Why him?"

She spat snot and spittle to the ground. "Why do you care? You've known him but hours."

It felt much longer. At least seven years.

"Sorry, but I made a promise to his dyin' mother to see him taken care of. I don't think this is what she meant."

Baba Yuveleva leaned forward, conspiratorially. "What if I told you you'll die in five years? Would you still want to be responsible for him?"

Forrest squinted, trying to gauge her words. "You sayin' that's just a possibility, or do ya know somethin'?"

She waved her hand nonchalantly. "I dabble in the arcane. No fortune telling, but I hear things in the wind. No sense of him getting attached to a father figure that'll die horribly."

Forrest knew from the moment he signed on as sheriff

that he'd be unlikely to leave Drowned Horse alive. A man could fight a curse only so long, and evil tended to get smarter, not dumber, over time.

"Doesn't matter. I'll find others to look after him when I'm gone. It only matters that *you* don't get him." Seeing nothing around to fight with, Forrest held up his fists, ready to beat the old witch senseless if he had to.

His mind, however, kept working the angles.

Baba Yuveleva sighed. "I didn't want this, but I must have that child. His existence is unnatural. He should have died in that raid, but the natives somehow broke him free of that fate. That means he's filled with un-mined potential that I can tap into to make me the most powerful Baba ever."

Forrest didn't understand how one tapped someone's potential, but it didn't sound like it would be all that great for the boy. .

"He's not a well, you old hag. He's a person who has a right to choose his own destiny."

"Doesn't matter. He's fuel for my magic, and I want him...now!"

She stood and mumbled words under her breath.

"Wait!" Forrest shouted, waving his hands when he realized he'd hit upon a possible solution. "What if there was another way?"

Baba Yuveleva stopped mid-incantation and cocked her head.

"Such as?"

"Such as, why *don't* you let him decide? I can't speak for him, as I'm not his pa, and he's not been educated in the world as to make a sound choice yet. Wouldn't you rather wait 'til he's older and you have a willing sacrifice versus an unwillin' one? I know a spring is easier to tap than an aquifer."

The old woman sat back down and tapped her talons again. "The power derived from someone willingly offering themselves *is* much stronger." She clucked. "Oh, some say fear powers spells better, but I've always been more of a 'love wins' believer." She stopped tapping. "But! He must come of his own free will. Nor can you speak of our deal. Leave him a note to be delivered after your death." Baba Yuveleva pointed to a table where paper and quill resided. "Write it now! I'll charm you so you won't be able to tear it up after you leave."

Forrest drafted the letter. He'd have five years to find a way to break the curse and warn the boy.

After approving the note, Baba Yuveleva threw chicken bones and sparkly dust in his face.

"Now, get out. You may have bought yourselves time, but that boy will be mine. One way or another."

Forrest pushed the boy through the reappeared archway and out into the summer sun.

From a nearby hilltop, they spotted the Verde River. They would be back in Drowned Horse by nightfall.

Only...

Drowned Horse wasn't anywhere to be found. In fact, all evidence pointed to it never having been built.

---

Arizona Territory
???


"THAT DAMNED WITCH SENT US BACK IN TIME!"

How far? Was this even still America, or the *Terra Incognita* that existed before? What would the locals think of two *higow'ah* suddenly staking a claim here?

They needed shelter. Forrest pointed them toward the caves within the Black Hills. The next morning, he speared fish instead of hunting as he only had so many bullets left.

The boy stopped abnormally aging at about age eight, and then grew like any child thereafter. Forrest taught him to trap, and how to hide from Indians. He still had no name, as "Boy" or "Son" worked most of the time. Forrest figured if he wanted one, that'd be his choice, as well.

Together, they built a makeshift shelter out of fallen trees and made clothes from animal skins.

As was inevitable, they eventually encountered the natives.

Forrest sighed in relief when he recognized their markings as Wiipukepaya. He spoke just enough *Paya* to promise they meant them no harm and asked if they would like to trade. He offered them a selection of furs he and the boy had collected. Deal struck, the duo now had tools to fashion a cabin and some clay pots to cook with.

Word spread of the strange pair, and others like the *Yavaþé*, *Diné*, and several mixed tribes came to trade. Over time, Forrest and his son became fluent in the local dialect and variations of it. They joined the tribe for ceremonies, hunting parties, and there was even talk of Forrest picking a young woman from the tribe to marry. Forrest declined, not sure if he still had only the five years left the Baba predicted. Plus, while the curse hadn't shown itself yet, every sense told him it waited there for them.

Two years later, Forrest and his son met a group of Mormons coming up the Verde River by boat, led by Lieutenant Amiel Whipple and a French Trapper named Antoine Leroux.

They answered Forrest's biggest question since their final time jump...

———

Arizona Territory
May 13th, 1854
6:57 P.M.

They'd traveled back twelve years!

Armed with that knowledge, Forrest made a plan. He and the boy took furs to a trading post over a week's walk away, where they bartered for better tools, dry goods, and weapons. Then they returned to the place where Drowned Horse would someday reside.

"Son, we're going to build a saloon here."

"Why, Pa?"

"Because, this town will need one. Believe me."

They worked the rest of the summer and fall. Forrest told his son about the curse, and what type of things they would face in the future. He taught him how to recognize it; fight it. Forrest recalled tales he'd been told as a child around the Roma campfires. Then, together, they sought out the legends of the Yavapai, the Apache, the Hopi, and the Zuni.

By the next summer, they'd built, at least in Forrest's mind, a decent replica of the Sagebrush Saloon, the heart of Drowned Horse. More trips to the trading post followed where they exchanged pelts for booze and smoked meats for the coming winter.

At about age 13, the boy took to shaving his head, saying he preferred that to washing it. Forrest laughed, finally understanding who he'd been chosen to guard by the whim of the gods.

"It looks fine, Owner."

The lad tilted his head. "Owner?"

"Yeah, it's your saloon. You're the owner."

Owner laughed nervously. "It's *our* place, Papa, unless you're leaving?"

Forrest rubbed the top of his son's head. "Not intentionally. And if'n I do, it won't be for long."

Matter settled, Owner nodded.

It'd be nigh on seven years before Forrest's younger self would arrive as part of the first expedition to settle the Verde Valley. Only, instead of empty land, they'd found a fully functioning saloon and a bald man tending bar. It made no sense to anyone at the time, but now Forrest understood. He would die and leave Owner here alone, but not before he taught the young man everything he'd need to know who would then teach those things to a naïve Levi Forrest in 1865.

And all would be right.

---

Arizona Territory
February 13th, 1856
Let's say it was about mid-morning

FORREST'S PARENTS HAD BEEN ROMANI, THOUGH most knew them in America by the slur "Gypsies," as if none were ever to be trusted. However, the world *he* grew up in treated religion like a bountiful harvest, each sermon containing whatever was ripe at the time. Some days they were Catholic. Others, Jewish. Occasionally even Muslim. They let the moment guide them to the divine.

Forrest instructed Owner on theology, but unfortunately, he could only find a missionary's bible to study from. It had grown worn, and Forrest promised he'd get the boy a new one in the near future.

Lessons finished, Forrest put the book back on the shelf, and slid the five-year-old letter he'd written under the Baba's watchful gaze, inside of it. He had faith that his son would figure out how to best the old crone. He'd prepared him for that day without muttering a single word about her. Instead, he imbued Owner with reason and knowledge and ingenuity. The boy, now a young man, had never brought up the old woman with the chicken in the years since. Nor did he have any recollection of time skipping, or anything really, before they settled there, nearly five years ago. When Forrest would ask, Owner just shrugged and moved on to another topic. It made him wonder if he wasn't the only one enchanted by the witch.

Forrest planned to slip the letter from the old bible into a new one, but life, or the whims of gods one might say, enjoyed messing with the plans of men. As soon as the letter was placed, Forrest forgot it existed. New bible bought, the old one sat on the shelf in their room gathering dust for many years.

That winter turned out to be the worst they'd experienced. Even the Verde River had a sheet of ice on it, though not strong enough to ford, which was fine as the Wiipukepaya had been their only visitors lately, and they mostly huddled together during those kinds of weather conditions.

Thus, when Forrest and Owner heard the cracking ice and a high-pitched scream of a girl, they'd been caught completely unawares. Grabbing their coats, they raced outside.

Halfway across the Verde, a Wiipukepaya girl thrashed in the ice; her thick pelts weighting her down. She wouldn't survive long.

Forrest pulled off his coat and boots.

"Get the rope from the storeroom. I'll get her free, and you toss us the rope."

Owner, panicking more than Forrest expected him to be after all his years of training, begged, "No, Pa! It's too—"

"Go! Now, boy!"

Forrest never needed to raise his voice before, so Owner kicked into action.

Testing the ice as Forrest traversed the river, he called to the girl. "Just hold still. Let the water refreeze around you with your head above ice."

Though scared, the girl did as he commanded.

The color of the ice lightened under him, and cracks formed with each step. Forrest reckoned he'd be a good twenty feet away from her when he'd go under. He waited until he heard Owner call from behind him.

"I got the rope, Pa!"

Measuring in his mind, Forrest ran forward, skipping across breaking ice until he could leap into the air. He busted through not far from her, but still far enough he had to swim under the ice until he reached her legs. Diving deep, Forrest pushed up quickly, using his head as a ram, surfacing next to the girl and wrapping himself around her.

Now that he wasn't moving, the effects of the frozen river took hold. Through chattering teeth, Forrest guided Owner until the boy could safely stand and throw the line. On his second try, it came close enough for Forrest to reach.

He told the girl, "I'm going to take off your coat, and you're going to let my son drag you to him."

Owner shouted, "I can pull you both!"

Forrest disagreed. "I'm too heavy. Bring her to you first, and then you both can pull me out."

"No, Pa. I need to save you."

A father's love warmed his words. "You will, son. You will."

Forrest smashed the ice encasing the girl. "Pull!"

With Forrest holding onto her coat, the girl slipped free, and Owner dragged her to safety. Forrest let the pelts sink as ice reformed around him. He felt nothing, above or below the ice. His mind slowed, and he barely registered the rope —or the begging cries for him from his son to take it—as it fell repeatedly nearby him.

Then the once and future sheriff of Drowned Horse closed his eyes and chuckled. The curse wouldn't get him after all.

Just his…

Big…

Damn…

Heart.

---

Arizona Territory
February 13th, 1866

6:57 A.M.

BULLETS HITTING THE FRONT SIDE OF THE boulder rained shards of rock down on Sheriff Levi Forrest, who hid behind it.

"Dammit! I'm not even supposed to be here."

Which was true. The Tontos had raided a wagon train headed for Utah, and Forrest arrived just in time to hear a dying woman's wish that she be buried with a locket containing a silhouette of her dead husband.

Well, didn't he just make a stupid vow to go fetch it?

Though sneaking into a secured Apache encampment—nestled securely cliffside—at night turned out to be more daunting than that description would imply. All it took was him accidentally kicking a rock to alert their sentries. Now, he found himself pinned down, too far away from Roland.

Beaver Creek rolled just over the embankment from where he hunkered down. If he could get there without taking a bullet in the back, he could follow it downstream, and circle back for his horse once E Company arrived for their planned morning assault.

As if on cue, the cavalry's bugle sounded. Relieved, Forrest would wait out the attack there.

Only...

A Tonto warrior jumped atop of the boulder Forrest used for cover, screaming his intention to kill the *higow'ah*.

Rolling forward onto his back, Forrest drew and shot him.

The brave fell dead beside him.

*That's another life I'll have to account for to whatever celestial being awaits me up there.*

But Forrest hoped that'd be a long time off. Checking to make sure he still had the locket, the sheriff slunk away as the cavalry charged.

A WHISKEY WAITED FOR HIM WHEN HE GOT BACK to the Sagebrush.

Forrest plopped the jewelry piece on the counter. "Can you make sure that Craddick gets that before he buries the Mormon girl? I'm too tired to move."

"Sure thing," Owner said. He picked it up, but paused. "You didn't find a baby the Apaches might have taken from the settlers, did you?"

Forrest raised an eyebrow. "No. Why? You hear somethin'?"

Owner shook his head, as if to clear it. "No, must be déjà vu. Seems like I recalled something about a child."

"Don't know." Forrest shrugged and started in on the whiskey. "You were here when Gallegos from Camp Lincoln came recruitin' for volunteers. Maybe he said somethin'."

The Fort was struggling. When ordered to the region, they'd not been given proper clothing, food stores, or horses. They were, however, given plenty of weapons to arm the new settlers and often asked for help defending the camp. Sometime, if relations with the Indians were bad, they'd get plenty of volunteers. When things were good in Drowned Horse, no one wanted to stir up trouble and face reprisal.

Owner smiled at his sheriff. "I'm the only one who does the recruiting around here." He turned to leave.

"Hey," Forrest said with sleep-deprived weariness. "Remember when you did that?"

Owner paused. "Did what?"

"Recruited me. You said, 'It's about time you got here.' What was that all about?"

Owner stepped out from behind his bar and put on his father's coat; the one the man had worn just before sacrificing his life to save an Indian girl. Since he vanished in a flash of light before he could be pulled safely from the river, Owner figured his pa wouldn't mind if he inherited it. It kept him warm those long, lonely nights as he finished preparations on the Sagebrush for the time when his father would return.

"Maybe I'll tell you when the time is right."

Forrest shrugged again. Owner had his secrets, and the sheriff knew to leave well enough alone.

Feeling much older than his years, the lawman said, "Suit yourself. I'm going to pour a hot bath and sleep for a whole year."

Owner walked from the saloon and whispered under his breath, "Or nine. But then, who can predict the future? Right, Pa?"

# FOUR
# "TAXES ARE HEAVY"

Prescott, Arizona Territory
April, 1866

"I DON'T WANT TO DO THIS."

"You have to."

"No, we can just pretend there's no one there."

Yavapai County Sheriff John P. Bourke gave his county recorder, Silas Neurink, a cross-eyed glare from the saddle of his horse, ending the debate. While less than three-hundred people lived on the other side of the Black Hills from the county seat, they were still to be taxed as residents. The notion the residents of the Verde Valley lived on cursed land would not excuse the two of them from their sworn duty.

"Collecting taxes pays for my office and yours," the Sheriff reminded him.

Silas sighed and got onto his horse, so he was level with the lawman. "Probably no one who's made $800 or more down there yet."

Leading his horse to the trail that would take them down

Grief Hill, Bourke said, "There's a saloon, a livery, and ranchers. If there's money to be found, we'll find it."

Neurink urged his mount after the Sheriff's.

*Maybe the 3% we gather would be worth our lives,* he wanted to say, but kept those thoughts to himself.

---

THEY APPROACHED THE TOWN WHICH WAS LITTLE more than a saloon and a couple buildings. Drowned Horse had trouble taking serious root in the area due to the Indian attacks, lack of continuous Army presence, and the sudden and violent deaths of many who decided to make the valley their home.

Neurink could still see the appeal, though. Cottonwood trees were beginning to bud after a moderate winter. The rivers swelled with runoff, but had not gotten to the raging levels that gave Drowned Horse its ominous name. They passed a few ranches and farms that seemed to be preparing for planting. So far, nothing unusual to lend to the rumors that kept floating up to Prescott.

Bourke interrupted Neurink's musings. "We'll check in with the saloon owner. He'll have records of who's settled here in the last year."

"Why again are there two sheriffs for one county?"

On that, Bourke just said, "Well, you see, it's a long way between my office and the Verde Valley. Seemed prudent and expeditious. That's why they're formulizing an Army camp down here, after all."

He didn't sound all that convincing to Neurink.

They tethered their horses in front of the Sheriff's office. Levi Forrest came out to greet them.

"Bourke."

"Forrest."

They shook hands. "Thanks for the warnin' you were on the way. This is Mr. Neurink, I assume?"

"Indeed it is," Silas said and also shook hands with the

short man. Whereas Bourke was large and intimidating, Forrest was compact and reminded him of a badger.

*Maybe that's what kept the strange happenings at bay? Someone with dogged tenacity like this man.*

Instead of walking into the Sheriff's office and jail, Forrest led them over to the Sagebrush, the town's only saloon, and the whole reason there was a town. A plaque hung just next to the door that read, "Established 1855," which couldn't be right. Prescott had been founded only two years prior and the area was largely unsettled before that.

*Maybe it was a misprint and the owner didn't want to pay for a new sign to be made?*

A table piled with ledgers had been prepped with beers poured for each newcomer. A man, bald before his years, welcomed them in.

"I'm Owner. Thanks for coming such a long way."

Silas, confused, asked, "Did you just say your name was Owner, or that you were *the* Owner?"

Dropping into a seat, Owner confirmed, "It's just Owner. No last name. Only name I've ever known. If there was another, it's long forgotten."

The county clerk slowly sat down, less sure that he was actually in Drowned Horse.

*Maybe I fell asleep on my horse, and this is all a dream?*

They went over the books, the two sheriffs mostly just answering questions asked by Silas. Owner was the brains of the area, having kept meticulous entries on each person who settled there.

"And what about this property owned by James Polk and Enos Barnett?" Silas asked to clear up an irregularity. "You list only Polk on their revenue statement."

Forrest spoke up. "Oh, sorry, Yeah, Enos got carried off and beheaded by a giant bat."

Silas stared at the Sheriff in disbelief.

"A giant bat?"

"Yup," he said with a straight face. "Sacrificed to a Mexican god."

Bourke leaned toward Silas. "Just put him down as 'deceased, 'k?"

Silas made the notation. "And Joseph-Marie Dubois?"

"We think it was a rougarou."

The clerk raised an eyebrow, but didn't look up from his ledger. "A rougarou?"

Owner answered, "It's like a giant man-dog-like thing. You can write 'killed by wild dogs,' if you'd like."

Bourke nodded, knowingly. "What he said."

This continued through a dozen different names, each death they described more horrific than the next until he reached his final query

Silas breathed a sigh of relief at the complete normalcy of that death. "Okay, that balances all the old records. Anyone move into the region recently you've not accounted for and that could have earned over $800 in that last fiscal year?"

An awkward glance went between Forrest and Owner. Forrest opened his mouth and then closed it. Owner began to speak, but stopped mid-syllable. "Um…"

Bourke squirmed. "I'm not going to like this, am I?"

The two local men simultaneously said, "No."

---

BOURKE, FORREST, AND NEURINK APPROACHED the cave slowly, the sheriffs with their guns drawn.

"He's not a bad sort, really. He's just got kind of a temper." Forrest's softened voice pleaded for understanding and patience.

"Y'know," Bourke said in a hushed tone, "we had an agreement. You'd handle this sort of thing, and I'd handle the normal stuff."

Forrest moved up from one boulder to a closer one, whispering back to his peer, "You're the one who decided to personally collect taxes. I coulda just done it and sent it on the next stage."

Bourke shook his head. "Been too many stage robberies lately. We need these taxes this year especially."

"For what?"

"None your business. Let's just get this over with."

Silas wouldn't have taken what Forrest and Owner told them at the saloon seriously if they weren't about to enter its lair. *Spriggan*, they called it, or *spyryson*, in the original Cornish.

"Just don't offend him, and he'll be pleasant enough."

"Why didn't you just kill him like all the other monstrosities you've encountered?" Bourke had moved up beside Forrest as they prepared to enter the cave.

"Because he hasn't hurt no one. Not yet." He paused. "Well, not intentionally."

Silas slid up to join them. "It's hurt people *unintentionally?*"

Forrest blushed. "Well, you see, most of these strange things happen because someone who moved to the Valley had some personal issues. Gemtwinkle ain't no different."

"Its name is Gemtwinkle?" Bourke asked.

"Gemtwinkle came to be because of this greedy merchant Kenver Uglow. He set up a trading post at the base of the Mogollon Rim, but he overcharged everyone he dealt with, because, y'know, he could."

Bourke nodded. "I remember hearing about him. He vanished, right?"

Forrest sucked in air through his teeth. "Not exactly."

Bourke cocked his head, and Forrest nodded. Silas looked back and forth between the two.

"You don't mean..."

"Yup, the change was slow, at first. The more miserly Kenver got, the quicker he changed. One day, I found his shop empty and a tunnel out back." Forrest gazed into the cave. "It was months before some poor trapper, seeking shelter, stumbled upon ol' Gemtwinkle in here. I started out with the intent of putting him down, but it turned out

Uglow had become much nicer as a spriggan. He apologized for scaring the trapper and paid restitution."

"And that's why you think it, er, he will pay his taxes?" Silas asked.

Forrest held up his hand as if to say, *Who knows?*

The three slipped out from behind their shelter and drew closer to the opening.

Forrest called out, "*Hou sos,* Gemmy? It's Levi. Can we talk? I got a couple friends with me, and we mean you no harm."

A sonorous voice shook loose gravel from above the cave's entrance when it replied, "*Ha pur vysi.* Just hit a vein of obsidian the Pai will buy from me."

Bourke urged Forrest on.

"I know you're busy, but y'see, these folks came a long ways to see you. It's about, y'know, business."

When Gemtwinkle spoke again, he sounded closer and his accent thicker. "What kinda business? *A vyn'ta anjei brena?*"

"No, they're not here to buy anything. They're from the Territory seat up in Prescott. They say you owe some money for running a business in Arizona."

Slow, methodical stomps drew closer and closer to them, and Silas wondered just how big this spriggan was.

"How much money?"

The two lawmen turned to Neurink. It was his turn to shrug. "Depends on how much he made this year."

Forrest called out, "Did you sell more than $800 in minerals?"

Gemtwinkle said, "Ya…"

"3% of whatever you sold."

A shadow grew larger and larger as the fairie walked up the tunnel. Silas felt chills as the shadow reached from the ground to the roof, clearly thirty feet or more. Then, the clerk gasped when Gemtwinkle stepped into the light of day.

Not more than about four-feet-tall hunched over, the

lantern the spriggan carried is what had cast the big shadow. His brownish hair flowed from his head down his back and halfway down his arms. Spending most of his time underground, Gemtwinkle's skin had turned a mottled gray, and warts covered him from head to toe. The most unsettling part, to Silas, had to be the ears that hung down like wings from either side of his head.

*Maybe it's really just a miner who's spent too much time away from the light?* Silas had trouble selling that one to himself.

*"Henna oll?* That's nothing!" Gemtwinkle grinned, showing irregular, jagged teeth. *"Dydh da*, welcome, mates of Levi. Gemtwinkle ov ya! Kavos te?"

Forrest, relieved, waved Bourke and Neurink forward. "He's just put tea on. Come on."

---

THE ACCOUNTING WENT WELL. GEMTWINKLE KEPT better records than Owner and gratefully handed Silas a heavy canvas purse after they finished tea and cakes. "The faster the government opens this land for settlers, the more artists will want to buy my gems to make their pretties, *martesen?"*

Silas had a hard time looking at the disgusting creature, but the amount of money he was paying in taxes, the clerk would agree to anything.

"Indeed. Well, it's a long ride back."

Bourke and Forrest agreed. They all got up to leave.

*"Meur ras*, Gemmy," Forrest clasped arms with the spriggan.

*"Meur ras,"* the cursed being echoed.

They left the cave and worked their way through the rocks. They reached their steeds, mounted, and started back to Drowned Horse.

Bourke was pleased. "That went better than I'd thought. Sounds like it might be easier going forward."

Forrest nodded. "Yeah, and I think you'll find that purse

filled with enough coin to fund the county for the next year alone."

That pleased Silas. He'd be congratulated by the Governor, maybe even given a promotion. One thing nagged at him, though, so he asked Forrest, "Was he that ugly when he was Kenver Uglow?"

Forrest's eyes grew wide in alarm. "Ride!" He spurred his mount suddenly. Bourke followed quickly. Silas, confused, started after them but too late.

"What?" he yelled.

From Gemtwinkle's cave, an angry growl echoed through the whole valley.

Silas looked over his shoulder as he drove his horse.

The spriggan had grown easily over seventy feet tall, and his eyes glowed red. He picked up a boulder the size of a cabin, his intent very clear.

Panic gripped the clerk as he refocused on the trail ahead.

Forrest and Bourke split in opposite directions from the doomed target.

Silas rode straight down the trail alone, hoping he'd make it out of range in time.

A shadow circled him and traced his path. Too big to dodge, Silas Neurink suddenly put together Forrest's warning about offending the spriggan and just how big Gemtwinkle's ears were.

*Maybe I should've just stayed home.*

---

BOURKE AND FORREST STOOD NEXT TO THE boulder that they were pretty sure the Yavapai County Clerk was under.

"You going to take care Gemtwinkle now?" the county sheriff asked.

"Nope. I did warm your man. Plus, you see what happens when Gemmy gets mad."

Bourke, who took out the purse he'd wisely held onto instead of letting Neurink carry it, nodded. "Yeah." He hefted it, feeling its weight. "Mr. Gemtwinkle is a good citizen in fine standing with the county."

They remounted their horses.

Bourke tipped his hat. "Same time, next year?"

Forrest returned the salute. "Yup. Maybe you should just come alone?"

Bourke agreed as they headed back to their separate charges.

# FIVE

# "WHERE JUSTICE ENDS, VENGEANCE BEGINS"

Arizona Territory
June, 1866

IN THAT MOMENT, LEVI FORREST, DULY ELECTED sheriff of Drowned Horse, hated his position. Not for the first time, mind you...and not just because of the 1840 Musket pointed at his head.

Well, truth be told, it *was* mostly that.

"I've come for the girl, Sed," he exclaimed. "You've got no right to her."

The man holding the gun, Sedrick Davidovic, was obviously of a different opinion.

"I done bought her fair and square. The pastor married us and everythin', Sheriff."

Forrest regretted letting the situation get out of control. When word broke that Sed bought himself an Apache girl, he'd thought it just a nasty rumor. But then, he pictured the trapper—one large, weather-beaten, ugly son-of-a-bitch who even the whores at the Sagebrush charged a hazard fee for—and it struck him as completely plausible.

"You held him at gunpoint. Not sure God considers that

a legally bindin' agreement. 'Sides, slavery's illegal now. Haven't you heard of the thirteenth amendment?"

Sed's cabin was part home, part workshop. Several of the mountain man's recent catches hung around it in various states of drying, tanning, or just plain ol' rotting. A repugnant smell wafted through the air. Sed, there on the porch, smelled no better.

"I didn't buy no slave. This is one of those, what-do-ya-callits? Arranged marriages. Yeah. I gave those reds a dowry. Three of my best bear skins. You know what them are worth?"

That *was* a good deal, for the Indians. And it explained some of Sed's reluctance to part with his teenage bride.

"She wasn't theirs to sell. She's 'Che, and they're 'Pai. They found her and now word's gotten out. To keep the peace, she's got to go back to her people. You don't want them bringing a whole war party to your doorstep."

The girl in question appeared in the window, raising her head slowly until her eyes were visible. He placed her age at twelve or thirteen, but she hadn't been crying or anything yet. Forrest wondered if she understood what was in store for her that night.

The sheriff pleaded, "Now come on, Sed. This isn't going to end nice for anyone. Certainly, it will do that girl no good to see two grown men shoot each other. You can help us all out by lowering your gun."

It looked like the trapper was set to comply, dropping the barrel several inches to the right, but then his finger twitched, and he blew a hole in the dirt near Forrest's feet. Gravel shot up and pelted Forrest's boots. That move gave Forrest the right to return fire, but Sed'd switched guns and reacquired his original target quicker than the sheriff's eye could track. He had an old Springfield '55 trained on Forrest's head.

"Now, git off my land! It's my weddin' night."

"Sed. That's only got one shot." Forrest's implication didn't leave room for debate.

"I'll make sure you go first. Ain't kiddin' here, Sheriff. Don't come back 'less it's to bring us a weddin' gift."

The rifle wasn't Sed's only gun. The trapper had stacked enough weaponry on the front porch to take down a herd of buffalo.

Deciding to cut his losses, Forrest mounted up.

"This isn't the end of it, Sed. The new marshal just arrived at Fort Whipple, and I can have him back here tonight. He has jurisdiction over Indian stuff. Maybe you'll listen to him."

"Doubtful."

Forrest spat on the ground. "If those Apaches return, and she's been harmed in any way, well... let's just say scalping will seem like a mercy."

Sedrick snarled, the feral dog in him coming out. "Y'all will find trouble here—you, the marshals, the reds. Look after yer own and leave me the hell out of it!"

The lawman didn't need to turn around to know that the Springfield stayed on him until he rode out of range.

Bringing the newly-assigned marshal into this type of mess might be a good thing, Forrest considered. He could break the unsuspecting lawman in gently before any *real* trouble started.

———

IT JUST SO HAPPENED, AT THAT VERY SAME moment, Marshal Tucker Bandimere, recent of the Arizona Territory seat, hated *his* position for what would be the first of many times...and not just because outlaws had lit his house on fire while he was having dinner over at Fort Whipple.

Though, truth be told, it *was* mostly the fire. The words written in the dirt that read, "Go Hoom Mershell!" didn't help none.

That evening, while staring at the smoking remains of his home and belongings, and wondering why he'd signed on to the marshal's service in the first place, a short man wearing a sheriff's badge walked up to Tucker. The stranger stood reverently, observing of the last embers' glow.

"That's the marshal's home, right?" asked the man.

Tucker nodded.

"Marshal wasn't in there this time, was he?"

Tucker pulled back his duster, revealing his star.

"Good. Let's go stop another Indian war."

———

A DELUGE SWEPT OVER THE BLACK HILLS, delaying the lawmen's trip back to the Davidovic place. As Forrest sat in a cave, sharing a can of beans from his pack, he surveyed their sanctuary. Even in the poor firelight, Forrest could see thin copper veins.

Following his gaze, Marshal Bandimere, sighed. "One of General Cook's men, Al Seibert, I think, was talking over dinner about having seen a rich vein near here. Hopes to open a mine and leave the military life behind."

Forrest finished his beans. "They all say that. More to mining than just finding a claim." But the sheriff knew that it wouldn't be long before someone did find a big strike and mining would come to the Verde Valley.

Wanting to distract himself from those bad thoughts, Forrest surreptitiously turned his gaze to Tucker. A string bean of a man with an extended handlebar mustache, it was clear to Forrest from their discussions on the ride over that Tucker was greener than a bullfrog's sack when it came to being a lawman.

Not so much in regard to combat. The marshal served in the Colorado Cavalry honorably and had played a part in a couple of General Kit Carson's campaigns.

What the young man really lacked was the subtlety.

"So," Tucker asked, "This trapper. You think he's the reasonable type, or am I just going to have to shoot him?"

Forrest nearly choked on the water from his skin. "I'd

prefer he be reasonable." Then he sighed. "But yeah, we're probably gonna to have to shoot him."

*Perhaps I shoulda handled this on my own?* Forrest thought.

At first light, they approached Sedrick's cabin. Forrest envisioned finding a crying girl out on the front porch, having no idea why the man did what he did to her last night. If she'd been deflowered, the Apaches *might* kill her, as wont to happen, or they *might* keep her to see if the offspring was male—another warrior for the tribe. Certainly, they'd ask for restitution in a piece of Sedrick's hide or possibly money. That was the problem with the local tribes: If you meet one of them, you've *only* met the one. You could never tell what the rest of them thought.

The early morning air felt different as they walked toward the cabin; an unnaturalness hung over the trail. For one thing, no light shone through the windows. Sed must have covered the backside of his shutters with greased paper so no one could look in. The sheriff drew both his irons while Tucker shouldered a Colt shotgun to cover him. The marshal wanted to make sure he could punch through any pelts Sed might be wearing.

"Sed? I've got Marshal Tucker here. He just wants to have a talk with you. Seems he thinks we can come to some sorta 'mutually beneficial' arrangement to keep the peace. What do ya think, Sed?"

Nothing. Not a rustle of clothing, scraping of furniture, or whimpering of a child. In fact, other than their horses swatting flies, the whole area was silent.

"Sed? I'm going to come up to the door. Don't do anything stupid now…ya hear?"

Forrest moved to the porch, placing a foot on the bottom step, but just then a rancid smell made him gag and he stumbled backwards. Not the same smell from last night.

Something worse.

"What?" Tucker asked.

"Something's dead and cooking in the morning heat."

Tucker quick-stepped up the porch. "There's blood coming from under the door."

Forrest looked at the shutters close up. He could see shades of crimson. They hadn't been covered, but bloodied.

Kicking open the door, Tucker immediately leapt back to Forrest's side, as if repelled. The smell of rotten meat and burnt blood assaulted their nostrils. Flies escaped by the dozens and, through watery eyes, Forrest could see maggots crawling on the chunks of meat strewn about the cabin floor.

There was nothing solid left, nothing that could be identified as once being a man or girl. Only by wrapping a bandana around his nose and mouth did Forrest actually make it up to the doorway again. Sed's pants were on the floor, no body parts evident inside. Along the back of the cabin, however, his shirt had been stuck to the wall with blood, as if it'd been plastered there. The skeletal outline of hands, head, and lower body extended from the shirt as if it was a scarecrow meant to repel angels, not birds.

"Goddamn!" Tucker said, peering over Forrest's shoulder, "Any sign of the girl?"

"Nope."

Tucker shook his head pityingly. "They probably took her. Poor thing."

Forrest raised an eyebrow. "'They,' who?"

"Apaches, of course. They tracked the girl and made a message of your Sedrick here."

Forrest moved back down the steps and pulled off the bandana. He spat the taste of bile from his mouth. "Cavalry didn't tell you much about this territory, did they? No rumors? Half-truths? Nothin'?"

Tucker shook his head.

"See all Sed's guns in there?"

The marshal reluctantly glanced back, seeing several muskets and rifles lined up against the wall.

"Sed was a hunter and a good shot. He never got a chance to reach for one of those."

"So, they caught him by surprise?" Tucker still wasn't seeing Forrest's point.

"You got a lot to learn about Drowned Horse." They mounted up. "You know all those scary stories your pa told you around campfires? Boogie men, ancient evils, and monsters under your bed."

"Yeah?"

Forrest leaned forward conspiratorially. "Drowned Horse is the place those bad things call home."

———

To Tucker, Sheriff Forrest's office looked like a hundred others. The town itself looked no different than any town he rode through when he mapped out the area shortly after receiving the badge and being informed the Arizona Territory was his. His superiors told him it'd be a rough assignment, with outlaws and Indian wars. They told him he shouldn't marry, as he'd just be leaving a widow before long. He didn't tell them it was already too late for that. He'd left his wife, Piety, back in Kansas.

What they had *not* told him was anything about curses and demons.

Forrest, boots kicked up onto his desk, leaned back in his chair, taking everything in stride while the new marshal sat dumbfounded across from him.

"A demon?"

"Of some sort, yeah."

Tucker rolled his hand in deference. "And it probably has the little girl?"

"Probably." Forrest shrugged. "Or maybe not. Might have swallowed her whole. There are...other possibilities, too."

"You know, I'm having a hard time with all this. You could be crazy from the heat."

Forrest grinned in a way that made Tucker uneasy. The sheriff reached down into a drawer, and Tucker found his own hand sliding to his iron. But then Forrest tossed an item on the desktop with a resounding thunk.

A tooth. Definitely not human. Certainly not from a creature Tucker had ever seen. It curved like a fang, but the end was serrated and barbed.

"I'm guessing that's not a shark's."

"Never seen one," Forrest admitted, "but I'm pretty sure there're no land sharks."

"You're saying that's a demon 'of some sort's' tooth?"

"I'm saying that whatever killed Sed didn't start with him," Forrest clarified. "Found this laying near another dead trapper four months ago. I knew it was just a matter of time before its owner struck again."

Tucker stared at the razor-sharp instrument of death, questioning reality. "It could still be a beast, right? Doesn't necessarily mean something demonic."

Forrest got up. He chuckled as he walked over to a cabinet. "Doesn't matter if it's a bear, a dragon, or Satan himself..." He opened the cabinet and Tucker whistled. Inside were all manner of weapons. Something akin to what Tucker had once heard called an elephant gun filled the majority of the space, but there were also ancient swords, bone knives, and dynamite. Forrest grabbed the big one—a black-powder, muzzle-loaded, 4-bore rifle—and rested it on a shoulder. The short man looked ten-feet tall with the armament. "...it's got to be put down."

The two peace officers raced back to Davidovic's cabin and looked for tracks. Tucker tried his best to overcome his naivety in front of the very experienced Forrest, but if anything the man said was true, then his assignment was going to be worse than imagined. He found a track in the dirt; a single trench that weaved back and forth. "Looks as if something dragged the girl away from here."

Forrest approached and spit on the ground near the track. "Nah. There'd be a second set of tracks beside this one. Looks like a snake to me."

Tucker thought that'd have to be one big snake.

"Over here," the sheriff pointed. "I believe I've caught the girl's trail. She's running as if the heavenly host pursued her."

Tucker thought it an odd turn of phrase but bent down to look.

"That's some good eyes you've got there," he admitted.

Forrest waved it off. "You probably trained out east. Arizona's dirt is different. It messes with the eyes. You'll grow accustomed to it. She'd heading into the foothills, looking for higher elevation."

As they pursued the girl and monster, Forrest filled Tucker in on the area's history.

"The Verde Valley earned the title from the Spanish for its unexpected lushness, a product of the surrounding mountain range. The town of Drowned Horse received its ominous name due to the flash floods that brought carcasses, mostly horses, down into the valley from Mogollons.

"As for the curse, well, lots of people have ideas on that. I've spent a good deal of my time looking into it: reading old diaries, talking to the local tribes, when they've been willing to talk to a 'blue eye', and so forth."

"So, why would you stay in a cursed town? Seems like there's got to be other places in need of a sheriff."

Forrest said nothing for a couple of minutes, and Tucker wondered if he'd ignored the question.

"Someone's got to do it," Forrest finally confessed. "Don't have any kin. I'm the one willing to stick it out."

"That's noble, but also a bit suicidal, don't you think?"

"Nah. Well, maybe. Takes crazy to fight crazy, I guess."

The sheriff left it there, but Tucker, having only met the man two days ago, knew there had to be more. The man had unexpected levels, like everything Tucker had encountered so far in the new territory.

*I hope I can find some of that crazy,* he thought, *if this area is gonna be my responsibility from here on out.*

Forrest gave his horse, Roland, only subtle encouragement as they moved into the tree line. Tucker marveled at the sheriff and steed's relationship. The mount seemed to understand Forrest's directions without any use of the reins.

"Most the rest of Arizona is pretty normal compared to Drowned Horse. Bandits comin' up from Mexico, looking for a fight. Food is in short supply all over. The soldiers. The tribes. Everybody's hungry and everybody's angry. I find, if you just remember that everyone was here before you, and you don't try to change them too much, people will take to ya."

With a tip of his hat, Tucker thanked Forrest for his advice.

It didn't take long for the pair to pick up the girl's trail. She followed an old logging path that only trappers used anymore. Every so often, they spotted crimson on some leaves.

"She's trying to clean off the blood," Forrest suggested.

"Or bleeding herself," Tucker added. "The thing, whatever it is, might have injured her."

Forrest didn't act concerned, but he did dismount and squat near the tracks.

"What?"

"Did you get a good look at that cabin?"

Tucker shuddered. He'd gotten a better look than he would care to remember. "Hard to see anything with all that blood."

"It wasn't the amount of blood so much as to where it was. Think back."

He did, tracing the patterns of blood throughout the cabin in his mind. "Sedrick had his pants off when the demon attacked. They were on the floor."

"Yep. Still had his shirt on to hold his gut in, though."

The marshal scratched at a bug bite behind his ear. "Okay, what's that mean?"

"Means he was about to consummate his marriage."

"So, you think the monster was trying to stop that?"

"Yep."

"So, it's a monster with good intentions." A statement, not a question.

"Nope."

"Enough damn riddles! Tell me what's going on, Sheriff."

Forrest raised an assessing eyebrow. "You're not going to survive out here if you don't start putting two and two together and finding five."

Tucker played and replayed the grizzly scene through his mind.

"The blood. It sprayed away from the bed."

The sheriff nodded.

"If that was what was left of Sed on the wall, then he was blown back from the bed, as if…"

*He'd been attacked by something under him*, Tucker thought.

"Oh, shit."

Forrest stood over one of the footprints. He circled it with a finger. "Did you notice our little girl's footprints have grown in size?"

Tucker leaned over the side of his horse. The shape of the foot hadn't changed. It still looked delicate and feminine, just larger, like an adult's.

Tucker snapped, "When did you know?"

"I didn't. Well, not for sure."

By his expression, Tucker told Forrest he wasn't buying that. Sheepishly, Forrest confessed.

"Okay, maybe I sent a letter with a drawing of that tooth to an English professor at some fancy college after the first murder. Said I was writin' a book. Asked him what type of single-men preying monsters might have a tooth like that."

Tucker didn't want to ask, but did. "And?"

"Lamia."

"What the hell is that?"

"It's a vengeful demon from Greek mythology, ate children for breakfast, sometimes young men for dinner. Legends say her children were taken from her, and she went mad. She can change shape, and that's pretty much all the professor knew. A little girl, a beautiful woman. Whatever she needs to lure men in."

Tucker played with his mustache. "That's a hell of a notion you got there, Sheriff. That wouldn't account for her eating trappers. Maybe she goes after men that have, or would have, harmed a child?"

Forrest shrugged. "Beats me. It's a monster making a mess in my territory. I want it gone." He then flawlessly propelled himself up into his saddle. He led Roland forward, but Tucker didn't follow. Incredulously, the marshal stared at the sheriff's back. Forrest, finally noticing Tucker wasn't behind him, brought his mount around.

"When were you going to tell me this?" Tucker pointed. "*You* came to me for my help, after all. Is that how you hunt down Greek myths? Find the newest idiot and use them for bait?"

Tucker's words come out as angry bullets, but Forrest dodged them with another shrug. "Wasn't sure I was huntin' anything when I came for you. You can't ever be sure of anything," he said returning to his pursuit, "save that ya can't be sure of anything."

Farther along, the tracks grew closer together indicating the thing had slowed down.

"Rumor says Guilford O'Malley, the first dead trapper, had a lady with him the night of his dismemberment," Forrest revealed. "I found a shovel near his body. The tooth's probably one of hers. O'Malley must've knocked it out before she done him in. Could explain the monster's messy dinner etiquette, it missing a tooth an all."

"How'd your professor suggest killing it?"

"Just like a snake. Chop or blow the head clean off."

"That's it?" Tucker didn't think it could be *that* easy.

"Most these things bleed like normal folk. Biggest problem we had so far is ghosts. They're hard to put down."

Tucker opened his mouth to ask a question, and then thought better of it. Ignorance was bliss after all.

Forrest gave Tucker the "shush" sign when voices wafted through the trees.

Male speaker. "Oh, you poor thing. How'd ya get stuck in my trap?"

"I am such an idiot," a distressed female responded. "My husband. He is after me. I-I just couldn't take his temper anymore, so I ran away."

"There, there. A pretty young thing such as yourself shouldn't be treated that way."

A noise like the wrenching open of a trap sounded. The woman made a sharp yelp.

"Okay, got it off. Let's get ya back to my shelter so as to clean that wound."

The lawmen dismounted, Forrest pulling his enormous elephant gun from its saddle holster. Tucker rechecked his rifle, even though he remembered loading it earlier. They moved forward as a pair.

Two shapes resolved into that of an old man standing above a beautiful, voluptuous woman. Still Apache, her hair extended down to the small of her back. A red circle blistered just above the ankle of her left leg. The grizzled trapper assisted her as they hobbled through the forest. He hadn't noticed the stains on her clothes.

"Damn," Forrest whispered. "That's Isaiah. He and I don't get along so well."

"Why?" Tucker whispered back.

"I caught him trading skunk meat to the Yavapé as rabbit. Doubt he's going to believe me about that girl being some Greek monster."

"Maybe you should stay back, then. Let me try to get them separated."

Since Forrest didn't offer any other options, Tucker guessed that meant for him to go ahead. Checking his rifle for a third time, he set off to save the old trapper's life.

LEVI FORREST COULDN'T DECIDE IF THE NEW marshal was brave, stupid, or both. Just because Forrest's only weapon was the gun, didn't mean he didn't have a plan. Rushing into things got people killed. Forrest knew that all too well.

*Who said they didn't want to be bait?* he thought.

The sheriff hadn't told Tucker the whole truth about Drowned Horse. He'd shoveled enough fantastic details into the unprepared Tucker's mind already. Any more, and the poor boy might explode. Forrest spent two years now tracking down such anomalies and seeing to their demise. He always had a plan. Always.

Well, save for that first time that made him an orphan.

And this one other time.

And...

Okay, sure, his plans relied heavily on luck, but he sure as hell wasn't going to start his relationship with the new marshal that way.

The sheriff sighed and set off to save both the old trapper's *and* the new Marshal's life.

---

AFTER GETTING CLOSE ENOUGH, TUCKER MADE HIS presence known.

"Marshal's office! Isaiah? I need you to step away from the lady."

The lamia's face flashed irritation for a moment and then faked abject terror.

"No! That's my husband! Don't let him take me back! He's done horrible things to me!"

The trapper let the girl slide off his arm to the ground, but during the motion, Isaiah drew down on Tucker.

"I'm sorry, but this little lady's my concern now."

Tucker didn't have time to get his rifle fully positioned before the wizened old timer had him dead to rights.

"Now drop that there gun nice and slow now, Marshal," Isaiah demanded.

Tucker obliged. "You don't know what you're getting mixed up with, old man. The lady's wanted for murdering two other trappers."

"Ha! This little thing? No way in hell."

With Isaiah's attention firmly on him, Tucker figured he might be able to work the situation to his favor. "I'm being serious. She killed them in their sleep, stole all their possessions."

The trapper raised an eyebrow. "Who?"

"Sedrick Davidovic."

"Sed's dead?"

"Yessir, and O'Malley."

Isaiah's gun slacked. "I'd heard about Gully. Thought that was a bear?"

"We're keeping it hush-hush. Big investigation. Look at her dress."

But the girl was no longer there. Not, at least, in the form of a girl.

The world went white around the edges of Tucker's eyes. They must have been big as pie plates while the monster transformed. Truth be told, he hadn't really believed anything Forrest had told him until that exact moment.

The top half of the creature displayed the naked torso of the same beautiful woman he'd seen moments before. Tucker couldn't help but notice that she'd kept the enormous breasts, likely to do exactly what they did—distract from the rest of her. Below, she'd become a snake, bigger than pictures Tucker had seen of pythons or boa constrictors.

A demonic hiss caused Isaiah to finally turn around. The lamia swayed hypnotically, memorizing the trapper. Towering over him, her mouth opened to reveal one long, barbed fang parallel with a gap where a second fang should've resided. As she lunged, Isaiah screamed, holding his hands to his face.

Without preamble, Forrest burst from the trees on Roland, riding fast and, grabbing the back of the mountain man's coat, dragging him out of harm's way. The snake-demon's face planted into the ground as Forrest, trapper, and horse disappeared back into the trees.

The creature righted itself, spitting dirt and twigs from its mouth. A bifurcated tongue flicked out from between thin lips.

Tucker dove to the right, grabbing his gun as he rolled. He placed two good shots where he thought the heart should be. Both bullets hit home, but they appeared to only annoy the monster.

Scanning for Forrest, but not seeing him, Tucker ran. He didn't need to be Ulysses to know the creature slithered right after him. If he could make it to his horse, he might get out of the woods alive.

"Forrest? Forrest!" he yelled between breaths. "Anytime now!"

---

THE SHERIFF LEANED BACK ON ROLAND, ARMS crossed and slyly grinning. Isaiah had scurried off, leaving Forrest to decide what to do next.

Both the lamia and the marshal were kinda pathetic.

First, he'd informed Tucker what it would take to kill the beast, but the damn fool wanted to be a hero. And Tucker had called *him* suicidal?

Then there was the lamia. One tooth. If lamia ran in packs, that one would've been culled moons ago.

*Well,* Forrest decided, *time to do just that.*

He lined Roland up with Tucker's trajectory, supernatural predator close behind. Forrest let go of the reins and stood in the stirrups. Signaling Roland, they galloped towards the pair.

"Let's show them what you've learned."

Despite learning this stunt from the trick-riders in his

family's Romani traveling show, Forrest had never tried it with the rhino gun before and probably wouldn't again.

He interceded between marshal and monster just as Tucker caught his foot on a root and fell to the ground. The lamia reared up to strike. Forrest ignited the gun's powder with a snap of the trigger. It went off point blank range in the lamia's face. Blood geysered from its neck stump. The body fell to the ground after coating everything in a twenty-foot circumference.

There was a cost, though. Forrest flew sideways off Roland, crashing through two thick pine branches before finally dropping to the forest floor. His hat landed beside him, no worse for wear. The sheriff couldn't say the same. Air knocked from his lungs, he struggled several times to find his breath. Catching it just moments before passing out, he sucked in the cool breeze until he laughed.

Tucker pushed himself up from the ground, looking around until he spotted Forrest. He stared squarely into the Sheriff's twinkling eyes.

"What's so damn funny?" Tucker asked.

Forrest tipped his hat.

"Welcome to Drowned Horse, Tuck. Helluva place, huh?"

# SIX

# "KIT CARSON VERSUS THE TOAD MEN OF RIO GILA"

Arizona, Territory
August, 1866

KIT CARSON HELD HIS HANDS UP IN SURRENDER. It was far from the first time the former general and frontier tracker had been in such a predicament, but this was shaping up to be his last.

The Toad Men of the Rio Gila had pointed the nefarious weapon known as *Professor Justin Jeremiah Janikowski's Amazing Nattling Gun* at him. The good professor lay on the ground, a dozen nails from his own invention sticking out of his left arm. The teenager, Will Ragsdale, tended to the professor's wounds, pulling nails out and wrapping the holes with pieces of cloth handed to him by his sweetheart, Sarah Bakersfield, as she tore them off from her dress.

It struck Kit as ironic that this young lady happened to be one of the very people they'd come to save. The thought made him smirk, which did not make his captors any less nervous. The strange, amphibian-like men didn't like him, nor his attempt to free their breeding stock from captivity.

And here he thought his reputation as a friend to all

people, be they red, yellow, or, in this case, a lumpy-brownish, preceded him everywhere.

But then the Toad Men of Rio Gila had consideration for only three things in this world: food, shelter, and mating.

The sound of the Nattling gun increased, and Kit knew he had only seconds before the gun recharged to full and would pummel his body with a hundred nails. Other toad warriors kept their single-shot rifles trained on him, so Kit could make only the subtlest of moves.

He swallowed and thought of his wife and kids back on their farm in Colorado.

He shouldn't have come to Arizona at the request of a good friend.

He should've stayed retired as he was too old for these types of adventures.

But somewhere in that brain of his, something desired to be the man people thought he was in those damnable dime novels one more time.

The whistling reached its peak. Kit said a small prayer and waited.

---

Three Days Earlier

FOURTEEN-YEAR-OLD      WILLIAM      RAGSDALE couldn't reason how he'd lost track of his camp in the middle of a desert. Sure, it was late, but he'd only crossed two sandy mounds to relieve himself. That being done, he'd returned the way he came.

Or had he? As he squatted, did he rotate to avoid a prairie cactus? Could he have gotten pointed in the wrong direction half-asleep? Still, at most he had to be only a couple hundred feet away from where he started. He should be able to see the cook's campfire from the top of a dune.

Scampering up a mound, Will scanned his surroundings. No smoke. No lights. No music or horses nickering. His parents, gone. The cute girl he'd had his eye on since leaving Kansas City, Sarah Bakersfield, vanished.

He had no provisions, barely any clothes, and certainly no weapon. Sunrise would come in six hours, give or take. He needed to find his way in the dark, as the Arizona desert had a reputation for being unforgiving to the lone traveler.

He tried to follow his original footsteps, but he'd criss-crossed them too many times in the sliver of moonlight. Instead, Will laid out a hunting pattern as his grandfather had taught him when they went trapping in the Appalachians. But those mountains were much different than a desert at midnight.

Along the third path he'd chosen, Will spotted a glow warming the side of a hill and strands of music wafting in the air. Will didn't remember the hill when they'd set up camp, but who else would be out there this time of night?

He sprinted around the mound just as the music stopped. His heart stopped with it.

The light came not from a fire, but from a hundred little orbs that hung on the side of a wagon. Elaborate carvings and designs that felt like they belonged in a church had been etched into the wood trim. One side of the wagon extended up to form a roof, showcasing the interior. Inside, a collage of little wooden musicians, each face and body carved with the minutest details, stood at attention. The band held intricately crafted instruments in their tiny hands that moved by rods and strings that disappeared into the ceiling above them.

A blast of steam came from a stovepipe on the roof of the wagon, and the music played again; violinists bowed violins, trumpeters blew on trumpets, and drummers drummed. Will counted two dozen musicians in all. The music came from somewhere inside the wagon, but the marionette men and women had been choreographed perfectly to appear as if they played each note.

Will walked around the behemoth, but found neither his people hidden behind it, nor an operator of the mystery machine. He did find two camels tied to a cactus nearby. They honked and spit on the ground as Will approached. He petted them to make sure he wasn't dreaming. Sure enough, two single-humped camels eyed him with detached resolve.

A curse erupted from inside the wagon, and the music ground to a halt. A backdoor kicked open and a board slid out. With it came feet, then a waist, and then a beard. And then even more beard. It was unlike any beard Will had seen. Golden, curly rings cascaded across the man's belly like Mississippi River rapids after a big storm. But not just ringlets, there were tools tied on the end of many strands of hair; small, precise screwdrivers and wrenches, and hammers and devices Will couldn't fathom a use for.

Instead of a tool belt, this man had a tool beard.

The board tilted until the end touched dirt and the owner of the beard pushed himself up and off the ramp. He turned back toward the wagon and made an obscene gesture that made Will chuckle.

The man spun upon Will's laugh. At first, the anger at the wagon transferred to the new arrival, but then the man's eyes opened fully to take in the teen.

"Oh, my dear boy. I'm sorry. I didn't mean to give you such a fright. I obviously didn't hear your approach."

"My apologies, sir. I didn't mean to sneak up on you like that. Just got myself turned around, and I thought you were my people at first."

"People, you say? Are you part of a wagon train heading west?"

Will nodded, suspicion creeping into his mind. His pa told him to be wary of strangers asking too much about the caravan.

The man must be good at reading faces, for he said, "Oh, no. Don't you fret a bit. I'm no one to worry about." He stepped away from Will, motioning for the boy to follow. He reached to something on the top of the raised side panel and unfurled it. A canvas sign dropped down:

*Professor Justin Jeremiah Janikowski's Steam-powered Orchestra!*

"I, my wayward lad, am a scientist and entertainer."

Will scratched his head. "You're both?"

The Professor sidled up to Will, slipping an arm around his shoulder and guiding him to a seat in front of his "stage."

"A true performer must be a student of science. A lot goes into all those notes you hear, my boy. There're numbers on sheet music for a reason. Calculations that go way beyond the understanding of non-musical types. It takes scientific artistry to make those instruments, too. One does not just make a Stradivarius the way one carves a whistle from a reed." The Professor waved with a flourish. "And this is my greatest musical invention!"

Will admitted it looked impressive.

"Like the player piano, I've built an automation that can play any song in the history of man; be it Mozart or hymnal. If there's sheet music to it, I can program it!" He held up a finger. "Let me show you. Pick a song, any song."

"Camptown Races?" Will loved that song from his days at his grandfather's cabin.

"Just the song I was working on! Let me see if I can finish the brass section."

Professor Janikowski drew himself back into the machinery. Another string of curses erupted from its bowels, however, the good professor must have remembered he had an audience. "Sorry!"

Will's nervousness increased. Surely, his parents must be wondering why he hadn't returned. Will craned his ear, yet he hadn't heard his name called. Just how far *had* he walked?

Steam belched forth and the music started again. Listening closer, Will could pick out the familiar tune. Will recognized it as the one playing when he arrived at the professor's camp. He just wasn't used to all the extra instruments. It sounded more like something sung in church than something sung around a campfire.

The Professor appeared beside him.

"You don't look happy. Is the brass section still amiss?"

"No. I should be getting back. I don't know how my camp disappeared so quickly."

Professor Janikowski opened his mouth to say something, froze in mid-thought, and then looked slightly alarmed.

"Did you say 'disappeared'?"

When the teenager confirmed, the Professor closed the up wagon rapidly.

"Quick, my boy! Grab the camels. Hitch them up. Don't worry. They're docile."

"What? What's going on?"

Not waiting for an answer, Will hooked the animals to the front of the wagon, while Janikowski bounded up to the driver's seat. He reached his hand down indicating Will should join him.

"Please. Hurry. Your family may be in grave peril!"

While the professor tried to prepare Will on the way to the camp for what they might find, the reality of what he saw tore his soul asunder.

Wagons had been tipped over, some still burned. Clothes and items strewn hither and yon. Horses missing. And not a soul to be found anywhere.

Will yelled for his parents, then Sarah, then for anybody.

No one replied.

His family's wagon remarkably stood intact. Will climbed into it grabbing clothes and strapping the six-gun his father gave him to his hip before tucking his mother's hold out in his boot. He collected other weapons, whatever he could find. His people would need them whenever he tracked them down.

The professor called out, "Will, my boy. You better come here."

Will rushed over to where the old man's voice came from, only to discover the professor looked down at a pair of boots sticking straight up; boots with their owner still in them. The lad swallowed hard and approached to see who the dead man was.

---

Two Days Earlier

KIT CARSON HATED DROWNED HORSE, ARIZONA. The place felt wrong. The whole area felt odd from the first time he'd explored it. He'd told the Army and anyone who'd listened not to build there. The 'Che, the 'Pai, even that Navajos all had legends about a great evil lurking in the red rocks that surrounded the valley. When he'd gotten word that a town had been built right where he said not to, he sighed and wondered why anyone ever asked his advice on anything.

His wife, Josefa, had been even more reluctant than usual letting him leave. They had a farm to run, kids to raise, and he'd retired from the negotiator business.

"I can't tell you enough how much I appreciate this," Marshal Tucker Bandimere said for the third time that evening.

Tucker bought Kit's dinner, room, and whiskey as a thank you. They leaned in camaraderie against the bar of the town's only saloon, *The Sagebrush*, but Tucker's gratitude grew quickly tedious.

"As I said, Tuck, I owed ye. I never forget a debt. Plus, Indian negotiations is tough business, 'pecially with the 'Che."

Kit hoped his actions would help the new U.S. Marshal establish himself in his territory. Tucker stood a string bean of a man with a handlebar mustache. Kit remembered him from when he could barely grow one; a lad manning the walls of Fort Lupton. Those were dangerous times, but Tuck had persevered.

"Yes, but to convince a very proud chief to allow his son's arrest for the raiding of a settler's homestead, instead of letting it escalate...well, that was pure artistry. And just after you'd arrived from a week on the road."

"Made the trip from Colorado to Arizona more times than one could count," Carson bragged. Though, it took Kit a good deal longer than it ever had before; a product of his advancing age. "Both sides were weary from all the fighting, and the lad hadn't killed them, so he had that on his side. It will strengthen the chief's son to do the time. When he gets out in a year, hopefully this whole situation will be different, and the man who emerges will be a better example for his tribe."

A commotion rose up outside the saloon. Inside, the sound of hooves galloping in fast echoed, but Kit's trained ear recognized they didn't belong to horses. Curiosity piqued, Kit made his way to the window where others had gathered to stare slack-jawed.

A wagon pulled into town drawn by two camels.

Kit looked again.

Two camels drew to a halt outside the sheriff's office; a man with a beard so long and thick, he could wear it as clothing sat in the driver's seat. Next to him sat a boy, no more than fourteen, a mixture of fear and anger evident on his face. On the roof, a body lay strapped down under a bloodstained blanket, his boots sticking straight up to heaven.

Sheriff Levi Forrest, the local lawman, approached the wagon as the two men got down.

*Don't get involved*, Kit told himself.

Tucker left the saloon in a hurry to join the sheriff.

*It has nothing to do with you*, Kit reminded himself.

Tucker listened to the man intently, and then pointed toward the saloon as if he'd sent an arrow right at Kit.

*You can leave out the back and be home in five days of hard riding*, his mind pleaded with him.

Kit's feet, however, had other plans as he walked out of the front.

---

WILL COULDN'T BELIEVE THAT *THE* KIT CARSON actually sat across from him. The teen tried to act more mature around his idol, but the mix of grief from finding his family's camp raided, and the discovery of the dead wagon master, left Will with uncontrollable emotions.

They sat in the local undertaker's wake room. A coffin rested on a dais nearby, but it was thankfully unoccupied. Drowned Horse's sheriff brought them there, not only because the wagon master's body needed to go there, which it did, but because the building had the largest sitting room in town away from nosey people.

Will did his best not to stare at the legend. He practically tripped over himself saying hi.

"General Carson, sir? It's an honor to meet you. I've read all your books."

General Carson kept an even expression as he moved past the teen to address the adults. "Don't believe anything ye read and only half of what ye see."

Will didn't register the brush off. So star-struck by the famous tracker, Will found it hard to focus on what Sheriff Forrest was saying.

"So, when you got back to Ragsdale's camp, the wagons were there, but the people were missing?"

Professor Janikowski stroked his beard. "Yes, yes. All save for the body of the unfortunate wagon master, who as you saw, died of multiple nail wounds."

Marshal Bandimere, Will believed he was called, asked, "About a hundred, give or take a nail or two, you say? And this was caused by your invention?"

The Professor winced. "I used to build forts before I

retired and moved into the performance arts. I designed Fort Garland, a place the General should be familiar with."

General Carson corrected him. "Just Mister, now."

"A loss for the Army, I'm sure," the professor said. "But even Ulysses had to go home eventually. Yes, to answer the marshal's question. I invented a machine to save me and the men exorbitant time. Professor Justin Jeremiah Janikowski's Nattling Gun." He beamed. "I used the principal of a Gatling gun, only smaller and it fires nails instead of bullets."

Will heard all that on the ride to Drowned Horse, still finding it hard to believe something like the guns he'd seen mounted at forts could be made portable. He had even more trouble stomaching the next part.

"I headed to California to meet with an investor who wanted to reproduce them," Janikowski continued. "But on the way, I stopped near the Rio Gila for a couple of nights to work on my orchestra." He leaned forward conspiratorial. "I saw their slanted, yellow eyes just outside my campfire. They were entranced by the music, barely able to breathe. I didn't know what to make of them as they approached."

"Toad Men?" Forrest echoed the term Professor Janikowski used earlier.

"Hideous creatures! Flat faces covered with bumps and warts, hardly human. Webbed fingers, barely able to hold their purloined rifles." He crooked a finger as if he held one of the guns. "Barely, but still able. I discovered this when the music irrevocably stopped, and they grew angry. They took me hostage, collected my belongings. They wanted me to, um…"

The Professor looked at Will, seeming to not know what to say next.

Will nodded. "Oh, don't worry, Professor. Ain't nuthin' I haven't seen on a farm."

Still wary, Professor Janikowski chose his words carefully. "They're trying to breed the deformity out of them. From what I gathered, each generation looks less toad-like."

Forrest raised an eyebrow. "You mean to say, they wanted you to lay with their toad women? Now I've heard it all!"

Will stood up. "They have my family, sir. This is not a laughing matter. And...well, they have others I care about, too. If the professor's right, these toadies might kill them if they refuse to help them. Or worse!"

The thought of the kidnapped females brought somber reality to the group.

Mister Carson asked the Professor, "How'd you escape?"

"I begged them to let me go back to my wagon. They'd taken the horses, so I couldn't leave. I had managed to get the orchestra working well enough, and while my guards were transfixed, I wacked them over the head. After days of walking, I saw the camels, at first thinking them a mirage. Well trained, I led them back to the wagon and have been driving around Arizona for weeks, trying to figure out what my next move would be. Then I came across young Will here, or truthfully, he found me."

Tucker's voice remained skeptical. "And you thought not to tell anyone?"

"Who in their right mind would believe me?"

Forrest cuffed the Marshal on the shoulder. "You can't tell me this is the weirdest thing you've seen or heard?"

Sheepishly, Tucker agreed.

"Well, I've covered every inch of the Gila over the years." Carson didn't look happy. "I'm sure that's why Tucker pointed me out."

"Yes sir, Mister Carson." Will couldn't stop himself. "First, you led an expedition from California to the Colorado River, despite being attacked by a thousand Pima warriors. Then, along with a division of Dragoons, you went down the Gila to get a message to the President during the Mexican-America—"

When Mister Carson harrumphed, and held up a hand to cut him off, Will stopped his yammering, mortified.

"There were no thousand Pima warriors. We traded with

them, mostly peacefully. We weren't taking their land back then. Jes' explorin'. Plus, in all my trips down the Gila, I certainly never seen a settlement of frog-like men."

"Toad."

The negotiator broke in his cool demeanor, but only slightly. "Frog. Toad. Lizard. Don't care if they're thirty-foot pythons."

Forrest and Tucker shot a look at each other as if they shared a private joke.

"I'm just saying," Mister Carson continued, "there isn't a place to hide a tribe of pioneer-stealing, lily-pad hopping, fly-eating, water-sucking monsters."

---

## Last Night

KIT CARSON, PROFESSOR JANIKOWSKI, AND WILL Ragsdale peered over a ledge and down into the river-worn canyon of Rio Gila. In a secluded bend, roughly two dozen toad men, women, and children went about their daily business. They moved about simple huts, painted the colors of the red sandstone of the canyon walls, camouflaging them. Meanwhile, eight normal-looking and unharmed humans could be spotted, captive in a prison carved out of the rock wall.

Kit grumbled, "Exactly the reason I retired. Just when I think I've seen it all…"

"What was that, Mister Carson?" the boy asked.

Kit couldn't decide what was more annoying; his inner-voice or the teenager who treated him as his lord and savior. He wanted to leave Will back in town, but seeing as it *was* his family captured, the boy couldn't be discouraged.

"Nothin'. See those boulders there? Those had to have been loosened by a monsoon, or forcibly removed. That bend wasn't here when I went through with the Dragoons in '46."

"That's okay, sir. You couldn't have known."

"But I should have." *Been too long away. What good am I as a tracker if I don't know the area I'm tracking?* Bile rose in his throat.

"You can't be everywhere. You're an important man. The President—"

Kit's anger came as a horse whisper, but the emotion was clear to all.

"*Was* an important man. *Was!* Nobody calls on Kit Carson for matters of national importance anymore, kid. They put me out to pasture, like they do old horses. Life ain't like novels. Heroes don't always show up in time. And when they don't, people die. That's the truth of it."

The boy's father had taught Will right. He didn't cry, even though it looked as if he wanted to. Instead, he left Kit and Janikowski to walk back over by the wagon.

"A little hard on the lad...and yourself...weren't you, General?" the Professor asked.

"It's Mister. Sorry, but the kid's gotta learn. This ain't no fairy tale."

The Professor stroked his beard. "True, true, but remember, those *are* his parents down there and a girl he fancies. Don't you have a son about that age? Do you talk to him like that?"

*Didja fight Injuns, papa? Were you outgunned twenty to one?*

Kit son's, Billy, became increasingly disheartened when Kit came home without new stories. He experienced his father going from tracker to war hero to messenger to farmer, losing more respect for him each time.

*Is that why, when a man pulled up in a camel-led wagon, you leapt at it, Kit? To have a story to take home to yer son? But it ain't so easy anymore. The world changed around ye, and yer too stubborn to change with it?*

Kit looked over to where Will kicked some rocks. It'd be better if the boy understood the world sooner than later.

Will glanced up, and Kit recognized eyes as disheartened as Billy's had been.

The Professor whispered, "Maybe talking about people dying right now isn't the best tact. He needs to know there's a plan. Do you have one? How many toads do you count?"

They moved away from the cliff's edge.

*Too many*, Kit thought, but said, "Thirty *if* ye include the women and children."

"The women might fight," Professor Janikowski thought carefully, "but mostly to protect their children. They're the only ones the men can count on to break the curse."

"Curse?" Will questioned, close enough to hear them.

"People don't turn into toads for nothing, my boy. Either they're diseased or been cursed."

Kit raised a disbelieving eyebrow. "Ye call yourself a man of science, and yet ye believe in magic?"

"I found two camels wandering in the desert, General. How could I not?"

"It's mister," corrected Kit once again, "and those camels were part of a scheme gone bad. A guy brought them from Africa thinking they'd be the answer to desert travel. Turns out people still preferred horses, so he just let them loose. There've been sightings of them for years."

"Yes, but to find two right when I needed them? That's the magic." The professor indicated his orchestra. "I make music that soothes savage beasts. I invent things no one has dreamed of..."

Kit interrupted, "One could say ye dreamed of them."

The bearded man pinched his eyes at Kit. "Fine, *Mr.* Sour-Puss, then I won't loan you any of my 'magic' to beat my *obviously* normal Nattling Gun."

Will spoke up. "You have something that will stop it?"

The professor held up his hands in mock protest. "I do, but if Mr. Carson is too grounded in reality to use it, then I couldn't possibly..."

"Mister Carson, you've got to convince him to let you use it. Please, Mister Carson, Please!"

Will's pleading face made Kit chuckle. Without Tucker or Forrest—who were due at a trial up in Prescott—they were outnumbered four to one. Kit held his hands up in mock-surrender. "I apologize, Professor. Yer a wizard of the first order, and those are cursed toads down there. Lend me your magic so I may smite them."

Will beamed, and Kit tussled his hair.

"To be sure, I said a curse was *one* possibility." Professor Janikowski winked. "It's probably just a disease."

---

THOUGH HE HADN'T SAID THE WORDS, WILL KNEW his idol was sorry for his earlier words. Mister Carson smiled reassuringly at him from time to time.

Professor Janikowski unloaded inventions. Will received a bandolier strap with several of the glowing orbs attached, unlit at the moment.

"We're approaching at night," the professor explained. "If you get caught, my boy, just pull this string." The string hung loosely over Will's shoulder and connected to several small Leyden jars on his back. "The orbs will blaze to life, blinding your captors long enough for you to take action."

"Thanks, Professor. What will Mister Carson's do?"

A square buckle replaced the one normally on the tracker's belt, while wires ran around to a small canister Janikowski had strapped to Mister Carson's back.

The professor held up a finger. "That's a surprise. Unfortunately, it's got a steam-driven battery of my invention, with only one use or I'd demonstrate it. Let's hope we don't need it twice."

Will wondered how reliable any of the scientist's inventions were after seeing how much time he spent fixing the orchestra. The professor ran tubes from the wagon to the edge of the canyon. He didn't elaborate what they were for, either.

The plan Mister Carson thought up would take precise

timing. Will's part would be to free the captives. All and all, not the easiest of tasks, but better than taking on the whole of the toad clan, which the professor and Mister Carson planned to do. Will needed to climb down from above the prison cave, surprise the two guards, and spring his people from jail.

That part of the canyon wasn't deep, maybe a hundred feet at its farthest. Mister Carson had pointed out the best place for Will to descend, showing him the ledges and hand-holds that he would use. The teenager memorized them until he could picture them with his eyes closed. The professor secured a rope to a big, ol' cactus, bigger than any Will had seen on the trip west. Then he brought out a box, which he threaded the rope through until it reached the knot. He ran the rope through again creating a loop which the box sat nestled in.

"*Professor Justin Jeremiah Janikowski's Incredible Recoiling Rope*," the professor announced. "If you get in a bind, press this button and you'll find yourself wheeled back up."

Will thanked him and got into position. As the sun set, he waited for the signal. He got it in a wave from Mister Carson. Will began the laborious climb down, careful not to send any loose rocks below. The wall had worn raggedly over the years, providing several adequate footholds. Will mis-stepped only once and slammed against the side. Worried he'd break the orbs, Will swung the strap around his body so the more delicate lights were behind him and the thicker jars up front. Almost to the ledge above the cave, Will thanked the lord he'd encountered no problems.

Two toads—younger and less toadish than others he'd seen—guarded the entrance to the cell. Will felt pretty confident he could get the drop on them. Except, at the moment, two torches bobbed their way toward the cell. They'd cast enough light, he'd be spotted hanging above the toads. He didn't have time to finish his descent. Unhooking himself from the rope, Will dropped about ten feet to the ledge and lay flat.

He drew his gun and waited.

---

TWO LARGE TOAD MEN WALKED TOWARD THE prison. Kit held his breath as they got within visual range of Will.

Aiming his rifle, Kit would have a difficult shot in the near-dark. He doubted he'd get four shots off before others spotted his position.

The two smaller guards moved aside to let the newcomers into the cell. Kit relaxed for the moment, figuring amphibian eyes must not be as good at night.

A young girl screamed while one of the toad men dragged her from the cave. A man, probably Mr. Bakersfield, protested and the other guard beat him to the ground.

Kit's intuition sent up a warning fire.

"Oh, sheet!"

Will cried out, "Sarah!" and leapt down from the ledge. He landed on the toad man holding the girl, slamming its head to the dirt. The teen looked up just in time to avoid the butt end of a rifle swung at his head by another guard. He rolled off the prone toad, drawing and firing at the same time. The shot was true, and the guard dropped.

The younger pair of toads croaked in alarm. They moved toward Will, and Kit took a shot. It wasn't a kill shot, but the gun arm of the leftmost toad was rendered useless.

More croaks sounded from the camp, and Kit caught movement in his peripheral vision. In amongst the toads, two carried a device that could only be the professor's Nattling gun. One carried the gun itself, several barrels strapped together and connected to a big stock. The second toad wore a pack on his back. He quickly pumped a lever on the side, and increasing whine resounded through the canyon.

And then...

Toad people froze in their tracks as the orchestral sound

of *Camptown Races* wafted down, piped in from the tubes the Professor had laid out. Kit scanned the rim until he spotted the Professor waving one of his glowing orbs.

However, be it that they were too far away or too focused, the toad Will faced pressed their attack. Foregoing guns, the trio fought *mano a mano*. Kit broke cover, sprinting to where the teen and toads grappled with each other in mutual death grips.

"Use the orbs!" Kit called.

Will must've forgotten all about them. Letting go with one hand, Will pulled on the string.

White light blared in front of Kit. Everything lost detail and became a painful blur of black spots and rainbows. Kit brought his hands to his eyes, rubbing them. He blinked, trying his best to see something, anything, but he was effectively blind to the world.

Kit heard the thump of someone hitting the ground.

"Will? Will?"

"Oh, lord! Mister Carson! I'm so sorry. I had spun them to the—"

"Never mind! What happened to the guards?"

Will chuckled. "Sarah clocked one over the head with his own rifle. He's out cold. I was able to get the other."

Will took Kit's arm and guided him over to a rock where the old man could sit.

"And the rest?"

"They're still swaying to the music. Like they ain't got a care in the world."

Vision slowly returning, Kit could see torches as flicking orange blurs.

"Where's the professor?"

"He's moving through the camp. He's almost to his nail-shooter."

And then... the music stopped.

Now

MISTER CARSON HELD HIS HANDS UP IN surrender. While Will knew this wasn't the first time Kit had been in such a predicament, though, it looked to be his hero's last.

After the wagon broke down, the toad men sprung to life pretty fast. They surrounded Mister Carson, his vision having fully returned. The professor, making a mad dash for the Nattling Gun, took a blast to the arm and lay bleeding on the ground. Their captors gathered the would-be rescuers together and looked to execute Kit first seeing as he was the most dangerous or at least less useful for fathering children.

"I'm sorry, my boy," the professor said, "I guess I'm neither a good inventor nor entertainer. I've failed you and your lady here."

He looked as if he would weep, but Will patted his good arm reassuringly. "That's not true. Those orbs worked fine. Plus, Mister Carson will think of something. He always does."

But Will wondered *when* Mister Carson would do that, as the whine of the Nattling Gun increased. A dozen toad men covered them. Sarah slid in close, wrapping herself around Will's arm. Even after days of captivity, she still was the prettiest woman he'd ever seen.

"Sarah, in case we don't make it out of here…"

She put a finger to his lips and nodded. She leaned forward to kiss him, but at that moment, the whining reaching its peak.

The Toad Men's laugh was guttural and watery. One reached for the trigger and pulled.

Quicker than Will could see, Mr. Carson pressed a button on his belt. An explosion of steam burst forth from the device on his back. Metal blades unfolded from Kit's buckle. They sprung out like a woman's fan, growing bigger and bigger until they made a giant shield like a British knight Will had read about in school.

The nails shot out from the professor's device, but bounced off the shield in a dozen directions. Several of the surrounding toad men were punctured.

Will pulled his mom's two-shot hold out from his boot. He aimed at the toads holding the Nattling Gun and hit both. Mister Carson grabbed his fallen pistol and took down several more of armed creatures.

Gunfire sounded on the ridge and Will looked up to see Marshal Tucker, Sheriff Forrest, and a company of Mexican soldiers arrive. They rode down into the canyon and surrounded the whole toad clan. Will and Sarah helped the Professor to his feet, propping him up as the surviving toad men laid down their weapons.

———

FAMILIES REUNITED, KIT FELT HE DID LITTLE TO actually change the outcome of events and said as much. As expected, the boy disagreed.

"Sir, if it wasn't for you, I wouldn't have climbed down a cliff, faced a bunch of water-sucking toads unafraid, nor seen my loved ones again."

Will gazed lovingly at Sarah when he said "loved ones," and Kit knew it wouldn't be long before those kids would need to get married.

But a future husband needed a job...

"Hey, Forrest. I noticed ye didn't have a deputy. That right?"

Sheriff Forrest came over to them. "You looking for a job, Kit?"

The tracker laughed. "Nope, but I know a lad who'd make a fine one. Good in a fight. Thinks with his head. Well, most the time." Kit tussled Will's hair again. "He's old for his age. If his family settles in the area, I think he'd make a fine addition to yer team. Plus, he already has a glimmer about how strange the territory is."

Forrest looked the lad over. "Can't make it legal until you're sixteen, but we could start you working around the office, teach you the ropes."

Will's eyes lit up. "Really! Thank you, Sheriff!" He turned to Kit. "And thank you, Mister Carson." He offered his hand.

Kit drew him in for a hug, instead.

"It's Kit from now on. Ye earned it."

Stepping back, Kit said, "Now I got to get home, so as I can tell my son the story of Will Ragsdale, and how he faced down a hundred lizardmen."

"Toad Men."

"Whatever."

The professor walked up as Will and Sarah left to talk to their parents. The inventor escorted a toad woman with a slightly rounded belly.

"Seems my nights here, um, bore some fruit. I'm going to stick around and see if I can't help figure out what really happened to these people. *Curse...*" He winked at Kit. "...or science. I should be able to keep them out of trouble from now on. They seem more content to live *with* society as to attack it." He leaned toward the group and spoke in a stage whisper. "Plus, they love my music. Nothing like a captive audience."

"And maybe you can train them to build stuff...working stuff. Make a name for themselves." Marshal Tucker suggested. "Oh, and speaking of." He pulled an envelope from his pocket and handed it to Kit.

"Seems word that Kit Carson was in Arizona got out and this came by stage before we left. Driver said it held a priority directive."

Kit turned it over and found the seal of the President of the United States on it. He looked up. Everyone smiled, and the Professor prodded him to open it.

"It's a request to escort four Navajo Chiefs to Washington, D.C. to have a sit down with the President. He says I'm the only man he trusts for the job."

Tucker patted Kit on the shoulder.

"You better get going then. Don't want to keep President Johnson waiting."

The former general scratched his chin for a moment, eyes playing out a story in his mind and then he nodded decisively.

"He can wait. I want to see my family."

And so Kit Carson, former tracker, former general, and former toad man fighter, made the president wait for a week...and nine months later, he welcomed a daughter to the world.

# SEVEN

# "THE WIDOW WORE GLASS SPURS"

Arizona Territory
September, 1866

SIX MEXICAN RIDERS RACED AROUND UP AND down Main Street trying to pull a chicken that had been buried up to its neck from the dirt. They jousted like medieval knights, not to win the favor of a queen, but for a bird. This wasn't the strangest thing I'd witnessed since becomin' the law of Drowned Horse, but it was one of the stupidest.

One rider, with impressive skill, leaned far enough over his saddle to grab the hen by the neck and yank her free. Cheers erupted around me from the spectators. This was our first festival and everyone from the region came out to celebrate. Celebrate what, I wasn't sure. Chicken slaughter, I guessed.

As the leader fled with his prize, the other five closed in on him. A tall dude with a long reach slammed his horse against the leader and got a hold on the chicken's leg. They wrestled over the squawking bird, feathers flying everywhere. While being pulled taunt between the two, a third rider swooped low under the chicken bridge, and tore it out from both of their grips.

More feathers.

More screaming fowl.

More cheers.

This tug-o-chicken continued until one rider eventually crossed the finish with most, not all, of a dead bird. He raised the bloody carcass over his head and yelled something in Spanish. Declared the winner, people surrounded him tossing accolades and the like.

I sat back on the porch in front of my office trying to decide if I'd wasted an afternoon or not. Owner, Sagebrush's patron saint of booze, women, and gambling, collected money from losing bettors, paid out the winners, and collected a healthy cut for himself. At least that still made sense.

I watched over him, gun across my lap, in case someone decided his purse looked a lot like a chicken and wanted to abscond with it. No one did, and soon he stepped up to the sidewalk, taking the empty seat next to me.

"That was profitable," he said, clearly satisfied.

"That was...disgustin'."

"The town seemed to enjoy themselves."

"The chicken didn't."

Owner leaned forward, elbows on his knees, trying to catch my eye. "You're in a mood today."

He was right, but I kept my gaze on the people in the street.

"I just don't think killin' things for people's fun is my idea of a good time."

Sighing, Owner said, "It's getting to you, isn't it?"

"What is?"

"This town. The curse. Always having to be vigilant. Prepared."

I looked at him out of the corner of my eye, then back to Main Street.

"Nope, not at all," I responded, keeping my tone flat. "I

find it relaxin' to wait for someone to tell me someone I know, or knew, is dead. Then, comes the rush of excitement when I find out it's an unnatural death. I live for this."

"Ha. Ha." Owner didn't appreciate my sarcasm as much as I did. "Maybe you need a vacation? Head south down to Tucson. Drink. Find a woman for a night or two that you won't have to see again. Get away from the job for a couple days."

My turn to stare him down. "And what happens durin' those days I'm gone? What if some big monster comes through town eatin' up everyone? No one here's prepared as I am to take it on."

Owner acted wounded. "I'm the one who taught you a lot of this stuff. I'm sure I can keep the town safe for a few days."

I harrumphed. It wasn't that Owner couldn't. He probably could. He just never showed much inclination to take on the sacred trust he handed out. He stood in the background, supportin' me, supportin my mission. "And if somethin' were to happen to you? Ain't going to do this town any good to lose its heart. It'd die as quickly as you would."

I didn't mean it to come out belittling, but it did even to my own ears.

Without a word, Owner headed back over to the Sagebrush. I opened my mouth to apologize, but the words stuck in my throat.

Not an hour later, Hiram Craddick, the undertaker, and I were on our way to the Spanish C Ranch. Cesar Raul Mendoza, the Verde Valley's first cattle rancher, had been murdered.

---

MENDOZA'S BODY STILL LAY IN THE PASTURE where his staff found him, they being too scared or too suspicious to move it. That didn't stop them from staring and crossing themselves. I couldn't be sure, but I'm sure I saw baked spit on him, too. The summer sun hadn't done him no favors, either, browning him like a piece of jerky. I wonder how long ago he'd been killed, or more to the point, how long they waited to fetch me? The gawkers dispersed quickly after I arrived.

All around his prone form were footprints, mostly bare. If there'd been any trackable prints, they'd be long erased.

"Who found him?" I asked the man who'd brought me to his body.

Luka, Mendoza's lead ranch hand, shrugged. The scars on his face and hands told his story better than asking him directly. "No idea, *Señor*. By the time someone get me, there were many people around. I ask but they not tell me."

"And no one noticed he was missing before then?"

"*El Patrón* and I ride out to inspect the herd in the morning. I figure he went alone, which was not uncommon. It wasn't until he miss dinner that Señora Mendoza send someone to look for him."

The Mexican had a hard time meeting my eyes as he talked. It wasn't unusual. There was a fear of reprisal for saying too much built into his culture. Didn't matter that I tried to deal square with everyone. I was the law, and the law never worked in their favor.

But he also could know more that he was telling me. That, too, wasn't unusual. Rich folk often forget their underlings are around and spill secrets.

Hiram knelt over Mendoza's stinking corpse.

"Seems like a stab wound, Levi. Right through the chest. Pierced the heart. Should be blood soaked into the dirt all around him, if he'd been killed. I think he was drug here to be found."

"So, probably a human killer, then."

Luka crossed himself. Anyone living in the Valley prayed to their gods when the curse was mentioned. Gods who mostly ignored those prayers for reasons of their own.

"One could hope," Hiram agreed.

Hope was not something I was in much supply of those

days. Hiram said he'd get the body to town and do a more thorough examination of the wound before prepping the rancher for burial.

I asked Luka to take me to Cesar's widow.

Estanfani Mendoza—Stefani to friends and family—sat in the parlor, gazin' out the glass windows that made up the back of the massive ranch house. That, in itself, spoke of his money. Mendoza was warned against building anything so lavish in the middle of Indian territory, as it would be a signal fire to all who saw it that he had money. He swore there was nothing to worry about. He had a new bride, a new herd, and a plan that would make him even richer.

She addressed me without tearing her eyes away when I entered the room.

"Welcome, Sheriff. I'm sorry we meet under such tragic circumstances."

Mrs. Mendoza's breathy voice still had the accent of her youth. Mormon missionaries found the girl and adopted her after the Mexican-American war. Spoiled, the orphan had received the best education, the best clothing, and the best husband picked out for her. Cesar, who had fought in the war, became enamored with her and courted her parents voraciously until they gave in. He brought her to Arizona and treated her as a queen.

If rumors held true, she demanded no less.

She wore a fine white cotton summer dress in the Mexican style, conforming to her slight figure. The wide-rimmed, flat, black hat with a thick lace veil covered half her face, leaving her delicate cheeks exposed to evidence of tear tracks.

I took off my own hat and held it to my chest.

"My condolences on your loss, ma'am."

She dabbed a kerchief under the veil. "Thank you. That is very kind." She adjusted her posture so she was at an angle to me, but not directly.

"If you don't mind, I have some questions," I asked respectfully.

"Of what nature?"

That was an odd response. I fiddled with my hat.

"Well, to find out who killed your husband. Now, did he have any—"

The Widow Mendoza held up the hand with the kerchief to stop me.

"That won't be necessary. I know who killed my husband."

This was going to be an easier day than I thought. "And would you care to share that information with me? I'd like to arrest and hang that person as soon as possible."

She coughed in a way that came off more like a laugh. My gut told me I wasn't going to like the answer.

"Certainly. But you'll have a hard time arresting and hanging the man." Stefani stood in one swift motion, gracefully like queens were supposed to. She walked over to me, almost passing me by, before stopping parallel. I, not being a tall man, was only slightly taller, so when she leaned over to speak into my ear, her lips almost kissed it.

In words just above a whisper, she told me, "He's already dead. It was the ghost of Galvarino the *Mapuche* come to exact revenge on Cesar's bloodline."

———

"THEN SHE TOLD ME THAT CESAR WAS RELATED TO *the* García Hurtado de Mendoza, the Spanish Marquis that subjected and slaughtered the Mapuche people."

"Uh-huh." Owner continued wiping down the bar top.

"Cesar apparently started seeing Galvarino's ghost a few days ago, but mistook him for an Indian trying to scare him off the land."

"You don't say?" Owner rinsed glasses in a bucket of water.

"Mrs. Mendoza believes that because her husband was the last 'pureblood' of his line, that Galvarino's ghost should be satisfied and finally at peace."

Owner said nothing.

I finally had to confront him. "Is this how it's going to be now? I say somethin' out of sorts and you get your feelin's hurt?"

Owner cocked his head, eyebrows scrunched as if he could barely see me. "Did you say something wrong? I would have never guessed it."

"Listen, I—"

Owner went back to cleaning glasses. "You seem to be happy now, so that's all that matters, right? This was an easy one. Almost *like* a vacation. Didn't have to exorcise anything. Didn't have to hunt a demon down. Take the win. You've earned it." He gathered up a crate of clean glasses and headed to his storeroom. When he didn't immediately come out, I finished my beer and stood up to leave.

"He is right, of course."

I spun toward the voice, my hand quickly to my holster. I hadn't seen anyone else in the Sagebrush when I walked in. It was morning, and Owner hadn't thrown open the doors yet. There were guests upstairs after the festival, but they hadn't even made sounds yet, having spent the previous evening drinking and doing other activities.

The native wasn't dressed like any of the tribes in the area. He was old, but not so much that he looked infirmed. I pegged him in his late sixties to early seventies. His nose was crooked, bent out of shape. He draped himself in a bandito—a poncho from one of the coastal regions of Mexico—and topped himself with a stovepipe hat. A giant eagle's feather stuck out from the rim. He sat at the far end of the bar, two snakeskin boots rocking back and forth underneath him, making him shorter than me. And then, there were the turquoise earrings of a style you didn't see around that region anymore, because most jewelry of any value had been traded away for food, clothing, or guns. He, too, had just finished his beer.

"I'm sorry," I told him as I moved my hand away from my gun. "I didn't see you there."

He waved it away. "No problem. Protector has got to protect, correct?" I nodded. "I was saying that your friend, if he is still such, if correct. You did catch a break this time."

The stranger's English was very good, with very little accent left. I figured he must be East Coast trained, maybe someone like Mrs. Mendoza, adopted at a young age and run through all the proper schooling.

"Never said he wasn't."

"Your friend or correct?" His smile was broad and disarming, which put me on guard.

"Both," I assured him. "But somehow, I'm guessin' you have something to add." I walked over, pulled out the stool next to him, and twirled it around to sit rodeo-style.

"Maybe, maybe I do."

"I didn't catch your name."

He ignored the implied question. "I could tell you more, but I think I'd rather make it more of a game. Care for a wager?"

"I'm not a betting man. Owner's always on me about that. Says it'd give guests confidence at the tables. 'Must be a fair game, if the sheriff is playing.' Stuff like that. Only, don't want to be in debt to someone who I just might have to shoot later." I hoped my drinking buddy got *that* implied suggestion. "So, you were about to tell me what you know."

"No, I was about to suggest a bet, one I think you will like." He faced me. "You have not seen the last of Cesar Raul Mendoza's murderer, but if you do finally catch them, you will not be able to do your job. You will choose poorly, and they *will* get away."

I scoffed. "You're definitely not from around here, however, you seem to know about our little situation here, so I'll be blunt. I've faced monsters, demons, and things that if I tried to explain, would send that hat of yours to the moon." I leaned in closer. "I've questioned my actions, and even felt guilty afterwards, but I have never shirked my duty as a lawman." I made sure we were eye-to-eye when I told him, "I'd die before that."

Not flinching, not blinking, he replied, "That you may, so then how about you bet me?"

I got up, tired of the old Indian's game. I'd made it halfway to the door, before he said, "I will give you something you desperately want if you win."

I stopped but didn't turn around. "There's nothing I want that much."

"I know who started the curse *and* how to break it."

My soul chilled. The room swam around me, and I thought I might pass out. Reflexively, I had a handful of the stranger's bandito and pulled him close to me.

"How could you possibly know that?"

He grinned. "I have in my possession a document—a very, very old document that explains in detail how the Verde Valley came to be like this and...how to fix it."

I growled. "I want that, now."

He shook a finger at me. "Ah, Ah, Ah. That's not how this works. You cannot threaten me with violence. It would look bad to all the local tribes if the lawman who constantly asks them to trust him beat up an old man, such as myself. Now, sit down, and I will lay out my terms."

Reluctantly, I let him go.

"Very good. The bet will be as such. *If* you find whoever killed Cesar Raul Mendoza, I will give you a journal that reveals who cursed the Verde Valley and why they did it. Then if you fulfill your duty as protector of the people of this land, and make sure the culprit sees justice for their crimes, I will add the pages to the journal that also explains how to lift it."

These types of bets are too one-sided. I knew there had to be a catch. "And if I lose?"

He got up from his chair. Standing in front of me, he barely reached my shoulders. "If you do not find Cesar's murderer, I demand you leave this area for good. If you cannot do something as simple as that, then you don't belong here anyhow."

The old man wasn't wrong.

"And if I don't fulfill my duty, as you say, as 'protector of the people of this land'? What is my penalty then?"

He sized me up, from boots to hat. "You will be indebted to me for the rest of your life and will do anything I ask you to."

This was a loser's bet. He held all the cards, already knew how the endgame would play out. "I will accept your terms, under one condition."

The Indian rubbed his hands. "This should be good."

"I need one answer. Was Cesar Raul Mendoza truly the last of his line?"

"If I answer that question, we are agreed to terms?"

I nodded.

"Go to your office and wait. You'll get your answer soon."

Owner stepped out of the storeroom, and my attention drew away from the Indian for a split-second. When I looked back, the old man had vanished.

"What are you still doing here?" Owner asked.

I headed for the door. Over my shoulder, I said, "My duty."

———

I WAITED IN MY OFFICE MOST OF THE DAY, PULLIN' apart the conversation with the old gambler, trying to figure out what game he played. I recognized real magic when I saw it, but what flavor his was, I didn't know. He dressed like the cross between a Guatemalan shaman and a Caribbean houngan. And yet, he was clearly a native, maybe Apache or Navajo. That vanishing act was nothing I hadn't seen before, but it was too well timed, as if he kept Owner frozen in the back until that exact moment, as if to make a point.

I hated magic. More specifically, I hated the advantage magical beings had over me. That was what wore me down more than anything else. I had to be twice the man as anyone in this town to keep them all safe. And I had to do it every day. Owner dangled a vacation in front of me...like I could let down my guard that long?

I had Will Ragsdale to train before I could do that, and the lad was still young. Did I have a right to place this burden on his shoulders, knowing that he'd feel like this one day? I should send him and that girl he's fond of far from the area. I guess if I end up having to leave town, that's what I'd suggest they do, too, lest he end up like me.

Sauntering footsteps approached my front door. It opened to allow the Widow Mendoza in. She wore a thinner veil over her hat so I was better able to see her features. Her heavily-lidded eyes sought me behind my desk. Her soft voice breathed relief. "Thank God, Sheriff, you're here."

I sat up. "What can I do for you now, Mrs. Mendoza?"

She took five steps to me and nearly fell onto me. I stood quickly to catch her, her arms going around my neck. She sobered into my shoulder. "I'm so scared. Galvarino's going to kill me."

"Huh? Why would that ghost come for you now?"

She looked up with deep, pleading, brown eyes. "I'm pregnant."

———

GHOSTS ARE THE HARDEST OF OTHERWORLDLY beings to disperse. You can shoot, stab, behead, throw a bag of mystical herbs or bones at just about anything else. Not spirits. Nope, you got to give them what they want, reason with them, or find a priest to cast them into hell.

Closest one of those to Drowned Horse, that wasn't a native medicine man, had to be at the Mormon settlement far to the northwest. There might be someone ordained down in Tucson, but that wasn't any better. Every once in a while the Army sent a Chaplin out with the cavalry, but to my knowledge there wasn't one currently up at Whipple;

Lincoln barely had men, let alone holy ones. No, it'd be up to me to think up something clever.

I'd been requesting all sorts of books from libraries back East on mythology, religions, and demons. Those librarians who didn't think me crazy would forward what they had to me, which mostly turned out to be useless: children's bedtime stories, fairy tales, and the like. The theology books only referenced the Bible. Last I read the King James, there wasn't much in the way of casting out three-hundred-year-old vengeful ghosts.

I thought about the old bible that sat on a shelf in my room above the Sagebrush. I didn't recall buying it. It was worn, like it'd been read quite a bit, but I couldn't remember ever thumbing through it myself. No one had ever been in that room before Owner offered it to me, but the moment I took possession of it, it felt like I'd lived there my whole life. I considered going up to my room and grabbing it, but I had another copy in my office, and I could avoid bumping into Owner. Plus, you don't survive a curse without picking up a few non-theological tricks along the way that I hoped would give me an advantage when Galvarino showed his ghostly face.

I didn't fancy fighting him one on one. The way legend had it, during the Arauco War, Governor Mendoza chopped off both of the Mapuche warrior's hands. Undeterred, Galvarino strapped long blades to his mutilated stumps and returned to fight Mendoza's conquistadors, almost taking out the brutal tyrant before being captured once again. The Spaniard fed Galvarino to his dogs.

Yeah, I might be motivated to come back from the dead to seek revenge after that.

―――――

NOT KNOWING WHEN MY OPPONENT WOULD SHOW up, I moved into the Spanish C Ranch. I was unloading my stuff into the bunkhouse trunk when the Widow Mendoza checked on me.

"Will this be acceptable?" she asked.

I went to answer her but swallowed hard instead.

She no longer wore the hat or the veil. It was easy to see why Cesar became obsessed with her. Her flawless skins had the color of warm sand, and those sleepy eyes took a man's breath away. She wore a coat over a dressing gown and moccasins.

"Yes, ma'am. I've slept in much worse growin' up."

Mrs. Mendoza slipped into the room and stepped over to a small table. The previous occupant had left cigarettes in a cup. She took one and lit it with a match. Drawing in deeply, she exhaled the smoke in rings, clearly familiar the with process.

"That feels better." She titled the cup my way. "Would you care? I don't think he's coming back. I don't think any of them are."

I politely declined. "Why is that?"

She angled herself on the bunk so that her posterior barely dented the mattress. She hovered there, not wanting to stand, but not entirely committed to sitting.

"My husband was not a good man, Sheriff Forrest. He knew the land was harsh, so he became harsh to tame it. He understood that any one of a dozen groups wanted him gone. The Apache. The Wiipukepaya . Even my own people. He represented everything they all hated. So, he expected betrayal, expected death." She shivered and crossed her arms. "But not that way. No one could have expected that."

I saved unpacking my special case for last. "He should've. We tell everyone who chooses to settle here. It'd be right unfair to not do so."

"He knew. That is why he paid to have a medicine man place wards around the ranch. And hired hardened men as ranch hands. He even traded meat at Fort Lincoln to assure that they'd come when called. Pointless, in the end. His arrogance has left me alone with child, and at the mercy of a vengeful spirit." She spit on the floor. "*Bastardo.*"

I took a necklace out of the case and handed it to the widow for her to examine.

She held it up to the window, letting the last rays of the setting sun catch the green gemstone. The walls of the bunkhouse reflected off the facets twisting back and forth as it spun.

"It's beautiful," she said. "What is it?"

"Peridot." I retrieved it and hovered behind her "May I?" Mrs. Mendoza gathered her black hair into a ponytail and pulled it to the side. I bent down and tied the cord around her neck. "According to local beliefs, it's supposed to protect against evil spirits."

She giggled, the first one I'd heard since meeting her. "If this is so, then why do I need you?"

"It's just a legend. No idea if'n it'll work."

Mrs. Mendoza got up to leave, holding the gem out in front of her to admire it. Before she exited, she paused. "Well, then. I *might* just have to keep you around then."

After she left, I could still smell her in the hot, moist air of the bunk house, and it wasn't the tobacco.

---

I woke to a different aroma: beans and coffee.

Apparently, not all the staff had left. Luka, the ranch hand I'd met previously, still hung around in the distance, doing ranching stuff, and two Mexican women, Mrs. Mendoza's attendants, cleaned.

Breakfast, however, was made by the queen herself.

"Please come in," the Widow Mendoza invited, as I entered the kitchen. "Breakfast will be ready shortly."

"I should get back into town, Mrs. Mendoza. They're not...well, I'm not used to bein' away for long periods of time. It makes me nervous."

She pointed a wooden spoon at me. "It's Stefani from now on. You stay in *mí casa*, you will be treated as family." She waved the spoon over the food. In addition to the beans, she'd made eggs, tortillas, and bacon. "I bet you're also not used to a good meal before a long day. Please eat. It'll give me great comfort when you leave me."

I pulled out a chair at the table. "I'll be back before sundown. Never seen a ghost appear in broad daylight. Mind you, they might be there and I just don't see them, but I feel you'll be safe enough while I take care of some business."

Stefani nodded and served up a pile of everything. She wouldn't let me leave until I had a second helping. During the meal, she often played with the necklace I'd given her. "I slept much better last night. The first real sleep I had since Cesar's murder." She blushed. "Thank you for that."

I cleaned my plate, savoring the final bites. She wasn't wrong. Owner's meals never tasted that good. "I'm glad to hear. You should be fine today. Do me a favor, if'n you would. Sometimes ghosts are connected to certain objects, especially ancient ones. Make sure your late husband didn't have any relics that might be tied to Chili or the Mapuche people."

She saw me to the door and watched me get on Roland, who Luka had fed and brushed that morning. "I will look." She cast her eyes down, but gave me a rueful grin. "And I wait for you to come back this evening."

I tipped my hat to her. Roland nickered as we rode out from the ranch. "None of that. She's just someone who lost a husband and needs reassurin' she and her baby gonna by okay."

Roland snorted in reply.

"Yeah," I agreed. "I don't believe me either."

I THOUGHT ABOUT STEFANI THROUGHOUT THE DAY, embarrassed that each time I did, I grinned. It wasn't a bad idea, really. Her kid would need a father, and I'd treat them better than most of the types that came through here. Trappers. Laborers. Prospectors. Soldiers. Gamblers.

Gamblers. That took me back to the bet I'd made with the old Indian, erasing any thoughts of joy or a bright future from my day. If I didn't stop Galvarino, then Stefani and the baby would be dead, and I'd be o the first stage outta town. I focused back on my preparations for my second night at the Spanish C ranch.

I stopped by Hiram's to see if he had any news for me after dressing Cesar's body. We went to his workroom, where he pulled off the shroud over the rancher.

"With him so damaged by the heat, I can't be sure of all the details, but I can confirm he died by stabbing."

"That's in line with the idea of Galvarino's ghost."

Hiram shrugged. "Maybe, but maybe not." He grabbed a set of pliers and pulled back the jerkied flesh around the wound. "This cut, you see, is very clean. Like a sword or knife. Up close and personal, too."

I raised an eyebrow. "But don't the legends say Galvarino had blades instead of hands?"

"True, but think about the time. That's three-hundred years ago. Sure, the Spanish had forged blades, but do you think a primitive warrior tribe had access to that fine a weapon?" He went over to set of drawers and pulled one all the way out. He dumped the contents on the table.

A dozen knives clattered and clinked as they fell in front of me.

"Look at some of these," Hiram said, holding up an Apache knife. "I've pulled a lot of these out of bodies. See? It's from when we first got here." The blade was stone and rough around the edges. It'd been carved from rock and honed against a whetstone. "That doesn't look forged, right? And that was just two years ago. What do you think the Mapuche used?"

I wasn't convinced. "They could have taken swords from the Spaniards."

Hiram agreed. "Possibly, but would Galvarino feel comfortable wielding the weapons of his enemies?" He crossed his arms and smirked knowingly. "I would bet he'd use his own people's weapons. Better to fight with what he already knew."

He made sense, but ghosts didn't always make sense. "He's a ghost, Hiram. Who knows what damage it might leave? Anything else?"

The undertaker titled his head, as if to say, *Isn't that enough?* He coughed and admitted he had nothing specific to confirm a supernatural death. "No residue indicating some sort of ghostly presence. The rigor mortis on his face indicates surprise, but not necessarily fear. I got nothing to help you beat this ghost, if there was one."

I snapped. "Well, that doesn't do me a lot of good. I got a widow and a baby to keep safe."

Hiram took a stepped back and held up his hands. "Whoa, there, Sheriff. Don't shoot the messenger. I call 'em like I see 'em. You want more, you might want to visit a medium. I just stitch up the dead because I wasn't very good at keeping people alive."

Craddick had been a field surgeon during the war and left feeling as if he could've saved more lives. Instead, he cut off a lot of limbs and buried a lot of good men. He swore he'd only work with the dead after that.

"Sorry. Don't know where my head is these days."

Hiram laid a hand on my arm. "You want to talk about it? I'm good at listening."

"I'm running out of time, Hiram. To protect Drowned Horse. To stop the curse. I can't seem to catch a break. I put one thing down, and before long, something else shows up. I've got no reprieve." I pulled away, letting his hand drop. "I've got no sanctuary of my own."

He walked out of the workshop with me. "Sanctuary is where you make it, Levi." The sounds of his wife and son in the kitchen preparing dinner reached us. He looked in the direction of the noise, contentment bringing color to his cheeks. "I couldn't do what I do without them. I'd go mad." We shook hands. "You're doing honorably by us. We all know it, even if we don't show it all the time."

I left still feeling awash in conflicting emotions. My gut told me I'd missed something. The old Indian's bet indicated as much.

I sat in my office for hours, pouring through books, old parchments, and notes I'd scribbled down over the last two years. I wasn't seeing it. As I mounted Roland, Owner exited the Sagebrush to sweep the sidewalk before the evening crowds arrived. I coulda gone over to talk to him. I shoulda been the one to say something first.

He beat me to it.

"Will you be joining us for dinner, or do you have...other obligations?"

"I'll be back tomorrow, hopefully."

I spurred Roland and tried to beat the setting sun.

***

LANTERNS ILLUMINATED THE FRONT OF THE ranch house as we pulled up to it. A scream broke the quiet of the night. I'd barely dismounted when Stefani fled out the door. The front of her dress was blood-stained.

"Levi! He's here!"

She wrapped herself around me, but I held her back far enough to check the wound. The gash crossed her collarbone wasn't deep.

"What happened?"

"My necklace!" Her panic turning to sobs. "Something cut the string, and I didn't notice it'd fallen off until I reached the garden and saw him."

I lifted her into Roland's saddle.

"If I don't return, ride until you reach the Sagebrush. Tell Owner what happen. Got that?"

Stefani nodded.

I yanked my shotgun out from its saddle holster. No idea if my plan would work, but I had little else. I marched around the house to the rock garden. More torches led the way. I stepped down the gravel path between the cotton-wood trees, annoyed by the tinkling of glass ornaments and wind chimes that hung from their branches.

Galvarino appeared at the far end of the garden. He wore the ceremonial dress of the Mapuche: high leather boots, a loin cloth around his waist, a poncho over his shoulders, and a scarf around his head with three feathers sticking out of it, and all of it ghostly white. The features of his face I could not see clearly in the shadows, but I could hear his snarl. He crossed his arms over his chest, and then pointed them at me. Each arm capped with a blade, long as a sword, which he aimed at my heart. He swiped one blade then the other through the air. Something struck my face and my shoulder. Blood leaked from the gashes the mystical blades created. Behind me, I could hear the ornaments shatter from the force of Galvarino's attack.

He crisscrossed the air again and again, resulting in more and more invisible blades cutting my body. I tried dodging, but I couldn't get a clear shot at him. The closer I got, the farther away he seemed to be.

With little recourse, I dove forward, laid flat on the ground, and brought the gun to my shoulder. I fired up at an angle, the blast ripping apart the night. The salt load I'd replaced the pellets with hit Galvarino in the chest. He flew backward into the dark and vanished.

I rolled onto my back, breathing hard. The cuts weren't any deeper than Stefani's, but they stung.

She came into my vision, hovering over me. Her tears of relief dripped down onto my face.

"Is it over?" she asked.

"I don't know."

She helped me to sitting, then to standing. We entered

the house, and she took me to her bedroom where she took off my shirt and cleaned my wounds, gently, thoroughly.

"I thought he might kill you."

"Ouch! Yeah, I thought that, too."

When Stefani mended the cuts on my face, I winced.

"You're a big baby," she teased.

Then she kissed my cheek.

"Yup, a big baby."

Then she kissed the non-existent cut on my lips.

"The biggest," she whispered.

I kissed her back.

Our bloody clothes came off urgently as we continued kissing. She stepped back, her deep brown eyes cast down, to let me admire her body. "Do I please you?"

As an answer, I swooped her into my arms and carried her to the bed. I showed her how much she pleased me, and let her return the affirmations until we fell asleep spent.

---

I WOKE DISORIENTATED AS ONE DOES WHEN YOU'RE looking up at an unfamiliar ceiling. It took me looking all around to remember where I was and what happened the night before.

Stefani had left an indentation in the feather mattress where her body previously lay. I placed my hand on it, finding it cold. She'd been up awhile. That was good, seeing as I had some thoughts that needed answers.

Before that, I needed new clothes, seeing as my others had been shredded by Galvarino. I found Cesar's trunk and searched for a shirt and trousers that fit well enough so I wouldn't have to walk through the house obscene.

A set of Texas Ranger clothes sat at the bottom. I'd almost forgotten he'd fought in the Mexican-American war. Stepping back, I noticed a shelf above the washbasin. It was just long enough that a veteran might store a saber there as a memento of his time in the service.

Quietly, I slid the dressing chair over and stood on it to examine the shelf. The dust pattern indicated that a sword had rested there, possibly for a year or so, until recently.

I got down onto my belly and looked between the stone tiles on the floor. I pinched some sand and ran in between my thumb and forefinger. Sure, much of the Arizona sand is a reddish color, but not *that* red.

I returned the chair and went downstairs. Stefani humming in the kitchen. A wall separated us, so I was able to slip on my boots and sneak out through the front door.

Retracing my steps from the attack, I carefully walked the garden path. Glass had been strewn everywhere. A lot of glass. Much more glass than there were broken ornaments. Digging through the shards, I found one very unusual one. Cylindrical in shape, it looked the right size to be an arrow shaft.

I walked out to where I'd seen Galvarino. Scanning the ground, I discovered traces of blood.

Now, I might not be up on every supernatural creature that shows its multi-horned head in Drowned Horse, but it has been my experience that ghosts don't bleed.

Nor did they leave footprints.

Two sets, to be exact. Some effort had been made to brush them away, but it was sloppy work.

I followed them out of the yard and to an almost empty cattle barn. That couldn't be right. Cesar often bragged that his cattle were doing so well that he had enough head to donate some to the Camp Lincoln. Stefani had indicated, as much. But there were less than a dozen with the **SÍ** branded on their hides.

I kept exploring and came across a cattle trough; the water milky white. An acidic taste bubbled up my throat as I reached down into the dank liquid, already assuming what I was going to find.

The rocks holding Luka's body down slipped away, allowing me to drag him to the surface; white paint still covered parts of his face. The bladed gauntlets fit over his hands perfectly.

*Wham!* An arrow slammed into my back but ricocheted off my shoulder blade. The shot had been at the wrong angle. The force of it, though, caused me to lunge forward. I almost ended up in the trough with Luka, but instead, I let my momentum carry me up and over. Laying against the wood planks, numbness traveled down my left arm leaving it useless. I reached for my holster, but it wasn't there. Where had I placed it last night? Why didn't I put it on this morning?

Whoever my assailant was, they'd find me easy pickins if I stuck my head up. They had the advantage. I pressed harder against the trough causing it to give.

Seeing a way out, I rocked the bin until enough water sloshed out that I could tip the whole thing over. Several arrows impacted around me, the archer taking pot shots hoping to spook me into running. With the trough now empty, I flipped it over and crawled under it. It hurt like hell, but I lifted it up onto my bruised shoulders and duck-walked out of the barn. The thump, thump, thump the arrows hitting the roof moved me faster. Outside the barn, I kept heading toward Roland. I kept a hold-out piece in his saddle.

"I'd stop, if I were you."

I tiled my impromptu shield up enough to see Mrs. Mendoza's riding boots standing next to Roland. I lifted it further until I could see she had an apple in one hand, my pistol in the other.

"Come on out. It's all right."

I dropped the trough.

The Widow, clearly no longer grieving, wore riding pants and a blouse as if she planned to be leaving soon. She bit her lip, as if I'd ruined some great surprise.

"What gave me away?"

I held my hands up in surrender. "Ghosts don't miss. It's sorta in their nature. They can pop up anywhere. Galvarino ran your husband through up close. Why would he then just cut you so gently and leave you alive to come running to me? I knew then, this was all your plan. I put you on Roland to make sure you wouldn't leave. He's trained well."

"I can see that," she chided while feeding the apple to my horse.

"Traitor."

She cocked her head. "Me...or the horse?"

"Both. Why'd you kill Cesar?"

Her expression told me the answer should have been obvious. "He was a horrible rancher. Between what the Pai stole and what he gave away to the Fort to keep the Pai from stealing, he never made any money. All his fortune went into building this ranch and replacing livestock. We were going to lose everything."

Footsteps crunched on gravel, and I prepped myself to meet Stefani's partner. The Apache was big and strong and painted head to toe in black, making him impossible to see in the dark. "I had to protect me. I stayed out in the field one night, waiting for whoever was stealing our cattle to arrive. My plan was to shoot them, but Night Wind and I worked out an arrangement instead." Never taking eyes off of me, or letting the gun waver, she reached an arm around the brave and pulled him closer to her.

Wonderful.

"Years ago, he traded the life of a merchant for the secret to glassblowing. He made me all those ornaments during our courtship. His glass arrows are a work of genius." I couldn't tell if Night Wind seemed prouder of his artistic skills or his lover. The Widow Mendoza blushed with embarrassment. "Cesar caught us, one night when he was supposed to be in Prescott. While he and Night Wind fought, they knocked his sword of the stand, and...well, I'm sure you've figured out the rest."

I had. I needed to keep her bragging so I could finish this. Stopping *her* wouldn't be hard, but Breaking Wind would be more challenging. In addition to the bow, he had a very large dagger strapped to his belt. I had to count on her hold over him.

"So, knowing Mendoza's family line, you used the ghost of Galvarino to cover up his death. Poor Luka—who clearly hated his boss—was more than willing to help. Can I lower my arms, now? They're getting tired." She nodded, but Foul Wind tensed. I paced while summarizing the events I'd put together. "But you still worried that I'd figure out somethin', or that maybe I wouldn't be satisfied that Galvarino's ghost wouldn't return."

Mrs. Mendoza nodded. "You do have that reputation."

I angled myself to get in line of sight with Roland. As a rule, I tended to talk with my hands, but now, I made specific gestures that my horse would recognize.

Trained well, indeed.

"You set up this elaborate ruse to get me on your side, hoping I'd take out Luka, the weak thread in your plan." I slowly clapped in appreciation for her cleverness. "Well done."

Roland took a step back, snorting that he'd received my command.

"So, what now?"

The widow actually appeared torn. "I really didn't have a contingency. I mostly wanted your cooperation." She sighed. "I figured after you killed 'the ghost,' our business would be done. I'd sell the ranch, leave this cursed valley, and never return."

"There's no baby, is there?"

She barked. "Ha! I did not want that man's spawn in me. His kind slaughtered my people for generations. It would be a betrayal of everything I am." She rubbed a hand across Night Sweat's chest. "But I might have to put one in there once we dispose of you."

They shared a quick gaze of lust between them, and I seized the moment. I whistled and Roland reared back on his hind legs, knocking the gun from the widow's hand. Mrs. Mendoza's "injun brave" swung her out of harm's way, as I hoped he would, and I whistled my second command. Roland sprinted forward, getting close enough I could fling myself up into the saddle. I stayed low as we galloped out of range of Night Jerk's arrows.

By the time I returned with a posse, they were gone.

---

ESTANFANI MENDOZA AND NIGHT WIND GOT caught in Tucson while arranging to cross into Mexico. He died fighting the law, but they took her alive. Despite all my efforts to the contrary, I did find myself on a vacation of sorts to testify at her trial. The widow put on a convincin' act, claiming the cruelty of her late husband, but I did my duty and testified against her. When the subject of whether or not I'd bedded her, in an attempt by her lawyer to discredit me as a scorned lover, I lied. I told the jury with a straight face, that it'd never happened.

If she hadn't been already willing to kill me, she certainly would have then.

Mendoza was set to hang two days later, being the first woman to be executed in Arizona, but then the Governor, wanting to keep such negative tidings from the papers, stayed her fate, choosing instead to banish her from the United States forever.

As the U.S. Marshals escorted her to the border, they were attacked by a band of 'Che, a long way from home. No lawmen were killed, but Mrs. Mendoza joined her late husband and her lover in that big ranch in the sky...or hell, which was much more likely.

I returned home where Owner and I had patched things up.    .

"You were right," I told him. "The job *was* getting to me. I couldn't see what was in front of my face. I've been wound tighter than a Swiss clock, and I forgot that I'm not just our protector against a curse."

Owner poured me a beer. "You're also our keeper of law and order."

Not every event that crossed my path was due to the curse. Some evil just came from the hearts of men. Or in this case, a woman.

I looked up to thank Owner for the beer, but he was gone. The noise of the saloon quieted. I swirled my stool around. The whole place had emptied, save for one person.

If he was indeed, a person.

The old man appeared identical to when we'd first met. He, too, had a beer, which he drew from as if it tasted like love. He wiped his upper lip of alcohol with the back of his sleeve and exhaled.

"That is good beer. Do you know where he gets it from?"

"He buys it from a guy up in Prescott."

The enigma took another sip, a smaller one, and smirked. "Nothing like a beer after a job well done, eh?"

"Who are you?"

Again, he ignored the question. "I have to admit, I didn't think you would lie on the witness stand. Is that not against the lawman code or something?"

"My duty was to see her pay for her crimes."

"Even though you loved her?"

I laughed sharp and hard. "I didn't love her. Love isn't one night in a hay loft. Love comes from trust. I didn't have that with her. I don't have that with anyone." I gave him a lopsided grin. "She was a vacation, and one sorely needed."

He held up a finger. "Ah, but people trust you. How would they feel if they knew you betrayed that trust by lying?"

Owner walked out of the back, which caused the old man a lot of concern.

"How did you...You are supposed..."

The barkeep picked up a towel and wiped down the counter. "I've been here a long time. Some magics just don't work on me." The Indian harrumphed. "As for your question, there isn't a person in this town that would judge Levi for doing exactly what you bet he wouldn't do."

"You heard that, too, huh? Not many can reject my spells."

Owner nodded. "Let's just say, I've learned a thing or two over time. Now, I believe you have something for him? A document about the curse? There were two conditions, but we both know the first was a given."

Twisting back and forth on his stool, the mystic challenged, "Oh, really? Was it?"

"Certainly." Owner walked out from behind the bar to stand beside me. "You couldn't win what you wanted, which was Levi's servitude, unless he found the killer."

Grinning ear-to-ear, the Indian nodded. "That is true. I would not have even tasked him, were he not up to the job."

Owner continued, "Which means your plan all along was for him to fail. And the only way he could have done *that*, was to tell the truth on the stand, letting the Widow Mendoza go free. You bet that our sheriff was too honorable a man to see justice done."

"Boy, did you get that wrong." I thought back to the festival. "You bet on me as if I was a rider, when I'm actually the chicken, who just kicked your old man's ass." I drew my gun and pointed it at him. "Now, my winnings, please."

The old man frowned. With a wave of his hand, he produced a leather-bound journal. After setting it down on the counter, he snapped his fingers, conjuring coins, which he lay next to it. "For the beer."

Owner picked up the book and flipped through it quickly.

"What's this horseshit?"

"What?" I asked.

He opened the book wide for me to see. The words were in a script I'd never seen. Neither had Owner.

"We can't read this. That wasn't the bet."

The old man held up a finger. "Ah. Ah. Ah. I said I would give you a document that had the truth about the Verde

Valley curse and how to lift it. I never said that it would be in a language you could understand."

I moved on the old man, but despite being two steps away, he vanished before I could reach him.

———————

I TOOK THE TOME TO EVERY TRIBE IN THE territory. None admitted to understanding it, though when I reached a band of Navajo's to the far north, almost to Colorado, they drew guns on me when I showed them the journal. After they calmed down, a tribal elder said that they knew of the script, but not how to read it. That ability had been lost over generations. He told me it was the language of the First World.

Of the Gods.

He studied the words carefully, trying his best to translate them, but all he managed to do was decipher a name.

"I can tell you *who* this story is about, but not *what* it says." He took a long drag of his pipe. "Some time before, there had descended among the Pueblos, from the heavens, a divine gambler, or gambling-god, named *Noqoìlpi…*"

# EIGHT
# "TWICE TAXED FOR IDLENESS"

Prescott, Arizona Territory
February, 1867

YAVAPAI COUNTY RECORDER JOHN P. BOURKE looked at his journal and sighed. Tax day brought him both excitement and nervousness. One year ago, Bourke collected his biggest business tithe as the county sheriff, but it cost the life of the last clerk. His cut from that payday funded his campaign to be that man's replacement. The return to Gemtwinkle's cave had come way too quickly, but Bourke had already devised a different approach than before. He had goals beyond sheriff or county clerk, and those plans would take more money than he'd get from his normal cut.

Luckily, the current County sheriff, Johnny Moore, had other things to contend with, so escorting the tax collector, who'd once been a sheriff, wasn't on his agenda. Bourke had been given leave to ride down to Drowned Horse, meet with the local sheriff Levi Forrest, and do his duty. That had been fine by Bourke.

The two-day ride went without a hitch. One could never be

sure where the line was between what was cursed land and what wasn't. Even in his time as lawman, some of the strangeness of the Verde Valley had leaked up to the North West where Prescott resided. The current Marshal, Tucker Bandimere, took a certain pride in settling those particular events, having been trained, in part, by Forrest. Bourke's one and only goal was to deal with the creature called a *spriggan*, and leave with as many precious gems as possible. Most would end up in the treasury, but a healthy chunk would end up in his election fund.

*Governor Bourke had a nice ring to it*, he thought.

In the town of Drowned Horse, a lot had changed since the previous year. More buildings. More people. More gambling and women upstairs at the Sagebrush Saloon. Bourke paid only partial attention to the saloon's owner, named Owner, as he went over the town's books with him.

"Fine. Fine. Excellent work, as always. I'm sure everything is to the letter of the law."

"Thank you," Owner said with pride clearly all over his face. "It's been another tough year, but I made sure to account for all of the…unusual events and adjust the taxes accordingly."

Sheriff Forrest, who sat at the table with them, brought up the uncomfortable topic of Gemtwinkle. "Speaking of unusual, I had a talk with our miner friend, and straightened him out on his poor behavior last time. He sure feels bad about what happened." Forrest took off his hat and placed it over his heart. "He had me send Silas's widow a donation that'll set her up for a while."

"Yes," Bourke recalled. "She came by after the anonymous package arrived. She thought it'd come from me, and I figured it was best she believed that, instead of asking too many questions."

Forrest agreed that it'd been the best course of action.

Bourke felt his palms get sweaty in anticipation. "So, shall we pay Mr. Gemtwinkle a visit?"

Forrest and Bourke got up. Outside, though, the sheriff

called a young lad over. He looked to be about fifteen or so, with sandy-brown hair and fair complexion.

"John, this is Will Ragsdale. I'm training him to be my new deputy. He's still got a ways to go, but this'll be a good experience for him."

The county clerk didn't like this new twist to his well thought out plan, but smiled and greeted the boy. "How do you do, boy?"

Will took Bourke's hand and shook it firmly. "Very well, sir. It'll be an honor to ride with two sheriffs today. I hope you'll share with me a story or two along the way. I'd love to hear them."

Bourke laughed. "Former sheriff, but sure, I've got a tale or two that doesn't," he looked directly at Forrest, "involve monsters...outside the human kind, that is."

Will grinned, and they set off for the spriggan's cave.

---

FORREST LED THEM TO THE CAVE WITHOUT THE trepidation he had a year ago.

"He's expecting us this time."

As they approached, Bourke heard the sounds of music coming from inside the mountain. Someone played a flute or pipe beautifully, the notes floating on the breeze like the smell of honeysuckle. Just inside the entrance, Gemtwinkle, still looking small and ugly, danced and blew on an onyx flute appearing no less like Pan in *A Midsummer Night's Dream*.

Then he sang:

> *Ow huv kolon gwra dos,*
> *A ny glewydh y'n koos,*
> *An eos ow kana pur hweg?*
> *A ny glewydh hy lev,*
> *A-woles a sev,*
> *Y'n nansow ow kana mar deg?*

*Y'n nansow ow kana mar deg?*

Seeing the trio coming near, the spriggan switched to English. Forrest clapped, and Will danced a gig alongside Gemtwinkle.

> *My sweetheart, come a-long,*
> *Don't you hear the fond song,*
> *The sweet notes of the nightingale flow*
> *Don't you hear the fond tale,*
> *Of the sweet nightingale,*
> *As she sings in the valley below?*
> *As she sings in the valley below?*

The song stirred Bourke's heart, and he regretted what he was going to do to the little monster, but he also knew campaigns didn't fund themselves. After the song ended, Gemtwinkle bade them join him for tea and cakes as he'd done the time before. They sat around a campfire, drank and ate, and spoke of events and changes to local tribal leadership. The spriggan was especially sensitive to what was happening between the Army and the Apache, growing maudlin when talk turned to the purge of them from the land.

"There's a reason you don't hear of my kind in England anymore. The fae folk were slaughtered in much the same way. What remains of our blood is in the humans we bred with, coming out only when powerful magic deems it so. *My a dyb y vos hwedhel trist.*"

Forrest agreed. "Yup, it *is* sad. But more and more people are coming to settle in this area. There's going to be a fight for land. Not much I can do other than make sure the fight stays fair."

While everyone was in a moment of quiet contemplation, Bourke seized the opportunity to spill his tea onto his lap.

"Damn," he shouted, jumping up and brushing the liquid from his coat. "I'm as clumsy as a floundered stud!"

There were queries as to if he was okay from the others, to which he said he was. Bourke took off his coat and shook it off to the side, and then he turned it inside out and put it back on.

The effect was immediate.

Gemtwinkle screeched like a banshee and backed away from the fire pit.

Bourke feigned total surprise. "What's happening?"

Forrest ran to Bourke and yanked off his coat. "Not your fault. You didn't know."

Gemtwinkle visibly calmed down, slowly coming back to the circle.

Will, who'd drawn his gun reflexively, looked back and forth between Bourke and the spriggan. "What's going on?"

Forrest checked on Gemtwinkle, speaking in Cornish to the creature, making sure they were all good. Over his shoulder, the sheriff said, "So, fae folk have this thing about inside out clothes. You wouldn't know unless you studied the legends."

Bourke apologized profusely, trying not to overdo it. "Mr. Gemtwinkle. I had no idea. Please, please accept my apologies."

The spriggan nodded. "Vydh sallow. You could not know of our ways."

They continued on with the accounting, Gemtwinkle handing over a sizable purse to the clerk. Bourke thanked him, apologized again, and exited the cavern with Forrest and Ragsdale.

"Whew!" Forrest exclaimed. "That was a close one. Would hate it if dead county clerks became a regular thing. Might cause some problems."

"Well, you'll have no problems from me," Bourke lied.

They all shook hands and headed their separate ways.

But Bourke didn't take the trail back up Grief Hill. Instead, he found a place to wait out the day. When night fell, he undressed, flipped his clothes inside out, and redressed. He even flipped his hat. He covered his face with a mask backside forward, wore his gloves wrong-side out, and put on a reversed set of moccasins. Feeling like he'd made himself as disheveled as possible, Bourke found his way back to Gemtwinkle's horde.

Humming came from a tunnel heading deep underground, leading Bourke to believe the spriggan was hard at work mining for more gems. Taking advantage of the low light, he moved through the cave toward the room he'd witnessed the monster go in and out of to retrieve his governmental tithe. Bourke stopped dead when he entered.

Almost reaching the ceiling, piles of gold bars, coins, gems, and even paper notes filled the room. Bourke had never seen so many riches in one place. He'd never be able to carry it all, but he knew what items looked the most valuable. He carefully chose a select few gems, a handful of gold coins, and some of the larger bills, tucking them into his pockets.

As soon as he had, the humming stopped, only to be replaced by running feet. Bourke knew that a spell guarding the treasure was a possibility, so he grabbed a couple last items and left the room. He'd almost gotten out of the cave, when cries of "Thief!" reached his ears. Gemtwinkle sped around a corner and found his intruder. He slid to a stop, gasping as Bourke loomed large in his disordered garb.

"Boo!" he said.

Gemtwinkle scrambled backwards, cowering in a recessed spot in the cave wall. He chattered, "E-v-vil! Loot-t-ter! Y-you'll never get away from m-m-my wrath!"

Bourke chuckled and left the lair.

*He'll never find me, and if he tries, I'll send all the men from Fort Whipple to kill him. Giant or not, they have enough guns to take him down.*

But the clerk and former sheriff didn't have an easy ride back to Prescott. Winds picked up and battered him and his horse. They followed him even as he sought shelter. What should have been a two-day trip became a three, then a four. The winds never let up. Bourke ran low on provisions and grew sick with hunger and exhaustion.

A patrol found him, still alive, next to the carcass of his horse. They were pretty sure he'd taken a bite out of the hide.

John P. Bourke was taken to the army hospital, where he lasted for the better part of a month before dying on March 7th, 1867. The only money left on him had been just enough to pay for his funeral.

# NINE

# "NEVER WAGE WAR IN DROWNED HORSE DURING WINTER"

Arizona Territory
December, 1967

TUCKING HIS COAT AROUND HIM TIGHTLY WITH one hand and holding his hat down with the other, Sheriff Levi Forrest walked determinedly from his office to the Sagebrush Saloon. Despite his best efforts, the wind and ice tore at his skin. By the time he got through the door, he was sure he'd lose an ear to frostbite.

"Godammit," he said as he shook crystals from his coat. "Never had a winter like this before."

Owner, quick with hot towels to drape around his friend's neck replied, "Only other one like it I can remember was before your time."

A shiver from deep in his soul caused Levi to spasm. "Brrrr! This isn't going to do a whole lot for anyone tryin' to visit town. You expectin' comany?"

Owner took Levi's coat and hung it over by a fireplace where three or four coats also dried. "The stage was supposed to arrive five days ago, which is never good. Just before the blizzard rolled in. There're a couple scouts that got lost in the storm getting warmed upstairs."

Marching over to the fire himself, Levi plopped down into a chair and took off his boots, dumping slush from them onto the hearth where it quickly melted and steamed. He undid his socks next.

"Luckily, got no one in the cells, so don't need to worry about them freezing to death. Degory's got the horses all tucked in, so they should be fine. You hear from any of the homesteaders?"

Owner said he'd not. "No one's going to come out in this unless it's an emergency. We've been warning them for months, especially after Motha came by with his tribe's predictions." He walked back over to Levi and handed him a warm brandy.

Levi thought fondly of how quickly the Paya boy had grown. "Yeah, but he says that every winter hoping to scare us off. Hard to know when he's tellin' the truth." Levi took a sip, burning his lip. "Ahchaha! That's hot."

Owner laughed. "It's supposed to be." He leaned sideways to look out the front door. "No Will?"

"I told him to stay home. No way to do any trainin' today."

"Cards?" Owner asked, rifling through a deck.

Smirking, Levi said, "No, I thought maybe we'd work on this a bit." He reached into his back pocket, pulled out a journal, and waved it in the air. "We've got a little break due to this weather, so why not try to get ahead of his game?"

Owner frowned. "We've been at that book for a year with nothing to go on. I don't think we're going to crack it without some sort of code or translator."

That discouraged the sheriff. "C'mon, Owner. It's everythin' we've been lookin' for. All the answers are right here." He patted the cover. "We just need to figure out some more words that aren't his name, and maybe we crack this."

When a gambling god gave them the tome as a reward for

winning a bet, and told them all the secrets to the curse were inside, he hadn't warned them that those secrets were in the language of the beings of the First World; the world the natives' gods come from. For a year, Levi, Will Ragsdale, his deputy, and Owner had interviewed every native that would speak to them about it. All they found out was the identity of the god that'd placed the curse on the Verde Valley.

Noqoìlpi.

"Old Noqoi's got to have some sort of weakness to exploit. If we can find out why he cursed us, we should be able to get him to undo it."

Owner reached under the counter where he kept all the charts he'd made to decipher the text. He gathered all the rolls of paper and took them over to a table. Levi joined him, pushing another table together.

They had just begun to work, when someone opened the saloon's doors, letting wind, and cold in. The papers flew hither and yon.

"Hey!" Levi shouted, but then saw the haunted eyes of the man who'd entered.

Terrorized, those eyes darted around the room until they landed on Levi's badge shining in the firelight. He moved in closer, furs not tied closed, just hanging loose on his body. His teeth chattered like a rattlesnake's tail, and his skin had the red marks of frost burns. He pulled his coonskin cap down around his head, as if it somehow protected him from what he'd seen.

"S-sherif-f. Ya-ya gotta come l-look a' this."

The man pointed behind him.

Dreading what he'd find out there, Levi got up and walked toward the door, stopping only when Owner called out.

"Levi? Boots? Coat?"

"Oh, yeah."

He borrowed one of the scout's drier boots and coat, pleased they fit him. Then, he followed the man outside.

In front of the saloon was the overdue stage, the horses nearly half-dead from the treacherous journey they'd taken.

Levi called over the wind, "How'd you even make it down?"

The driver yelled back, "H-had no choice. When I-I f-f-found him." He directed the sheriff's gaze to a spot behind the coach.

Tied to the stage was a block of ice and on top of it, lay another man. Levi stepped off the patio and approached the prone form. Someone had sealed the man's hands and feet inside the ice, making a stockade of sorts. That was bad enough, but while they held the victim this way, they drilled a hole through his chest deep into the block.

A body's worth of warm blood melted a channel into the ice, staining it scarlet.

Forrest and the driver went back into the Sagebrush where Owner thawed them both out.

"Found him at the base of Oak Creek Canyon." The driver crossed himself. "Took me two days to dig him out, while trying to keep myself and my horses alive. Knew no one would come all that way out until after the storm. Weren't sure he'd even still be there or dragged off by animals."

Levi thanked him. "You did right." To Owner, he asked, "Apache warning?"

"Like, 'Don't use our canyon'? Hard to say. Never heard about this type of message before. Might know more when Hiram looks at the body."

"Damn. I hate to bother the man in this weather, but I don't suppose it can wait."

After drying out a second time, Levi dressed again and made his way over to the undertaker's office.

---

"THE WOUNDS INDICATE A DRILL OF SOME SORT," Hiram said, pointing inside the hole to a circular twist to the bored flesh. "But not metal, wood, or rock. There'd be chips, flakes of some sort left over when it passed through bone."

The victim, a prospector who occasionally visited town, but didn't talk much, must have been alive when the torture happened: his face cemented in agony. Hiram didn't know if he could fix that, even when the man defrosted.

"That seems a bit sophisticated for the Tontos." Levi never underestimated the cleverness of the Indians, but something like a large drill wasn't anything he'd seen in any of their camps.

Hiram walked around the slab. "He was laid down when his hands and feet were locked in the ice, but wounds suggest he was held down by one person, while another poured water over his limbs."

"Was he robbed? Could be he found a claim and his competition did this to get its location from him?"

Holding up a finger as to indicate he was still talking, Hiram pointed to the blood's path through the ice. "Then, the whole slab was lifted to standing before they drilled the hole in him."

The block must be six foot by four foot, making it close to 500 lbs. That'd be a daunting task for five men, let alone two.

"A ritual with a lot of followers?" Levi said, holding onto hope it wasn't a supernatural creature.

"Or two very strong believers." Hiram answered.

Oak Creek Canyon was nearly two days by horse, even longer walking. Levi looked at the closed shutters as if he could see through them all the way there. He'd have to wait until the storm blew over, then he'd gather up his deputy, maybe the Marshal, too. Hunting monsters was tough enough in fair conditions. Whatever killed this man had no problems with the climate, which worried Levi. He'd read myths about several snow demons, ice creatures, and winter warlocks, but he'd not come across any that drilled holes into folk. He didn't like being unprepared,

and he didn't have time to write someone more knowl-
edgeable.

Levi stared down at the prospector's unnerving face.

*No, don't like this one bit.*

---

THE WIND AND SLEET LET UP, BUT THE COLD
didn't abate. Marshal Tucker wouldn't get over the mountain from Prescott anytime soon, so it'd just be Will and
Levi going to check out Oak Creek Canyon.

Many a wagon slid off the winding trail on the way
down, dropping hundreds of feet into Oak Creek below.
There were "safer" routes from Whipple's Trail into the
Verde Valley but they passed right through the heart of
Apache land. For those in a hurry, Oak Creek Canyon
offered the fastest reward with the highest risk. Reaching
the bottom left a person's nerves shot and them vulnerable
to all sorts of attacks. The Army sent occasional patrols into
the area, but too few, and often too late.

Sheriff Forrest and Will dressed for the cold and armed
themselves with as many items as they thought prudent.
Levi had dug through a whole bunch of old gear looking for
a few things that might give them an advantage if and when
they faced their adversaries.

Roland and Blaze trotted through the snow, seeming to
enjoy the change of pace from sand and gravel.

"They're having fun," Will said.

Forrest agreed. "I just hope they don't step on a buried
rock and break a hoof."

That caused Will to hold Blaze's reins tighter, resuming
control over his horse.

The Sheriff chuckled. The boy—well, not so much a boy
anymore—overthought every word Levi told him. He added
extra weight to each correction Forrest made, letting it
fester in his mind like a criticism of his very nature. Levi
didn't think he was being too harsh on him, which had him

considering that Will might have confidence issues beyond living up to his expectations. Not being a parent, Levi had no idea how to help him.

*I'm sure when he marries that girl of his, he'll be less stressed.*

He hoped that'd be soon. They were at the right age, and already their desire for each other made her parents nervous. They restricted the amount of time the kids were together and only during the day.

"You goin' to make Sarah an honest woman soon?"

Will snapped his head around. "Where'd that come from?"

He'd overstepped. Wasn't his business. "Never mind."

But Will didn't let it go. "I mean, yeah, I want to. Just haven't picked the right time."

"This is Drowned Horse, son. Who knows when your time is done here. Best grab some happiness while you can."

Will raised an eyebrow. "Like you did?"

Levi looked down at his horse. "Yeah, well. I'm...complicated."

Grinning, Will said, "Sure you are."

They rode in silence until they got into Tonto territory. They found tracks in the snow. Horses. Fur-lined feet. If they hadn't already been spotted, they would be soon.

Forrest reached back into his saddlebags and drew out the white flag and tied it around Roland's bridle.

Red rocks towered over them, and Levi thought back to his first hunt with Long Tooth. How naive he was back then. Even with some coaching from Owner, the new sheriff immediately got in over his head and only by fortune and sacrifice did he live long enough to learn just how deep. He tried to prepare his deputy better.

A band of Tontos stepped out from behind the monoliths. Bows drawn, they tracked the two lawmen as they rode forward to greet their leader.

"Why do you enter our hunting ground, *higow'ah*?"

"We're hunting, but not for your game. *Dilhilé*. Evil creatures. Maybe two. Maybe more."

The leader looked to his people, checking to see if any would question his judgment, then back to Levi. "Something moved into our land. Something not of the *Dilzhę'é*, but they are clever hunters. They do not hunt us, only blue eyes, so we leave them be. Does not your army have a saying when they turn our tribes against each other? 'Enemy of my enemy is my friend'?"

He had Levi there. "Well, you know how it is. If that same army gets wind of dead prospectors, or settlers, or any of their own, they'll blame you first."

Will added, "And the longer this cold continues, the more likely this evil will come for your people."

Again, the leader gave eye to his pack, and seeing no doubt in his command, he stepped aside. "They reside near the base of the canyon. We think they use the creek to hide in and attack from. They may breathe in water."

Levi nodded. As he urged Roland past the warrior, he leaned back and drew a bundle from his saddlebags. He tossed it to the leader. "We just got a new butcher in town. I thought I might run into someone who could make use of these."

The Tonto unrolled the wrappings to find salted elk jerky. He smelled it, then cautiously took a small bite. Finding it not poisoned, he tore off a bigger bite. "*Áho.*"

"No," Levi said as he tipped his hat, "Thank *you.*"

---

LEVI CONSIDERED THE NOTION THAT ONE OFTEN had to go down before they could go up. The trail took them at a steep angle down to where Oak Creek cut through the massive rocks on either side. With snow still everywhere, it was only by the slight discoloration, the smoothness of the covering, and the gap between trees, that he was able to find the creek proper. They set themselves parallel to it and took a slow gate as they rode deeper in. The large rock formations blotted the afternoon sun, and the leafless trees took on an eerie continence, like arms reaching down to grab travelers passing by.

The creek bed extended out far enough, the horses slipped and stumbled as they found the buried stones round and smooth. Fearing his prophesy about broken hoofs true, Levi had the two of them dismount and go in by foot. Levi pulled his 4-bore from its saddle holster. Will stepped lightly, his Sharps raised and ready.

They moved in tandem, alternating forward and cover. At wider parts of the creek, the current underneath broke the thin ice, exposing the dark water. Levi watched these spots extra carefully.

The creature peeled itself from the top of a tree, its gaunt form camouflaged perfectly within the branches, and dropped on Will. Long sinewy arms wrapped around the lad and pinned him to the ground before Will could fire.

Forrest spun to aim at the thing, which looked up at him with black eyes, an elongated face, and rows of serrated teeth. Reflexes honed by years of surprise attacks saved the sheriff, who felt more than heard the water erupt behind him. He dodged to the right and the second creature, a female version of the other, landed in the spot he'd just been. It moved like mercury in the thermometer, its silvery complexion adding to the effect. Forrest leveled his gun, but by then, the she-beast had already dove back into the creek.

Will yelled as fingers sharp as knives pierced his arms. Levi ran forward, dropping the larger gun for his side irons, which would give him more accuracy. He fired high, hoping for a head shot, but like a fish dodging a spear, the male twisted around causing Levi to miss. When he got into fighting range, the creature launched back into the trees, scampering from branch to branch more agile than a squirrel.

Levi kept his gaze on both the river and the trees as he leaned down to check on Will. Blood seeped from wounds on both his arms. "Can you get up?"

His deputy put his arms under him and pushed, but fell right back to the ground. "My arms...they're going numb."

Some sort of poison. Levi prayed it was only a paralyzing one, and not fatal. But then, these monsters had plans for them, so not deadly, he reasoned.

Levi hoisted Will up by getting under his shoulder. The deputy could walk, so he pushed him forward, tracking his gun back and forth from creek to treetops.

*If we can get to the horses...*

If night fell before they did, the sheriff had no doubt these creatures saw perfectly well in the dark. The ice cracked to his left, and a shape exploded from the creek, tackling Will into the snow. As Levi aimed, its mate or sibling swung from a branch like a monkey, striking him in the back and sending him flying face forward. He planted in the snow hard, the creature on his back in seconds. Multiple stings lanced his arms and within moments, Levi blacked out.

———

WHEN LEVI WOKE, HE HUNG SUSPENDED IN A block of ice. It was nearly pitch black around him. He sought his deputy in the dark. "Will? Will!"

"Huh?" Will hung secured to his left. "Sheriff?"

"You see them?"

The lad struggled against his bonds.

"Don't waste time with that. We thought this might happen. Do you see them or their drill?"

Levi counted on younger eyes to be sharper in the dark. "We're not far from the creek. The girl, she's spinning the water like someone making a pot. It's becoming a cone, no, it's an ice drill."

That explained why Hiram couldn't find splinters.

"Keep your head, Will. You remember the plan."

"It's not my head, it's my guts I'm worried about."

Levi smiled. If Will could joke, then he wasn't so scared to act.

While waiting for the storm to calm down, Levi went through all the different items, and weapons he'd collected over the years, seeing if there was something that would give them an advantage if this exact situation happened.

He found two.

The creatures approached, carrying the ice drill. They got close enough, Levi could make them out in the shadows. The female beamed with pride as she held the drill in her arms like a baby. The male stood behind the ice shard and spun it with its supple hands. It picked up speed, the female guiding it toward Will's chest.

*Wait*, Levi commanded Will in his mind. *Wait for it.*

Just as the tip was about to pierce the young man's abdomen, Will bent his head down into the collar of his jacket. His teeth locked onto the pull string hidden there and yanked it with all the strength he had in his neck.

From his belt buckle, metal blades sprung out to form a round fan. The ice drill's tip impacted on it and shattered. The creatures screamed angrily. Levi bit down on his own pull string and glowing orbs ignited, lighting up the whole creek area.

Blinded, the creatures stumbled around.

Whooping echoed through the canyon. The Tonto pack the lawmen had met earlier ran out from the trees. Some bore torches, others arrows, and others knives. The monsters, whatever they were, made to get away but stunned as they were, fell to the warriors quickly.

After the Tontos cut them free of the ice, Levi thanked the pack leader. "You got my note."

He held up the cloth the jerky was wrapped in. Written in Apache was the request to follow a couple hours behind them if they wanted glory and more jerky.

"I hope you do not mind, but we already took the extra jerky from your saddle when we passed your horses."

"Not at all. Just glad you decided to come."

The native grinned. "It is good shit."

"Ouch!" the sheriff said, as feeling returned to his arms. "Yeah, it is."

---

THE SNOW WAS GONE, AND THE VERDE VALLEY returned to its normal temperature. The stage had dropped off mail for the town and Sheriff Levi Forrest read the one addressed to him.

"*Ikuutayuq,*" He told Will, slapping the paper down in his desk. "Inuit."

"All the way down here? That's a long way to travel just to kill some folks."

"No idea. Ain't seen anyone matching an Eskimo around these parts. Usually someone brings them in with them."

There was little rhyme or reason to the curse, just Levi's suspicion that settlers brought their demons with them, some more literal than others.

"Back to work then?" Will asked.

Levi reached into a desk drawer and retrieved Noqoi's journal. He stood, motioning for Will to lead the way to the Sagebrush.

"Back to work."

# INTERMEZZO
## "THE DRAGON AND THE SHARK"

Meanwhile on
the Mississippi River...

IT DIDN'T TAKE A GENIUS TO KNOW SEBASTIAN Maher would lose the last hand of the poker game, if he called the fifty-dollar bet. The person sitting across the felt table from him was too confident, and while Maher's cards were good, they weren't *that* good.

Problem was, he'd let himself be goaded into betting his entire stack on the two cards he had swapped out. They'd been the cards he wanted, but whatever his nemesis had drawn must have been better. The dim-witted cowpoke glowed like a streetlight in New Orleans.

This left Maher with two choices; bow out gracefully and try to start over from the last dollar secured in his boot...or cheat. Seeing as their riverboat would arrive at the Memphis dock in just under an hour, cheating seemed the best course of action.

Maher apologized. "Ah'm sorry, but Ah do believe you have me at a disadvantage, sir. Ah can tell from the way you just cannot contain your enthusiasm that you must have received something special from that last exchange of cards."

"Believe what you want, Dandy," his slack-jawed opponent said. "Yer gonna have to pay to see if yer right."

The term "dandy" had been thrown at Maher before, as if it meant he preferred the company of men or something to that effect. The gambler considered himself a gentleman, educated at better schools, bred from better stock. If the cretins south of St. Louis couldn't tell the difference between a true man of the world and a poof, that was their ignorance.

"Sir, since you're going to take me for all my winnings, then please indulge me a chance to tell you a tale before Ah have to leave the table. It won't take long, and you might find it fascinating."

The man, who hadn't seen a lick of soap in months, grimaced. "What does 'indulge' mean?"

"It means, 'grant me a favor,' a boon, if you will." Maher waved his hand in a simple gesture of penitence.

"What does a boo—"

"I want to tell you a story."

Maher wondered what ancient god he must have offended to draw only a full house against such a buffoon.

"You tell yer story, then I git all yer money?"

The gambler nodded.

"Fine. Tell yer story. But if I smell any sort of trick, I'll shoot ya where ya stand." The cowpoke placed his gun on top of his cards to emphasize the point.

They were both sitting, but not wanting to point out the semantics, Maher let the lapse in grammar pass.

Leaning back in his chair, the gambler made sure all eyes were on him as he spoke. He'd done a bit of theatrical training and knew how to capture a crowd.

"A long time ago, a couple hundred years, truth be told, seven men sought the Mississippi River in hopes that it'd lead them to the Pacific Ocean."

A man who'd folded early in the game interrupted, "I know this one. That was them Lewis and Clark fellas."

"Not quite," corrected the gambler, "This was before them. It was led by a French missionary, Jacques Marquette, and a fur-trader named Jolliet."

The assembled men and waitresses spat on the floor at the word "French." They waited to see what Maher would do, a test of his allegiances.

"Oh, yes. I forgot." He made a spitting attempt at the floor. "Fuck the French."

That satisfied everyone around him, so he continued. "After they passed the Straits of Mackinac, they encountered a savage tribe of natives. The *Illini* were fierce warriors, but having encountered other servants of God before, they did not attack the Father and his group. Instead, they passed on a warning to them."

"What type of warning?" asked another player, the one who'd folded last, leaving just Maher and his cowboy opponent. The man swallowed hard, anxious for the answer.

Maher obliged. "They warned the men of a winged beast that would devour whole any man who dared travel near its nest."

"Git out," said the cowpoke. "Ain't no bird that big in the territories. We'd a heard of that by now."

Maher shook a finger at him. "No, sir. This was no bird but an ancient beast still alive from the dawn of man. A monster left over from the flood that had managed to escape doom and flew above the waves, through the rain, and survived to find land after the waters subsided. It was a creature whose only kin might be the great leviathan that gobbled Jonah up whole."

Eyes widened, and a few men crossed themselves.

"The good Father and the trapper ignored the warning and continued on. It wasn't even three days southbound on the Mississippi until they saw them."

"T-them?" asked the early folder.

"Yes, two of them." Maher said in hushed tones. "A male

and female. They were high on a bluff, overlooking the mighty Miss. Horrible winged demons with feathers of yellow and green and red and black."

Seeing as he had his audience enthralled, the gambler recited the legend exactly as it'd been told him. "They were as large as a steer with horns on their heads like those of a deer. Red eyes glared down at the explorers. Each had a beard like a tiger's, one a horrible mannish face, the other a hideous lady's. A long tail that wound all around the bodies and passed above their heads and going back between their legs, ending in fish tails."

Shifting eyes tried to envision what Father Marquette witnessed and Maher relayed.

"The female creature spotted the craft in the water and swooped down to snatch one of the oarsmen from the canoe. Screaming, she carried him back to the nest where her mate ripped him apart to serve as breakfast for the winged monster's brood, who, incidentally, were just starting to hatch from their eggs."

Maher took off his hat and pressed it against his chest. He bowed his head in reverence and all the players did the same. In that moment, Maher quickly switched one of his cards with a sleeve card, giving himself four of a kind. Moment passed, he continued.

"Deciding he would grab dinner for them, too, the male descended toward the expedition. The remaining men were ready. Father Marquette held the Holy Book of God aloft and prayed for divine intervention. The men filled the air between them and the beast with shot, but they bounced off its thick hide. One, however, as if guided by God himself, hit the creature in the eye, where it entered the beast's brain, killing it. It dropped in the big river; the splash nearly capsizing their canoe." There was a whoop from late folder.

"Enraged, the female monstrosity dove at the crew, vengeance in her angry, red eyes. Trapper Jolliet, seeing a shadow below in the water, paddled their canoe directly over it. When he said the word, all jumped out of the boat as the winged demon drove itself into the canoe, expecting vengeance. Instead, it found a large boulder waiting on the river's floor. The creature broke its neck and floated to the surface."

Everyone drew a breath of relief. Maher waited for the question someone would eventually ask.

"What happened to those babies?"

"The expedition climbed up the bluff and slew each and every one of them. The end."

Maher bowed slightly at the round of clapping.

"In honor of your allowing me that reprieve, Ah will pay to see your cards." Maher reached down and pulled out his last bit of money out of his boot to match the bet. "Call. Let's see how badly Ah am undone."

The cowpoke returned his mind to the game, having been completely drawn in by the tale. "Um, yeah. Well, I've got a straight flush." He flipped over a seven to Jack straight, all of the club variety.

"Oh, dear. That is an almost unbeatable hand."

The cowpoke grinned and reached for the pot.

"However, Ah was sure you had a royal flush. Ah do, indeed, have you beat. Good thing Ah didn't fold."

Maher flipped over his four queens. The crowd exploded at his success, all save for the cowpoke, who looked angrily at the gambler.

"Yer a goddam cheat, that's what ya are! Ya done distracted us and did some sort of switch." He lifted his gun to aim it at Maher.

"Now, now, kind sir. There were witnesses here. Ah count a dozen men who stared at me the whole time. When could Ah have pulled some sort of ruse? At what point did anyone not gaze with rapt attention at me?" He scanned the crowd. "Who saw me touch my cards? Anyone?"

No one answered. No one spoke up. That seemed to anger the cowpoke even more.

"I had ya beat. Ya knows it, and I knows it."

"Well, then," said Maher, holding up his hands, "we

seem to be at a bit of an impasse. What would you suggest to settle this like men?"

"I suggest I kill you and take my winnings."

"Ah have a better idea. How about we go up on deck and stage one of those gun fights your breed love so much?"

This brought a round of laughter from the crowd. None would have bet on the gambler to be able to even hold a gun.

The cowpoke laughed, too. "Okay. Let's do it yer way. Ya own a gun?"

"Oh, I'm fine. You bring yours, and I'll bring my own weapon." The gambler reached into his sleeve and pulled out a whistle.

This brought more laughter. The cowpoke looked at the small silver object.

"Yer gonna beat me with that?"

Maher nodded. "Shall we be off?" To the dealer, he said, "Please collect the pot and store it until one of us returns."

The deck of the steamboat had enough space for five paces. Both men agreed that would suffice. They stood back-to-back and counted off steps. Maher placed the whistle in his mouth and blew it once for each step. On the fifth step, he blew it long and hard.

The cowpoke spun and drew. His finger slid into place, but he never got the chance to pull the trigger before he was lifted off the deck by a creature from nightmares. It had feathers the color of yellow and green and red and black. Its face, a hideous distortion of a woman's, bit down on the cowpoke as she dragged him skyward. His scream was cut short as his body was constricted and gulped down in three swallows. The creature disappeared into the night sky before anyone blinked.

"Oh," said Maher, as he took in the crowd, "I left off one part of the story. You see there were two Piasa eggs that hadn't hatched yet." He leaned conspiratorially toward the early folder. "Piasa being the Illini Indians' name for the creatures."

Maher straightened back up and continued. "Trapper Jolliet took them and kept them warm, wrapped in pelts. When they hatched, he raised them and trained them. He headed south and hid among the people of Mexico. There he kept the piasa, then known as a Quetzalcoatl, safe and, with each generation, the oldest male of his line is given a chick to raise as his own personal guardian. Interesting story, right?"

The riverboat passengers rhetorically agreed.

"Well, looks as if we're getting close to dock. If you all don't mind, Ah'm going to collect my winnings and catch the next ferry to Little Rock. Ah hope to make the Arizona Territory in a week. Ah'm sure Ah can trust everyone to keep mum about this, right?" He tapped the whistle still sticking out of the corner of his mouth. Again, everyone promised his secret was safe with them.

"Thank you all very much for your support. Speaking of legends, Ah've heard whisper of one near a town called Drowned Horse. Supposedly, there's an amazing gambler there." Maher bowed to the stunned crowd. "Feel free to join me anytime."

But he doubted any of the passengers would. If anything, none of them would ever come close to the territory and that was just dandy with him.

# ACT TWO

BEGINNINGS AND ENDINGS

TEN

# "TAXED THREE TIMES FOR PRIDE"

Arizona Territory
March, 1868

SHERIFF LEVI FORREST DECIDED NOT TO TAKE ANY chances that year in regards to collecting taxes from Gemtwinkle, the spriggan who lived in the caves under the Black Hills. Having lost two of Yavapai's county clerks to the faerie, he wrote the county seat to say he'd bring the Verde Valley's collected taxes to them himself. Well, he and his deputy, William Ragsdale.

The boy's training had gone well. He studied hard, practiced his skills every day, and begged for more opportunities to prove himself. Levi hoped that, by next year, Will could do this run on his own.

They rode side by side toward Gemmy's canyon.

"It must have been a huge effort for Mr. Gemtwinkle to move," Will supposed.

Levi agreed. "After getting robbed, he wasn't takin' no chances. Took me a fair bit to find him and ease his concerns. He still wants to contribute his fair share, but that's the reason good faerie folk like him hide from humans. Either we shoot first or find a way to exploit them."

"Doesn't seem fair."

"Nope, it doesn't. There's enough really bad stuff out there tryin' to do us in. No sense upsettin' those who'd prefer to be left alone."

Gemtwinkle's new location sat at the end of a box canyon. Levi felt eyes upon them the moment they crossed into it.

"We're being tracked."

Will, suddenly alert, scanned the rock walls trying to spot a lookout.

"Not there." Forrest motioned with his eyes for Will to look down.

Will had to squint to find them. Tiny elf-like beings poked their heads out from behind rocks along the trail. The skittered around, darting from cover to cover, following the two riders as they proceeded farther in.

"Chaneque?" Will asked, thinking them the miniature humans that often caused trouble in the valley.

"Nope. Korrigan. Cornish gnomes. Don't know how Gemtwinkle got them here, or why they're working for him, but things just got a lot more complicated."

One thing that had not changed was Gemtwinkle's hospitality. He still had tea and cakes ready for the duo, but he didn't look as happy as he had before the move.

"You doin' okay there, Gemmy?"

"*Skith esov*," Gemtwinkle said with a long sigh. "I don't sleep well anymore. Finding a new vein in a securable location and digging out a new home took more effort than I predicted. Plus, I now have dozens of small mouths to feed. Mind ya, the Korries don't eat much individually, but they make it up in volume."

The spriggan tossed a cake over his head to land about twenty feet behind him. Fifty Korrigan, about half a shin high, scampered out of cracks all over the cave to wash over the pastry like ants, devouring and then disappearing back into the shadows, not a crumb left on the ground.

"I'm not making as much as I used to," the spriggan continued. "I can't show myself to most humans, and there are fewer 'Pai or 'Che each year. The demand for what I dig for lessens with each battle, each skirmish."

Levi had an idea where the conversation was going. "I really can't do much to stop the influx of settlers, Gemmy. They're coming, whether you or I or the locals want them to or not."

Maybe it was the size of the new cavern, or the angle of the lights, but the sheriff thought that Gemtwinkle looked different. Not just tired, but also…bigger.

"*Konvedhav*, mate, I get it. But if I cannot keep my fortune doing what I've done in the past, then I must find other lines of work."

"Like what. Mr. Gemtwinkle?"

The monster smiled at Will. "Please, call me Gemmy, like your *mester* here does."

Levi sat up straighter. "You remember the rules, right? You start killin' settlers or Indians, and that's going to make a whole lotta trouble for me that'll be hard to ignore."

Gemtwinkle waved that notion away. "No, no. Nothing like that. I'm getting too old for war. No, I'm hoping to find something that makes use of my talents to help people, not hurt them."

That allowed Levi to relax. He didn't want to get into a fight with a creature that could grow taller than an oak. "'K, long as we still have our understandin'."

"We do, *koth*. We do." Gemtwinkle produced the purse with that year's taxes and handed it to Will. The lawmen left the cave shortly thereafter, but Levi held on to his anxiety all the way back to Drowned Horse and for weeks after.

THREE MONTHS LATER, LEVI AND WILL WERE summoned to the homestead of Sean McGannon and his wife, Riley. Mrs. McGannon rocked in a chair on their porch, weeping inconsolably.

The duo dismounted and were met by McGannon, whose face was beet-red in anger.

"The basterd! That little basterd! I'll kill him. I kill the whole lot of them."

Levi held up his hands. "Whoa, there, Sean. Before you go on a rampage, why don't you tell me what's goin' on? Is the baby all right?"

McGannon spun on his heel and marched into his house. "Come see for yourself!"

The McGannons had just welcomed their first child, a little girl, Poppy, into the world. Last Levi had heard, the tike was doing fine.

In the child's room, he stood next to a crib. Levi could see the child's sleeping form there, wrapped in a blanket.

"What's wrong?" Will asked, seeing the same thing Levi did.

"This!" McGannon yanked off the blanket for a flourish.

Instead of a sleeping child, a Korrigan lay in its place, thumb in its mouth.

"Dah dah," it cooed with a Cornish accent.

Mrs. McGannon's wails pitched higher as she grieved.

McGannon produced a note. "This was in the crib when it…" He jerked a thumb at the Korrigan. "…arrived."

The penmanship was excellent, but then Gemtwinkle was once human.

*Dear Mr. McGannon,*

*I'd like you to know that your child is safe, for the moment. We are holding her temporarily on behalf of a Síofra Dunleavy, a young lady you had relations with while you wife was with child. She has employed me to settle a dispute that arose when you severed your arrangement once your wife gave birth.*

*It seems you ended things quite abruptly and rudely with Miss*

*Dunleavy, who you had once promised your heart to. You told her that, and I relay her quote as she gave it to me, "If ye ever come 'round me or my family, I'll kill ya." Despondent, Miss Dunleavy took her own life, then was buried in a grave beneath a cedar tree, only to be reborn a few days later in the form of a dearg-due.*

*No longer fearing your threats, she attacked you one night outside the Sagebrush Saloon, which she now understands was a mistake brought on by womanly emotions. After you successfully got away, it appears as if you have placed wards from that same tree around your farm. You also carved necklaces from the wood to keep her away. However, you did not think to protect little Poppy. Since your wards could not stop the Korrigan in my employ, it was simple to abscond with the mite.*

*This brings us to the problem at hand. Miss Dunleavy wishes you to honor the verbal contract you made with her and give her your heart. Not in a romantic sense, but in a physical one. She would prefer it was still beating when you surrender it, but she will accept it in a gift-wrapped box, if you so choose. If she does not get what is owed her, she will instead take your heart in a more metaphorical sense, and claim baby Poppy's as in-kind trade.*

*You have two days, Mr. McGannon. Please make the proper arrangements. Either give the packaged heart to my agent currently filling in for your child, or allow him to escort you to my location where it can be properly retrieved by Miss Dunleavy.*

*Yours,*

*Gemtwinkle*

*Solicitor to the Supernatural.*

Levi wanted to read the whole note again, disbelieving what he'd read the first time.

Will, who read it over his shoulder, asked, "What's a da-rug-du-ah?"

McGannon answered. "She's a bloodsucking whore, that's what she is. Vengeful harlot come back from the grave to suck men's blood."

Levi admonished McGannon. "Did you have a relationship with this woman?"

The Irishman blushed. "I mighta, a wee bit of fun and games, you see. She'd be knowin' I was returnin' to Riley once she popped. I dinnea know where this whole 'gave her my heart' thing she's goin' on about came from. It's shite!"

The sheriff took the moment to use this situation as a teaching lesson for his deputy. Forrest leaned toward him and spoke in a loud whisper, "Y'see, William, men, in the heat of passion, often will promise anything. My guess is Sean here made some sort of deal he had no intention of keepin' to earn access to Miss Dunleavy's, um, virtues."

"Now, wait a bloody moment, Levi."

Ignoring McGannon, Levi went on. "And when a man such as he gets what he wants, he no longer finds it as appealing as it was when he first sought it out."

McGannon went to punch the sheriff. "You lyin'—"

Forrest, however, struck the cheater across the chin first, knocking him to the floor. McGannon rubbed his reddening jaw and tried to get up, but Levi knelt down next to him and sapped him again, knocking him out.

"Help me get him on the back of Roland."

The two carried the prone form of McGannon out the door.

Riley paused crying. "You'll get my Poppy back?"

"Yes, ma'am, we'll do our best."

"And will ya be bringin' this pile of shite back, as well?"

"If that's your wish."

Mrs. McGannon walked over to Sean's body, draped over the back of Levi's horse. She spit on him and said a few well-rehearsed Celtic curses. She returned to the porch, angry. "Do wit him what ye will."

Forrest and Will tipped their hats. "Ma'am" and rode toward Gemtwinkle's cave.

---

"AVODYA, SHERIFF. LEAVE IT BE. THIS IS NO concern of yours."

Gemtwinkle had indeed enlarged himself, though not to full size. Even sitting, he had a foot over Levi.

"Can't do that, Gemmy. I told you, if any business you're doin' harms anyone under my protection, I was goin' have to step in."

The spriggan held out its hands. "I have harmed no one, nor do I plan to. However, my client is another story. Since she has not...yet, there is no reason to intervene."

McGannon woke up half-way to Gemtwinkle's lair. He told the lawmen where to find the tree where Síofra Dunleavy had been interred. Will was sent to grab a branch off the tree and make a weapon Levi could use against the dearg-due. That left Levi stalling for time. The unfaithful husband sat just outside the cave entrance, listening, as the sheriff tried to save his unworthy ass.

"If you're going to pretend to be a lawyer, you learn the law. We have a thing called 'bein' an accessory,' which means if you allow her to kill McGannon, you're just as guilty."

Gemtwinkle contemplated that, his oversized hand twirling strands of his hair. "You should understand the need for *justis*, Levi. There isn't anyone around to defend the beings drug here by the curse."

Levi shook his head. "You've had me, haven't you? I didn't haul you in for killing that clerk, Neurink, 'cause he broke the rules first, even after being warned. I also never looked too closely at Bourke's death despite them finding a few familiar gems on his body. Nice of you to leave his widow somethin'."

"He broke the rules, too."

Levi stepped closer into the cavern, angling to the best place where he could dive for cover, if need be. "I'm sure he did. So, you know I'll keep my trap shut when things are fair. This isn't fair."

"*Grrr!* How is it not? He broke that poor girl's heart and look at her now." Síofra stood off to the side of the spriggan. She must have been quite the lady to behold when alive, but death had done her no favors. Her skin, pale and sallow, gave her a ghostly shine. Red trails ran from her eyes where she'd been crying. Síofra glared at McGannon and Levi couldn't gauge if she hated him, loved him, or just wanted to eat him.

Women were much too complicated for Forrest, he acknowledged.

"I understand there needs to be some sort of recompense here. I'm not sayin' she ain't entitled to justice. Ripping poor Sean's heart out, though, is not going to give her that."

Síofra spoke for the first time. "What else will? Look at me! Think I wanted to end up like this? How am I ever supposed to find love when every eligible man I meet I want to drain his blood from?" She pointed at McGannon, who cringed. "That's *his* fault! If I'm going to drink blood, it should be his."

Gemtwinkle nodded and made motions with his hands. Korrigan came out from holes in the walls and poured over McGannon. They lifted him up and carried the struggling man into the cave.

Levi knew he had little time left to settle things down. If he didn't, that meant he'd have to kill the girl, the spriggan, and a whole lot of fairies.

He stepped in front of the procession. "Wait! Stop!" He looked at the dearg-due. "Do you have to drink *all* of his blood?"

Gemtwinkle stopped rubbing his hands.

Síofra stopped drooling.

The Korrigan stopped marching.

Sean, on his back, titled his head up, and asked, "Wha?"

Levi spoke fast. "No, hear me out. Is there any rule that says you have to drink all his blood?"

The dearg-due thought about it a moment. "No, I don't think so. I'm still new at this y'know, Sheriff." Síofra spoke bashfully, embarrassed she didn't have all the answers. "I've been real hungry since this whole thing happened, but Gemmy convinced me I should only kill animals, until I got

Sean's heart." Gemtwinkle nodded, giving her a warm smile. "He said you'd make my death quick, then, since I only killed the man who'd hurt me."

"This true, Gemmy?"

Gemtwinkle said it was. "That's no life for a young lady, Levi. She gets justice, and you do, too."

"And you get paid."

Gemmy blushed. "Hey, I told you the market was bad."

Levi sighed.

Will ran into the cave, a whittled sword in hand. "Ah ha! Stop your evil, witch, or I'll…" He noticed everyone staring at him. "…or I'll…" No one was attacking or killing anyone. "I'll show up too late, and you're already working things out, that 'bout right, Sheriff?"

Levi sighed again. "Yup, that's about the shape of things." He gauged his words carefully. "Here's the deal. Sean?"

McGannon held up his head. "Yessir?"

To the Korrigan, Forrest asked, "Can you just set him down?"

The fairies dissipated, dropped McGannon with an *umph!*

"Sean, your wife doesn't want you back, and I can't rightly blame her. However, if I'm not mistaken, there's a lady over there who does. Am I right?"

What blood she had left over from the last creature she ate brought crimson to her cheeks. "Well, yeah, I mean sorta. If he wasn't such a liar!"

Levi stood next to McGannon and placed an arm over his shoulders. "We'll get to that. Sean, you need to be an honorable man here. You're going to marry this young lady, and then you're going to let her drink *some* of your blood when she gets hungry."

"Immagunnawha?"

"You heard me." The sheriff pushed the Irishman toward the creature of his own making. "You caused this mess, you're going to fix it. Otherwise, I let her drain you, then I stab her with that branch, blow up this cave with Gemtwinkle in it, and step on a whole bunch of runts."

A resounding, *ooohhh!* came from every crack in the cavern.

"But, she's dead. How canna marry her?"

"No problem. It's not a real marriage because I'm not a real minister." Levi asked the lady, "That work for you?"

She nodded. "And Sean? As long as I feed, I'm pretty sure I'll never rot." She ran a hand down the sides of her stunning body. "I'll be young like this forever."

Levi slapped McGannon on the back. "See? Isn't that a good deal? And just to make sure you don't go back on it, if she, or I, or my deputy, or the honorable Mr. Gemtwinkle, or any of the Korrigan... Hey, you guys okay with this?"

Again, a disembodied, "Yep."

"...or any of the Korrigan hear of you steppin' out on this nice lady, then she has all of our permission to do exactly what she intended to do today. You understand me, McGannon?" Levi moved his hand to behind the stunned man's head and nodded for him, seeing as he was having trouble speaking.

And so the wedding of Sean McGannon to Síofra Dunleavy commenced at the residence of Mr. Gemtwinkle, solicitor to the supernatural. It was performed by Sheriff Levi Forrest, witnessed by Deputy William Ragsdale and attended by about fifty of their tiniest, but closest friends, who respectfully paired off in equal measure for the bride and the groom. Gemtwinkle caught the bouquet.

When Levi and Will brought Poppy home to her mother, no worse for the journey, she burst out crying again, but this time for joy. Levi explained the situation and that her husband was otherwise engaged. That made her even happier.

Sheriff and deputy made to leave, but Gemmy's Korrigan from the baby swap still hung around. "You can head back now," Levi informed him.

Riley shook her head. "He doesn't like working for

Gemtwinkle, so we made a deal. He's going to stick around here and help me with Poppy." She blushed, and averted her eyes. "He says he has no problem reaching certain...places Sean dinnea want to go."

The Korrigan winked.

Levi shrugged. "Deputy, this place gets stranger and stranger."

# ELEVEN
# "LOVE...IN THE TIME OF THE WEIRD WEST"

Arizona Territory
June, 1868

SARAH BAKERSFIELD WAITED IMPATIENTLY ATOP A twenty-foot, red rock boulder for the man she planned to marry.

Problem was...a twelve-foot tall scorpion had come between them.

Almost twelve, certainly, more than ten, if she gauged its size correctly. Her perch rose about fifteen feet from where its whip-like tail kept trying to sting her, making her estimate of the creature to easily be...about the size of a house.

The aberration patrolled the space between her and her potential betrothed, Deputy William Ragsdale. William and his boss, Sheriff Levi Forrest, hid behind a row of similar rocks, concocting some cockamamie plan to rescue her. Most times, their plans actually worked.

Sarah scowled down at the scorpion's many eyes. *Stupid bug! How dare you mess up our picnic?*

She and William couldn't catch a break. The only reason she stayed in Drowned Horse—cursed as it was—was because of him. Three years ago, he'd rescued her from becoming a breeding stick of the Toad Men. Well, wasn't that just the type of thing that captured a young girl's heart?

They'd been just teenagers at the time, barely beyond childhood, but William's gangly body grew into the handsome and strong man she so adored today. His brown eyes, like fine mahogany, melted her every time he asked her to dine with him, or go look out at the stars, wishing on falling ones that they'd be together forever, and also praying that the meteor wasn't another alien come to invade Drowned Horse. It was a ridiculous notion to court someone in a place where demons just show up in the middle of a church service, but William and Sheriff Forrest had become real good at clearing up such messes before communion was served.

They had gotten so good at it, Sarah thought it past time she and William got hitched. She wanted babies, and despite William's best efforts—and some amazing willpower of her own—she wanted to be wed first.

"You okay up there, Sarah?" William called. He and the Sheriff had secured themselves out of reach of the bug's pointy tail. That thing could skewer a buffalo.

"Getting a bit hot up here," she replied.

The remains of their picnic had been trampled into the Arizona sand. It certainly was much too early in the season for giant bugs, which is why William picked this spot. She'd barely got the blanket laid out and put marmalade on the biscuits when William recognized the chittering sound of something unholy coming their way. "Stabby" had rounded the corner a moment later.

While William distracted the scorpion, Sarah had climbed the nearest rock formation. Neither of them came prepared for battle, so William rode back into town for help. But not even Sheriff Forrest's monster 4-bore gun worked against the creature's thick shell. The bullet just ricocheted off.

Sheriff Forrest asked her, "You're book smart, Sarah. Whadda ya think? Magical or something ancient?"

"Could be something mad scientist-y," William offered.

Sarah cocked her head. "I don't care if this thing swallowed Egypt whole, boys. Get me down."

Thank the lord she hadn't lost her hat while climbing. It was getting on noon, and Sarah didn't want to smell unladylike when William proposed.

If that's what he intended to do, after all. When he suggested the picnic, he told her he had something very important he wanted to ask her. However, he hadn't clarified what that was. Sarah assumed, of course, that it would be a proposal. She'd dropped enough subtle hints over the last few weeks, like telling William that she couldn't wait until they had their own children like the ones the yeti up on Black Mountain had killed those miners to protect. Or when a hogbear tore apart the town looking for its mate a trapper had captured, she clearly stated that she wished she had a man willing to make a public declaration of their love like that. How could he miss her insinuations?

Sarah decided she'd better check.

"Honey, weren't you gonna to ask me something earlier?"

William, poking his head from behind the rock, furrowed his brow. "Right now? Isn't the man-eating scorpion kinda a priority?"

The scorpion, apparently tired of scuttling back and forth between Sarah and the lawmen, waited off to one side.

"Stabby don't seem to be in a hurry at the moment."

William looked to Forrest who held up his hands indicating it was his deputy's problem. William took off his Stetson and swallowed hard.

"Sarah?"

"Yes, William?"

"You 'member the day I came to rescue you from the Toadies?"

She blushed. "Best day of my life, how could I forget?"

William sheepishly looked at his feet, which nearly made her kinda swoon. He was so cute when he did that.

"Well, I knew right then that, a few years later, we'd be doing something special."

This was it! "I knew it, too, honey."

"Then will you..."

Sarah clasped her hands together expectantly.

"...go visit the toad men again with me?"

She couldn't have heard that right. "I'm sorry, but could you repeat that?"

William dusted off his hat. "Well, the Sheriff's caught wind of some trouble down there from the Professor, and you know the toadies are sweet on you, so I was hoping you'd come with me. Make a trip of it."

Sarah puffed her cheeks until they turned red before letting William have it with both barrels.

"William Ragsdale, you insensitive, oblivious, narrow-minded, horse's behind!" William cringed as if each insult was a hit to his face. "How dare you drag me out here, nearly get us killed, just to ask if I wanted to check if some slimy, frog people were still behaving themselves!"

"They're toads, actually," Forrest corrected.

"I don't care if they're gooses that pooped gold. I got no interest in spending days on horseback in this godforsaken desert just to be bait for no *toad* people neither."

Sarah carefully descended the rock. She'd had enough foolish behavior.

"Wait!" William grew more agitated the farther she climbed down. "Stop that, ya hear me?"

"Now, don't be silly, girl," the Sheriff begged. "Stay up there where it's safe."

Sarah had waited long enough to be rescued.

"Now, listen here, gentlemen. I'm done being some precious figurine on a shelf to just be admired." She huffed as she reached for each foothold. "William...Ragsdale? If... you...love...me, you'll come out from behind those rocks... and...propose to me."

At the bottom, Sarah turned to face the unholy monster and her fate. "If you don't, then I'm better off being scorpion feed."

Sensing the opening it'd been waiting for, the scorpion raced forward.

William rushed out of hiding to intercept it.

"Damn, woman! You go crazy from the heat, or somethin'? Get outta there!"

Sarah crossed her arms and closed her eyes defiantly. "No. You figure it out or go find another damsel in distress."

William fired his pistols at the monster. He shot out one eye, making the scorpion redirect from Sarah to him. Enraged, it batted William with one of its man-sized claws, sending him tumbling.

Sarah suddenly realized the folly of her plan. It might kill William instead!

Panicking, she ran forward, waving at it. "Here! Over here!"

William, flat on his back, kept shooting. "No, forget her! Stay right here!"

The monster grabbed at Sarah with its massive pinchers. Sarah rolled under them and then crawled over to be next to her man.

"If we die, we die together," she swore.

"Together."

As the scorpion reared its back side, readying its strike, the sound of Forrest's elephant gun echoed around them. The underbelly of the creature exploded outward covering both of the young lovers in shell and guts. When it collapsed, they discovered the Sheriff standing behind the remains. He had found a place not covered by thick shell to fire his elephant gun into.

A very inappropriate place.

Sheriff Forrest bowed to them.

"Got the idea when you mentioned goose poop."

William stood first, and offered a hand to Sarah. Once upright, he took both her hands in his and before they'd even had a chance to wipe the goo off of their faces, he knelt in front of her.

"Before something else tries to kill us, hear me out. I wasn't asking you to be bait. I just figured we could celebrate our honeymoon in the place where we first met...a cruise down the Rio Gila."

From his pocket, William pulled out a ring.

# TWELVE

# "THE BOSE IKARD WAR"

Arizona Territory
August, 1869

"SO THERE WE WERE, BACKS PINNED AGAINST A cliff with a hundred foot drop to the Rio Verde, a war party of Apache comin' at us from the South—"

"North. They were coming from the North."

"North, then, and Smirking Igor's Gang coming from the south. And if that wasn't enough, there was easily two dozen pigmies shooting at us from the West."

"Pig-*men*, Tuck. I keep telling you they were *kamapauas*. Big difference."

"Who's telling this story, Levi? Me or you?"

"Please, go ahead. I'm now curious how we get out of it."

"You know damn well how we got out of it."

"But you haven't told them how we got *into* it, right?"

"No, not yet. I was getting to that."

"You just wanted to get the stuff at the end because it shows just how clever you are, huh?"

"Hmmm. Maybe so. I should start at the beginning." I

took a swig of whiskey from the glass someone had placed in front of me. I don't, as a habit, drink that much. I've worked with men up in Prescott who do a little too much sipping on the job. But when you live adjacent to land cursed by a Navajo god, you need to have your wits about you, or you don't survive things like the Bose Ikard War.

"So, you see there was this man, a negro actually, come to Drowned Horse looking to sell a few head of cattle..."

---

Three Days Earlier

"I SURE DO APPRECIATE YOU ACTING AS DEPUTY while Sarah and Will are enjoying their brand new baby, Tuck."

I sat across from Sheriff Levi Forrest, my first friend I made in the Arizona Territory when I took over the post of U.S. Marshal. I'd stopped in to visit the new parents and their girl, Trina. It made me miss my wife, who I'd not been home long enough with to give children a serious try yet. I would've moved her out with me, but Levi's revelation about the curse three years earlier had made me write to tell her to stay put.

"It's my pleasure, seeing I don't get down here all that much. There're lots of miles to cover, and you generally have things well in hand." I smoothed down my itchy mustache. I'd run out of wax and thought I could pick up some while in town. "But to be clear, if anything you're *my* deputy, seeing as I outrank you."

Levi tipped his Stetson at me. "I live to serve." He had his feet up on his desk, as he usually did. "Honestly, we're entering harvest season here. Crops are being pulled up and brought into town. Wagons are coming in with supplies as we prep for winter."

"Hopefully not like last year's."

My friend crossed himself and echoed my sentiment, which was interesting as I'd never seen him profess to be any sort of religious man. Actually, I thought maybe he was Jewish.

"Town's fillin' up. More shops are being raised trying to beat the weather. In addition to the butcher, we now have a dress maker for the women, a smithy, a second mercantile, which was bound to happen, but doesn't make the owner of the other none-too-happy."

"No second saloon, though?"

"That'll be the day!" Levi laughed. "I'm sure Owner made some sort of deal with the devil to be the only watering hole in the valley."

"And by that, do you mean…"

Holding up his hands, the Sheriff corrected my assumption. "No, no, no. Don't even mention that guy's name. Owner'd never do that. My guess? There'll be others, just farther out."

I'd been waiting for the right time to drop this news. "Looks like there's going to be a mine coming in. Just at the base of the Black Hills."

He responded with a long, drawn-out sigh, followed by, "Guess it had to happen eventually. Folks been talking about copper in those hills for ages. I've seen it. You've seen it."

Indeed we had. "That means workers, women, drinking, gambling in the camp town, but there'll be plenty of over-flow into Drowned Horse."

"Plenty of thievin', fightin', stabbin', and shootin'. Like I don't have anything else to do."

I knew he had to keep the curse that plagued the Verde Valley in check, but that wasn't all Levi was good at. "You'll keep the peace. You always do."

Levi didn't seem to take the compliment as it was meant. He grew sullen. I was working out a way to get his mind off of this news, when the stage arrived outside. We moved to the porch. As was usual, the driver handed Levi a rolled package. This would be the new wanted posters come up from Tucson, which I would normally get a set of at my office, too.

"What do we got?" I asked.

Levi unwrapped the tie and peeled one poster at a time.

"James Kettle of the Crab Rock Gang's reward went up."

"'Bout time."

"Smiling Igor, Russian cattle rustler."

"Nice to know we're attracting new foreign elements to the area. Makes us seem like a real state, even if we aren't yet."

"Oh, now this is interstin'…"

"What?" I looked over Levi's shoulder to see there was a list of recent arrests. I immediately saw the one that'd caught his eye.

*Bose Ikard: A negro arrested for possible cattle theft.*

"That can't be our first freed slave in the territory?" Levi asked.

"Certainly our first arrest of one, in any case."

Levi read the charges out loud. "Mr. Ikard came to Arizona with three herd of cattle to sell. Suspicious of the claim, Commander George Sanford of Fort McDowell took Mr. Ikard into custody suspecting Ikard of having stolen the cattle from their proper owner and came to the territory to make a sale before word of his crimes reached here. Sheriff Brady of Pima County awaited confirmation from Texas and Colorado, where Mr. Ikard has previously worked as a ranch hand for Mr. Charles Goodnight and Mr. Oliver Loving."

I crumbled the notice. "Oh, shit."

"What?" Levi asked.

"Goodnight and Loving?" I stared at him disbelieving. "Don't you ever read anything other than stuff on myths and legends?"

"Not really."

I strode toward my horse. "The Goodnight-Loving Trail,

Levi. Big cattle drive from Texas to Colorado. Lots of inter-
views with Goodnight in the papers. He kept highlighting
the efforts of his lead rustler, a negro named—"

"Bose Ikard, I get it." Levi, on my heel, said, "See? I'm
not the only sheriff who doesn't read the papers."

---

WE REACHED FORT McDOWELL THE NEXT DAY. TOO
bad Ikard wasn't held at Camp Verde, the formerly named
Camp Lincoln, but they didn't have holding cells at the
smaller camp. Even four years on, Camp Verde struggled to
keep its men fed or even paid, in part to supplies from Fort
Whipple not making it to them due to outlaws or Indians.

I appreciated Levi's company on the trail, but I worried
about him leaving Drowned Horse unguarded.

"Owner's taking the watch. He'll get word to me if
anything worthy of my intervention is needed."

We showed our badges and were escorted directly into
Commander Sanford's office.

He stood, offering us a hand, which we shook. The
man's immaculately groomed muttonchops spoke to his
position there. Most cavalrymen couldn't get the good stuff
like beard cream. "Gentlemen, what can we do for you?"

"Well, for starters, you can free a man you've taken prisoner here. Bose Ikard."

Sanford frowned. "Even if I could, why would I? Caught
the man in possession of stolen cattle."

Levi took a chair. "Are you sure of that? What makes you
think they're stolen?"

The commander stared at him as if he was dumb. "The
man's a negro. I've never known one to own that many
head."

I, in turn, gave Sanford the same glare. "You do realize
that we now exist in an emancipated America, don't you?
Or hasn't word reached you yet that the Confederates lost?"

The Confederacy claimed Arizona as one of theirs, but

that didn't sit well with most of the folks living there, many who headed west to avoid being drawn into the war.

Sanford blustered, "Well, yes. But still, who would sell to a negro? How'd they even have the skills, the brains, to manage such a task?" He sat down, as if he'd said all that needed to be said.

"Charles Goodnight, for one," I countered. "In *The Journal*, upon his retirement, Goodnight remarked Ikard, and mind you, I'm quoting from memory, 'I have trusted him farther than any living man. He's my detective, banker, and everything else I needed him to be.' Sounds like a man who might stake his most loyal employee a few head of cattle."

Not to be proven wrong, Sanford said, "Well, we've sent a letter to Mr. Goodnight for confirmation. We'll just see."

Levi cocked his head. "Not a telegraph? You just supposed to let the man sit in a cell until a reply comes God knows when?"

"Of course. If he turns out to be what I've suspected him to be, then I don't have to send men out to retrieve him."

I hated to pull rank like I was about to, but the man had left me no choice. I placed my hands on his desk and leaned in, fixing him with my most serious expression. "General George Sanford, in my capacity of United States Marshal, I am taking custody of the prisoner named Bose Ikard. If you need to find him, he'll be held at Drowned Horse's jail under the supervision of Sheriff Levi Forrest."

"That's me." Levi pointed to his badge.

Since Ikard was neither a military nor an Indian prisoner, Sanford had no authority to keep him.

The General interlocked his fingers and spoke pensively. "Sheriff Brady's not going to like this."

"Have him take it up with me. I'll take my prisoner, now."

I signed a few papers clearing the Army from any responsibility, and soon, Mr. Bose Ikard was brought to Levi and me. Years on the range etched Ikard's face. Sun, wind, touches of frost burn. His hands were scarred from ropes, knives, and who knew what else. Yet, despite being arrested for something he hadn't done, and certainly treated poorly by the garrison, he greeted us with dignity.

"Sahs, what is happenin' here, if I may ask?"

He accent was thick with the south, especially Texas.

"I'm Marshal Bandimere, and this is Sheriff Forrest. We're taking you with us. We believe you are innocent."

Gratefulness shown in his eyes. "I t'ought to tell them that, but no one cared t' listen."

Levi grasped the man's shoulder. "Let's go get your herd. I know some ranchers in the Verde Valley that might take them off your hands."

Ikard tipped his head our direction. "Much obliged, sah."

Only, when we went to the Army quartermaster, we discovered we'd arrived too late.

"Someone came and claimed them."

"What? How?"

The clerk showed us a poorly written document that stated the cattle in custody were the property of the Crazy I Ranch. "The brand matched," the clerk explained.

Levi, livid, asked, "Where were the cows kept?"

"Down range of the Fort."

"Was anyone guarding them?"

The clerk shrugged. "Occasionally."

"So, anyone could have walked up to a cow, scribbled the brand down, and added to a clearly fake document?"

Embarrassed, the clerk admitted, "Maybe?"

I asked, "What did this person look like?"

The man he described was large, thick mustache, smiled a lot, and spoke with a Russian accent.

Levi pulled out the wanted poster for Smilin' Igor.

The clerk pointed, "Yeah, that's the guy...oh."

---

THE HERD HAD BEEN CLAIMED THREE DAYS PRIOR. That meant we could catch up after a full day of hard riding.

We retrieved Ikard's horse, which had not been stolen, and the three of us set out. The tracks had Igor heading north, which worked for us. We knew the territory he was heading into.

"Igor can't sell in any town that might have his picture up." Levi suggested. "He might drive them toward Drowned Horse, thinkin' the only sheriff in the area is in Prescott."

"That *is* a common misconception."

That night, we sat around a fire, sharing the rations we always kept in our saddlebags. Ikard mostly kept to himself, thanking us for allowing him to partake in the sparse food. He finally got the courage to ask, "Sahs? Why you so intent on helpin' me?"

I wanted to say because it was the right thing to do, but I didn't, thinking it was trite. I wanted to tell him that I fought for the North, but I held that back, too. I could've said that my wife, Piety, back in Kansas had grown up on a plantation in Louisiana and never felt her father treated their slaves with dignity, so she moved north as soon as she was able. We hired freed slaves to help her around the house while I was away. I could have told Ikard that all that.

I threw a fresh branch into the fire. "It's hard enough watching events happen around me I have no power to control. Military strikes on the tribes. Indian raids attacking settlers. Evil preying on the weak. Hope destroyed with every wagon train that doesn't reach California, Utah, or Nevada." I revealed more than I planned to. "When I saw the notice, I thought to myself, 'Here's something you *do* have control over. Here's something you can make right.'"

"I thank ya," Ikard replied. "I been lucky t' find t' good folk. First my owner, Mister Ikard, then Mister Goodnight and Mr. Loving. T'ey see sumthin' in me, and I work'd hard t' never let t'em down." Levi asked him what type of jobs he'd done for them. "Whatever t'ey ask, sah. Drove two thousand cattle from Texas t' Colorado. Fought Comanches. Broke broncs. Even learn'd to cook pretty good."

Both Levi and I were impressed.

"You should think about settling in the area. We're not much now, but we will be."

Ikard shook his head. "Got my wife and kids back home. T'is my last drive, just t' finish up what Mr. Goodnight stake me. After t'at, I want t' live simply."

I couldn't deny the desire a simple life had its appeal.

We slept briefly, breaking camp before daylight. As we followed the tracks, Levi grew concerned.

"Igor's driving them too far east."

That worried me, too. "That's sending them right through Apache country."

"Not only that..." Levi leaned over in the saddle to tell me in a hushed tone, "I recently got word of something... else making camp in that direction."

I could only imagine what fresh hell the curse had brought to Arizona.

"What type of else?"

Levi cast a quick glance at Ikard, finding the man studying the tracks. "If the description holds up, they're called kamapauas."

"Kamapauas?"

"Yeah," Levi said, dropping his volume down more. "They live in a colony and hunt as a pack."

"So, like the natives?"

The sheriff grimaced. "Not dissimilar, but these little bastards are more savage killers as a group. They're sort of pig men, with tusks and everything."

"Pigmies, got it."

"No, not pigmies. Pig men. Their leader got cast out of some island. Banished him and his kids to a place never to see the ocean again as some sort of punishment."

"Arizona."

"Yup, and they're real angry about it."

I didn't understand, other than the standard concern over dangerous creatures.

"They're really big on things called lou-ows, where they roast meat over a pit and have a party. So far, they've only stolen a few chickens, a couple of turkeys, but if Igor drives a herd of cows right past them..."

I got it. "*Big* party."

Ikard came over to join us. "Is t'ere a problem, sahs?"

Levi hesitantly said, "First, I'd prefer if you called us by our names and not 'sirs'. We're not your betters. Second, yeah. There's brewing to be quite a scrap over your cattle. How badly you need them? Really."

Ikard thought a moment. "T'ese t' last of the stake Mr. Goodnight gave me. It's all the money t'at'll keep my family until I die. Would hate t' lose it, but I'd feel bad if anyone got hurt 'cause of it."

I looked at Levi, who without discussion said, "Let's go get us some cows."

At Ikard's urging, we would steal his herd back at night, when Igor's men would be tired, and the cowboy assured us he could wrangle the cattle at night. "Once t'was a storm so dark, I gathered t'em cows by t'eir glowing ears. Didn't miss a one."

I'd witnessed an electric storm causing my horse's ears to glow, but still, to gather a whole heard that way...

Night fell, and we made our way to Igor's camp. Smilin' Igor had a dozen men working for him; family he'd brought over with him, as I understood.

"Where's your men?" Levi whispered to Ikard. "You didn't bring that many head across two states alone."

"Army done run t'em off when I got took. Mostly Mexicans didn't want trouble."

We could've used a few more men, but then we didn't have to go far from here to Drowned Horse.

Igor had camped on the lee side of the Rio Verde, meaning we'd have to cross the herd over the river. What worked in our favor, being late summer, was that the river was at its lowest.

The outlaws slept in shifts, and we waited until the retiring men wanted sleep, and the recently woken weren't quite awake yet.

"Four men. Two for you. Two for me," Levi said.

Ikard wanted in, but Levi told him, "No, you focus on getting those steers pointed in the right way. Get the herd moving toward the Verde. Once they're forded, we'll be in a much better position to fight."

Ikard slipped off into the night.

Levi and I drew as close to the camp as we could, then picked our targets. I had my Sharps out, stepping carefully to within a few feet of the half-awake sentry. I brought the butt of the rifle down right at the base of his skull, snapping his head back. He stumbled forward, dazed, which gave me the moment to reach around, cover his mouth, and drag him away from any assistance. He didn't put up a struggle as I gagged and handcuffed him.

When I returned, another sentry was no longer on patrol, leaving two.

One of the men, noticing two of his brethren were missing, called in hushed tones, as not to wake the others, "Aton? Rudin? *Щхере аре йоу?*"

I could see Levi peeking around a boulder. He shrugged. Then in the worst Russian accent I'd ever heard, he said, "Over here. Taking a shet."

I followed with the second worst accent. "*Da.* Me, too."

One guard looked at the other, and they both appeared satisfied.

We waited until they were at the farthest position from each other, and then we relieved them of duty. I knew at any moment, one of Igor's men could wake needing to *actually* vacate themselves, so we joined Ikard in driving the herd across the river. That noise would wake the whole lot, and did. Only half the cattle had forded by the time the first cries of alarms went up.

"The herd! Someone's stealing them! *Тхиевес!* Thieves!"

Levi and I stayed to the rear, rifles out. The outlaws came stumbling down the hill from their camp, firing their guns in the air as a ridiculous warning that armed men were coming. The flashes, brief as they were, lit them up for us.

Levi and I each shot two, slung the rifles, and drew pistols. The next wave learned from their dead comrades to hide behind boulders before shooting. We rode back and forth, making difficult targets to hit even if it was daylight. Roland, Levi's horse, was especially good at moving in patterns that gave the sheriff freedom to aim at will. I counted on the moon to find me outlaws to shoot.

When the last of the herd made the water, we turned and entered the river ourselves. Igor's men would have to mount up before giving pursuit.

Ikard, to his credit, kept the cattle running, even in the little hours of that morning. We had three maybe four hours to sun up.

Levi and I stopped often to slow the outlaws down. We managed to cut their numbers in half, but we still had two to one against us.

We reached a plateau just as the sun showed itself. "Keep them moving west," Levi shouted to Ikard. "Get to Drowned Horse. Find a man named Owner at the Sagebrush."

He planned to make a stand, and I figured he had the right idea. We found ourselves a good vantage point, dismounting and grabbing as much ammo as we could. We reloaded, set ourselves, and prepared to turn Smilin' Igor into Cryin' Igor. As the world warmed, we discovered that right behind us was a drop off with nothing but air and the Rio Verde below.

The outlaws were working their way toward us between massive boulders, occasionally taking pot shots for sport. They could also see Ikard driving the herd across the desert, but decided that if we were dead, they'd have an easier time retrieving it.

"No, no, no. Not now!"

I didn't know what Levi was going on about until I spotted them coming down from the North.

A raiding party of Apache must have seen the cattle and thought they'd take a few back to their camp. That's when *I* caught a similar dust cloud heading for the same spot from the west.

"What the…"

Levi chose that moment to teach me all the different words he knew to offend God.

"Those the pigmies?" I asked.

"Pig-men! And yeah."

I held my rifle to my chest, said some words to my wife who was *my* God, and prepared to launch myself from the rocks in hopeless attempt to do the right thing.

———

"SO THERE WE WERE, BACKS PINNED AGAINST A cliff with a hundred-foot drop to the Rio Verde, a war party of Apache comin' at us from the North, Smirking Igor's Gang coming from the south, and two dozen pig-*men* arriving from the West." I checked Levi to see if I'd gotten it right. He waved me on.

By then, everyone at the Sagebrush's attention was focused exclusively on me. The trappers, the citizens of Drowned Horse, even the ladies from the second floor. When we stumbled in a couple hours ago looking bedraggled and near death, and with three herd of cattle which currently grazed in the middle of town, it hadn't taken long for word to get out we were back. By then, even Bose Ikard was no longer being stared at with a mix of curiosity and fear. He'd been given some food and beer at some point. Levi must have drank three shots during my tale and looked more relaxed than I'd seen him in days.

I paused for dramatic effect, until someone, one of the women, begged, "Are you going to tell us what happened or what?"

Giving her a cocked smile, I lifted my whiskey to my lips, took a pull, and leaned forward, gazing out at all the rapt faces.

"So, you'll never believe what happened next…"

# THIRTEEN

# "TAXED FOUR TIMES FOR FOLLY"

Arizona Territory
May, 1870

"THIS ONE'S ALL YOU," SHERIFF FORREST told him.

Hearing that made Will Ragsdale's day. In the years since he settled to Drowned Horse, he hadn't had as many opportunities to prove himself as he would've liked. Sure, he watched over the town when his boss was away, but often nothing much happened during those times. How was the town going to trust him someday when Levi retired? *Did* sheriffs retire? Will wasn't sure. None he'd known, or heard of, ever left their post willingly. Most in a pine box.

But he and his mentor would be the exception. They were getting closer to understanding the curse that lay over the Verde Valley. In fact, just the other day, they got a lead on a cave up the Mogollon that had that funny type of writing Noqoi had left them in his journal.

Will hadn't met the strange Indian man...god, whatever he was, and the gambler god might be the only being that truly scared the young man. Monsters, outlaws, ne'er-do-wells; they didn't bother him. He just kept his wife and baby girl in his heart, and he could overcome everything. A vengeful all-powerful being like Noqoi? Will didn't know what it'd take to stop someone like that.

"I'll get right on it, Sheriff."

Will hurried out the door and got on Blaze, his horse. Unlike his boss, whose horse, Roland, had been picked for his agility and strength, Will chose Blaze for her speed. Often, Levi sent him to get some item or clue to balance the odds against the stuff they faced together. Will needed to get it and get back before Levi was the one carried out in a pine box...if there was enough left to bury. He'd never let the man who'd been like a father to him down. Will wouldn't that day, either.

The trip to Gemtwinkle's cave took Will past his homestead, so he decided to check in on Sarah and Trina. His wife waved from the kitchen window when she heard him arrive. She stepped outside when he dismounted.

"Trina's asleep," she whispered. Not that she needed to. They'd been blessed with a child that slept through anything.

Will hugged Sarah and kissed her like a man still in love.

"To what do I owe this visit?" Sarah asked as they stepped up to the porch.

"Levi's got me riding solo. It's tax day."

Sarah furrowed her brow. "You're going to go visit that spriggan, Gemtwinkle? Y'know he gives me the willies."

"Ah, he's harmless. Well, mostly." Clearly, his wife had not heard the part about him handling it on his own.

"His kind steal babies, Will. Switch them for their own." She shuddered.

The deputy continued to play down and concern. "Gemmy's only done that once." He thought a moment. "Maybe twice. But he's a good sort. Plus, as I said, Sheriff is trusting me to do this by myself." Will preened. "It's a big responsibility."

Sarah reached up and kissed her husband on the cheek.

"I'm very proud of you. Just be careful. Don't make him mad. I like our daughter right where she's at."

Will considered Sarah's words as he continued along the trail to Gemtwinkle's box canyon.

"Why can't she be more supportive?" he asked Blaze. "It's not like I can't handle this type of thing. I've done much more dangerous stuff than picking up taxes."

He would've done the tax collection last year, but the spriggan sent runners to Drowned Horse with the tithe, saying he was too busy to meet. The Korrigan collapsed exhausted after the heavy purse was lifted off their shoulders. Owner gave them all shots of beer for their efforts, which meant, of course, they stuck around for the next two days drinking and generally being a nuisance. Will, Owner, and Levi finally ran them off with a broom.

When no Korries showed up over the last couple of weeks, the sheriff decided it was time to go collect the money in person. He felt Will ready for the task. The young man just wished his wife had been more excited. "Maybe she'll be when I come home and nothin' went wrong. Yeah, that's it."

Will spurred Blaze on to a gallop. The sooner he returned with the taxes, the sooner he'd show everyone they could count on him not to mess things up.

---

EVEN THOUGH IT'D BEEN TWO YEARS, WILL FELT something was off the second he crossed the threshold. The Korrigan escorting him were quieter, more subservient, than when he last encountered them.

The lanterns that hung on the cave walls flickered eerily, creating deep, dark shadows almost anything could be hiding in. The smell of sweat and fear lingered in the air. The looming shape of a ten-foot-tall Gemtwinkle sent a warning sign to Will. Gemmy never grew big unless he was mad at someone.

Instead of tea and cakes on a table, the spriggan sat behind a large desk. How it was built and by who, Will wasn't about to ask. The Korries led Will to a chair and announced him to their boss.

"The deputy. Ragsdale, was it? I remember you. It is nice of you to visit. How may I be of service to the constabulary of Drowned Horse?" Gone was most of the spriggan's Cornish accent, as if he wanted to make sure every word was understood. He kept his eyes closed, and breathed heavily, as if he labored under an illness.

Will spoke slowly and carefully. "Good afternoon, Gemmy. As you know, it is that time of year when we pick up the Yavapai County taxes under the Revenue Act of 186—"

"Oh, that? I've lost track of time down here. I rarely go out anymore, as most of my business is handled by proxies."

"We expected the Korries, and I only come because they never arrived."

Gemtwinkle chuckled. "They aren't the only beings in my employ these days."

"Are you still working as a solicitor?"

Shaking his head, the spriggan said, "No, I now work in what you'd call...security, for others affected by the curse, such as I was." He snapped his fingers and two four-legged nightmares stepped into the scant light. Almost dog-like, their eyes glowed red-hot like iron pokers, and flames licked their lips as they panted. "Meet the Kent Boys, a pair of highwaymen who preyed on settlers, Indians, cavalry, and anyone who got in their way. They were fine looking lads until they killed a person while traveling through the Verde Valley and became *gwyllgi*." He chuckled again. "Well, you know what I do. I managed to reason with them, and they came to work for me."

Will knew there was a notice about the Kent Boys sitting on the board outside the sheriff's office, but he wisely thought best not to mention it at that moment. Instead, he played the game like he thought Levi would. "It's nice that you have company down here, sir. Now as for the t—"

But again, Gemtwinkle wouldn't let him finish. "They're really good at making sure other creatures such as ourselves don't get into trouble here, or if they do, making sure nothing tragic happens to them."

That didn't sound at all like the person he'd met on two previous occasions. "Are you suggesting that you would protect a creature that harmed citizens of this area? That you'd send these..." he swallowed his first words, "employees of yours to stop us from seeing justice done?"

Gemmy leaned forward and opened his eyes slightly. Milky-white irises stared down at Will, dull but not entirely blind yet. "I'm saying that my protective services are available for those that couldn't hire the Pinkertons or that the 8th Cavalry might shoot first, ask questions later. I'll work for anyone, Deputy. Humans, the Yavapai, the Apache, and those of my kind." He waved his fat, blistered hand in circles. "And yes, I'll protect them from *any* threat that might come their way. That includes you and your boss."

Will stood and both the gwyllgi tensed. The deputy resisted the temptation to move his hand by his holster and instead straightened up. "I would like to settle our accounts, if you would please, and then I'll be on my way."

"I think," Gemtwinkle began, "that it's time for a new arrangement. I think, it'd be more financially responsible if the Town of Drowned Horse paid me for protection, instead of you and Levi Forrest. We're better suited for the type of work you boys do. In fact, you can take that message back to your people, Will Ragsdale. If Drowned Horse wishes to continue feeling safe, I'll expect a tithe equal to fifty percent of all earnings starting three days from today."

"Fifty! Ain't no one gonna pay that, Gemmy."

Gemtwinkle pushed his desk back and stood, growing to half the size of the cavern. "It's Mister Gemtwinkle now, boy! And you will all pay, or I can no longer guarantee anyone's safety." He stepped forward forcing Will back.

"Now, you run back to your master and tell him, Gemtwinkle is the new law in the Verde Valley!"

Will backed out of the cave and jumped on Blaze, panic and worry trailing behind him.

———

BEFORE HE REACHED TOWN, WILL REINED BLAZE to a stop. He got down and stomped around, kicking rocks and the occasional prickly pear.

"Dammit! Dammit! Dammit!"

How did things go so badly so quickly? Gemtwinkle changed the rules, that's how! Now he had to drag his tail back to Levi and tell him he'd failed on the biggest job the sheriff had given him, so far. His mentor would be disappointed in him, and it'd be years before he trusted him to do anything but sweep out the jail.

"Think it over, Will. You can do this."

What had changed in Gemmy over the year? Maybe even two years, since no one had seen him in that time.

Or maybe someone had. Certainly, someone must have dealings with him. The giant had mentioned he was already hiring himself out, but to who?

The Paya or other tribes, maybe? Monsters unable to defend themselves? He was kind of a troll, so maybe he charged people to cross a bridge, or something? Where to begin?

Will got back on his horse and rode toward the former McGannon homestead. Maybe the Korrigan was still there and could answer some questions.

Poppy McGannon played in the dirt outside, as three-year-olds tended to do. She reminded Will that his own daughter, Trina, would be that age soon enough. Her mother, ever watchful, stepped onto the porch when she heard the horse approach.

Riley had bags under her eyes, and her hair hadn't been combed in some time. Her clothes had the wear of someone who worked hard and went to bed exhausted. She gathered Poppy into her arms, the child squirming to get out and continue playing.

"Deputy Ragsdale? What brings ye out here? Not that two-timin' basterd of a husband of mine?"

Will assured her quickly it wasn't. "I'm lookin' for the Korrigan that you were, um, friends with last we spoke."

"Jori? Yeah, he'll be under foot somewhere. Jori!" she called out. "Get your little butt out here."

Jori the Korrigan appeared beside her shin in a blink. "Yes, dear?" he said in the nasally, squeaky voice of his kind. He looked worse for wear than Riley. When he noticed Will standing there, a wave of what the deputy guessed was relief washed over him. He bowed. "Welcome, sir. How may I serve you?"

Will didn't have time to figure out what was going on there, so he got to the point. "Jori, you still in touch with Gemtwinkle or any of your kin in his employ?"

The Korrie shook his head violently, making his long pointy ears flap back and forth. "No, sir. I would have *nothing* to do with that shyster anymore. Nor have I had *any* communication with my brethren in this last two years, truly, sir."

The only one of them who would have bought that pile of horse shit would be Poppy, and I think she even looked at him in disbelief.

Riley stared down at him. "Joriii…"

Will pleaded, "It's real important, or I wouldn't have come to you."

Jori looked back and forth between his woman and the deputy and finally fessed up.

"Fine, I play cards with some of the boys on Thursdays after you fall asleep, my lamb."

"I knew it! That's why I find you nappin' when you're s'posed be watchin' Poppy on Friday mornings." She side-kicked him.

Jori squealed. "I'm sorry, my love. I just getting to missing people, you know, my own size."

The lady squinted at him. "Are you sayin' I've gotten big too big?"

The Korrigan looked to Will and then back to Riley. His face betrayed that there was no right answer here. "No, you're perfect, my bonnie lamb." He mouthed to Will, *Help me!*

"Ma'am? Might I have a word with Jori in private? He may have information vital to me."

Riley turned on her heels, flipped her hair behind her, as to suggest she couldn't care, and marched into the house, slamming the door.

Will got on one knee to talk to the tiny elf.

"See what I have to deal with?" Jori said. "You have no idea what that lady makes me do. Take care of the baby. Mend her socks. Do I look like a cobbler to you?"

"Sorry for your troubles, but I really need you to tell me what's going on with Gemtwinkle."

Jori pulled a tiny flask from his vest pocket, uncapped it, took a swig, and turning grim, said, "That spriggan was always miserly. I mean, that was his curse, right? Of course, it wouldn't give him the power to redeem himself, but make use of his darkest traits."

Will scrunched his face. "He always seemed to play fair with us."

"That was all an act. The sheriff of yours scared the hell out of him. How many supernatural creatures has he taken down? Dozens? More? Gemtwinkle knew it was only a matter of time, though. The rumor is five years."

"Huh? Five years?"

Nodding, Jori said, "Yeah, there's a rumor that your sheriff has a clock running, and he's supposed to die after five years of guarding the valley."

Will fell backwards on his rump. It couldn't be possible.

"Who says?" Will asked.

Jori shrugged and took another swig. He offered the flask

to Will, who declined. "Not sure where it started. It's just been whispered in conversations. No idea of it's true or not."

*Levi? Dead? In five years?*

"So, he's got five years, so what?" Will buried the feelings down. He still had a job. "What does that have to do with now?"

The Korrigan hopped down the steps to place a hand on Will's arm. "Sorry to say, but that prophesy was given nearly four years ago. Gemtwinkle is betting on Sheriff Forrest pushing up daisies any time now. That's why he's being so bold."

The world spun around, and Will Ragsdale threw up. Luckily, he didn't do it on Jori.

---

HE WOKE WITH A WET RAG ON HIS HEAD AND RILEY McGannon leaning over him. He was still outside, on the ground next to Blaze.

"Are ye bein' alright there, Will?"

Will got to sitting, then managed to get to his feet with some help.

"I'll be fine," he told her. To Jori, he asked, "How do I stop Gemtwinkle? What's his weakness?"

Jori shrugged. "Don't know that he's had one since before, when he was a human."

Human. Jori had just reminded him that the spriggan used to be a human! If a curse could be placed, one could also be removed.

"Thank you," he told the Korrigan. "Thank you," he said to Riley. He got into his saddle. Before leaving, he mouthed to Jori, "Not a word. To anyone."

Jori nodded.

Will had to go place a bet.

---

WILL STOPPED BY HIS HOUSE TO TELL HIS WIFE HE was going to be gone overnight.

"What's wrong?" Sarah asked. "Did everything go well with Gemtwinkle?"

He wanted to tell her everything, and he would eventually. Instead, he took her into his arms and hugged her tightly. Stunned, she held him and didn't ask any more questions. Then he went to Trina's crib and bent over to kiss his precious little lady.

*Heaven help anyone who does her harm.*

He gathered up the notes he'd made on Noqoi's journal. He and Sarah played around with the impossible script at nights, after Trina fell asleep. They hadn't really decoded anything substantial, but he'd be able to recognize the same words if written on a cave wall.

Finally, Will grabbed a parchment of his own and a quill and wrote a note for his mentor, explaining what had happened and what he was about to do. He handed it to Sarah.

"If I'm not back in two days, give this to Levi. Don't," he pointed at her, "read it before then. Two days. I need you to give me that."

Sarah nodded, concern marring her beautiful face. "Be careful," she said, and kissed him.

He hated leaving her this way, scared for his safety, but he'd never feel safe, never feel confident in his own abilities, if he didn't try this. One last kiss, then he was out the door.

---

THE RIDE WAS HARD, BLAZE HAVING TO CLIMB UP several rocky trails. A trapper told Owner about the cave one night while drinking at the Sagebrush, though he hadn't been real clear exactly where it was. Just in a general sense. He said he'd sought shelter in it when a sudden storm swept over the valley. He'd recite the tale to anyone who'd buy him a drink that he could feel their place was different, holy even. Not that he'd been in a church since he was five. But when he described some of the markings he'd seen, Owner fetched Will and Levi, and the journal. The trapper confirmed the symbols he saw matched the ones in the tome.

Levi sobered the drunk up, and got him to narrow down where the cave might be. Owner and Levi shared a look between them that Will asked about. At first, they were hesitant to tell the young man, but Levi decided it was time.

"There's a cave, a special cave, that plays into the Apache and Yavapai story of creation," Levi explained. "They believe that there was this flood that wiped out all the people save for this one woman and a bird."

Will scratched his head. "A flood? Like in the bible?"

Owner confirmed. "Yeah, spooky, huh? Well, this woman *Kamalapukwi* is the first woman, and she survived the flood because she was put in a hollow log by the bird and told to stay in there until the waters receded."

Levi took back the narration. "When she did, she was high up on those red rocks we can see from the hills, deep in Apache territory."

"Like that place you and Long Tooth fought the camazotz?"

"Yup, but not that place. Someplace not easily gotten to. Then, well, it gets a little crazy from there, but she and the sun had a baby, and that's who the whole lot of them came to be."

As part of Will's training, Levi had taught him a lot of myths and legends, but this was one he'd left out. Now that he was hearing it, he understood the mentality of the local tribes better. No one knew where the Eden of the Bible was, but if your people knew their whole race came from a place just over the hill, you'd fight and die to protect it.

The Sheriff and Owner planned to make an expedition to find the cave, but they wanted to get approval, maybe even an escort, from one of the White Mountain chiefs, as it fell within their territory. Levi wasn't about to go to their holiest of places without their permission.

Will hoped he wasn't going to make things worse by doing exactly the opposite of that. He spent the better part of the first day just getting to the area. Then he camped. The next day, he left Blaze tied up, threw a pack over his shoulders, and climbed from there. The places Levi had chosen to search would not be easily reached, but Levi was older than him, and he'd been shot, stabbed, trampled, and tossed about for nearly four years already. Will was still at his peak.

*Don't think about it.*

But of course, he did.

*Does he know? If there're rumors, he must've heard them. Why wouldn't he tell anyone?*

Will couldn't bring it up. Either way, that conversation wouldn't go well.

As he hung on a cliff face, the sun reached over the mountains, shining its rays onto the range across from him. The light illuminated a cave Will couldn't see in the shadows. It matched the description of the one the trapper sought shelter in. It would mean another half day, but Will thought he could reach it before dark.

Entering it, Will felt the same pulse of energy the lost hunter had. His breath slowed and a hum echoed in his brain. He lit a torch from his pack.

The script on the walls matched the ones in the journal exactly.

Will walked around, tracing some of them with his hand, looking for the word he needed. He found it far in the back. He reached into the pack and pulled out a deck of cards and a pile of chips from the Sagebrush.

Setting them down in front of the script, he stepped back and shouted, "Noqoi! I've come to play!"

Nothing happened.

At first.

Then the cave lit up with dozens of torches in wall sconces Will was sure hadn't been there a moment before.

When he looked at the offering again, a short, aged Indian sat cross-legged, looking just as Levi had described him, right down to the feather in his stovepipe hat.

"You did your homework, boy." He clapped. "Very good. What are we betting on?"

Will suddenly realized he'd made a big mistake.

———

NOQOI GOT UP AND WALKED OVER TO A TABLE that appeared out of thin air. Two chairs waited, and the Gambler God took one.

"It wasn't easy coming all the way up here. Just to let you know in the future, you can find me many places, not just in Kamalapukwi's old place." He motioned for Will to sit. "So, you've defied everything your mentor told you to do just play a game with me. Why do you look like then that you are about to piss your britches?"

The insult lit a fire in Will, returning him to his senses.

"I'm here to get you to take your curse off of one person. A man who goes by Gemtwinkle."

Noqoi raised an eyebrow. "Oh, the spriggan, they call that race. What has he done to rate such a punishment?"

Will took the seat across from the old man. "He's stirring up trouble, and he's too powerful to just be dealt with."

"Too strong for your Sheriff Forrest or just too much for you?"

Levi had warned Will that, should he encounter Noqoi, the entity also liked to play mind games. Will could do that, too.

"He's building an army of supernatural creatures," Will said, exaggerating the truth. "He's going to take over Drowned Horse, and that'll throw off your curse, won't it? Upset whatever plans you have down there."

Noqoi picked up the deck of cards and shuffled them with alarming skill and speed. "Oh? You think I have plans down there?"

Will leaned in. "Of course you do. Why else would you want the Sheriff gone or under your control?"

Nodding, the old god said, "That's the logical assumption. But I don't like a quick game. My plans, whatever they are, extend long past the lifespan of you and your family."

"My family?" Will wasn't expecting that shift. His voice cracked a bit. "What about my family?"

"I already know what you want me to do, but it pains me to do so. The only way I'll do it, is if you place a wager with me."

Will expected this part, but slid his chair back. "I won't bet my wife or child's lives, like the legends say."

"Ha! Legends." Noqoi dealt three cards down. "You've been in bars, boy. When have you ever known a person to give you the whole truth when they're telling you a story? You think gods are different?" He studied Will's stymied reaction. "Of course not. They will always make themselves look better, and everyone else worse. Gambling is my hobby. Does that make me a villain?"

Will calmed down. What the old man said made sense. "So, what am I betting?"

"You're going to turn over these three cards representing three items. Then you'll pick one of them. I'm going to bet that you won't give the item they represent to either your wife or your daughter or your sheriff because you're too scared of the outcome."

"And if I do, you'll turn the curse off of Gemtwinkle?"

Noqoi held up his hands. "More or less. Curses are tricky to place. Harder to remove."

"And if I won't play?"

"That's easy. I won't do anything." He pointed out the cave's entrance. "You'll find yourself facing the spriggan alone, unable to stop his plans, and a failure in front of the man you respect and the woman you love. Your daughter will die someday knowing her father could have saved her, but chose not to."

The gambling god had gotten him. He summed up Will's

every fear and made them a chip in his game. The deputy had little choice. He held his hand over the cards. "I just have to pick one of these three things?"

Noqoi nodded. "And take it to the person it was intended for."

Will turned over the first card. It became a photo of a tombstone with the marker, "Here lies Levi Forrest, Sheriff of Drowned Horse." It listed the date of his death as September 17th, 1871.

"Is this real?"

Noqoi nodded.

Showing this to Levi would put a death mark on the man. He would know for sure that he was going to die and when. He could prepare for it, or possibly reject it, because it came from the trickster god. If Levi didn't know, it gave Will time to figure out how to avoid this fate for his friend and mentor.

Will lifted the second card. Again it was a photo, but not one taken in any reality that existed. It showed the deputy lying drunk in bed naked with the three saloon girls of the Sagebrush similarly attired. "That's horseshit. This never happened and never will."

Shrugging, Noqoi admitted, "Does it matter? Will Sarah believe you if she sees this? You can swear that it didn't happen." He chuckled at his own caginess. "When she goes to talk to the girls, she'll find that they remember this event quite intimately."

Will growled and got up, but then a wizened finger tapped the third card.

"At least see what the last card is before you storm out."

Grabbing it, Will slammed the last card down on the table forcefully, his hand covering it. He stared at Noqoi, no longer afraid, rage wafting off him in waves. For his part, the god just smiled knowingly. Will slid his hand off the card.

It was a Kachina ragdoll, like many he'd seen Paya or 'Che children carry around. That's all it seemed to be. Simple. Unassuming. Safe.

Which meant it wasn't.

"Is it cursed or something?"

"No, not at all."

Will didn't believe him.

"I know my word holds no weight with you, but if you think about it, I haven't lied once. I may have omitted some facts, but I have never lied. The game isn't fun if I cheat. I'll give you my word. No harm will come to Trina because of this doll."

But cheat was exactly what Noqoi was doing. Will could feel it in his soul.

So, his choice was to assure his boss's death, break his wife's heart and possibly lose her, or bet the word of a devious being on his child's safety.

Will left the cave with card in hand.

---

"GEMTWINKLE!" WILL CALLED INTO THE SPACIOUS cavern. "I've come with an answer to your demands."

The spriggan stepped out from a side tunnel, his fae drooling, fire-breathing dogs lapping on either side of him. The spriggan grew until he towered over the deputy.

"You have too much fire in your voice to have come with my payment and the town's surrender."

Will stood his ground. "No, sir, I have not. Instead, I'm placing you and the Kent boys under arrest. Them for murder. And you for extortion."

Gemtwinkle laughed so hard, Will thought the cave would come down around them. When he stopped to catch his breath, he said, "This is what you did with your two days? I know from my Korrie spies, you didn't even go into town, didn't present my request to Levi, Owner, or anyone. You ran away, and came back to challenge me in my own home?" Gemtwinkle bent toward Will. "You have some balls, kid. My boys will love eating them."

The pocket watch in Will's coat chimed.

Smiling, Will held up his hand and snapped.

Gemtwinkle disappeared to be replaced by a shivering Kenver Uglow, as he must have looked before the curse. He sat in a pile of giant clothes his spriggan form had been wearing just a moment before. Beside him, two naked shivering men knelt on all fours.

Will took out the three pairs of handcuffs he'd brought with him, tossed one to each man, and drew his piece. "Please put those on, and any attempt to run out of the cave or down into the tunnels will result in me placing a bullet tax in your asses."

---

THREE CRIMINALS IN JAIL AND A BAG OF GEMS TO give to the county, Will basked under the respect Sheriff Forrest showed him.

"That's some good work there, Will. How'd you remove the curse?"

"Came to me in a dream, Sheriff," Will recalled. "That if I was at a certain place, at a certain time, the curse would be broken. Don't know why or how."

The sheriff grasped the young man by the shoulder. "Well, not like people 'round here don't have visions like that, but you shoulda filled me in. Three men, two known-to-be killers, was too much to take on alone. You did well this time, but let's make sure we're watchin' each other's backs in the future."

It was merely a slight admonishment that only dulled the praise a tiny bit, but Will let it go. He knew he was fortunate the vision turned out to be true.

As Will opened his mouth to ask what would happen next, Sean McGannon burst through the door. "I dinnea know how you did it, Sheriff! But thank you!"

Levi scrunched his face. "I have no idea what you're talkin' about, Sean. I haven't thought of you in two years."

Sean winked. "Aw, Levi. You dinnea have to be so

modest. Síofra? The dearg-due? One moment she's sucklin' my neck, as she's done for two years, and the next, she's dead. Like two years' worth of dead. All gross and decayed." He stepped forward and forcibly shook the sheriff's hand. "Thank you. I'm going to go and try to win Riley's heart back."

At that moment, as if summoned, Riley McGannon burst through the office door. "Sheriff! Jori's gone! He just van—" She nearly ran into her husband. "You! You had something to do with this!"

Now Sean was confused. "Do with what? Riley, I was just coming to see you."

"Where's yer undead whore, Sean? I hear you can't be goin' anywhere without her."

Sean opened his arms. "That's just it. She's gone, too. I miss ye and little Poppy."

Riley clubbed Sean across the chin. "Ye basterd! Ye think we missed you? Jori was a better father and damn better lover than you." She kicked him in the shin. While her ex hopped on one leg, she turned to the lawmen. "I want to report a murder. This man killed Jori the Korrie."

Sean laughed. "That's who you left me for? A wee man? You probably sat on him with that big ol' arse of yours."

Riley slapped Sean. Sean slapped Riley back. Then they really began to fight.

Levi said, "Yeah, that'll win her back," and launched into the fray to break them up. Once the sheriff and Will got them separated and into separate cells, Levi asked, "Did you see any of the Korrigan when you left Gem...I mean Kenver's cave?"

Will hadn't.

Over the next few days it was clear that any human that had been transformed into something else had reverted back. And any resident creatures, even the nice ones, had vanished.

A month later, Sheriff Levi Forrest and Deputy Will

Ragsdale took down a scarecrow that'd come to life and started killing farmers. The curse was clearly still there.

Will returned home that night, spent.

Sarah greeted him at the door, picking straw out of his hair. "Go get undressed. I'll fetch a pail and let's see if we can clean all this straw off you."

He kissed her. "I want to check on Trina, first." He'd felt more protective of her lately. He wasn't sure why.

"Okay, she's in her crib."

Will walked into Trina's room. She gazed up at him, grinning a toothless smile. She held her arms out to be picked up. He obliged, holding his daughter against his chest and rocking her back and forth, feeling the warmth of her love through his entire being. He turned when his wife joined them.

"Speaking of hay, she loves that ragdoll you gave her."

"I gave her?" Will asked. "I thought you got it for her?"

"No," Sarah said, uncertain. "Now that I think of it, it must have been Levi."

Will nodded, certain Sarah was right. He studied the small kachina in his daughter's grasp. He recognized it as the one representing *Shalako* or good fortune. He hoped that it would watch over his daughter and protect her from the curse, whatever form it took next.

*I must remember to thank Levi again for the doll,* Will thought, *but then I've got all the time in the world for that.*

## FOURTEEN
# "TO DANCE WITH THE HIGHWAYMAN"

Camp Verde
June, 1870

MRS. YVONNE ARMSTRONG STOOD OVER THE grave of the young Private Ollie Cox, dabbing her eyes with her kerchief.

"Don't cry, Vonnie," her husband, Second Lieutenant Jonas Armstrong whispered. He leaned in close to her she could feel his whiskers on her earlobe.

Vonnie, still new to being an Army wife, gasped. She tilted toward him in a similar manner. "Why ever not?"

Jonas stood tall and firm, unwavering. "When Ollie enlisted, he knew the risks. See the men looking at you? Your sadness could demoralize them, make them question their own roles."

To Vonnie, it was absurd. "Certainly, they understand that I'm grieving not only for myself, but the poor man's family. He must have a mother, a wife, a sister back east."

But as she looked over at the other men and their wives, each held in any outward displays of emotion. She was the only one dabbing a kerchief to her eyes.

The cavalry band struck up a lighthearted tune. "See?" Jonas pointed. "We play gay music to keep their spirits up. You'll get used to it over time."

She doubted she would. She'd been with her quarter-master husband for less than three months in the Arizona Territories, and she already wished to return to New England, or at least back to San Francisco where the 8th Cavalry had launched from. Considering the treacherous journey there, she sometimes considered going back to her native Germany, were she not so much in love with the man she'd become betrothed through family connections. Already, they had taken a treacherous boat ride across the Colorado River. A second, almost as dangerous, steamer ship took them up the Gila River, leaving them still to march from Fort Yuma to Camp Verde, the only bastion of order in the lawless Verde Valley.

That was not necessarily true, Vonnie knew. There was a town, not too far from the fort that developed, however, its ominous name evoked images that had kept her away from it so far.

Drowned Horse.

*Who named a town as such?*

Having a quartermaster for a husband meant they had better than average lodgings at the camp, which actually didn't mean much. No one wanted to inconvenience the man who ordered their supplies. They'd also been fortunate enough to be given one of the enlisted men as a cook and a local Mexican girl to do cleaning, which really left Vonnie little to do other than knit, talk with the other commanders' wives, attend dances, and meet her husband's needs.

That last part meant before long, she would find herself in *that* way, something she was in no hurry to be. The land around them remained untamed despite treaties, wars, and increased military presence. It was no place, and those were no times, to bring a child into the world.

And yet, many of the company wives already had one or two little ones running around them, and each had an

Indian or Mexican nanny to help, so maybe it wouldn't be as bad as she imagined. Maybe *nothing* was as bad.

It would be then, three days after the funeral, that Jonas convinced Vonnie to join two of her contemporaries on a trip into the town of Drowned Horse.

The smell of fresh timber and horse droppings greeted them as their three-man escort led the procession down the main street: one wagon for the ladies and a second empty wagon for the items they were sure to buy. Several of the dozen buildings were new, including a mercantile. Jonas was very frugal when it came to the type of personal items he would request for anyone at the camp, seeing that it would be months for the supplies to arrive, if at all, as the wagons traveled much the same route the soldiers did and faced Indians, outlaws, and environmental obstacles.

Armed with some of his soldier's back pay, which had just arrived, Vonnie decided it was time she got a few things for herself. A Dutch oven was the top of her list, as she missed the smell of baking bread she'd grown up with back in Hanover. Her luck won out as the store had only just received one, and she beat out the other women to the clerk to buy it. They would be looking at her cross on the way back, though she knew all would be forgiven when she delivered fresh loaves of *Roggenmischbrot* to them.

After acquiring a few more personal needs, she tipped the store's clerk to place everything in the second wagon. According to their schedule, she had nearly an hour before setting back for the camp. Vonnie, no longer as fearful of the town, decided she'd take a stroll past the other buildings to see what was there.

The town seemed built around a saloon called the Sagebrush. The sounds of men, music, and sin leaked out its front door, so she moved well away from it. A stable, a butcher, and an undertaker confirmed her suspicions of the types of places she expected to find.

And then there was the Sheriff's office.

There were whispers among the men and their spouses

when Vonnie had arrived at the camp. Rumors about Drowned Horse's lawman. Levi Forrest, they had named him. From where Vonnie stood, she was sure that must be him sitting on the porch of his jail, feet up on the railing, taking in all the comings and goings of the town. He wasn't tall, nor broad shouldered. In fact, he struck her as being more agile than strong. Dark curls of hair stuck out under his hat, and he wrapped his hands behind his head to keep it from resting against the outside wall he leaned against. She recognized his Romani blood, as such travelers passed through her town often when she was a child. The town guards wouldn't let them stay for long, for fear of looting or other nonsense.

Vonnie walked opposite him across the street, taking in the enigma, when he tilted his hat at her. Realizing two things quickly: one, that he'd caught her staring, and two, he had excellent vision. She blushed and ducked her head down before moving quickly away.

She purchased some game hens from the butcher for their cook to prepare for supper that night. As Vonnie headed back to the wagon, she couldn't avoid passing right in front of the sheriff's office again without being obvious about it, so she breathed a sigh of relief that he was no longer out front.

Vonnie stopped short, however, when she saw a notice hung on a board near the office's front door. It was a warning to be on the lookout for army deserter, Corporal Rolf Morbach. He'd fled from Fort Whipple and had been seen in the Verde Valley area. It went on to give details of what he looked like—medium build, brown hair, gray eyes— and who should be notified if spotted.

Desertion was a cowardly act, and despite the hardships she'd endured coming West, Vonnie would never really abandon her husband or his post. What had made this man do so? The constant Indian attacks? A reluctance to follow orders? Or something else entirely? She would have to ask Jonas when she got back if he knew any other details.

Vonnie rarely told anyone this fact, but in addition to the dances, the baking, the knitting, and time with her husband, she loved, loved, *loved* a good mystery.

———————

THAT NIGHT, DURING DINNER, VONNIE STARTED her gentle inquisition with, "Is it common for men to desert the cavalry?"

Jonas, not expecting such a question over braised hens, nearly choked. He sputtered, "T-tarnation, Vonnie. What?" As he wiped food from his chin, Jonas studied his wife. "Where'd that come from?"

Vonnie tried to look as if she had no idea her idle inquiry would be so out of the ordinary. "I was just wondering, as I'm still new to this life, whether or not some soldiers finding all the fighting, the hard travel, the being away from their loved ones, enough to drive them to do something so cowardly as to run away?"

His composure returned, he set about to the bird once more, cutting smaller bites from then on. "It does happen. Madness takes some of the men who can't handle the isolation. Some become despondent after seeing so much death. But fear of being caught deserting keeps the sane ones in place."

"Was that the case with Corporal Morbach? I happened to see a wanted poster for him while in town."

Jonas pointed his fork at Vonnie, and looked slyly at her. "Ah, that's what this is about?" He laughed. "Well, Morbach is certainly an unusual case. We got word of him via the helio."

When Vonnie had arrived at the camp, one of the first things she asked about were the large reflective dishes on top of tall towers. Jonas had explained they were part of the heliograph: a communication device that could send messages up to Fort Whipple, a hundred miles away in Prescott.

"It seems he and his company got lost for days in the canyons north of Whipple and came across a group of Havasupai women with carts filled with food, having just traded with another tribe. The men decided to help themselves of their rations, forcefully. When one the squaws attacked him, Morbach pushed her down. Tragically, she hit her head on the cart and died."

Vonnie held her hand to her mouth. "How horrible."

Jonas continued. "Needless to say, their men hunted down the soldiers and made short work of them, except for Morbach, who somehow survived to report to his commander. Only…"

Knowing he had her on the edge of her seat, Jonas raised an eyebrow at his wife, waiting.

"Jonas, don't tease me so. Such suspense will kill me. What happened?"

Jonas grinned. "Morbach disappeared a few nights later, under the light of a hunter's moon. He's been spotted a couple of times by patrols, and yet, no one seems able to bring him in." He lowered his voice conspiratorially. "Ironically, he's been known to steal from wagon trains, or sneak into Drowned Horse where all anyone ever sees of him is his shadow before he vanishes again."

Vonnie ate up all her husband's tale, completely forgetting her meal. She just sat there, unspeaking, twirling her blonde locks, and pondering many possibilities. When Jonas pointed out that it wouldn't be fair to waste such good food, he startled her from her mind's wanderings, and she began to eat again.

Had Morbach left the service out of guilt? Had he been taken hostage by the Havasupai warriors and escaped, only to still be hunted by them? Where was he hiding? Vonnie understood caves riddled the Black Hills and the Verde Mountains to the west. Even to the south were plenty of canyons, but which one would keep him safe from two groups, the Paya and the Army, that sought his end?

And why did she care?

Upon going to bed, Vonnie fondly recalled her days as a young lady reading the penny dreadfuls her father brought back home from trips to London which, according to her strict grandmother, were exactly what a "lady" shouldn't be reading. There'd been campaigns by their Government to crack down on such trashy literature. For Vonnie, though, it helped her learn English, especially some of the spicier words. *The Mysteries of London*, and the author's later works, *The Mysteries of London Court*, were her favorites, though she loved the highwaymen tales, like *Spring Heel Jack* and *the Scarlet Pimpernel*.

Maybe that's why Corporal Morbach fascinated her so much? He was living the life of a brigand, though not as noble as the ones she'd read, but hunted by all sides for what amounted to an accident. He certainly didn't mean to kill that Indian girl, right?

The thoughts about Morbach had her tossing through the night.

August

ONE FINE SUMMER MORNING, VONNIE HAD JUST stepped outside her quarters when she saw Jonas, the camp commander Lt Charles King, and Sheriff Forrest gathered together with a tall native male. The adornments on his clothing told her he was someone of importance. Jonas had instructed her on few of the local different Wiipukepaya, Apache, and Tonto customs should she encounter any of them in Drowned Horse, where they sometimes came to trade. Her husband explained that the *Paya* were less aggressive than the Apaches to the north, telling her she should stay as far away from the 'Che as possible. Despite all being aggressive when challenged, the *Paya* could normally be reasoned with.

This one seemed to be not as such.

"I'm telling you for the fourth time, it's none of my people stealing your corn and beans," the Major said.

"My men saw one dressed as you," the native rebutted. "He was fast and gathered much of our harvest into a satchel and ran off when he was spotted. My men could not keep up with him." He peered past Jonas's shoulder. "He is probably here, now."

Sheriff Forrest offered, "Listen. While these men are often under-supplied, they get their stuff from the Army, or grow their own out back. Heck, they just got a new quartermaster. And what they don't have, they get money to go buy in town. How can we convince you this wasn't one of them?"

Jonas stepped aside. "Please, you may tour our storeroom and see if we have anything of yours."

King didn't like that idea. "That will not happen. I don't want this savage to see our supplies. Good god, man! He'll lead a party back here to clean us dry."

That comment didn't sit well with any of the others, especially Forrest. "My job is to keep the peace between you two set of bullheaded groups. Unwarranted accusations from either side make my ass pucker and my job harder."

That's when the sheriff noticed Vonnie listening in and tipped his hat. "Pardon me, ma'am. Still not used to women at the camp."

Everyone suddenly focused on her, causing her to feel self-conscious. "No need to apologize, sheriff. I live among soldiers. I've heard worse."

"Vonnie, what *are* you doing here? Can't you see we are having an official discussion?"

Vonnie apologized again, but would not be deterred. "It seems you have not landed upon a third possibility, that of the missing Corporal Rolf Morbach."

"Damn if she ain't right," Forrest said, then apologized

for his language again. "I bet it's that little weasel. Thank you, Miss…?"

Jonas answered for her. "Mrs. Armstrong, my wife. I also apologize for her speaking out of turn."

However, two of the three men didn't seem comfortable with Jonas putting Vonnie in her place. While the *Paya* chief clearly wanted to say something, it would be Forrest who spoke for them both.

"Mr. Armstrong, as I'm sure you know, we're out here all on our own, and sometimes decisions have to be made in the blink of an eye, or we end up with things like what we have here, a misunderstandin' that could lead to people being killed." He tipped his hat to Vonnie. "If a lady, be she a wife or one of the gals at the Sagebrush…" He cleared his throat. "Well, I would welcome such an interruption if it saved lives. Waitin' for a man to give a woman permission to speak her mind is akin to tellin' a horse not to drop a foul. It's nature and tryin' to stop it just delays the inevitable."

Both King and Armstrong didn't look happy at being reprimanded in such a manner, but Vonnie couldn't help but stifle a chuckle in her gloved hand.

Jonas opened his mouth to offer a rebuttal, but Lt. King interrupted him. "Sheriff, when you're in Drowned Horse, you can see fit to do as you will. In my camp, we will stick to the time-honored traditions that keep this man's army moving forward." He made it clear that was the last word on that. "As for Mrs. Armstrong's suggestion, she is right that we had not considered that deserter as he hasn't been mischievous in some time. Chief Tecoomthaya, I offer my apologies as this man raiding your farms, while no longer a member of *our* tribe, he once was and, thus, I am prepared to make a recompense equivalent to what you lost."

The Chief looked back and forth from the commander to Forrest.

"He says he'll give you some of his corn to make up for it."

That pleased the *Pé*, who nodded.

As they turned to leave, the Sheriff once again tipped his hat toward Jonas and Vonnie. "Mr. Armstrong. Mrs. Armstrong."

Jonas took his wife's arm and turned her back toward their quarters.

---

November

---

VONNIE HEARD MORBACH'S NAME MENTIONED again in town on a supply run. At six months into their assignment, the time approached when Company K would be transferred farther into dangerous territory to a place aptly named Camp Apache.

That unsettled Vonnie, and she told her husband so. He agreed that it was time she learned how to defend herself in case of attack. They'd practiced firing pistols and rifles behind the camp. Vonnie picked up on it quick, though she'd never consider herself a sharp-shooter.

The trip into Drowned Horse had been to find herself a pistol and holster. Jonas could have requisitioned them, as he considered those essential supplies, however, this was a purchase she decided to make herself. Vonnie wanted her own gun, not one handed to her from the Army, which then could be taken away from her at their whim. No, this was going to be *her* gun.

Correction. *Guns*.

Vonnie bought two. It was all the money she'd brought, but she felt better for it. The gunsmith threw in cleaning and oiling for her, as they were "previously used." She didn't want to think about who had used them before, and why they were now for sale. That could be a bad omen.

The first was a pocket revolver the smithy called a "Baby

Dragoon," which he swore breathed plenty of fire for a woman her size. It had a five-inch barrel and wasn't too heavy for her. The next was a Starr carbine, which weighed less than eight pounds despite a nearly two-foot barrel. The smithy, Frank Chalker, let her fire a few rounds out back of his shop to make sure she liked the feel.

She did, especially the pistol.

Using all her money left Vonnie with the problem of having none for dinner, and she still had a couple hours before the wagon returned to the camp. Unsure what she was going to do, except maybe go to one of her companions and ask for their kindness, she noticed Sheriff Forrest leaving his office with another man. The tall, red-haired stranger wore an apron covered in blood. Suddenly no longer thinking of food, Vonnie found herself wandering the way they'd gone.

They entered the last building on the street, and Vonnie got a weird shiver up her spine when she read the sign.

*Hiram Craddick.*
*Undertaker.*

Then this was "official" business. Just like the official business Vonnie's husband tried to warn her away from. Which, led by her stubbornness and curiousness, meant she *had* to find out what was going on.

Vonnie crept down the alleyway between the mortuary and the next building over. She kept her head low so it wouldn't be seen through the windows, should anyone be inside. The voices she wanted to hear were in the rear of the place. She got to the corner, content to just listen in, lest she be discovered.

"How'd Morbach get himself a wolf?"

The voice belonged to Sheriff Forrest.

"Dammed if I know, Levi, but that's what the dead man's hunting partner said." That would most likely be the undertaker, Craddick. "They discovered a drifter in ragged cavalry clothes rummaging through their cabin. He fled through the back wall and into the woods. They chased after him, taking the occasional shot."

"And that's when the wolf leapt out of the bushes and ripped this man's throat out?"

"That's the way the survivor told it."

Forrest cursed. "How could he be so sure it wasn't just a random wolf attack?"

"I can't say for sure, but the Mexican, well, he kept saying *Cuetzlachcojotl* over and over. I know that's one of their words for wolves."

"Cuetzlachcojotl? Not *lobo*?"

Craddick answered, "Nope. The man hauled the body here, dropped some coins for me to give him a Christian burial, crossed himself, and left town faster than a sinner on Sunday."

"Shit."

"What?"

"That name. That's not just any wolf. That's a guardian wolf. It's bred to protect its master."

"Morbach?"

"Morbach."

The two men's voice faded as they retreated deeper into the mortuary. When she was sure they were out of sight and earshot, Vonnie poked her head around the corner to look at the deceased trapper.

He was Mexican, as his partner had been, and waited for Craddick's return on a bench. Medium height and build, dried blood matted one side of his dark, curly hair. Directly under his chin, the source of the blood was clear. Most of the man's neck had been ripped clean, chewed off by a wild predator with no concern for human life. He lay in that state, his arms crossed over his chest, and his hat resting on top of them, his eyes open staring up into heaven.

Vonnie didn't know why, but the eyes disturbed her more than his manner of death, and she slipped from the alleyway shadows intent on closing them.

Vonnie only made it three steps before gravity tugged at the victim's head causing it to lilt to the side toward her. Suddenly, Vonnie was eye-to-eye with the dead man, his unseeing gaze boring into her soul. She yelped and fled back into the alleyway.

---

VONNIE WOULD SEE THOSE EYES IN HER DREAMS in the weeks after. Often, a set of wolf's eyes, or a howl in the distance, would accompany them. She'd wake up with a start and reach for the gun she kept in the side drawer next to the bed.

Jonas might mutter "Go back to sleep," or "It's just wind," or some other nonsense.

To his wife, though, she now felt like someone watched her at all times.

Camp Apache took her mind off of Morbach and dead trappers for a while, as everyday they walked a thin line between security and sure death. The White Mountain Apache were at once kind, obliging, even helpful, while still being fierce and cruel. One evening they could be taking shots at the camp with stolen rifles, and the next day invite the soldiers to come watch a ceremonial dance. The strength of the garrison kept the 'Che mostly in line with counts done regularly to receive what rations the current treaty had afforded them.

It was one such evening that the Company commander accepted the invitation of Chief Diablo to attend a ceremony, along with several other officers. They proceeded to a canyon that made for an excellent amphitheater rivaling that of the coliseum in Greece. The dance the Apache performed, though, might have been considered scandalous even in Paris.

A large fire blazed in the middle, while many Apaches sat in a ring outside it beating tom-toms. Naked, or nearly naked, the dancers wore ceremonial paints to indicate the characters they were portraying. Adding to the act, some wore large helmet-like animal heads supported by frames on their backs, allowing the masks to be as twice as tall as they were.

An Apache squaw translated for the soldiers and their wives.

"The first ceremony is a prayer to the gods called the *Gáŭn Bagúdziĭtash*. It honors the Gods of the East, North, South, West, and the…" She paused seeking the word. "fun-maker? The sly one?"

Vonnie offered, "He plays tricks? Like a trickster god?"

The young woman nodded. "Trickster."

Jonas grimaced. "Doesn't sound like a nice god."

The dancers transformed from moment to moment as they twirled and gyrated, bells on their necks and arms jingled as the drums beat faster driving them into a wild fervor. Vonnie was mesmerized, thinking of some of the pagan sacrifices described in the penny dreadfuls she'd read. It terrified her to see such reenactments performed right in front of her, but also excited her in parts of her mind she never dared believe she possessed.

And then it was over and everyone from the camp got up to leave.

Except for Vonnie.

"Please tell me there's more."

The translator stared at her, not sure she'd hear right.

"You wish to see more?"

"Yes, I do."

Jonas laid a hand on her shoulder. "Come, Vonnie. Everyone will be heading back. I don't want to take these trails at night without escort."

But Vonnie did not budge. She couldn't. Her legs would not move.

Seeing there was some sort of commotion, Chief Diablo approached them. Even in full make-up, Vonnie could see why the women at the camp whispered about him. With that body, he might be a god in his own right.

The woman and the chief talked in their own language for a moment. He nodded, and the translator returned.

"There is one more story to tell, but it is normally forbidden for the white people to see. Diablo says, if you," she pointed at Vonnie, "wish to stay," she smiled at Vonnie's husband sarcastically, "with your permission, the chief will guarantee your safe return."

"She's not staying without me," Jonas said, unwaveringly.

The translator looked to Diablo, who shrugged.

"He says, 'Fine.' But he has been told by the gods that this story is for your wife. I will not translate it, as it is forbidden within the tribe to talk about such things, however, I do not think it will need translation."

Thus they agreed that Jonas and Vonnie would stay behind, and if they did not arrive back at the camp within a certain time, the commander promised a rain of justice would fall upon the White Mountain tribe.

Jonas sat next to his wife, arms crossed. "This better be worth it."

Vonnie, excitement causing her hands to shake, promised, "How could it not, Jonas? We are about to see something no one else has ever gotten to see."

Jonas harrumphed.

The dance began as it had before, with beating of drums, and figures adorned with various costumes, but shortly thereafter, only three figures remained dancing. Two men and a woman with no paint or masks, only the bells. The couple danced joyfully around each other, while the third followed from afar with menace in every step. Soon, they were dancing in circles around each other, the palpable hatred of one towards the oblivious love of the others.

And then the evil warrior struck the male with such force, it was clear he had committed murder. The killer danced over the body joyfully, as the woman's steps exemplified her grief. The jealous one reached for the girl, but she resisted. She scratched at the warrior, and he jumped back. Without mercy, he slew the woman.

The dead rose from the places and danced a similar dance to the one they performed earlier. The five gods reappeared, but the trickster god was in the lead. The slain couple's dance begged for justice, which the trickster god seemed to hear.

Now the Gods danced around the murderous man, encircling him. Vonnie could see his movement between their steps. The evil one tossed and turned and...transformed.

When the gods parted, the warrior had been painted and masked in the most hideous of costumes. Nothing human remained of his human visage: only something tortured, something almost canine in form. The dancer now moved on all fours, begging the Gods to undo his curse, but they all turned their backs to him.

Except for the trickster god who laughed and laughed and laughed.

The dance ended.

Vonnie breathed for the first time in minutes.

Jonas uncrossed his arms. "Well, I didn't understand a bit of it. I don't know why the chief wanted you to see that."

Vonnie, watching spellbound as the tribe extinguished the fire, thought she did.

February, 1871

BY THE TIME THE ARMSTRONGS AND COMPANY K left Camp Apache, word had reached them that Camp Verde had been evacuated and a new camp was being built close by. Malaria had struck the soldiers, and the place had been quarantined. The new camp wouldn't be started until spring.

The cavalry left instead for Fort Whipple in Prescott which, from where they were at Camp Apache, would take them over the treacherous Mogollon Mountains. Jonas informed Vonnie that it would be the hardest trips they'd taken to date.

The Tonto Basin, to Vonnie's surprise, presented a feast for the eyes, but only briefly before their ascent truly began. On trails barely wide enough for the prairie schooners, the men pushed wagons from behind as the worn-out mules pulled. Vonnie and the others' items needed to be discarded over the ledge to lighten the load. Even this was not enough for one wagon, which did tumble over the side. All six mules, along with the hapless driver, were dragged down. Their death screams made Vonnie's blood curdle.

They made camp on the mesa, and several men went to hunt deer for supper.

Jonas and the women unpacked the remaining supplies to prep for a cold night ahead. Vonnie relished the colder temps, as it was closer to what she'd grown up with in Germany. As Jonas built the campfire, the wives and children layered themselves with blankets.

Vonnie took a stroll around the edge of the camp. When she heard someone coming through the brush, she assumed that it would be the mighty hunters returning with elk.

It was not.

The wolf took her in with questioning eyes. Its tongue hung loose from panting.

Vonnie froze in place, each gauging the other, waiting to see who'd make the first move. They stayed that way. For how long, she could no longer tell.

Going on instinct, she whispered, "Morbach? Rolf?"

The wolf jumped back and growled.

"Don't!" Vonnie cautioned. "One scream, and they'll all come. Not to mention…" She lifted her arm to reveal the gun she had holstered at her side. "I may not get this out before you kill me, but I will gut shoot you as you tear into my flesh. See how you like that!"

And then the wolf did something in all her years she didn't know a wolf could do.

It laughed. It sounded halfway between a human's chortle and a dog's bark, but Vonnie was sure it made light of her.

"That was not very nice. I'm fairly good with a pistol, I'll have you know." The wolf stopped laughing and regarded her with curiosity. "I should warn you. Our soldiers will be returning soon with a kill, I'm sure. If you follow the trail back toward Camp Apache, you'll discover we abandoned quite a few supplies into the crevice along the way. There might even be clothes for you in one of the trunks that'll fit. Unfortunately, they'll still be Army clothes. Unless, of course, you want to wear the dress I had made for the fall concert I'll now never get to wear?"

The wolf shook its head.

This time, Vonnie chuckled. "I didn't think so. Now go, before they return."

The beast turned to leave, but then Vonnie called out to him. "You've done horrible things, but a much more horrible thing was done to you. Someday, you'll have to make amends. For the squaw. For the trapper. Everything. If you don't..." Vonnie had no idea if she even knew what she said was right. It just felt right. "If you don't, you'll be like this forever."

The wolf didn't look back at her as it scampered back into the brush, but Vonnie swore the silhouette of a man stood up and ran away from the dying light of day.

In the morning, Vonnie's custom-tailored, fall concert dress hung off the back of her wagon.

———

San Francisco, California
April, 1871

THEY WINTERED IN PRESCOTT AT FORT WHIPPLE, but then one of the other company's wives chose to return to San Francisco because their toddler had taken ill, and the fort doctor recommended a better climate. The return trek back down the Colorado River to California promised to be rough so Vonnie offered to escort them. She bade goodbye to her husband and set off for the trip. There were spots along the way she thought the child wouldn't make it, and spots she thought none of them would, but within a couple months, they'd arrived to the seaside town.

Vonnie decided to stay awhile and help the mother, seeing as the woman had no family there. It afforded her a chance also to visit one of the local colleges to do a little research. Of the three available, she chose the medical school since the other two were religious in origin, and her queries might get her exorcized.

The Toland Medical College dwarfed any buildings she'd previously visited, outside maybe a few cathedrals and some government buildings. Students hustled in and out of doors, arms filled with books. She could tell the first-year students from the graduate ones by which ones still smiled and which looked like a soldier about to jump off a cliff rather than spend another day in the service.

When she found the professor she sought out, Dr. Elijah MacKeon, the Irishman had just finished a class. His students bustled out, tossing papers on his desk, and MacKeon gathered them up.

"Excuse me, Professor MacKeon?" Vonnie asked tentatively. "May I have a moment of your time?"

He took her in behind thick glasses. "Aye, lass? How may I help ye?"

She stepped into the room. "I understand you're an expert on diseases, specifically rare ones."

He made a motion for her to take a seat while he sat down at his desk.

"Aye, I've been called that. I've also been called a great

many things, some not too nice. Who is the inflicted? A family member?"

She shook her head. "No, a member of the cavalry back in the Arizona territories."

That caused his thick eyebrows to shoot up over the rim of the glasses. "That's a long ways from here, lass. Ye didna come all this way just for me? He'll be dead before ye ever get back."

Vonnie doubted it. "No, I arrived here on another errand, but this was so strange an ailment, I thought to seek your advice. See, Professor, the disease may have been given to him intentionally. You could even say—in certain circles—it might be considered..." She looked around, making sure no one was in earshot. "A curse."

That brought a guffaw from MacKeon. "I see why ye came to me. Certainly, I've written books on such things. Back home in Ireland, we have a long history of 'curses,' that turned out to be nothing more than someone sticking something somewhere he shouln'tna. If you get my meaning?"

"I'm a soldier's wife. I've heard plenty."

MacKeon nodded. "So what does this curse do? Cover him with warts? Turn him a shade of yellow?"

"It transformed him into a wolf, sir."

Now it was MacKeon's turn to cast his gaze around to make sure they were alone. "A wolf, ye say?"

Vonnie confirmed.

"Aye, now that's a condition that's got a bit of history to it." He leaned back and took a scholarly tone. "There are many legends of men or women changing forms. It's called lycanthrope, among those willing to even discuss it. The Greeks had many such tales, as did the Romans, the Norse, and others."

"The natives in my area also have such legends, but it's forbidden to discuss them outside their own people. I believe it was one such tribe that might have infected the lad."

MacKeon thought for a moment, his chin on his hand. He made noises as he considered his response. "Doth the man appear mad? Deranged?" Vonnie said he did not. "Then not rabies. Maybe hypertrichosis, which has been known to increase hair growth. I've seen a dog-man at a freak show that had a canine appearance."

Vonnie leaned forward. "He is not wolf-like, sir, but actually a wolf. Four legs. Snout. Big teeth."

The professor made to laugh again, then saw how serious she was, and stopped. "And ye saw this wolf?"

"Yes."

"And yer sure it was once a man?"

"Yes."

MacKeon *hmmmed* and finally snapped his fingers. "Aye, I've got it! Porphyrias! Not only would it account for the hair, but also the deformation."

Vonnie still wasn't convinced he understood, but then she heard the sounds of students outside the room, getting ready to come in. Her time was up.

"How would one treat such a condition, if it was that?"

He pointed a finger at her. "Colloidal silver. Should drive the dog right out of him, if that's indeed what it is. Often ye can find it in medicine kits as a disinfectant. If not, an apothecary should have some."

Vonnie thanked him and made to leave.

"If it does work, wouldya be so kind as to write me and let me know?"

She promised she would.

---

Camp Verde
July, 1871

THE SPRING THAW CAME, AND WITH IT, AN oversaturated Colorado River and River Gila. Vonnie wouldn't be able to return to the territory until summer. Finally, in July of 1871, she traveled alongside a different company set to replace her husband's at the newly christened Camp Verde site.

The railroads had yet to get to the Verde Valley, so Vonnie went by steamer from San Francisco south along the coast and then up north by smaller steamer from the Gulf of Mexico to Fort Yuma. At that point, she took a yet even smaller steamer up the Colorado, then the Gila farther north to disembark as close to Camp Verde as they could. After that, it was prairie schooner to "home."

Weathers and waters settled, it was a long trip, but not nearly as bad as the first time she'd traveled the route. Sitting in the back of the wagon, she heard the name that both filled her with delight and dread.

"Morbach killed a soldier, he did."

"No, really? One of his own?"

"Well, they ain't been his own for over a year. They say he's gone native. Runs with wolves, he does."

"And they're putting together a huntin' party just for him?"

"Yeah, both that sheriff from Drowned Horse and the 8th. They ain't going to stop this time until both Morbach and his devil wolf are dead."

Vonnie was too late. Even if the curse could be lifted, Morbach would be killed before she got there. She looked to see the two mounted escorts beside her wagon.

Calling out to one, she asked, "Are we close enough to the camp that I could pay you to take me into Drowned Horse?"

That stunned everyone.

"You don't want to go directly to home, ma'am?"

"I just remembered a pressing matter in the town I must attend to before reaching Camp Verde. I'll gladly pay you." She jingled a purse.

"We can't make good time in that skirt you're wearing."

Vonnie bent over and ripped the dress up the middle and tied the separated halves to her ankles, effectively created pantaloons.

"Good enough?"

The escorts looked to each other, and one finally agreed.

Thus Vonnie grabbed her satchel and jumped from the back of the wagon onto the back of the man's horse.

They rode wildfire over the trail to Drowned Horse.

---

THE RIDER HELPED VONNIE DOWN IN FRONT OF the Sheriff's office. Forrest had several men around him, all with horses at the ready. Many checked guns which ranged from derringers to Sharps.

Forrest noticed her and pushed back his hat.

"Mrs. Armstrong? You're joinin' this party?" He looked at her slyly. "Didja get your husband's permission first?"

"Ha ha. No, I'm not here to join it. I'm here to stop it."

That elicited several tawdry remarks aimed her direction.

The sheriff took her by the elbow. "Let's step into my office. I feel you might have some information I don't."

---

AFTER SHE FINISHED TELLING HER STORY, Forrest whistled. He sat back in the chair, feet up on his desk. "So, Morbach and the wolf are the same creature. Can't say I'm surprised, though. Curses are as common as corn in the area."

Vonnie furrowed her brow. "Whatever for? Why do you say 'this' area?"

Forrest told her about the unique nature of the Verde Valley.

Vonnie couldn't believe what he was saying at first, but it became more believable as he gave her examples.

"Does the army know this?"

Forrest chuckled. "You try to tell that ol' war dog, Crook, anything. You've met him, right?"

She had. General Crook could be a polite, courteous man until it came of talk about the Indians. Then he only saw them as the enemy to be defeated or exterminated.

"That brings up another problem," Forrest continued. "While I might get my guys to stand down, your husband is out there with a group of his fellow soldiers hunting Morbach now."

"Jonas? On a campaign? But he's a clerk. A quartermaster."

Forrest shrugged. "Crook asked for every able body from Camp Verde to go on the hunt. They came through town to tell us where they'd be searching."

Vonnie stood up suddenly. "Where?"

---

THE SHERIFF FOUND VONNIE SOME ACTUAL PANTS to wear before they headed out on back of Roland, his horse.

Vonnie sat behind him and held on tighter than she had with the previous rider. His horse and his knowledge of the area were confident, so they moved at greater speed. She worried about the vials of colloidal silver she had in her satchel breaking.

Dusk was just a couple hours off, and they hoped to find her husband's squad before dark. They came across part of Company K as they watered their horses near Cottonwood Wash.

"Is Jonas Armstrong here?" She asked, a touch of panic in her voice.

"No," someone answered. "He and three others headed closer to Grief Hill, checking the trail from Prescott to see if they could find sign."

Forrest leaned back. "There're a lot of caves that

Morbach could be hiding in. And those caves are easy to ambush from."

"Jonas." Vonnie grew more concerned about her husband. He might have a few ideas that she found tedious, but he was a good man and not a killer, unlike many of the men in his company.

Shadows elongated as they rode into the foothills. Every crop of trees reminded her of the forests back home, and the legends she'd been told as child. Those tales became the draw for the penny dreadful she'd read later on, but none of it prepared her to be racing into darkness on a quest to stop a wolf-man from killing her husband.

Gunshots erupted. Three.

Forrest turned Roland toward the direction he thought the shots came from. The climb grew steep, and they zigzagged between the trees. They got close enough to hear crashing up ahead.

Then howling.

They came across the first dead shortly after. Vonnie gasped and leapt down to see if it was her husband. Horrified, and yet relieved, the torn face of the soldier was not Jonas, but a captain she knew. His wife would be devastated, but Vonnie put that thought away as she ran through the thicket. She'd grieve later and in private.

Forrest, in a loud whisper, told her to stop.

The next victim she encountered had lost his right arm to Morbach. He leaned against a tree, blood still pumping out of it. His head turned to her, a wave of confusion and recognition.

"Miss-es Armstro...?" The light faded from his eyes right in front of her.

Another shot further up.

Growling.

A cry.

"Jonas!" Vonnie yelled and forged on.

The cave might've revealed its insides if it'd been middle of the day, but by then it offered nothing but a black hole set on a dark hillside. Without thought of her safety, she lunged forward, only to be grabbed around the waist by Sheriff Forrest.

"Unhand me! My husband!"

"We'll get him, but we must be smart about it."

Forrest took a flint from his coat pocket and lit a torch he'd retrieved from his saddlebag. He went first through the opening, Peacemaker in his free hand. Vonnie drew her Dragoon.

She had come to save Morbach but, if he'd hurt her husband, then she would see justice done.

They discovered the two of them in an alcove. Jonas held his wrist tight against his chest. It was wounded, but still attached.

Morbach, in wolf form, gnashed his teeth under snarling lips.

Forrest aimed at him. "Rolf Morbach, as duly christened Sheriff of Drowned Horse, I'm arrestin' you for the murder of four people. Will you come peacefully?"

But Vonnie stepped in front of Forrest's gun.

"Thank you," she said to Morbach. "For not killing him."

The wolf spoke in a raspy voice. "I recog...nized his smell...on you...from first time...we met."

Jonas looked back and forth between his wife and the wolf. "Vonnie?" he asked weakly.

Ignoring him, Vonnie continued. "I have something, a potion that should help. It might remove the curse."

Morbach shook his head. "Tried to...do what...you said. Be...better. The wolf...I cannot control...when afraid."

Vonnie got down on her knees and pulled the vials from her satchel. "I know. It is so hard to behave like people ask of you. I feel your pain. Let me try to heal you." She pulled a stopper from one of the vials and held the glass jar out. "Try this, please? If you're going to die, die as a man."

Hesitantly, Morbach limped forward. Only then did she see he'd been wounded, as well. The chunk from his right front haunch glistened in the torch light.

"Vonnie," Jonas cautioned, but she held out a hand to shush him.

The wolf stood in front of her now, its face even with hers. She looked deeply into its—his—gray eyes, seeking the man behind the mask. Morbach opened his mouth, and she poured the contents in. She repeated the same action with the other two vials, not sure what the liquid-to-wolf ratio should be.

Morbach gagged and coughed. He jumped back away from Vonnie, she was sure, to keep the wolf part of him from attacking her. He retreated into the shadows of the cave while continuing to cough, followed by the sounds of vomiting. The silhouette of the wolf dropped to its belly and whimpered, slowly curling into a ball.

Forrest, still keeping an eye on the shape, stepped over to Jonas. "Let me look at that bite, Mr. Armstrong."

Jonas, still flabbergasted at his wife and everything happening in front of him, offered his wrist for the sheriff to bandage.

"You knew him?" he asked Vonnie.

"No, not really. I met him on the Mogollon Mesa when we were coming back from Camp Apache."

"And where'd you come by this supposed cure?"

Vonnie told him she'd explain it all later. She refused to move until she knew if the silver had saved Morbach...or killed him.

After close to a half hour, a voice called out from the darkness.

"I don't suppose someone could go over to the next cave and retrieve my clothes?"

Vonnie said she would gladly.

Dressed, Morbach stepped out of the dark into the torch-light. His gaunt face no longer looked like the drawing she had seen over a year ago. The clothes barely fit him for the weight he'd lost.

Embarrassed, he said, "Being good was hard. I turned away from a lot of meals that would have been easy."

Vonnie smiled. "I'm sure you did."

The Sheriff took out a pair of handcuffs and locked Morbach's wrists in.

When they stepped out of the cave, a dozen men from the 8th Cavalry waited, led by Crook, torches in the air, guns drawn.

"I have him," Forrest told them. "He'll face trial in Prescott."

General Crook didn't lower his gun, nor did any of the men. The imposing man had muttonchops that extended beyond his shoulders, giving him the look of a high-bred, but mean, Scottish Terrier.

"This is a military matter, Sheriff. He's a deserter and is responsible for the death of three of my men."

Vonnie spoke up. "He couldn't help it. He was—"

Forrest cut her off. "Poisoned by the Yavaþé he'd wronged, and it drove him mad."

Vonnie looked at Forrest who wouldn't meet her gaze. Jonas, however, indicated with a nod that she should let the sheriff do what he did best.

"And what of his wolf?" Crook asked.

"Dead," Forrest lied. "Shot by Mr. Armstrong."

"Well, Armstrong? Can you confirm this?"

Jonas said, "I can. What they said is true. Morbach was poisoned, and my wife found a cure in San Francisco. Once she administered it, Morbach returned to his right mind."

Crook considered it all, then said, "It doesn't excuse his desertion, and his responsibility in multiple deaths. He'll come before a military tribunal and, if found guilty, will be hung."

Morbach, maybe with a bit of the wolf still in him, moved like lightning. He grabbed Vonnie's gun from its holster and stepped in front of her. With his back to the soldiers, he aimed at her.

"Thank you," he mouthed.

Forrest wrapped his arms around both Vonnie and Jonas and pushed all three of them out of harm's way as dozens of bullets struck Morbach. The gun fell from his grip, his finger never on the trigger. He slumped to the ground in a heap. He lay there, his now empty eyes turned upward, seeking heavenly absolution.

Vonnie, hand outstretched, couldn't find her voice to cry out.

---

VONNIE ARMSTRONG SAT AT A TABLE IN THE Sagebrush Saloon, her husband not meeting her gaze. He'd been offered a reward for capturing Morbach, but he turned it down. He did, however, take the medal for bravery the Army gave him only because it meant that he'd be buried with honors: a legacy to leave for his wife and any children they might have.

Sheriff Forrest came in through the swinging doors and tipped his hat to the couple.

"Mind if I join you?"

They offered him a seat.

"How's the wrist?" he asked Jonas.

The quartermaster held up the bandaged arm. "Much better, thank you. The camp doctor said the wol—I mean, Morbach didn't bite through any tendons, which I guess I have Vonnie to thank for."

Vonnie blushed.

Forrest leaned in close. "The Army will never understand the Verde Valley curse, but I'm suspectin' you two do."

They nodded.

"Well, then, this might work well for me and the town."

Vonnie asked, "What do you mean?"

The sheriff grinned in a way that clearly made Jonas uncomfortable, but Vonnie found engaging.

"Having an inside man," he bobbed his head toward Vonnie, "and lady, at the camp could help when the curse rears its ugly head. Supplies only the Army can get. Movements only shared with the troops. Stuff like that."

Vonnie grew fully engaged. "Men, and their wives, gossip. It would be easy to collect rumors and share them with you."

Jonas set his jaw. "That's akin to treason. If we were caught, I could be court-martialed or worse."

Yvonne Armstrong thought back to the highwaymen heroes of her youth. They, too, always faced a certain death if caught. She pictured herself like the Scarlet Pimpernel, committing crimes, but to benefit the people of her village.

"True," she said, her grin matching Forrest's, "but what's life without a little risk?"

She winked at her husband and set about to create mischief.

# FIFTEEN

# "UNLOCKING THE GATE OF FEAR"

*Love is the master key that opens the gates of*
*happiness,*
*of hatred, of jealousy, and, most easily of all,*
*the gate of fear.*

- Oliver Wendell Jones

Arizona Territory
November, 1871

LEOPOLD REINHOLDSSON, RENAMED LEO
Rheingold by the United States government, got up from
the shelter that he and his partner, Farlan Wellmann—now
Frank Wellman—had found to wait out the night in. The
rocks formed a cave of sorts, enough to keep the snowstorm
outside. It didn't make the night any less cold, but the fire
Leo tended to during his watch helped some.

He kicked Frank lightly.

"Gotta sheet."

Frank numbly replied.

His cousin made for a good companion, and they watched each other's backs. They split everything equally, even when one or the other had a bad run, like Frank currently experienced. He knew it bothered Frank that Leo's pelts brought them more money than his did, but Frank was family and having someone trustworthy to travel America with made it worthwhile.

Frank got up to a sitting position and grabbed his Sharps from nearby. Just like the animals they hunted, trappers knew they were most vulnerable when squatting. Together, they stumbled through the snow-covered scrub brush that lined the Verde Valley foothills, until they got far enough away from the shelter to not accidentally step in shit later.

Leo couldn't believe how cold it had grown since they arrived. Wasn't Arizona supposed to be a desert or something, like the Sahara? With each breath he took, he felt like a hundred little icicle shards went into his lungs. It was unnatural.

It took nearly five minutes for Leopold to get down to his long johns.

"Hurry up, will ya?" Frank entreated. "Da fire'll be out."

"So damn cold, dontcha know? Hard to get started."

Leo grunted, trying to rush, but then a sound from nearby stopped all other thoughts.

An animal—a predator—growled hungrily.

As they stood motionless, something moved around them. The noise bounced off the rock formations, making it hard to gauge how close or from where the hunter lurked. Its snarl—an eerie echo.

Ethereal.

Haunting.

"Get up!" Frank whispered.

Leo gathered his pants to tie them as he stood.

The creature struck.

Its large maw clamped over Leo's shoulder, teeth digging into his neck and chest. Steaming blood sprayed out far enough to hit Frank's boots. Leo screamed as the creature tossed him around like a rag doll.

With only the sparse moonlight, Frank could only see its glowing yellow eyes. The monster, for he couldn't make out any sort of recognizable animal, had to be the size of small horse. Placing the rifle to his shoulder, Frank aimed for the spot between those eyes.

It paused long enough from rending his partner's flesh to study him.

Frank fired from only ten feet away, but the creature only blinked as the bullet bounced off its thick skull.

It dropped Leo and roared like no creature Frank recognized. From the scream, the world around Frank froze like a fresh coat of ice had covered it. Frank backed away from the encroaching freeze as the creature eyed new prey, and Frank knew he would be lying next to his cousin in moments.

Keeping his wits about him, Frank dropped the rifle, as there would be no time to reload, and, with speed only a man facing death could have, whipped out his other gun, tucked under his pelt coat. He ran forward, sliding across the frozen ground, to jam the gun's barrel down the creature's throat. He fired, hoping to send lead careening through the creature's organs.

A massive paw swatted Frank like a fly. Luckily, Frank's thick furs saved him from any serious damage. The creature coughed up the gun before turning and running off into the dark.

Farlan Wellmann, now Frank Wellman, crawled over to where Leo Rheingold, once Leopold Reinholdsson, lay twitching; the gurgling of life escaping his cousin's throat guiding Frank to him. And then Leo released a single word with his dying breath.

Frank drug his partner over near the shelter and took up a pick-ax to dig Leo a grave as deep as he could. When he cleared about two feet of clay and sand, Frank wrapped Leo's head in a cloth, as was their custom, and filled back in the hole. He placed rocks over the grave to keep it safe from predators. He stayed alert the whole time, but did not hear the haunting growl again. Frank stoked the fire as high and bright as he could through the night and, at day's break, walked into Drowned Horse, the closest settlement.

Frank thought about what he'd seen and the final word his cousin spoke as a warning. He must have misheard, because Frank recognized that word, and it was no *thing* known to inhabit America, let alone the territories.

No! A *gulon* could not have made it all the way to Arizona.

No way in hell!

———

SHERIFF LEVI FORREST SHOT HIS FIFTH EMPTY bourbon bottle off of the fence out back of the Sagebrush Saloon, and yet it didn't relieve his discontentment. The Sagebrush's owner let him do this, from time to time believing Forrest worked through his frustrations that way.

Forrest faced a two-fold dilemma. Whereas a few years back his ratio of bullets to bottles was one to one, today it sat closer to three to one. His hand wasn't as steady. His eyes not as sharp. Not a good combination for a lawman protecting his town from the evil that all-too-often threatened it. Day was coming that someone, or some *thing*, would get the drop on him...and thus the second issue.

Deputy William Ragsdale hadn't come along as quick or as clean as Forrest hoped he would when he brought him on. He figured that hiring him young, as he did, meant that he'd have years to hone the boy's talents. Only, as Will grew into manhood, his tendency to let anger cloud his judgment had become an issue.

Just the other day, Will dragged a gambler out into the street by the man's collar and deposited him in a fresh pile of manure, all 'cause the cheat offered the deputy a bribe. Forrest arrived just as Will finished kicking the man senseless.

"I'm no crook!" Will screamed at the man while Forrest helped the card cheat up and sent him on his way.

"What's gotten into you?" Forrest demanded. "That's not how we handle this kind of thing."

"He thought me dirty, Sheriff. He figured I was like him." He shouted at the gambler's quickly retreating backside, "I'm not! I'm not like you!"

Forrest noticed that Will's hand twitched near his holster.

"Let's go back to the jail and sit a spell, 'k?"

Forrest led Will to the office they shared, but the deputy would not sit. He paced back and forth, mumbling under his breath about being better than a damn cheat.

"Something eatin' at you, boy?"

A storm flashed in Will's eyes as his head snapped up to stare at Forrest.

"I ain't no boy no more, Sheriff. What does it take to get a little respect from you?"

Forrest leaned forward in his chair and pointed to his chest. "Me? Whadda I do?"

Years ago, when Will was but a lad, he'd helped Forrest and the great tracker Kit Carson out of a mess. Seeing potential in him, Forrest trained him as a lawman. Will's naturally keen senses, quick draw, and previously level-headedness made him the perfect heir to the office. When Will's parents moved on to California, he stayed, and Forrest thought of him like a son. He made Forrest proud when he married his long-time love, Sarah. The couple had a little one, a girl named Trina. Will should be the happiest man alive.

"Now listen up, *William*. I don't know what's got you in such a state, and maybe you don't trust me enough to tell me, but that's your decision. However, I won't allow Drowned Horse to get the reputation as a town that drags crooked gamblers into the street and beats them bloody. We've enough other stuff to overcome if we're to keep this town afloat."

Other stuff…like the curse.

Forrest stood and walked over to the lad. He placed a comforting hand on his shoulder. "So I need you to get your head on straight, all right?"

Will looked a bit emotional but, as if sensing this, the deputy twisted out of Forrest's grip and marched out of the office.

"Well, that didn't go as planned," Forrest had said to no one.

But then little did in Drowned Horse.

Sixth bottle destroyed after a fifth attempt, Forrest stomped through the ankle-deep snow to have a drink and decide what to do next.

---

DROWNED HORSE SAT NESTLED IN AN AREA NAMED the Verde Valley for its lush vegetation, though none of that was right visible due to the snow coming over the mountains that boxed the valley in to the west and north. The Oak Creek came down from Mormon Lake and became the Cottonwood Wash, which often got plugged with horse carcasses in the spring, thus the all-too-true name of the place Forrest called home.

But that was far from the most interesting thing about Drowned Horse.

Further back than anyone can remember, a curse had been placed on the area by a gambler god, Noqoi, for reasons no one yet knew. The curse made it so that none who settled there should know a day's rest from the evils of the universe.

In Forrest's time as sheriff he'd fought creatures from mythology, demons from hell, and things dropped down from the stars. He felt it was his calling to protect the settlers that chose to stay in the area, but could it be that William had developed second thoughts about the mission? He'd been so young when he wound up here that now, as a man with a wife and baby, maybe he wanted to leave and didn't know how to say it. Drowned Horse wasn't the best place to have a family.

It could also just be the unseasonably long winter they'd experienced. The boy, er, young man, could have a touch of cabin fever.

However, before Forrest could gather the wits around him enough to go talk to his deputy, the town's undertaker, Ram, stepped into the office.

"Sheriff? You're going to want to come see this."

Adoniram G. Craddick had inherited the business from his father, one of Drowned Horse's many unfortunate victims. Ram, a young man close to Will in age, impressed the sheriff when he sent his pappy to his final resting place in a very mature and professional way. It took something serious to shake the calm demeanor of the tall, broad-shouldered man, but Ram looked downright white, as if Satan himself had shown up to pay respects.

"It's going to be that sort of day, isn't it?"

Ram nodded, and the sheriff unlocked his special cabinet for those sorts of days.

———

THERE WASN'T ANYTHING LEFT THAT COULD BE called a corpse, or even remains for that matter. The dark splotch in the impromptu grave looked more like what the butcher had left over when he finished making sausage.

Both Forrest and Will fought hard to keep their breakfast down. Not that either hadn't seen dead men before, but never so...chunky.

Pieces that could only be identified as once human by the bits of clothing or buckles, lay scattered around. Rocks that Frank must've used to cover the grave had been tossed about like skipping stones. Whatever thing unearthed Leo Rheingold's resting place must've been really big. The only thing that worked to their advantage was that the whole area lay frozen even in the heat of day and kept the scene intact like it was sealed under glass.

Ram pointed to the desecrated grave. "Leo was a trapper with Frank, over there. They'd been heading up to Prescott, but the pass closed due to the storm. They bunked down with plans to try again this morning."

Frank waited in said outcropping, his knees pulled up to his chest.

Ram continued. "Frank walked into town at first light to fetch me and a cart, as to bring the body back for proper burial. When we got here, though, the creature had dug up Leo's grave and ripped him apart."

Will spat. "Carrion eater. Must've had a hell of nose, too."

Forrest agreed. "No badger, wolf, fox, or other grave digger would've dug that far down. Or eat that much."

"*Vielfras*," Frank called out, his German accent thick. "Leo call it 'gulon,' but my people known it as vielfras."

Forrest approached the trapper. He wore a pelt thick with fox, ermine, and wolf—many of which seemed to still be looking up at the Sheriff. Only Frank's face, covered in a long beard, identified him as human.

"What is a gulon or vielfras?"

"Monster," Frank answered. "Would not have think such a thing come to America, but then I see Leo's grave and know it to be true. Dey eat the dead."

Will joined his boss. "What's it look like?"

"Beeg. It gorge itself then quickly take a sheet before eating more. Da vielfras always hungry."

That worried Forrest. There were a lot of settlers spread out farther from town than he'd like.

Frank continued, "Could gobble up whole family, then eat the sheep later, dontcha know?"

"Sarah!" Will ran back to Blaze and, after launching himself into the saddle, raced off.

Forrest barely got a "No. Wait," past his gums before his deputy had vanished.

While the Ragsdale residence sat on the opposite side of Drowned Horse from where they were now, Forrest understood the young man's fears. It's one of the reasons the sheriff never settled down himself. Once Will made sure his wife and baby were safe, he'd be back. He would probably take them into town where others could look after them, which, knowing the town, really didn't make them all that much safer.

"What other than 'beeg' can you use to describe it?" the sheriff asked.

Frank ran down its legendary traits from dog-like body, cat-like ears, to fox-like tail, leaving Forrest to wonder if it wasn't really a bear or something.

"Too fast for bear, especially in da winter. It stop the world with its breath. When it scream, it freezes everything around it."

Forrest thought that odd, even for some of the creatures he'd fought in the past. Well, whatever it was, Forrest needed to kill it. That was his job.

Ram motioned for Forrest to join him.

"I'd like to look at where Leo was killed. I found one of the scat piles Frank mentioned not far from here. He wasn't kidding. Huge pile between two trees, like it'd pushed the poop through a piping bag."

Forrest was sure he'd never get rid of that image until his dying day.

Forrest asked Frank to take them there.

"Why?" Frank looked at them both with trepidation. "Bad memories. Just want to leave."

"Well, we need a place to start hunting this thing before it kills other people."

After some discussion, Frank finally agreed.

At the kill site, blood-soaked snow had frozen into ice, pink as a lady's bonnet, to boot. Forrest crouched down to examine the gulon's tracks while Ram, carrying a knife that Forrest thought just a few inches short of a sword, circled out from the trampled area, searching.

Frank stared at the scarlet evidence, seemingly replaying the events in his mind.

"Shot it. Did your undertaker tell you that? Hit right in da head." Frank pointed at a spot right between his eyes. "When dat did nothing, then I ram my gun down its throat, shot again, but did not stop it."

Looking at a print in the snow, Forrest did mental calculations of the paw size to what that meant for the creature. "That's all a man can do. You're lucky to be alive." He looked up. "It's funny that you two come from the same place this thing originated from."

Frank, acting as if the question took a moment to register, answered, "I am, as you say, from Germany. Leopold from Denmark. His mother, half of each. He was cousin, of sorts. Both countries have same legend."

"Yeah. Strange coincidence."

Frank took in the sheriff, now aware that Forrest studied him.

"What? You think I do this? Bring vielfras here?"

Forrest stood up and then shrugged. "Maybe. Maybe not. I just don't believe in coincidences. People bring things to America, sometimes without even knowing it. They bring their culture, right? But also, their demons." Forrest spat on the ground. "You have demons, Frank?"

Frank nervously glanced to the sheriff's holster and back.

Ram arrived a second later. "Just as I thought. There's game carcasses scattered around, staked to the ground. Even tied to trees, but not like a trap. Just a lure. Someone tried to attract big game here. Maybe that person lured something he wasn't expecting."

Despite the cold, Frank's brow dripped sweat across his face.

"Wouldn't know anything 'bout that, would you, Frank?" Forrest asked.

Frank stared at each of them, going back and forth with shifty eyes. He stuttered, "N-not supposed to be vielfras.

Just mountain l-lion. Something I could kill and make good money. My traps not catching what Leopold's were. He must think to cut me loose. I just wanted to..."

Forrest swore. "Dammit, man! This land is cursed! Evil draws out evil. Your greed must've brought the vielfras here, a nightmare from your own minds."

Frank looked back and forth between the two men, seemingly to gauge whether to run or shoot it out.

"Not greedy. Hungry. He not supposed to die. Maybe injured. Then must keep me as partner."

Ram took a fighting stance, knife extended, while Forrest's hand hovered near his piece. Frank's arms were hidden under his thick pelt. He could have a throwing knife, iron, or a rifle under there, Forrest couldn't tell.

The pelt parted and the double barrels of a shortened shotgun peeked out.

Forrest placed a bullet in Frank's chest. He could hardly miss at that range, and the pelts made him a big target. He dropped flat as a grave.

Ram hadn't even gotten a step forward.

"Jesus, Sheriff. What was he thinking?"

"He was thinking he could shoot me first, then you." He cocked an eyebrow. "Any questions?"

The undertaker shook his head.

"Good, now let's go bury the body. Then we watch and wait."

———

Dusk had settled in by the time they finished filling in Frank's grave.

They scampered up a series of nearby boulders, to give them a bird's eye view.

Forrest positioned his 4-bore rifle in a nice crook that would allow him to steady it. Not only because it was a beast to hold, but he knew he'd gotten lucky with Frank. The pelts had weighed down the man's gun as he lifted it to shoot the sheriff and undertaker. If Forrest hadn't hit him with the first shot, it would be he and Ram down there as gulon bait, not Frank.

When Ram set his Colt rifle same as Forrest had, the sheriff felt relieved. He didn't want word getting around yet that his skills had faded. Ram's rifle wouldn't have the range or the stopping power of Forrest's "elephant gun," as some called it, but it might be useful as a distraction.

As if almost on cue, they both caught movement through the brush near the grave. A dark shape crawled low.

*It could still be a mountain lion*, Forrest hoped, but all thoughts of that fled his mind when the creature reached the mound. Twice as big as any mountain lion Forrest had ever seen, Frank's description of the monster hit it pretty close, though Forrest would've said the tail was more whip-like than a fox's; long and sinewy with a tuff of fur at the end.

He and Ram followed it through their sights as it breathed on the burial mound, turning it brittle, and then hungrily chipped away at it with its large paws.

But as the sheriff made to tighten on his trigger, a noise drew all three of their attentions away from their tasks.

The sound of hoof beats.

Deputy William Ragsdale rode hard along the range to catch up with the party he'd abandoned, oblivious to the notion he would run right into the "always hungry" gulon.

Forrest didn't know how far a gulon could jump, but it could easily take down the horse and rider, making a meal of one, before squeezing out a shit and eating the other.

Ram made to get up, but Forrest held him down.

"That's my friend," Ram said.

"He's mine, too. But if we do this wrong, we'll miss our chance, and he could still die. This is a powder load, and I'll only get one shot off in time."

Ram settled back in to his spot.

"When I say, shoot right in front of Will's horse."

Ram slowly turned his head to check if Forrest was serious. Seeing that he was, he returned to sight in the advancing deputy.

The gulon crouched, back end high lifted—an indication it prepared to pounce.

Forrest exhaled and held the gun exactly at the place the gulon should arc.

He counted down from three as Will arrived at the intersection point.

"Now."

Ram fired a shot hitting the rocks right in front of Will's mare. As she'd been trained to do, Blaze darted the opposite direction as the gulon leapt. Forrest fired his gun, the boom shaking the foothills. Ram covered his ears, though Forrest had grown deaf to it.

The gulon took the large caliber bullet right in the side of the head. The force punched through, removing most of its skull.

The white of Will's eyes could be seen even from up high as they were. The now-carcass passed by him in the air, blood gushing everywhere. Will leaned forward to dodge the gulon's claws, which acted as if they didn't know the rest of it was already dead. Still, the gulon's icy breath hit the side of Will's head and hat, turning the blood into frosting.

Once clear, William brought his horse around, side iron drawn and ready for whatever came next.

The body of the gulon twitched, and blood gurgled out of it, soaking the late-winter snow crimson.

Forrest was all grins as he walked up to his deputy.

Will punched him across the jaw.

"You used me as BAIT?"

Ram ran up between the two, placing a hand on Will's chest. "To be fair, he used Frank's body as bait. You just got between them."

Deputy Ragsdale paused, fists still balled, as he processed the new information.

"That trapper, Frank, is dead?"

Ram nodded. "He called the gulon here, intentional or

not. When the Sheriff figured it out, he drew on him, and you know what that gets."

"Yeah, sucker punches aside." Forrest rubbed his chin.

"Still don't make it right." Will stomped around, still looking for an outlet for his fear-driven rage. He swung at the air. "Not right."

"Wouldya preferred I let the damn thing eat you?" Forrest felt like he, too, wanted to knock the young man down a notch. He'd been dealing with Will's temper all too long. "You wanted me to bring your body back to your wife; your baby girl growing up without her daddy? That sound better to you?"

"No!" Will said. "But I sure as hell didn't want to go back to her covered in blood. Not again."

The two angry men stared at each other, tensed, ready to come to blows when they laughed.

They laughed so hard, Forrest had to hold his side. Will bent over and grabbed his thighs, thawing blood cascading off his hat like a waterfall, which only made them laugh harder.

Ram looked back and forth between them, his expression indicating he thought them both insane.

Forrest composed himself first. "Yeah, don't want to have that conversation with Sarah again. She still hasn't forgiven me for blasting giant scorpion guts all over you."

"Well, how could she? She was under Ol' Stabby, too!"

They continued to laugh all the way back to Drowned Horse.

---

WILLIAM RAGSDALE CALMED DOWN, SOMEWHAT, soon after that, Forrest noticed gratefully. They never did talk about what burned a hole in his deputy's soul, but in the end, it really didn't matter. Forrest's instincts told him his own time in Drowned Horse drew close to an end. The curse wouldn't be his problem much longer, and he could only hope he'd done right by the boy...and the town.

Sheriff Levi Forrest lined up five more empty bottles on the fence, feeling the cold right down into his bones.

It would be a long winter, and he needed to be ready for what came next.

# SIXTEEN
## JOURNEY TO THE CENTER OF DROWNED HORSE

Arizona Territory
June, 1871

"It looks like a coffin, Jonas."

Yvonne "Vonnie" Armstrong's husband and another man, Adoniram "Ram" Craddick, examined their handiwork while she looked on aghast.

"Don't be so glum," Jonas responded. "That's just your imagination."

Ram defended her, though. "It does, actually. I'm the town's undertaker. I don't make bathtubs. I make coffins."

Jonas scowled for a moment, but then went back to admiring the tub. "Coffins don't need caulking, though, and you did a fine job on that. We could sail this down the Gila."

Ram sucked in air through his teeth. "Well, until the Toad Men attack you." Vonnie and Jonas slowly turned their gaze to the young man, who shrugged. "It's a thing. Levi said you both knew about the curse."

They did. The Verde Valley curse drew all sorts of monsters, demons, and apparently toad men to the area. Since encountering it, the Armstrongs had become informants of a sort for Levi Forrest, the town of Drowned Horse's sheriff and guardian against all manner of things. They reported to him any news that came through Army channels at Camp Verde, where Jonas held position as quartermaster. There was no rhyme nor reason to the curse or how it manifested, but nearly a year into Jonas's stationing in the area, they had experienced more of it than they cared to.

Jonas handed Ram payment and moved to one side of the tub. The undertaker took the other side, and Vonnie guided them through the back door to the wagon that waited to haul the contraption back to camp.

"And Grover is okay with this idea?" Vonnie asked for what must've been the eleventh time.

"Yes, dear. The Major-General thought it a fine concept. With the other parts that arrived today, we'll all be enjoying a fine sulfur spring bath in no time."

Vonnie had agreed to come west with Jonas' commission because she not-so secretly craved adventure. Nevertheless, she did miss many of the creature comforts of New England homes, none more-so than a good bath. However, she has reservations about her husband's plan.

Behind the new location of the camp, one of the patrols had found a small hot sulfur spring bubbling up in the Arizona desert. Jonas, being the type of resourceful person that made an excellent quartermaster, came up with the idea to cap the spring, add a pump, and attach a large basin to make a bathtub. He felt that the men would enjoy relieving all the stress from riding through Apache territory, and their wives would enjoy a taste of luxury. Plus, people traveled miles for a chance to relieve ailments such as rheumatism.

Most of the items Jonas needed to construct his spa were not accessible through the Army, or at least none that wouldn't raise a few eyes back in Washington, thus the trip to Drowned Horse. He commissioned the tub while a couple of the enlisted men worked back at the camp on digging the well.

By the time the Armstrongs arrived back at the outpost, the men had just finished drilling the well using four horses working as a team. The soldiers quickly got the pipes and pump unloaded from the wagon and spent most of the day capping the spring. Now with the sulfur water controlled, they filled in the sopping ground with fresh dirt until the spa had a foundation.

Over the next week, off duty soldiers took shifts working on the bathhouse. It was a simple affair with a changing area containing a small bench behind a curtain and the coffin tub. Vonnie and the other wives marveled at how eagerly their men threw themselves into the project. Even though the troops were assigned and reassigned often, since the new camp, those stationed there took a sense of pride and ownership in the Verde during its construction. Half of the bathhouse sat about one hundred yards behind the quarters, so rules were put into place that no one should visit it alone and certainly not at night.

Vonnie had to say, despite her initial reservations, that she now had scandalous thoughts of sharing a bath with her husband, but Ram didn't build coffins for two, apparently. Still, since it was Jonas' project, the Armstrongs were allowed to be the first to try it.

Jonas manned the pump while Vonnie changed. A sulfur-infused smell filled the room quickly, even though vents had been installed to draw in fresh air. The scent invoked images of hell in her mind. When Vonnie stepped out, she had not expected the water to be black as Satan's soul: oily and pungent to boot.

"You expect me to get into that?"

Jonas persuaded, "It'll feel wonderful when it touches you skin." He ran his arm through it and pulled it free. "See? Nothing to be concerned about." He kept spurring her on until she finally acquiesced.

She did not like it. To her, it felt more like bathing in broth than water. She did, however, not let her husband know as he watched with puppy eyes, begging to be called a genius in that moment.

"It's delightful. I can feel my lungs," she coughed, "already getting healthier."

That was all the prompting he needed. Jonas beamed like he'd just gotten a promotion.

Vonnie kept her bath short, so Jonas could have his turn. As she dressed, she giggled to his "ohhs" and "mmms." When they finally left, and Jonas pronounced the Camp Verde Bathhouse open, there was applause from the men and women waiting for their turn. Vonnie wasn't sure she would ever smell anything but rotten eggs for the rest of her life.

As the weeks stretched on, most thought it a success. Unfortunately, for some, the sulfur spring had the nasty side effect of turning the skin a queer color, akin to a mottled green. When the victims questioned Jonas about it, he swore that it was just proof that the water was working and that it would wear off in a few days. Mostly, though, the bathers seemed happy not to have to go into town for a bath.

Three months after its instillation, Vonnie sat on the changing room bench as Jonas bathed. She had passed on her own bath, as she had in each visit since the first, claiming it wasn't a "good time" for her to be using a communal tub. Jonas, who kept perfect track of shipments and inventories, did not actually ever track such feminine things, which was typical of most husbands. This was how Vonnie managed to keep from getting pregnant, so far.

Jonas had reserved them the last slot of the day so he could take his time, but it also meant that night quickly approached.

"Dear, we should really consider getting back. Our cook will have supper ready soon."

Jonas mumbled an agreement, but his face registered such contentment, that Vonnie didn't press. She often wondered if his love of the bath was really due to its "healing" effects or that his pride would never admit to *not* enjoying it as much as he pretended to?

After his head bobbed for the third time, and he threatened to slip under the water, Vonnie got up to rouse him from his stupor.

When she took a step forward, however, the floor shook slightly.

She paused.

Waiting a moment, she took another step, and again, the floor trembled again as if scared.

"Jonas?"

"Hmm?"

The floor rumbled in earnest now.

"Jonas!"

Hearing the alarm in his wife's voice, Jonas came to alert. The water in the tub broke like ocean waves. He grabbed the sides of the coffin tightly, as if he could steady the whole world.

"What's happening?" he demanded.

Vonnie didn't have a clue. She looked for some sort of purchase, but only the spa's doorjamb could be reached quickly. Vonnie clung to it as floorboards groaned and creaked like the gnashing of teeth.

Jonas, panic-stricken, stayed in the tub, as if that would protect him.

The floorboards cracked wide around the water-laden bathtub, and Jonas caught his wife's eyes, fear in his own.

"Vonnie?"

Before she could reply, the ground split open and swallowed Jonas, tub and all.

———

THE PIT WENT DOWN FAR ENOUGH THAT SHINING A lantern or dropping torches did nothing to dispel the dark. Calls to Jonas by Vonnie or others had not brought a reply. Grover ordered the bathhouse torn down immediately and the wood used to build a hoist frame around the hole that they could lower men into it. The plan was to get their missing quartermaster back to the surface while there was still a chance to save him.

Vonnie fretted and feared the worst, especially after the first soldier hoisted down reported that the shaft didn't look to be a natural phenomenon but man-made.

"I can clearly see the evidence of digging tools on the sidewalls," he yelled up. "Someone wanted the spa to collapse."

That alarmed everyone, but none more than Vonnie.

"Apaches? Yavapai? Who'd do such a thing and why?" Brevet Major-General Cuvier Grover asked rhetorically.

Vonnie, however, already suspected something else. Something more difficult to explain. The solider, having finally reached the pit's bottom, confirmed those grim fancies when he pulled on the rope, only to return empty handed.

He said, resignedly, "I found the tub, but no Armstrong. There was a tunnel, though, and I saw lots of footprints in the dirt, but nothing..." His words trailed off.

Grover barked, "What, man? What did you see?"

The soldier shook his head. "The tracks, well, I could see Armstrong's footprints, so he walked off on his own, but around his were prints that weren't...human."

He went on to describe each foot having three distinct toes that ended in something akin to a circle, like the sucker on an octopus. The Major-General discounted it as a trick of the light.

Vonnie had no doubt something unfathomable had taken her husband hostage.

And she knew only one man who could get him back.

---

Sheriff Levi Forrest liked it when the territory marshal, Tucker Bandimere, came to visit.

"So, Tuck, what's going on up in Prescott these days?"

Tuck, a lean man with a thick, horseshoe mustache, groaned. "If it isn't one thing, Levi, it's another. Some prospector named, of all things, Miner, got everyone up in their boots about a gold claim somewhere up in the Pinals. Well, word got out, and now there's nearly three hundred men searching up there, including Governor Safford!"

Levi whistled. "That's a stew waiting to boil over."

The marshal nodded. "Already had several run-ins and a couple of shootings. I needed a break, left my deputies to handle it, and thought a day or two down here would be fine."

"Timing couldn't be better. Will's running an errand down to Fort McDowell, Owner's off getting a new supply of barrel whiskey. I was startin' to get downright bored."

"Bored sounds good. I could use a day or two of nice and quiet."

The sounds of a horse galloping with a full head of steam, reining to a stop in front of Levi's office brought a smirk to the sheriff's lips.

"Nice and quiet, you say?"

Tucker cursed. "When will I learn to keep my trap shut?"

As Levi stood and reached for his gun belt he'd left on its hook, he answered, "Probably never, but then what fun would that be?"

Yvonne Armstrong came through the door nearly as fast as her horse had ridden into town.

"It's Jonas. Something...took him."

That alarmed the sheriff. Jonas, a good man, was not one could call a smart man in a crisis. Quartermaster for the Army complimented the man's strengths, but he wasn't a fighter by anyone's reckoning.

"Took him where?" Tuck asked as he, too, stood.

Suddenly noticing the second man, Vonnie stepped forward. "Underground. Something dug a hole under his bathtub and kidnapped him."

Levi made introductions. "Mrs. Armstrong? Meet Marshal Tucker Bandimere, or as I like to call him, Tuck."

Vonnie faked pleasantries, clearly worried about her husband.

"How long has he been missing?" Levi asked.

"Going on ten hours. It took that long for the Major-General to get someone down the shaft to determine Jonas was no longer there. The soldier reported tracks like he'd never seen before. Like no one had seen before. The commander thinks it's the Apache, but I know better."

When she described the tracks as they'd been told to her, neither Levi or Tuck could place them.

"Toad men?" Tucker asked.

"Nah, four toes and webs in between, not suckers."

"Something new then?" Tucker surmised.

Levi nodded. He went over to his cabinet of goods for just such situations. "It's probably going to be cramped down there. Means we can't use most of the big stuff." He took out rope, a sword, three sticks of dynamite, torches, and a pair of strange pistols he'd been saving for such a day. He handed one to the marshal. "These are LeMat revolvers. They shoot both bullets and grapeshot."

Tucker accepted it with awe. "Didn't think too many of these made it out of the war. They stopped production early on." He took the .40 rounds Levi offered him.

"Yeah, you'd be surprised what people are willing to bet at the tables." Levi tossed Tucker the bag of pellets for the second barrel. "You got nine shots with the first barrel, but you only get one with the second. Then you got to take time to reload it, so make it count."

Vonnie looked back and forth at the two men as they armed up. She admitted to them that she'd left her little dragoon in her quarters in her haste. "So, then, what do you have for me?"

Levi, expecting her desire to join their expedition, knew that trying to discourage Mrs. Armstrong would only make her more stubborn. "For you, I have something even more unique." Levi reached back into the cabinet and pulled out a pistol with a knife welded on to the bottom. "Took this off a bandit who decided to add his own bayonet to the gun. When you run out of bullets, just stick them with the pointy end."

Vonnie took the gun gratefully. "This will do."

They rode back to the base just as a squadron of men were about to set off. Grover, looking as displeased as he always did when the sheriff showed up, held up his hand to stop the trio. "Your presence is not needed nor wanted, Sheriff. We have this all in hand."

Levi, knowing that this was not true, humored him by asking, "And what is your plan for rescuing your man, Armstrong?"

Grumbling, the Major-General said, "We have it on good authority that the Tonto Apaches dug the tunnel and have taken him to one of their camps. We're going to go retrieve him now."

Tucker brought his horse up a little closer so he could join the conversation. "In other words, you're going to go surprise a bunch of Indians that probably have nothing to do with this and set off another slaughter?"

The camp's commander, recognizing the Marshal, nodded to him. "Ah, Marshal Bandimere. Long way from Prescott, aren't you?"

"I go where I'm needed. And I would respectfully ask that you let the Sheriff and myself see if we can find Mr. Armstrong before you make my life more difficult."

Setting his jaw, Grover challenged, "You have no authority here. This is a United States Military matter."

But Tuck was not to be discouraged. "I'm sorry, but kidnappings of any sort do fall under my jurisdiction, military or not. And I'm going to go get him back. Now, again, I ask if you'll please hold off attacking anyone until we return. I'm sure myself *and* Governor Safford would be most pleased. I know he's having dinner with your boss, General Crook, this weekend."

Tuck was smart to mention Crook's name. While the man would most likely authorize any slaughter of natives, Grover was brought up short, not being sure if his actions might displease either the governor or the general.

"You have until morning. If he's not back here by the break of day, we'll do things the way the Army trained us to do."

Tuck accepted the conditions, and the three continued on to the well. The Army had been kind enough to leave the hoist in place.

"Okay, Tuck, I'll lower you first, Mrs. Armstrong next, then I'll shimmy down."

Tuck pulled the sheriff aside and whispered, "Are you sure taking her with us is a good idea?"

Levi put an arm over the marshal's shoulders. "She'll just come after us if we leave her here. Better I know where she is. Plus, she does have a stake in the outcome, good or bad."

Tuck shrugged and moved over the place the rope loop around his boot. "Your plan."

"My plan."

One by one they descended into the dark.

---

Vonnie knew neither of the men wanted her along, which was a common sentiment among men, period. The Army tolerated women because they kept the morale up, kept the men from leaving their posts, and kept them from bringing diseases into the camp from the local prostitutes. Mostly.

However, the wives were to be *kept* out of the way and were not to do exactly the type of dangerous things Vonnie often found herself drawn to. Being an insider about the Verde Valley curse created both sensations of fear and excitement in equal measure. Her life in Arizona had provided her the opportunity to experience the type of adventures she read about as a child back in Germany. Her gratefulness at joining the rescue mission did not lessen her fear for her husband. He'd been missing for a long time, and who knew what the ones who took Jonas wanted him for. Was he to be a sacrifice to an angry God or served up as a meal to a monster? Vonnie shuddered at either notion.

The Marshal kept the torch in his left hand raised high, while his gun in his right tracked back and forth between each shadow the light produced. The tunnel was not very big, but too smooth to be natural. Forrest pointed out places where clearly some sort of digging tool had been used. Of the sulfur spring itself there was no sign. It had been diverted somehow from the aquifer it originated from.

And then there were the strange footprints. Even close up now, none of their party had a clue what made them. They were, as the soldier had described them, three-toed with little circular impressions that could only serve as some sort of suction device. There was also a third track, a long thin one that the Sheriff suggested might be a tail.

"Nothing like this in any of the mythological creature books I've been reading," Levi said.

"Yeah, can't rightly say I've seen anything like it either," echoed the Marshal.

That didn't make Vonnie feel any better about Jonas' fate. If these two, who clearly had faced many evil spawn of the curse, were ill-prepared for what lay ahead of them, then what chance did Jonas, or she, have?

The tunnel sloped down over time. Vonnie no longer knew how long they'd walked, or how far they'd descended, but the surface world seemed much farther away with each branch they took. The tracks were easy to follow until the ground changed from clay to rock, obscuring the tracks. By then, though, the men had gotten a fair sense of the direction the kidnappers had gone and relied on instinct the rest of the way. Levi wisely kept the party together, instead of having them separate to try different branches. If they ran into a dead end, they backtracked. If it split, they chose one branch and stayed with it.

Vonnie noticed two things as they progressed farther. The first being that the tunnels widened and were now supported by "man-made" metal braces periodically.

Forrest had stopped to admire them. "I don't see any seams in these, like they'd been molded exactly to the right shape for holding up the rock."

The second piece of information she couldn't help but notice was how hot the air had become.

The marshal chuckled uncomfortably. "Lot of men wanted to send me to hell. Seems somehow fitting that I chose to go voluntarily."

"Yeah, I think we're getting' close to the source, whatever it is." Sheriff Forrest held up a hand, freezing them in their tracks. He waved the trio back into the shadow.

In a moment, Vonnie heard the sounds he'd caught first.

Something moved down one of the adjoining tunnels. It made a weird trudging sound: footsteps dragging something behind it.

The creature, when it emerged into view, came from the most depraved nightmare, and yet, Vonnie could not help but be fascinated. With about a foot on the tallest man Vonnie had ever seen, it stood upright, but its neck and head hunched over between thick shoulders. Skin that looked dried and cracked, like mud in the sun, had a sickly green hue reminiscent of the color that bathing in the sulfur bath produced. Both hands and feet ended with triple digits, each tipped with bowl like cups. The dragging noise was a tail that extended out five feet from the small of its back, ribbed with more cups. The face was the most disturbing, as it barely had one. No discernible mouth or nose, its craggy skin left one channel free for a mucus membrane covering a single eye that slid back and forth under it.

When the eye slid their direction, Vonnie and her escorts pushed back farther into the dark, hoping it couldn't see them. They stood rock still, holding their collective breath, lest the slightest sound gave them away.

The creature paused for a moment, then continued on.

Feeling they were in clear, Tucker spoke first.

"Levi, what in the hell…"

"I got nuthin'."

Vonnie whispered, "It was otherworldly."

That word sobered them.

"I've heard tales from the Paya about the different worlds their ancestors and their gods come from," Forrest recalled. "That ol' Montezuma's Well, as the Spaniards called it, was some sort of doorway. He pointed down the hall the thing traversed, "But that wasn't anythin' like any one of them described."

The "well" Forrest referenced wasn't far from Camp Verde. A large sinkhole with poisonous water that no one went into for a swim. A sibling of abandoned pueblos that once housed a long-vanished race of people conveniently named Montezuma's Castle surrounded it. Often, the soldiers and wives went there for picnics. Vonnie had done her fair share of exploring during those times.

"Could these creatures be the original inhabitants of the Castle?" Vonnie asked. "Somehow driven underground?"

Forrest shrugged. "Nothing I saw in those ruins indicated anything like that thing."

Tuck added, "Whatever they are, we now know what took your husband, Mrs. Armstrong."

The mention of Jonas returned Vonnie from her musings back to the task. "Should we follow it?"

They agreed to move carefully down the same tunnel that the being had. The trio paused several times as more of the same creatures entered or exited the corridor. They found some wooden crates to hide themselves behind when they drew closer to a main terminal of sorts. Their path ended in front of a massive cavern.

Forrest snuck up to the edge of the tunnel. Returning, he said, "The shaft is huge but is capped with something weird, like a big metal funnel attached to a larger metal box. Either the rock has grown around it, or it grew into the rock."

The description made little sense to Vonnie. "Did you see Jonas?"

He shook his head. "No, just lots of those creatures working like ants hauling crates like this one," he tapped on the one they hid behind, "upstairs into the box above the funnel. They're strong, though. They can carry three of these crates; one in each hand and one with their tail."

Marshal Tucker asked, "You think they speak English? Should we grab one and question it?"

Levi cocked his head. "Even if it does speak the language, it's got us in height, strength, and extra limbs. No, we need a plan."

Vonnie had one and, knowing that neither of the men would agree to it, didn't bother asking them before she stepped out from behind the crate and walked determinedly forward toward the cavern.

They called after her, "What the..." and "Don't do it!" but she didn't have time to debate. She looked back at them, resignation in her eyes.

"Rescue us," she begged the Sheriff.

Vonnie waved her arms frantically, yelling "Hey! I'm over here! Come get me!" She shouted until one of the creatures noticed her. However, it turned back to its task, apparently seeing her of no concern. Vonnie didn't like being disregarded in such a manner, so she took out her gun and blew a hole into the crate it carried.

The creature lifted its tail and a blast of air shot out its backside. Others around it repeated the action and soon, several different creatures came running out of various alcoves and headed toward her. These beings were slightly different than the loaders. Smaller, their arms ended in pinchers like a crab. A hard shell, like a beetle's, covered their body, but instead of the green tinge, a similar-colored mold appeared in spots.

Vonnie dropped the gun and held her hands up in

surrender. Then she thought she should also get down on her knees to look even less threatening. It must have worked, as the security monsters didn't immediately kill her, but took her arms in their claws and dragged her to her feet. They marched her away from the tunnel where Forrest and Tucker hid, and Vonnie hoped they were taking her to where Jonas was being kept and not actually leading her to their kitchen. Along the way, she prayed that her escorts would be able to follow.

---

"LEVI! DID YOU KNOW SHE WAS GOING DO A DAMN fool thing like that?"

Levi shrugged. "It was in the realm of possibility."

"And you didn't try to stop her?"

"How? Shoot her?"

Tuck put his hand up to his chin. "Well, not to kill."

Levi stared at his friend. "You have a wife, right? Back in Kansas?"

Tuck nodded.

"I don't, but I do have the Sagebrush's women and Mrs. Armstrong as examples of the gender. I've learned that when a woman gets something in her head, you have two choices: you can get out of the way or follow their lead. Is it any different with your wife? Is she some pretty, Midwestern wallflower that does everything you say and never, ever, ever goes off on her own?"

Tucker blushed and said nothing.

"Yeah, didn't think so. So, I got out of her way, and now we're going to follow her lead."

With a huff, the Arizona Marshal got ready to do just that.

In addition to the ones with suckers and the ones with claws, there was a third flavor of the species. These ones had human-like hands, though still three-fingered, and the silky skin coating their bodies seemed more like they'd been dipped in it rather than grown into it. They gave commands to both the other types of creatures, leading Forrest to believe they were the ones in charge.

Their language, if that was what Forrest heard, didn't remind him of any language he'd learned. It could be best summed up as burping. They burped a word, followed by a long, blown breath that Forrest hoped he'd never have to smell. The effect of the breath was instantaneous. Whenever a leader belched onto immediately dropped whatever else it was doing and launched into action.

"That must be some considerable whiffy smells those things are blowing on the lee side," Forrest whispered.

"It's like mating scent a mare gives off or something. Launches their workers into action."

Forrest agreed. "I've met some minin' barons who'd like to master that. Complete servitude."

Once all the security creatures retreated back into their alcoves, Tuck and Forrest crept into the main cavern. The workers seemed mostly oblivious to them, and even when they did catch sight of the duo, they kept focus on their assigned tasks.

"Let's make sure we stay out of sight of the other ones," Forrest suggested, to which Tuck agreed.

The guards drug Mrs. Armstrong up the long stairway to the top and into the giant box above the large funnel. Looking into it from below, it contained a fan, almost water-wheel in design.

"What happens when that thing spins?" Tuck wondered.

"Whatever it does, I wouldn't want to be under it."

Workers marched up and down the stairs, and guards waited in their alcoves all along the way.

"How we going to get up there?"

Forrest studied the whole process before answering Tuck.

"As freight."

VONNIE, WHO REFUSED TO SHOW HER CAPTORS how scared she was, actually marveled at the corridors they took her down. Everything was metal, like being inside a gun barrel or a pipe. Lights, which illuminated their way without flame, flickered slightly. The doors they passed were unlike anything she'd seen. At once, both like hatches of a ship but more like bank vaults with big wheels to open or close them. And nowhere did she find seams, just like those supports in the tunnels. When the creatures walked, their feet would make little annoying suck-pop noises as they stuck to, then pulled free from the floor. The thing that bothered her the most had to be the constant hum in the background that rattled her teeth worse than sitting in the back of a prairie schooner. The hum grew louder the farther in to the fortress they went.

Her escorts arrived at their destination hatch, and one spun the wheel and pressed its shoulder against the door to open it.

Noise, so loud, so powerful, it assaulted all of Vonnie's senses. She wanted to vomit. The guards kept her upright and carried her over the threshold into a mechanical room. Along the edges of the walls sat desks with millions of tiny lights radiating at her. At one such desk, Jonas sat hunched over the desktop studying the lights as if deciphering an ancient language.

"Jonas," Vonnie said weakly, still stunned from the noise.

More from the peripheral motion, and less from her words, Jonas turned and saw his wife. He jumped up from his chair, ran to her. The guards let her go just as he reached her and she collapsed into his hug.

"Vonnie! What in tarnation are you doing here?"

She smiled weakly up at him. "I came to rescue you."

"Heavens, woman." He helped her over to the chair he'd vacated and pulled another over. Without her having to explain, he reached into a small canister and pulled out a wax-like substance, which he quickly rolled between his fingers into two balls. He stuck each one in Vonnie's ears, and the motion sickness subsided.

Vonnie sat up straighter. "Thank you," she mouthed.

Jonas bent closer and kissed her. "You shouldn't have come," he said directly into her ear. It came through muffled, but she could hear him.

"I didn't come alone," she replied into his ear.

"Forrest?"

She nodded. "And another, the territory Marshal down from Prescott."

That pleased Jonas, she thought by his firm-set smile. "They are beings not from our world."

"Yes, Jonas. I got that impression."

"They don't speak so much as blow commands to the lower classes. They are obligated to do whatever the class above them tells them to do." Jonas blushed. "The highest on the food chain, the leaders, are the ones who ordered my capture."

Vonnie pleased a hand on his knee. "But why?"

"The sulfur spring was run off value from the impossible machine we're sitting above." He looked positively in love when he told her, "This whole thing is a vehicle, Vonnie! A vehicle they came to Earth in tens of thousands of years ago, when the planet was still new. Only, they got stuck, and they've been trying to get home."

To her religious upbringing, tens of thousands of years seemed much longer than the world had been around, but then few texts covered Native gods, supernatural creatures, and species from other planets, so she accepted what he said as truth.

"That still doesn't answer question of why they took you?"

He blushed deeper. "They think I'm some sort of genius engineer because of the spa. I tried to explain to them I didn't build it, but communication is difficult. They have these things," he spun in his chair, "that are like slate black-boards, only they're white." Jonas showed her a rectangular white space on the desktop. He picked up a small stick next to it and "drew" on the space. He wrote her name with the stick and black letters appeared. "And then I can press a button and it goes away." He did so and the space once again was blank. Jonas studied her bewildered expression. "Isn't it fabulous? I use this to communicate with them. I draw pictures on it, then press this other button over here, and whatever I write becomes a sound they can hear." He pointed at another spot on the desk, this higher up, closer to the level the beings' mouths would be at. "They in turn speak into that vent, and images appear on the slate. I was able to find out a lot." He yawned. "How long have I been down here?" Vonnie told him. "No wonder I'm exhausted."

Vonnie would have enjoyed exploring the aliens' technology all day, but there was a rescue that needed to happen. "What do they want you to build?"

A frustrated sigh. "They want me to figure out how to free their ship from under all the rock that has encrusted it over the years."

"And they think *you* can do that? Just because you built a bathtub?"

"Well..." Jonas flustered. "It wasn't *just* that. The spa had caused a back-up of their cooling system, I think that's what they called it. While I'm no engineer, I am pretty clever. I figured out an efficient way to cleanse the system, so they put me to work on this project."

Vonnie stood. "Jonas! Why ever did you do that?"

Jonas stood. "Because, my dearest," he said, a touch of anger in his voice, "they had me knee-deep in sulfur sludge mopping it up." He pointed down to his trousers where Vonnie could now see a discoloration that clearly proved his claims. "That's where you would have found me still—and probably where you would've been enlisted to assist me. I am done with sulfur baths from this point forward." Jonas noticed Vonnie's own attire. "Whose pants are *those*?"

Vonnie blushed. "The sheriff found them for me." When Jonas gave her a disapproving look, she crossed her arms.

"Well, I certainly couldn't go tunnel crawling in my Sunday best, could I?"

It wasn't so much that Jonas was jealous of her relationship with Sheriff Forrest. More that he never warmed to the idea of being the man's spy within the cavalry. He often challenged her over the things Forrest would ask of them, but then Vonnie always came to his defense, saying they were doing a better job protecting the settlers of the Verde Valley than the Army was. Jonas gave in as opposed to fighting her, since a loud argument might attract undo attention. He couldn't risk exposure.

"So, where is your knight-in-cowboy hat and spurs and, I guess, his squire?"

Vonnie cocked her head, looking at her "not-jealous" husband, and told him, "No idea. I left them back in the tunnels. They were taking too long to come up with a plan, so I came up with my own."

Jonas let his jaw hang loose only for a moment, remembering that this was the way his wife usually did things. He grinned adoringly at her. "So, then, what's *your* plan?"

She shrugged. "Find you. I did that. I can't think of everything. And you're the spa genius, after all." She winked and suddenly found herself drawn into his arms and given a long proper kiss.

*Maybe Jonas needs to be kidnapped more often*, she thought as she let the room melt away in his love.

---

IT TOOK THEM THREE CRATES TO FIND ONE THAT was empty enough to slip inside.

And there, they waited.

And waited.

Finally, Forrest poked his head out.

"They're gone."

"Gone?" Tuck asked.

"Yeah."

They got out of the crate and looked around. Not a single one of the creatures remained.

"What the hell?" the marshal exclaimed.

None of the workers or the guards could be found in the shaft. The duo made their way up the stairs carefully, guns out, checking every tunnel, every alcove, and found nothing. They had almost made it to the top, when they saw one creature slip down a side tunnel, its back to them.

"Should we find out where they're up to?" Tuck took a step forward, but his friend held him back.

"This is a rescue mission, first."

It became clear to the sheriff, though, Tuck really wanted to know.

"Okay," he gave in. "Go check it out. I'm gonna to find the Armstrongs."

Tuck tipped his hat and shuffled down the way he saw the creature go.

Forrest stepped into the fortress-like building and discovered it much as Vonnie had.

*It's like a vault.*

He had no idea how many doors he counted as he moved deeper into. He didn't know whether to go up or down. In a stairwell, though, he could feel a vibration coming from below. Thinking that even if he didn't find the couple, he'd find *something*, he headed down.

Forrest reached a door that hummed so much, he dared not try to open it. He stepped back one door earlier and tried that one. The wheel was meant for the odd beings but, with some effort, he got the wheel turned and pushed the door ajar.

On the other side, the hum was louder, but years of firing the 4-bore near his ear had ruined them to the point it was manageable. Forrest did make out a squeak of alarm as two figures darted into the shadows.

He thought he recognized the squeak.

"Mrs. Armstrong?"

"Levi? I mean, Sheriff?"

When Forrest stepped in, he found both Jonas and Vonnie scarlet red. Not exactly all of it came from embarrassment, but some from exertion. Their clothing was askew in places, and when Forrest raised an eyebrow, Mrs. Armstrong quickly checked them both over straightening what could be straightened.

"I see you found your husband. I take it they didn't torture him *too* badly?"

"Ahem, no, I'm fine," Jonas answered, not able to meet the sheriff's discerning gaze.

Vonnie recovered her wits first. "Sheriff, Jonas has an amazing story to tell."

After the quartermaster finished telling the same story he'd told his wife, Forrest thought "amazing" to be an understatement.

"So, they think you can remove a mountain from on top of this...space ship?"

Vonnie stepped in. "Yes. Do you still have those blasting sticks?"

The sheriff pulled the three sticks of dynamite out of his satchel. "You mean these? They won't blow the top of this formation. I've climbed one of those formations. Much too much rock. Not enough boom." He stuck the TNT back into the satchel, but handed it over to Vonnie anyway.

Jonas went over to the weird desk. "We don't need them to. We'll just drop them in the, what did they call it, the engine compartment, and we'll blow up the ship."

"Jonas!" Vonnie chided. "You're not going to kill a whole race of people, even if they don't much look like us, or kidnap handsome clerks."

The way they looked at each other had Forrest worries he might have to step back into the corridor. He dusted off his hat to get their attention. "Yeah, not big on wholesale slaughter, Armstrong. 'Nuff of that going 'round."

Jonas waved it off. "Oh, they won't be in the ship. This time, every day, they go down into the tunnels to 'the great pit,' they call it, to bathe and feed."

"The great what?" Forrest asked.

"Oh, it's this large underground sulfur pool where they hold a ritual cleansing. It's a very private ceremony, and no outsiders are allowed to see it under fear of death."

Forrest ran out of the room yelling something.

Vonnie turned to her husband. "He said, 'Tuck,' right?"

Jonas, crossing himself, said,. "Yes, let's go with that, dear."

---

TUCKER PLACED HIS HAND TO THE TUNNEL WALL. It almost seemed to sing to him, a chant of some sort like he'd heard from the natives or the Negros on plantations before the war. The actual music came from farther ahead, and step-by-step, he approached.

The passage ended above another large cave, but not as big as the main shaft. Below, a lake of blackish water resided. Most of the alien creatures frolicked either in or around it. The majority were the worker class of creatures, though the guards took turns guarding the passageways or soaking. The leaders all lounged to one side in mediation, each with their eye closed.

Other tunnels, like the one Tucker spied from, emptied into the cavern and some of the workers would jump into the pool, acting no less than like kids at a watering hole in summer.

Tucker found this amusing until he heard the sound behind him.

Slowly he turned around to find three of the workers staring at him. Unlike before in the main shaft performing their commanded duties, these three appeared alert, focused, and angry. They howled and sent their tails up in alarm, exuding a scent into the air.

Down below, Tucker caught the guardians leaving their posts or climbing out of the pool, heading into the tunnels he was sure lead to him. The leaders' collective eyes shot open, and they all went to where he stood gaping. They blew commands into the air, clearly furious at his arrival.

Tucker couldn't get past the three workers, and their enforcers would arrive any moment.

Without a second thought, Tucker leapt from the tunnel plummeting down into the inky lake below him, while praying he didn't land on anyone.

———

THE ALIEN SCREAMING AND GUNFIRE TOLD Forrest that he was too late to catch up to his friend, but hopefully not to save him. Like the previous tunnels, he made his way through a catacomb of dead ends and workarounds, until the smell of sulfur grew strong enough he could find the right path with his nose.

A main trunk angled downward, and he could see the edge of the pool now. Drawing his guns, he started down the slope when Tuck rounded the tunnel entrance from below running full speed. Covered head to toe in a wet, black ooze, Tucker's eyes were wide and wild even from a distance. The marshal pumped his arms furiously as he aimed not at Forrest but past him.

"Run!"

From behind him, a horde of angry alien creatures filled the passage, eyes glowing red with a rage that Forrest hadn't seen earlier.

The sheriff of Drowned Horse decided that Tuck had made a mighty fine choice, spun around, and followed him out the way he'd gone.

———

"SO, HOW IS IT THAT ALL THESE CREATURES HAVE been down here so long, and no one has taken notice of them before? Why now?"

Jonas smirked. "Ah, that's a fascinating question. Come over here."

Vonnie joined her husband. He pressed a button and a window suddenly lit up on the back of desk. She could see through the window into another room. There was a single chair in the center, and several more desk and chair sets around the parameter.

"Is that the next room over?"

Jonas shook his head. "Watch."

He pressed the button again, and the window changed, showing the two of them from above. Vonnie looked above them but saw no window that could be viewing down on them.

"And again."

He changed the window's view to a row of what looked like white metal coffins.

"This is where they've been. Sleeping. If I get this right, they sleep in there for hundreds of years, until the planets are aligned in such a way to make it easier for them to get home. Then something in the ship wakes them up."

Amazed by the window, Vonnie considered what other marvels these beings had at their disposal.

"And you're suggesting that now is one of those times?"

"Yes." Jonas drew a map on the white slate. "It's not the best time, but they thought about going for it. The next opportunity isn't for another 116 years. The journey back to their world will take them a millennia, so they'll go to sleep in those beds."

Vonnie paced back and forth, thinking.

"So, if you could free them from the rock encasing their ship, they'd all have to climb into those beds and go to sleep?"

Jonas confirmed.

When Vonnie grinned like she did right then, it often unnerved her husband.

"What?"

"Is there a way you could convince them that they're about to leave?"

Jonas snapped his fingers. "I see what you mean. If they think they're taking off, all the aliens will climb into those beds, fall asleep, and we won't have worried about them for over a century." He grabbed the sticks of dynamite from Forrest's satchel.

"The engine that powers this thing is activated in the room you saw with the single chair. It should be towards the top of this thing. There are three switches. When you hear the explosions, flip them one at a time."

Vonnie bit her lip. "You'll take all due caution, correct? I didn't come all this way just have you be blown up."

Jonas leaned in and kissed his wife with a promise he'd return to her.

After he left, Vonnie looked for the stairs heading up.

---

TUCKER AND FORREST REACHED THE GANGPLANK to the alien vessel just as Mr. Armstrong exited it.

"You need to get your wife and get out of here," Tucker warned.

The quartermaster shook his head. "We've got a plan. Can you stall them?"

"Stall them?" Tucker shouted. "We're just trying to survive them."

Forrest placed a hand on the tall man's shoulder. "Tuck, the man said they've got a plan. Let's give them a chance."

Tucker turned to the tunnel they'd just fled from, the sounds of hundreds of approaching workers and guards had gotten louder. Closer.

"Ah, hell." He asked the young soldier, "How much time?"

"Long enough for me to set these." Armstrong held up the three sticks of TNT.

Forrest shrugged. "We'll give you as much lead as we can."

Instead of heading into the ship, Tucker and Forrest headed down the stairs while Armstrong found a ladder and began his ascent. The lawmen reached the main shaft just as the horde piled out of the tunnel.

"Reckon, we've got a couple moments before they get here." Forrest bowed and waved his hand in a deferential motion. "Since you outrank me and are a former military man, I await your brilliance."

Tucker chewed his cheek. "That's low, Levi. Even for you." He could see the smile peeking out from Forrest's face. Sighing, he said, "I guess I had this coming."

Forrest straightened up. "Yup, guess you did."

Tucker surveyed the area. There were still lots of those giant crates around. They wouldn't be able to move them without a lot of effort. Thinking back to when the guards took Mrs. Armstrong, and when they chased him out of the pool, he couldn't remember them having weapons. Nor did they fly, it seemed. But they might be able to climb walls with those suction cups of theirs, so he disregarded taking the high ground.

"Tuck? They're gettin' closer."

The marshal knew they didn't have enough bullets to even slow them down, and even if Forrest hadn't give away his dynamite, the best they could hope for was to take a few of them down with them.

"They're almost here. Do you have a plan or not?"

Above them, their weird vessel hung, secured in the rock. Metal tubes snaked out from the rock and into it. Tucker pointed, "Any idea what's in those?"

Forrest said, "Accordin' to Armstrong, that's the same sulfur water that you were just bathing in."

He got an idea.

Forrest recognized the idea before he spoke it.

"Your plan."

"My plan."

They spotted a stack of crates that would do just fine.

Just as the creatures hit the ground floor, Tucker and Forrest scaled the tower of boxes. They took turns pulling the other one up. They'd gotten about four stories up when the horde saw them and headed their direction. Positioned as close as they could be to the pipes, the lawmen drew their LeMats, and popped holes in them. Dark sulfur water trickled out.

"We need more," Tucker directed.

They switched to the second barrel, the grapeshot, and each peppered the tubing. Now the water showered them, coating their bodies and the boxes they stood on, with the effect being that the creatures could no longer get a grip on the boxes below them. They slipped and slid off, their suckers unable to find purchase on the crates.

The workers stopped climbing, unsure of what to do. The guards, not having hands but claws, were also unable to climb.

Forrest slapped Tucker's back. "That should hold them for a bit."

However, about that time, the alien leaders arrived at the top of the stairway.

Tucker and Forrest waved, and then saluted the creatures.

The strange beings belched a command and blew it into the air.

A row of their subjects, dropped to all fours, while another group climbed onto their backs. That put them already halfway to the lawmen.

"Uh, oh," Forrest exclaimed.

Another group climbed to the top of the previous group. The guards rubbed their claws in anticipation. They'd form the top of the impromptu pyramid.

Forrest checked how many bullets he had left. "Not enough," he told Tucker.

"I'm already out. I wasted a lot getting out of that stinky pool of theirs."

Offering his hand, Forrest said, "It's been a fine run. Nice knowin' ya, Tuck."

Tucker shook firmly. "And you, Levi."

That's about when the roof above them exploded. Rubble cascade down on the horde. Not a lot, but certainly enough to make everyone suddenly focus on something completely different.

The giant fan under the ship revved up and steam billowed from the cone.

----

VONNIE FOUND THE ROOM SHE'D SEEN IN THE magic window. It was weird, though, in that unlike the rest of the ship, it was perpendicular to the corridor she entered from. She realized that the creatures' sucker feet must allow them to stick to smooth metal surfaces at any angle.

*How am I going to get to that chair?*

Remembering she still possessed the sheriff's satchel. She emptied its contents. He had placed a length of rope and a small sword in there. Quickly, she tied the rope to the sword, tested the weight, and then swung it a few times until she could get it to secure around the leg post of the chair. The hand-over-hand climb was tough, but she managed to grab a hold of the armrest and pull herself into the chair. It felt weird, laying down in it, but after a moment or two of acclimation, she liked it.

A large window, similar to the small one in the desk, filled the wall in front of her. She pressed a button similar to the one Jonas had, and the window came to life. At first, all she could see were shadows so she determined that she must be pointed at solid rock. She pressed the button again and again, rotating through images of different rooms in the vessel. Then, the view switched to outside. In the main shaft below, the sheriff and marshal were climbing some tall crates as a whole bunch of the aliens chased them.

"Oh, no."

She pressed the button again until she found Jonas. He had just finished planting the TNT in cracks toward the bow of the ship. He twisted the fuses together, lit them, and slid down out of the window's sight.

Vonnie changed the view back to the lawmen, who had now coated themselves, and the tower they stood on, with slimy, sulfur water. The aliens slipped off the crates, no longer able to reach them. She let loose the breath she held, and chuckled at their cleverness. Then, she watched in horror as the creatures stacked themselves up into a tower to attack Levi and Tucker. Anxious, she flipped back to the view of the dynamite, hoping that Jonas had gotten clear.

She counted in her head.

*3*

*2*

*1*

Vonnie shielded her eyes as a flash filled the window. The whole of the ship reverberated with the blast, forcing her to grip the chair's armrests. When she stopped blinking, the window no longer showed anything. Whatever they used to view that area of the ship had been destroyed in the explosion. Skipping to the area below the ship, Vonnie found it oddly disconcerting that all the masses of aliens, and her friends, all looked up at her.

Startled, she remembered what Jonas told her to do. She found the switches he'd described and toggled the first one. On the other desks, activated lights and beeps resounded. The armrest to her left vibrated. Vonnie discovered a gauge one might find on a steamship engine. It slowly climbed. It didn't take a space vessel scientist to realize that she would need to flip the next switch when the gauge read full.

But when the window showed her that now all the alien beings were running back up the stairs in her direction, she wondered which would happen first: the engines reaching ready or their masters reaching her.

THE EFFECT IN THE MAIN SHAFT WAS UNDENIABLE. All the creatures once again left the hangar and raced up the steps.

Forrest and Tuck carefully got down from the crates and waited for the Armstrongs to arrive. The aliens filed into their ship. When they did so, Jonas Armstrong stepped out from an alcove at the top of the stairs where he'd hidden. He waved down at them.

"Where's the Mrs.?" Forrest called to him.

"What?"

"Mrs. Armstrong?"

Armstrong held his hand to his ear, then apparently remembered he had something in it. He took what looked like wax out of both ears.

"Where's Vonnie?"

The quartermaster pointed to the ship.

That alarmed him. "You mean where all those creatures just went?"

Armstrong nodded, then, recognizing the flaw in his plan, turned ashen and went through the hatch to fetch his wife.

---

SHE HEARD THEM APPROACHING, JUST AS THE gauge filled. The window now focused on the hundreds of coffin beds as the worker drones climbed into them.

"It worked, Jonas," she whispered. Vonnie flipped the second switch, and a roar filled the whole ship. The sounds she and Jonas endured in the engine room pounded her ears through the pieces of wax. She pressed the palms of her hands against the sides of her head. Gritting her teeth, she made the decision to leave before a second gauge filled. She unhooked the sword and hung from the chair, so she could drop to the hatch.

Vonnie exited the command room just as the alien

leaders entered the corridor. The moment froze in time. She held up the sword, ready to go down swinging if she had to.

One of the leaders studied her for a moment, then gave her a dismissive gesture as if she was of no consequence to it. It and the other leaders moved past her, leaving her unmolested, to go climb into the room she'd just vacated.

"Well, so much for any swashbuckling," she said.

Vonnie met her husband half-way out of the ship. They hugged.

Looking at each other, they said simultaneously, "It worked!" Giggling, the couple left the ship together.

———————

"HEY, TUCK? WHAT DO YOU KNOW ABOUT SULFUR?"

"You mean that stuff we're covered in? A fair bit. I learned some in school. Why?"

"What happens when you apply a flame to it?"

"Oh, that's simple. It burns up. Heck, enough of it, and it'll even explode."

Forrest pointed up.

Tucker followed the finger to take in the flame that had ignited inside the big funnel below the alien space ship.

"Yeah, that's not good."

The Armstrongs escaped the ship at a solid pace but the lawmen urged them to, maybe, pick it up a bit.

"Sulfur—"

"Ignites, I know!" Mr. Armstrong yelled. "I order it to cauterize wounds."

"Then we'd best be out of here if they actually try to take off."

The lawmen hung by the tunnel they'd all arrived from, waving for the couple to run faster. When they got there, everyone sprinted through the passages doing their best to remember the way home from memory.

"Why didn't we mark our trail?" Tuck said.

"I don't know. 'Cause maybe I don't go rescuing cavalry

quartermasters with his wife every day, and it plum didn't occur to me."

Vonnie said, "Next time, we'll make sure to bring chalk."

"Next time?" all three men replied.

They found the bottom of the well under Camp Verde. They paused, breathing hard.

"Hello," came a voice from above. "Is that you, Sheriff? Marshal? Mrs. Armstrong?"

It was Grover.

"Yes, it's us!" Vonnie confirmed.

"Did you find your husband?"

"I'm here," Armstrong declared. "Can you pull us up in great haste? There's going to be a big explosion in just a moment."

"Dear God! What have you done?"

"Later," Forrest yelled. "Up! Now!"

Vonnie went first, then Armstrong, Tuck, and lastly Forrest. As soon as he broke the surface, he called for everyone to get away from the hole.

All of Company K backed up just in time. A rumble like an earthquake tossed most of the men off their feet, and then all were witness to the pillar of flame that extended forty-feet into the air.

If they'd been any closer, some would have lost eyebrows.

The fire dwindled, the noise subsided, and the hole collapsed in on itself.

Grover ordered his soldiers to make sure the well was completely filled in, and they posted warning signs around the area in case a sink hole should develop from the tunnels underneath. He approached Forrest.

"I see when you deal with those savages, you take care of business. Well done."

Forrest opened his mouth, but Tuck stepped in. "Just to let you know, it wasn't the Apache or any of the other local tribes. It was a group of outlaws who'd tug a tunnel and kidnapped your man in hopes of forcing him to steal weapons from your armory."

"My word! What a nefarious scheme." Grover looked to Armstrong. "Is this true?"

The quartermaster, who clearly had improved much at lying, said, "Unequivocally. Everything the marshal said is true."

That gave the Major-General pause, as if for just the briefest of moments he considered what his previous beliefs would have caused, then he shrugged it off. "Well, then, no harm, no foul." He turned to leave. "Carry on."

Armstrong and Tuck together grabbed Forrest before he could enact his beliefs on Grover. Mrs. Armstrong bit her knuckle.

When Forrest calmed down, they stood looking at each other. Dust, slime, and residue covered every spot on their clothes, faces, and bodies.

"Well we're quite a sight, aren't we?" Forrest suggested.

No one disagreed.

Jonas Armstrong turned to his wife and smirked. "You know what would be wonderful right now?"

Mrs. Armstrong pleaded, "Don't say it, Jonas."

"A good bat—"

The lawmen didn't let him finish that sentence.

# SEVENTEEN
## SINKING TO THE LEVEL OF DEMONS: PART I

Drowned Horse
September, 17th 1871

LEVI FORREST, SHERIFF OF THE TOWN OF
Drowned Horse in the Arizona territory, surveyed his
domain from the chair he propped up against the front of
his office and jail. What he saw, he liked.

When he arrived six years ago, he might as well have
still had peach fuzz on his nuts. There was no town, just a
saloon. There were hardly any settlers, just angry natives.
There was no garrison of armed soldiers keeping the tribes
at bay, just some tired and hungry volunteers.

However, there was still a curse, and until it was gone,
there'd never be peace. But that Sunday afternoon, it was as
peaceful as the town ever got.

The Fenskis, newly arrived in Drowned Horse, served as
preacher and teacher. He, Pawel, doing the lord's work, and
she, Klara, the state's. They stood with their teenage daughter, Martha, in front of the newly finished dual-purpose
church and school, which in Forrest's mind blew apart the
whole separation of church and state thing in the constitu-

tion. Building property was an expensive endeavor, though, and why have a building you only used on Sundays and holidays sit empty the rest of the time? If the town reached a certain number of ankle-biters to make it worthwhile to have two buildings, they'd discuss it then.

Other people strolled down Main Street that pleasant afternoon. Unlike many parts of Arizona, the Verde Valley cooled quickly in the fall. A little higher altitude. A little more vegetation. A nice mountain range to one side. Of course, winter wouldn't be far off, but then those were more often mild, too. Farther up north, Prescott or the Mogollons, would see deep snow. Even with the couple bad spells it'd had, Drowned Horse weathered them all.

"Weathered," Forrest chuckled to himself.

"Who ya talking to, boss?"

Deputy William Ragsdale came out of the office. His protégé was lean, had light brown hair, and sported the beginnings of what might be, someday, a serious mustache. It'd never come close to the ones Marshal Bandimere grew, but the young man had potential.

"Just musins', that's all. Hey, ain't ya supposed to be already out on patrol?"

Ragsdale slowly pushed the sheriff's hat down over his face. "I left about an hour ago. You're dreaming, old man."

Forrest listened to the retreating boot steps and didn't lift his hat back up until they'd faded away.

Will had grown since his "angry" years, as the sheriff called them. He still occasionally rushed into situations, relying more on quick reflexes instead of quick wits, but with his daughter, Trina, making it to two-years old, he calmed a bit. He'd do anything to protect his wife, Sarah, and that little girl.

Owner stepped out from *his* domain, the Sagebrush Saloon. The sounds of music and rabblerousing floated around him like a barkeep's perfume. He, too, studied the street, his wandering gaze inevitably landing on Forrest.

"Fine day, isn't it?"

The sheriff agreed. "Fine day, indeed. Things okay in there?"

Owner stretched, working kinks out of his muscles. Only a couple years his senior, in many ways he seemed much, much older. Maybe the fact that he preferred shaving his head bald led to that feeling, or that he only went by Owner, saying that was the only name he'd ever gone by. He was the first Anglo to build in the area. Built a saloon in the middle of nowhere. Kept it running against all odds until a town could form around it. He knew more about the Verde Valley and the curse than anyone.

Forrest had the honor to call him friend.

Owner answered Forrest's question. "Oh, sure. I've got one of the girls working the bar for the moment since she's not taking customers right now."

"Ah."

To make sure Owner's upstairs ladies didn't end up getting in "that" way too often, they'd take a certain week off each month. Mostly it worked though occasionally Forrest had been required to find a family to place a newborn with. There were enough settlers in the valley now that finding a couple who'd lost a child or wanted a sibling for one they already had wasn't difficult. If the mother had a fair guess as to who the father was, and if turned out to be the husband half of one of those settlers, Forrest possessed a certain skill in forceful persuasion that allowed him to place the child where it rightly belonged.

And so the citizenry grew. They'd come to trust him, and Will, to keep them safe from the curse. They trusted Camp Verde far more to keep them safe from the Wiipukepaya and Apache, since Forrest decided he no longer desired to get between clashing cultures. He knew too many good Indians, even called a few of them *Kiiyíi*, and just as many bad settlers. He'd still take down anyone who endangered his people, but forceful diplomacy was another important skill around there.

General Crook, that bastard, seemed to enjoy his job,

though. Too much. The battles increased. Thus, the raids increased in retaliation. Forrest felt it coming to a head, and he didn't like the future he saw. He knew what other states had done to curtail the "Indian Threat," and the notion made him sick. When Forrest first came to the valley, over 6000 natives occupied it. The number had been cut in half or more.

But since he had extra time by not getting involved in those troubles, it allowed him to focus on other things.

"Any luck on the tome?" Owner asked.

"Some. The drawings Will brought back from that cave helped, but there's still a lot we don't know."

The Verde Valley curse was not some whim of the gods, but the anger of one specific one.

The locals called him Noqoìlpi the Gambler, and he was every bit as bad as the legends say. What Forrest and Owner had gathered so far, from those even willing to mention his name, was that once upon a time, Noqoi made a bunch of other gods really angry when he enslaved an entire civilization by cheating at cards, or something like that. They sent a Navajo warrior to beat him at his own game, and exiled Noqoi south, where he was free to do the same thing to the Mexicans, if he so wanted to. Noqoi held a grudge, though.

At some point, Noqoi came back to Arizona territory and placed a curse on the land to the effect that no one who settled there would ever know a peaceful life. And he wasn't kidding, either. Demons, ghosts, monsters, beings from other worlds, you name it. If there is a legend or myth in any culture, it'd come to life.

Since Forrest arrived to the area, he'd been the sentinel against Noqoi's curse, a position that the gambler god took some offense at. More than once the sheriff had been targeted, only barely escaping each time. But after losing a bet, Noqoi was forced to turn over a bound journal that supposedly told the whole story of his curse and how to break it.

The god had failed to mention that the story had been

written in his own language, the language of the gods of the First World, the realm only reachable by surviving a dip in the poisonous waters of Montezuma's Well.

Since that wasn't going to happen anytime soon, Owner, Will, and Forrest took turns trying to decipher the words. Forrest sent Will to visit a cave that had drawings alongside some of those same words, and that led to translations of a few others. But ultimately, they were no closer to unlocking Noqoi's secrets and breaking his curse.

Owner walked over to Forrest and placed a hand on his shoulder. "We'll get there."

"Yup, that's what you hired me for."

Forrest became sheriff even before there was a town to protect. Whereas others balked at the idea of a curse or nightmares made real, Forrest had an intimate knowledge of them from his childhood. Upon being offered the role, he accepted as to make amends for what he couldn't do, wouldn't do, back then.

The stagecoach arrived right on schedule. Meant things were probably calm outside of town, too. Several passengers disembarked, the driver gathering their luggage from on top and the back. He'd also have letters and packages, maybe even some supplies for the mercantile.

"Time to go to work," Owner said, and he went to check in guests and receive deliveries.

One fellow who stepped out from the prairie schooner had the style and look of a gambler. Forrest grumbled a little. Even human gamblers knotted his stomach these days, as their craft often led to bar fights, shootings, or mischief.

The man caught Owner's attention. "Excuse me, sir," he said with a Southern lilt Forrest couldn't tell was real or affected. "Might Ah inquire if this is *the* famous Sagebrush Saloon where the best of gamblers gather?"

Owner ran a hand over his bald pate. "Well, I don't know if I'd say 'famous,' and I certainly wouldn't lead you to believe that the 'best' gamble here, but I run an honest faro game."

That seemed to please the man whose sly smile widened. "Thank you. Ah've traveled a long way to come here. It's exactly what Ah've been looking for." The gambler tipped his hat.

Before he stepped into the saloon, though, the gambler paused and studied the sky, as if expecting to find something there.

Forrest followed his trajectory and spotted a dot very high up that moved like a bird. The sheriff stood up and cupped a hand over his eyes as to get a better look, realized how silly that was since it actually did nothing to help him see the object better. He walked inside the office to get a spy glass. By the time he returned, it was gone, whatever it was. That gambler bore further consideration, and he'd follow up by having dinner with him at the Sagebrush that night.

Only, Levi Forrest, sheriff of the town of Drowned Horse in the Arizona territory, wouldn't make it back in time for dinner that evening.

Two hours later

"SHERIFF! SHERIFF FORREST! IT'S WILL. HE'S IN bad way!"

Forrest sprinted from his office at someone's call. A group of citizens surrounded the deputy, who lay prone in the center of the street. Owner, hearing the commotion, already sped out of the Sagebrush to join the crowd. The seamstress, Océane Giraud, knelt down and lifted Will's head into her lap.

"What happened?" Forrest demanded.

Chalker, the smithy, said, "Don't know. He walked into

town this way, draggin his feet, and collapsed before reaching your office."

The young man had bruises all over his face, a few already turning a nasty shade of black and purple. His clothes were torn in places and brambles clung to his pants. Will still breathed, but there was a rasp to it suggesting a broken rib or punctured lung.

Owner said, "I'll get the doctor," and left.

"No horse?" Forrest looked around but didn't see Blaze, Will's horse, anywhere.

Will managed to crack open one swollen eye and muttered, "D-ead."

Forrest crouched so his deputy wouldn't have to speak loud. "Are you able to tell me what happened, son?"

The eye closed, as if it helped him have strength to talk. "Found...tracks. Several horses...followed."

The sheriff knew that was a damned fool thing to do. Those tracks could have been anything from natives to outlaws. If there were tracks where there should've been none, he was supposed to come back for him. There was that impetuousness Forrest couldn't get out of Will. Not the time to scold him, though. Might never be the time, unless the Doc got there quickly.

"And? Whadda ya find?"

"Am-bush. J-Jimmy Ket-tle."

Owner dragged Doc Gedeon Rosen through the mass of people and bent down to take control of his patient. He placed a funnel to Will's chest and listened to him breathe for a moment. When he straightened, he pronounced, "Doesn't sound like he popped the lung, but there's something pressing against it. A rib, I'd wager." He gingerly felt Will's neck. "Bruised his throat, too. But until I get him on my table, I won't know if there's internal bleeding." Doc stood and instructed everyone. "We're going to need to lift him, but carefully. We can't take a chance on a sharp rib stabbing that lung. Let's get a pallet of some sort to carry the boy on."

The town threw together a gurney quickly and slid Will onto it. Someone was sent to fetch Sarah and to keep an eye on Trina.

Forrest couldn't do anything but watch.

"Did I hear him say Jim Kettle?" Owner looked over to the wanted board where posters hung in front of the jail. Right in the middle, the biggest announcement and largest reward was for James Kettle, leader of the Crab Rock Gang.

Forrest stepped up onto the porch and studied the notice. It claimed that Kettle was responsible for four wagon hold ups, three murders after bar fights, and at least suspected of one weapons raid at Fort Bowie while the majority of the soldiers were out on patrol. No one was killed in that raid, but Forrest had it on good authority that Kettle's gang had killed several Natives and Mexicans without mercy and savaged their women before killing them, as well. Number One on the marshal's list of wanted criminals, somehow Kettle always escaped capture.

Owner slid in next to Forrest and asked, "What are you going to do?"

Levi tore down the wanted poster, rolled it into a ball, and handed it to Owner.

"I'm going to bring Kettle in."

"Alone? I think not." He faced his friend. "You need a posse and don't think for a moment I don't know why you've been taking all my empty whiskey bottles. Your eyes aren't that good anymore. Or is it that your hand isn't that steady?" Forrest growled, but the barkeep held up a finger. "Don't take that tone with me. You know this. It's exactly what you'd tell that kid laying on the sawbone's table right now. Don't go off half-cocked."

Forrest knew that Owner was right, but he'd be damned if he would risk any of the settlers. He needed professional help. Since this wasn't some mythical monster, but one of the human kind, he knew where to get it. Tuck was too far away. The tracks would be gone by tomorrow, but Camp Verde should have great trackers.

He turned away from Owner and went to get his horse.

———

CAMP VERDE NEVER PUT ANY FANFARE WHEN Forrest arrived. The camp's acting commander, Lieutenant Griffin Creswell, tolerated the sheriff only because keeping the peace in the closest town to the encampment meant he could focus more on the Indian problem and less on the settlers. Forrest knew this, understood it, and thus it galled him to come to them for their help.

He got down off of Roland, his horse, and walked up to the commander's office. He knocked and was told to enter. Inside, Creswell sat behind his large desk, discussing supply issues with his quartermaster, Jonas Armstrong, a man Forrest knew and liked.

More than liked.

Sometimes used.

A fit, but mild, man, Armstrong along with his wife, Yvonne, knew about the curse and had been drawn into it on more than one occasion. That intimate connection resulted in Armstrong immediately tensing at Forrest's appearance in his superior's office.

"Sheriff Forrest," Creswell said, his tone indicating he did not appreciate the sight of him, "To what do I owe the interruption? Can you not see I'm dealing with important matters?"

The sheriff's knee-jerk reaction was to tell Creswell exactly what he could do with his 'important matters,' but then he remembered the sight of Will, and he stilled his tongue. Forrest took off his hat and held it respectfully.

"Listen, I know that Grover left you in charge while he's out on tour with Crook. It's a big ask, but I need your help. It's James Kettle. We have a line on him. I don't have the manpower to take him in, but you do."

Creswell raised an eyebrow. "Well, the Army does owe him for the raid, don't we?" He couldn't help but twist the blade, though. "Too much for you and that deputy of yours?"

Forrest tightened the grip on his hat. "That's the thing. Kettle ambushed Will alone and now he's bein' treated at Doc Rosen's."

Armstrong gasped. "Is he going to live?"

Shrugging, Forrest said he didn't know.

Clearly sensing he had an opportunity, Creswell stroked his beard. "If I send a company with you, what do I get in return?"

That caught Forrest off guard. "In return? The man is wanted not only by the territory, but also the government. *Your* government."

"I mean, soldiers cost money. We're here to protect the settlers against the Reds, not as your personal posse."

Fearing what he'd say next, Forrest turned to leave, but then Armstrong spoke up.

"I think what the acting commander is saying, Sheriff, is that it'd be nice to give the enlisted a free night at the Sagebrush?" The clerk looked back and forth between the two men.

Forrest swallowed. "No women. No gambling. Just booze and food."

Creswell leaned forward. "For the lower ranks, certainly. But as their leader, an exception could be made?" The letch practically drooled imagining carnal delights.

Armstrong tilted his head just slightly so Forrest would understand. If he wanted to bring this outlaw in, then this would be the only way to do it.

"Fine," Forrest agreed through gritted teeth. "But we need to leave soon."

Creswell stood and reached for his sword and gun hanging on the wall. "I'll get my men ready. It's fine motivation for them. Two rewards. One for Kettle's head." He turned to look Forrest directly in the eyes. "And one for you finally understanding your place."

As Forrest waited and fumed next to Roland, Mrs.

Armstrong came to join him. Golden hair pinned up, her accent revealed her German ancestry. She'd come to America specifically to marry Jonas, an arrangement Forrest never understood, but they worked well together. Her adventurous streak dragged Jonas out of his shell, while he tempered her wild side when necessary. They clearly loved each other.

Sometimes, Forrest wished he'd found a love like it.

Or her, first.

"Levi," Vonnie said, anxiously, "I just heard from Jonas about poor Will. Is there anything I can do?"

Normally, he tried to keep the Armstrongs out of any Drowned Horse business so they wouldn't be discovered as spies, but under the guise of not being too obvious about it, he'd arranged for Sarah Ragsdale and her to meet occasionally. To no one's surprise, Creswell disregarded women capable of anything but providing pleasure and creating problems. So, it was through their relationship, cultivated naturally, that Vonnie and Sarah passed secret messages back and forth.

"Sarah might need help, actually. No idea how long he'll be lame after this." He uttered a curse—something Vonnie never judged him for. "If he even survives."

Vonnie reached for the sheriff's hand, took it in her both of hers, and showed him the sympathy and affection he sorely needed. "Of course I will. I'll make plans to head right over."

He nodded once, grateful to her.

Creswell led six men to the front of the camp. The men smiled ruefully, suggesting the Lieutenant might not have told them the exact terms of the arrangement. "Shall we hunt?"

Forrest would deal with the situation he'd created later after he resolved the one Kettle had. Mounting his horse, he led Roland out of the camp to follow Will's patrol pattern in hopes of finding the Crab Rock Gang's hideout.

THE GANG GOT THEIR NAME NOT FROM THE
location of their camp, but where Jimmy Kettle made his
first kill. On his way to Utah, young Kettle's wagon train
was attacked by bandits. He watched in horror from the
shadows as their leader gunned down his father and several
other men. The boy, barely twelve, stayed hidden as the
outlaws raped then killed the women, including his mother.
In the middle of the night, when the gang had their fill of
greed and lust and fell asleep, Jimmy moved silently in the
dark, slitting the lead bandit's throat, and shooting the
other outlaws before they could reach their guns.

As he buried his family's bodies, they say that was the
last time Kettle wept. After that, Kettle set about to do unto
others as had been done to him. He provided much the
same end to settlers heading west, as if to say, "This was my
fate. Now it's also yours."

Forrest found his deputy's tracks and led the cavalry
soldiers on the same pattern he knew the young man took
each patrol. They wove south past several farms and even a
few Wiipukepaya settlements. They went deeper into the
foothills of the Verde Mountains that separated the Verde
Valley from the Prescott Valley. Forrest already suspected
that the trail would take them to one of the canyons that
snaked out across the front range.

When they lost the tracks the first time, Creswell said
nothing. That type of thing happened. They doubled back,
picked up the trail once more and lost it again. That time,
Creswell chastised Forrest for being a bad tracker, so he put
his best man on it.

As the sun descended, though, his best man also
reported that the scent had not just gone cold, but vanished.

That's when Forrest worried that maybe something more
than just a clever outlaw was at work there.

Upon returning to where Will and Kettle's marks
vanished, Forrest explored the area not with his weak eyes,

but with keen senses born from years of looking for the macabre, the magical, the cursed.

Creswell stared down at him. "What do you think you're doing, Sheriff? The trail's gone. We'll head back and try again tomorrow."

Forrest held up a hand and listened. He felt the warm breeze as it cooled. He walked forward, holding his hands out adjacent to his body, letting the Arizona air play over them. But he didn't look with his eyes, since they could be deceived.

Will's eyes could spot deception, too. He figured it right away, actually. Forrest smiled. Maybe he had taught him well, after all.

"That's it, Forrest. We're—"

The acting commander's voice must've stopped because Forrest disappeared before his wide-opened eyes.

Forrest looked around. There was something familiar about the illusion, something that itched his brain, but he couldn't place it. The boulders which must have taken a great effort to move were polished to almost mirror smoothness. They reflected off each other, giving the impression of being one large formation, not several individual ones. It was reminiscent of funhouse mirrors, or magician tricks...or something else.

*A similar illusion. A small boy. A chicken?*

He almost had it, the thing. The memory buried deep in his mind. He needed to pull at it, to yank it free, but then the first gunshot rang out, and Forrest ran back to the company.

"It's smoke and mirrors. Kettle's hideout is through there, but they already spotted me. It's going to be fish in a barrel if we go through that way."

Creswell considered the problem. "They'll be climbing up to high points, so ascending the hill and trying to drop down on them will be difficult."

One of his company said, "Plus, we don't know how far back this canyon goes."

The Lieutenant snapped his fingers. "You touched upon it, Sheriff. Smoke and mirrors. We'll smoke them out."

That was indeed an idea. Air had drawn him into the opening, meaning that it flowed toward the hideout, not away. Forrest agreed.

Creswell set his men to the task of finding or chopping down as much wood as they could gather quickly. Night wanted control of the sky, not leaving them much time. As is always possible, Kettle might have another way out, but if the smoke didn't drive them forward, the cavalry could then enter the canyon and find out where they went.

The bonfire they created held night at bay. Using branches that still had leaves on them, the posse pushed the smoke toward the illusionary entrance and watched in disbelief as it vanished. Higher they stoked the flames. Thicker they billowed the smoke.

Finally, from behind the polished stones, came the first sounds of coughing.

A man rushed out, guns blazing, but his watery eyes could hit nothing, especially with the brightness of the fire. The soldiers killed him cleanly. The second outlaw, smarter than the first, walked out coughing in one hand and surrendering his gun with the other. Five outlaws stepped forward, but none were James Kettle.

Forrest grabbed one of the men who'd been placed in irons and shook him.

"Where's Kettle?"

The outlaw said nothing.

"Where is he?"

The man grinned.

Forrest pushed him to the ground and looked back at the canyon. Kettle was in there, somewhere, and had figured a way to survive the smoke, or escape out the back.

He started forward, but Creswell grabbed his shoulder.

"Stick with the plan, Sheriff. He'll either come out, or we'll track him in the daylight."

Forrest shrugged off the commander's grip.

"We're too close." He took another step. "I'm too close. If he gets away, I can't..."

"You can't what?" Surprisingly, Creswell spoke with compassion. "Face your deputy? Your town? I know that feeling." He waved his hand to indicate the assembled company of the Army that served under him. "I take these men into danger every day, knowing that some won't return. I have to face their widows or the unspoken accusations of their fellow soldiers. It's the nature of what it means to lead, Sheriff. You can't always win."

"That's good advice there, *Generalisimo*."

The sarcastic voice wasn't any one of Creswell's men.

Forrest spun around, looking for origin of the words, his gun trying to find something to shoot at.

When James Kettle stepped from out of the dark into the firelight, he wasn't alone. Over a dozen men, well-armed, surrounded them.

Kettle had broad shoulders and a wicked shape to his face that recalled gargoyles on cathedral towers. He ordered his men to take the solders' guns and free the men that'd been sent out as bait. When Kettle had Forrest, Creswell, and the rest on their knees, he strutted back and forth in front of his prisoners.

"Well, let's see what we've gots here. A sainted Lieutenant in the royal Army of his holy President. And six disciples." He held his hand up to the side of his mouth, speaking as an aside to one of his men. "I thought there'd be twelve. There were twelve, right? Yeah, I thought so."

Creswell blustered, "You'll not get away with this. Once word gets out of our capture, the whole of General Crook's forces will come for you."

Kettle snorted. "Oh, I'm sure. I've seen that ol' tyrant slaughter a whole group of defenseless Injun women and children over just one of you lot being gunned down. I imagine you're quite right. So, we're not going to kill you, or even keep you very long."

That confused Creswell, but not Forrest.

"You left Will alive to draw me out, didn't you?"

"Correct! First guess, too." He walked over to hover over Forrest. "Ya see, there was this ancient Red, oldest I'd ever seen, and he made me a bet." Kettle spit in front of the sheriff. "Ya wanna know what he bet me?"

Forrest slowly lifted his head until he locked eyes with the outlaw. "Was it somethin' like, you couldn't kill me?"

Kettle's eyes and smile widened, and he pointed at Forrest. "Yeah, exactly so. He said there was this one sheriff who couldn't be killed. He'd tried many times himself and never could do it. He said if I killed you, then he'd give me something no other man possessed. A gift that'd make me immortal."

"I suppose that idea that he might be lyin' didn't cross your mind?"

Kettle nodded rapidly. "Indeed, it did." He paced around the fire, which, unattended, had begun to die out. "Then he showed me some stuff, including that mirror rock trick. He showed me some of *his* power, too. And it was real! He could give me the power that'd finally make me able to stop death." He bent at the waist and placed his hands on his knees. "I could finally stop waiting for it…because I'd be beyond it."

Forrest tried to use his forceful diplomacy. "He's usin' you to do what he can't. What he's not allowed to do. You're his patsy and all his gifts have a dark side, one you'd never suspect. It's a trick."

Holding his hand up to his chin, Kettle appeared to think about that revelation. "Tricks, huh? Like how I kept you busy smoking a canyon while we snucks up behind ya alls?"

Kettle's gang chortled at this.

"Or how you immediately came rushing to hunt me down after I gave that pup of yours a beatdown?"

More snickering.

"No, the only one pulling tricks is me." He pointed to his chest. "Me, James Kettle. Soon-to-be master of death." He held his pistol up and danced in a circle around the fire. "It'll be me, the one who brought the mighty Levi Forrest, the one the gods fear, down. Not the other way around." When he stopped dancing, Kettle aimed at Forrest.

Using his forceful persuasion, the sheriff demanded, "Least let me die on my feet, will ya?"

Kettle paused, raised the barrel, and motioned for his men to drag their captive to his feet.

"Thank you."

The outlaw tipped his head. "Least I can do. I'll be a merciful god, once I am one." He reacquired his target from his place on the opposite side of the fire. "I'd say it's nothing personal, since we've never met before now. But clearly you got some sort of problem with that old Red, so I guess it is, kinda." Kettle pulled back the hammer of his Peacemaker. "Sorry about this."

As Kettle's finger slid in front the trigger, Creswell's soldier training got the best of him, and he launched himself at Kettle with lightning speed, taking the bullet meant for the sheriff.

"No!" Forrest shouted.

Creswell's men, following his example, jumped up and bull-rushed the gang. Forrest had no idea how they'd freed themselves, since he was focused on Kettle, but then Kettle's men had been so focused on him, they were caught unawares.

Even outnumbered, the soldiers fought valiantly, some wrestling away guns and taking down their opponents.

Someone stepped up behind Forrest and whispered over the cacophony, "Don't turn around."

"Vonnie? I mean, Mrs. Armstrong?"

"Yes, and Jonas, as well. I, well, both of us, had a bad feeling, so we followed you." She worked at his bonds. "We stayed far enough back that we saw Kettle and his men sneaking up. I wanted to warn you, but Jonas wisely suggested we wait and approach at the right moment."

Forrest should have suspected that. Certainly from Mrs.

Armstrong. He spotted Armstrong gathering guns from fallen killers and tossing them to his fellow men.

Mrs. Armstrong cut through the ropes and handed Forrest her little dragoon pistol. "Sorry it's not more."

"Thank you. It's enough." She blushed, his praise pleasing her. Then Forrest looked for Kettle, who'd vanished.

He knew where he'd gotten to.

Stepping behind the illusionary rocks, Forrest entered the Crab Rock Gang's canyon.

———

THE FALL MOON BARELY ILLUMINATED THE PATH Forrest tread thanks to the heavy smoke that still lingered in the air. He covered his mouth with his sleeve, but kept the dragoon ready. He stepped slowly and carefully, moving behind boulders or trees, seeking any movement, questioning every shape.

When he rounded a turn in the canyon, though, he discovered a row of lanterns lighting the walkway forward. Great effort had been taken to clean the area up from detritus. Forrest could have been walking up to a wealthy rancher's homestead. Items—the spoils of the gang's deeds, such as furniture and statues, even a piano—had been arranged to give the hideout the feel of being just a normal residence. The path ended at a small house where James Kettle sat in a rocker, a Sharps rifle lying across his lap.

"Welcome, Levi. Can I call you Levi?"

Forrest aimed at the outlaw, coughing as he spoke. "James Kettle, as duly elected sheriff of Drowned Horse—"

"Oh, please. Stop that." He waved the words away. "You know you're not here to arrest me. You're here to kill me."

Forrest cocked his head. "No, why would you think that? Did Noqoi tell you that?"

Kettle stood. "Sort of. Ya see? You only got half the bet right." He stepped down from the porch, but didn't draw the rifle. "He did bet that I couldn't kill you. Said you'd always come up with some interesting way out of it, in the end. Said that you and I were quite alike in that way."

"Stop right...there," Forrest demanded.

But Jimmy kept walking. "He said, though, his bet was on you. He thought if you did get the drop on me, you'd kill me in cold blood." Kettle let the rifle fall to his feet. "That with no one looking," Kettle twirled with hands held high, indicating the emptiness of the canyon, "that you'd seek revenge for what I did to that pup of yours. Oh, did he live, by the way? They made sure to leave him off just outside of town so he might reach you before he died."

Forrest growled, though it cost him in hacks. "Will's stronger...than you thought. He'll live...all right."

Kettle clapped his hands. "Excellent! That means I can take another crack at him later, unless, what did you call him? Noqoi? Unless Noqoi is correct, and you are going to gun a defenseless man down." He held his arms out. "So, what's it going to be, Levi? Because if you don't kill me, I'm going to come back for you. And the pup. And whoever that skirt was that freed you. I'll come for her and rip that pretty dress off of her." Kettle gnashed his teeth. "And I'll bite into her flesh." Waggling his eyebrows, he drawled, "I'll make *you* a wager, that she'll love it."

Forrest's grip on the dragoon tightened as he coughed. Sweat beaded on his forehead. Had Kettle just moved? He straightened his arm, tried to hold the gun steady.

*Is he right? Am I gonna have to...*

"Nice piece. The gun, I mean. Seems to be getting heavy there, Levi. You best decide soon. That smoke y'all sent in here makes it hard to breathe, don't it?"

Forrest coughed more, barely able to stand still. Now he knew for certain Kettle had gotten closer. Forrest stepped back, wiped his forehead with his free hand, keeping his watering eyes on the outlaw.

"How are you..."

"Not affected by the smoke? Well, that's because I'm not James Kettle."

Kettle blurred, and Noqoi, the gambler god, stood in his place.

A noise behind him caused Forrest to reflexively spin around. He fired even before he finished turning, but...

James Kettle pulled the trigger on his pistol three times.

All three bullets hit the sheriff in the chest.

Levi felt each one as it struck. He'd been shot before, but this time it didn't feel like bullets, but more like lightning bolts passing through him and exiting out the back. He dropped the dragoon and stumbled backwards. Reflexively, he tried to raise his gun arm, but realized it held no weapon. He reached to his side, but no gun waited there either. He fell to his knees, looking for a gun, any weapon to make sure he didn't go alone, but everything had grown dark. He tried to draw in breath, but all he got was a wheeze.

That made him think of Will. The doctor had told him that his lungs were okay. Good. The boy would live. Live to take care of his family. No so in this case, Levi's primal logic told him. Clearly, Kettle'd punctured a lung, maybe both. He could feel his heart beating hard, trying to get blood that was seeping from his chest to the important parts of his body. His brain. His punctured lungs. Levi gasped in short bursts, each time the pain dulling as his brain stopped sending him messages that he was dying. He already knew that. He didn't need a brain to tell him that. He knew what death looked like. He'd seen it almost his whole life. His parents, slaughtered by some sort of a water creature while traveling through Louisiana. Leapt right out of the swamp where'd they'd camped for the night. Levi ran as it feasted on his mother, knowing that it would eventually fill and come for him. He wished he'd had the same courage Kettle had shown on the bandits that killed *his* family and took revenge on the beast. But he didn't. Running had been what he had been taught. So he did. He ran. He kept running until he reached the Arizona territories and finally found a home. Kettle. Yeah, Kettle had shot him. Not some being from another world, or another reality, or from a fairy tale book.

Mortal.

Just as

he was.

Mortal.

Kettle'd

die,

One day,

too.

Just like

he

was.

Levi Forrest stared at Kettle—a mere second after he'd been shot—and coughed, spraying blood from his mouth.

"Fuck...you..."

He collapsed after that. His eyes still open, he watched Noqoi approach.

The old god bent over him and snarled, "This is my land. My revenge! I'll kill anyone who gets in my way."

No longer able to keep his eyes open, the sheriff of Drowned Horse closed them and hung up his star.

———

THE LAST OF COMPANY K ENTERED THE CANYON after finishing the Crab Rock Gang. Of James Kettle, there was no sign.

Vonnie saw Forrest first, screamed and ran, sliding in next to him. She felt his cold face and hands. She held his hand to her own face, as if she could bring warmth to it. Her husband reached for her, pulling her away, but she didn't want to let go of the hand. She had to heal him. She had to keep him warm.

Only three soldiers survived, but none of Kettle's men had. Even Jonas had joined the fray, shooting two outlaws.

He stayed with his wife to watch over their friend's body as the rest went to fetch the undertaker from Drowned Horse.

Jonas kept looking at the body, expecting Forrest to stand up at any moment. To tell them it'd been a ruse to catch Kettle off guard. But the sheriff didn't move. Regardless of how Jonas wordlessly begged him, no matter how much he prayed to an uncaring god that let such a curse happen, he didn't move. Instead, he consoled his grieving wife.

When she calmed a bit, Jonas took off his jacket and covered the sheriff with it. It was respectful, and it helped him stop waiting for him to get up.

They came in the small hour: a procession led by Owner.

The bald man froze upon seeing the covered body. He held his arm up to his eyes and wept. His feet scraped the gravel as he walked forward, his legs acting on instinct, but no will left in his soul. Behind him, Adoniram Craddick, the undertaker, led a horse and cart. Several other people, who Jonas barely knew, filed in behind them, along with two of the three surviving soldiers from the night before. The third had diverted to Camp Verde to inform command through helio of their fallen leader.

Ram returned Jonas' jacket.

"I have a blanket."

Jonas nodded numbly.

Together, Owner, Ram, and the soldiers hoisted Forrest's body into the cart.

Owner walked over to Vonnie and Jonas, his eyes watery and red.

"Any sign of—"

Vonnie grabbed Owner and held him tightly. He hugged her back, and they cried together. Jonas looked over at Ram who also wiped away tears.

Jonas told the undertaker, "We must gather the dead outside."

Ram said he'd take the soldiers and Creswell back on that trip as the cart was just big enough for them. He'd leave the dead outlaws, and if there was anything left to claim, he'd come back for them later.

Jonas then wrapped his arm over his wife's shoulder and, together, they left that place of evil.

---

EVERY CITIZEN OF DROWNED HORSE CAME TO LEVI Forrest's funeral. They knew they owed him a debt that could never be repaid. Marshal Tucker Bandimere came with the "other" sheriff John Behran, who nobody actually knew because once he'd heard the word "curse," Behran stayed as far from the Verde Valley as possible. He didn't seem at all happy that arrangement might change. Even the Governor attended, as did General Crook, and the commanders of Fort McDowell and Fort Apache. Brevet Major-General Cuvier Grover represented Camp Verde, guilt marring his face after being responsible for his acting commander taking a bullet Grover believed he could have avoided had *he* been the one Levi asked for help.

Leaders of the Wiipukepaya, Yavaþé, Tonto Apache, and Apache tribes showed up, as well. Some had fought against him, some alongside him, but they all knew that of any of the *higow'ah*, Levi always kept his word, which was rare amongst the blue eyes. One in particular stood back from the rest. He wore white-man clothes and spoke very good English.

Owner came up to shake his hand when he'd arrived.

"Motha. Good to see you."

The man nodded. "They call me Mojave Charlie now."

Owner gazed at him sideways. "You know Levi preferred to address people by their actual names...when he could pronounce them."

Motha laughed. "Yes, even though he was terrible at it."

"He got better."

Motha raised an eyebrow.

"Well, he didn't start any wars over mistaken words."

That got them both smiling, until they didn't. They hugged.

When Motha excused himself, Tucker walked over. They embraced. "What happens after this?"

Owner shrugged. "Not sure. We'll need a new sheriff." He cast a gaze over to the lawman who'd ridden with Tuck. "I doubt Behran's up to the task."

"Not only that, but we're aiming for statehood and that means making the territory seat a shining beacon for any officials that come from Washington. The governor has him busy escorting dignitaries."

"You want the job?"

Tucker guffawed. "I've already been helping out down here at the cost of my own responsibilities." He unconsciously brushed down his mustache. "You know I'll continue to watch over the Valley until you can find a new protector."

To Owner, that seemed an impossible task. "Let's see how Will recovers. Levi groomed him to take over should this exact thing happen."

"Yeah, but..." They both studied Will who refused to miss the funeral despite the bruising, the bandages, and broken left hand. Sarah, his wife, walked next to him, holding him in her left hand and their daughter Trina's hand in her right. Ram and his wife, Sadie, had taken the other side, practically lifting the young man up as they moved toward the cemetery.

"Levi knew Will had a ways to go but, next to us, he knows more about the curse than anyone. He's got all of Levi's notes and various monsters he'd fought before, and which ones might yet still appear."

Tuck shook his head. "To think, after battling all those creatures, to get gunned down by just some outlaw? That's irony for you."

Owner wasn't sure. Levi had taken on outlaws before. It was the nature of the job. But even a clever bandit like James Kettle didn't strike the barkeep as being smarter than the man who'd secretly raised him as a child. And then there was that way Kettle had hidden the entrance to his canyon. Something bothered Owner about that, like a memory from his past.

Before he could consider the idea further, Ram tugged on his elbow.

"It's time."

Owner said he'd be right along. He closed the doors of the Sagebrush and fell in behind the rest of the mourners.

---

"COURAGE ISN'T JUST STANDING UP TO YOUR fear," Owner began. "It's standing up to your weakness. It's standing up to your friends when they tell you to give in. It's standing up to the night and telling it you're representing the day."

By his estimate, nearly five hundred people filled in and around the Drowned Horse cemetery. Chairs had been given to men like the Governor and his ilk, and one more for Will, who first refused to sit, until Sarah suggested that way he could hold Trina. Even though he was clearly in pain, he accepted the charge.

The rest stood, supporting each other where necessary.

"Sheriff Levi Forrest came here to teach us courage. To teach us what it's like to hold back the night. He showed us that even though we all have demons, we need not let them control us, claim our souls as theirs. In a place where demons sometimes do manifest in the most direct of ways..." Sheriff Behran squirmed at those words. "Levi gave us an example time and again of how we should answer them." Owner wiped a kerchief over his pate. The sun had picked a fine day to reinforce his words. "People often ask, when they hear about the nature of this valley, why any one of us would stay? Why here, when there are far more fertile, far less dangerous places? What makes anyone stay in Drowned Horse?" He chuckled. "It's a question I've asked

myself many a time myself, and I'm sure you have, too."
Owner gazed out over the masses. "I don't know *your*
answers, and mine wavers some days, but I knew Levi's.
When someone asked him why he stayed as protector of a
town that seemed set to kill him, he'd say, 'Because
someone had to.' Someone had to speak for the light.
Someone had to hold the torch of truth up high and make
those demons accountable. Then he'd say he was just crazy
enough to be that person." That got a few laughs and some
renewed sobbing. "So, maybe I do know my answer to that
question. Maybe we all do. And maybe someday we'll all be
called to stand in front of encroaching darkness that
threatens to swallow us." He paused and let everyone hang
for a moment. He hadn't prepared to say this part, but his
gut urged him on.

Owner stepped closer to Levi's coffin and placed a hand
on it. "Here's my answer. To whatever evil waits out there,
to whatever demons hide in the darkness, to the very god
who cursed this land, I say to you, I'll see your bet. I'll see
your bet against all of us, regardless of the color of our skin,
regardless of where we came from. I'll see your bet against
all the men, the women, the children who choose to stay in
this cursed land.

"Noqoi, wherever you are, I'll see your bet, and raise
you. I'll raise the bet and say we'll beat your curse one day,
and when that day comes, you won't just be exiled from this
land, we'll send you back down that damned well you slithered out of for good."

Owner slid his palm along the coffin lovingly.

"Because I'm just that crazy, too."

One by one, the citizens of Drowned Horse came up and
placed their hands on Levi's coffin. Some whispered thanks.
Some placed a flower. The natives said a word or two of
prayer to Noqoi's enemies.

Vonnie Armstrong and her husband Jonas stood next to
the coffin for a long moment, looking down at it, almost as
if they could see the man inside of it. As they turned to walk

away, Owner noticed that Jonas openly wept in view of everyone.

---

THE ARMSTRONGS WALKED INTO THE SAGEBRUSH after Levi had been lowered and the grave filled. They called Owner over but had a hard time meeting his eyes.

"What?" he asked.

"We've been—" Vonnie started.

"I've," Jonas corrected. "I've been transferred back to Washington. The new camp commander will be arriving shortly. Vonnie didn't want to leave, but we both agreed this is no place to start a family."

Vonnie's hands covered her midsection. After being so careful for so long, their little tryst in the alien spaceship had been ill-timed.

Owner congratulated them both. "That's wonderful, and yes, of course, you should get out of here while you can." He hugged her and shook Jonas's hand.

Still embarrassed, Vonnie said, "I'm sorry we can't be your spies anymore. There were a couple of the soldiers who had either experienced the curse, or were willing to believe in it, but the entire company is being transferred out."

"At least, what's left of us," her husband added. "Everyone's being assigned somewhere else, and it'll be all new men coming soon."

Owner understood. Soldiers unprepared for what they'd encounter on their new tour of duty. "I'll do my best to plant some seed among the recruits when they get here. They'll already have enough to deal with seeing as Crook is stepping up his endgame."

Word had hit town that the General had ordered an increase of soldiers at all the camps and forts, and that talk of reservations in the Valley became more of a reality. The natives didn't need a curse. They already had one with Crook.

The couple said their goodbyes, not staying for a drink, even on the house. They had packing to do. Vonnie hugged Owner one more time and left with a tear on her cheek.

But other people drank. They raised their glasses multiple times throughout the evening to Sheriff Levi Forrest. They told tales to the visitors of the various creatures he'd fought off. Someone had even composed an impromptu song and had the whole bar singing along.

It was the type of evening filled with entertainment that Levi would sometimes tell Owner that he'd grown up around. About growing up Romani. Traveling with his family to perform at such wakes, spinning tales and singing songs of the dead person, whether they be based in truth or complete myths.

To the citizens of Drowned Horse, on that cursed land, they knew such stories were actually one and the same.

# EIGHTEEN
## SINKING TO THE LEVEL OF DEMONS: PART TWO

Arizona Territory
December, 1871

DEPUTY WILLIAM RAGSDALE CONSIDERED THE sheriff's badge mocking him from the desk of his dead boss. He swore it even laughed at him, but then realized the noise came from his daughter, Trina, playing back by the jail cells. His wife Sarah, hovering anxiously near his side, took a tentative step closer to him and laid a hand on his arm.

"What are you going to do?"

"Do I have a choice?"

Sarah's eyes watered, but she refused to let them become actual tears.

"Of course you do. You can wait for Owner to appoint a new sheriff. You don't need to rush into this."

Will thought about that, but the longer they waited, the more likely Jimmy Kettle's Crab Rock Gang would come to town. They were drunk on blood, for the moment, but how long would that last?

At Forrest's funeral, Will noticed the gazes. The unasked

questions about whether he would be up to the task of filling the first sheriff of Drowned Horse's shoes. Even Will understood he wasn't at his best, still healing from Kettle's ambush.

*When they turned me into bait.*

Will flexed his left hand, which sent a shot of pain up his arm. He wouldn't be able to do much with it, but his plan, Forrest's plan, wouldn't take that much strength.

Levi Forrest, knowing that his days as guardian of the Verde Valley would ultimately result in his death, had for six years catalogued every fight he'd been in, be it human or other. That book was to be Will's bible when he took over as sheriff. None of them thought it'd be so soon. But that was death, wasn't it? Especially there. One could never predict it.

Trina emerged from the back and sidled up to her daddy. She hugged his leg; her ever-present rag doll hanging from her tight, little palm. He smiled down at her, his precious angel, and made his decision.

"I have to protect her." He picked up the badge with conviction. "I have to protect all of you. I have to see justice done." He stood and held his wife by her shoulders, staring deep into her eyes. "None of you will be safe until I do."

Will left them at the jail and walked over to the Sagebrush. Owner had a mixed expression when Will entered wearing the badge.

"You're going to do it, then?" the bald man asked.

"Yeah, I need to see it through. Wherever it takes me."

The barkeep sighed. The saloon was mostly empty. The last few months had seen a lot of change come over the Verde Valley. Crook had pushed through and gotten the Government to assign a reservation to the Yavapai and Apaches. Working out of Camp Verde, Camp McDowell, and Camp Whipple, he'd forced every last native into a few square miles. The pushback had been fierce. Many of the locals stayed home guarding what was theirs, trying to keep their heads down during that time.

Taking advantage of that was James Kettle, notorious outlaw and the one who'd murdered Sheriff Forrest, Will's spiritual father.

Owner continued to wipe the counter as he spoke. "Levi took a company with him to capture Kettle, and you know how that turned out."

Will wouldn't be deterred. "I won't need an army. Just me and Ram."

That got Owner's attention. "Now, wait a minute. Why do you need to get our undertaker involved?"

"He's already involved," Will countered, his anger growing. He pounded a fist on the bar top. "We're all involved. Only...most people here just want to hide, pretending like things aren't getting worse. That the curse isn't getting...I mean, why else would he be... He shouldn't be..." Will tamped down the welling emotions.

*Clear thinking. Use wits. Not anger.*

"Look. One of Levi's plans he used before...it'll work. Kettle isn't even bothering to hide his location now. Crook isn't doing anything about him because he's got Indians on the brain. I *have* to do this, Owner. *I* have to."

Owner leaned across the counter, conspiratorially. "Tell me the plan."

Will did, even though he wished the enigma would just trust him. After some tweaking, Owner gave him his blessing. But before Will left, he reminded the young man, "You're only the second person to wear that." He pointed at the badge. "Don't get blood on it."

"The only blood on this will be Kettle's," he assured Owner, but bravado aside, he knew he'd have a long way to go to live up to the example set before him.

----

ADONIRAM G. CRADDICK NEARLY SWALLOWED HIS mouthful of square nails when the newly christened sheriff poked his head around to the back of his business. He immediately noticed the badge and raised an eyebrow.

"Shaywiff."

Will stepped into the room. "Now don't start that shit up. Don't matter what title they hang on me. We've been on a first name basis since we met."

Lanky but not skeletal, Ram righted himself to his full six-foot-three frame. He examined the project he was abandoning, and then gave his guest his full attention. After setting down his hammer, Ram spit the nails into one hand. The other he offered to Will.

"Yeah, I s'pose I'd never get used to calling you that, anyhow. Offer you some lemonade in the parlor? Sadie just made it this morning."

Will looked down at the item Ram had been working on. "There isn't a rush on that, is there?"

"That?" Ram indicated the coffin. "Nah, just planning ahead. With the Crab Rock Gang around, it pays to have stock."

The statement stung Will visibly, so Ram quickly backtracked. "I mean, not that it'll always stay that way. I'm sure they'll get their comeuppance before long."

Will removed his Stetson and stared at the rim. "Yeah. Sorta why I needed to talk to you."

Drowned Horse's undertaker raised a wary eyebrow at his best friend. "Sounds like I might need to make that drink a bit harder." He opened a clay urn and pulled out a small flask. Ram blew off what Will hoped was only dust. "Whisky?"

---

CRAB ROCK SERVED AS THE BIRTHPLACE OF JIMMY Kettle's legend. It's where the future outlaw witnessed his family slaughtered by bandits and where he, in return, got his revenge on them. The red stone caves that ran under the crab claw-shaped monolith went back miles, people said. If there was a way out the back, though, no one had ever returned to speak of it.

The formation sat on Wiipukepaya land. Kettle traded food and money to the Indians for the right to claim the caves as his own. Starved and desperate as they'd become, they didn't care if one group of *higow'ah* killed another. While the natives still considered the area sacred, between the curse and Crook, they surrendered the area to Kettle without fuss.

Kettle studied military tactics and knew how to run patrols around their perimeter. They patrolled in pairs, in a pattern that crisscrossed each other so if a team wasn't seen at the appointed time, an alarm went up. Kettle had stolen enough money to draw plenty of men. He had Apaches, freed slaves, escaped convicts, cavalry deserters, and the like. He took care of his men, and they gave him loyalty in return.

But this arrogance made some of those men occasionally sloppy. They seemed to be on the lookout for large numbers: a posse. Crook's army. They kept their focus on the horizon, not right below their feet. It was here, Will saw the opportunity.

They crawled silently like lizards on their bellies, between the scrub brush and the boulders. Holding fast as the patrols approached, moving only when they were out of earshot.

"I'm not so sure 'bout this, Will," Ram whispered, "I'm more used to buryin' dead men, not makin' them."

"We need to take out four, maybe six men to get to the place we need to be," Will returned in hushed tones. "If this works, then the town's safe."

"If? You didn't say nothing 'bout no 'if'!"

Will pushed Ram's face into the sand because his voice crept up more than he thought advisable. Directly into Ram's ear he whispered, "Shush! They'll hear." When he let him back up, Ram spit sand from his lips. "There is always...how do those generals say it? Oh, yeah...a margin of error."

The undertaker shot daggers at Will.

The sound of approaching footsteps signaled the men to roll in separate directions, positioning themselves on either side of a small mound. The other problem with Kettle's patrol pattern was that it'd become well-worn, easy to find, and even easier to lay a trap over.

As soon as the outlaws stepped into the snares, the lawmen pulled them tight, tripping the guards. Will and Ram were on them before they could call out, bringing the butts of their six-guns down decisively on the patrols' heads, knocking them out quietly.

After securing them, Will badgered, "See? That's two we didn't have to kill, Deputy Craddick."

Ram huffed. "Don't call me that."

The second set of outlaws would expect those two in just a few moments, so Will and Ram quickly switched hats and other assorted garb. They got close enough to the next patrol to get the jump on them.

The final set of guards would place Will and Ram too close to the cave's entrance to risk any sort of protracted attack. Fortune struck when that duo stopped by a large rock to roll tobacco. Will and Ram slipped rags over their mouths and slit their throats. They fell without a sound.

Ram stared unblinking as their blood stained the sand.

Will whispered, "Every man in Kettle's gang has blood on his hand. These two are wanted for raping a girl down near Tucson. If we end their reign tonight, the blood on ours might be justified. Ain't this worth it to not have to fear Sadie's gonna end up that way?"

Ram shot back, "Yeah, yeah. That's how you got me out here in the first place, damn snake oil salesman that you are. I just never had to take another man's life before. Give me a moment."

Will gave him all the time they had to spare, which was as long as it took to drag the bodies behind the rock.

Forrest had pulled this stunt early in his career as a lawman. Blowing up the top of a cave and sealing the bad guys in, then coming back to dig them out after getting help.

Will didn't think he'd return that soon. Let Kettle rot in there a few days. If the murderer was even still alive when Will came back, he'd be too hungry and thirsty to put up much of a fight.

The height of the opening was easily thirty feet tall and curved out like a shell in the sand. The rock itself had a plateau above it where two more guards watched the horizon. In front of the cave, in a communal meeting spot, nearly a dozen men hustled around a cook fire, acting frenzied as if they prepared for something. Something big.

That bothered Will, as he feared they planned to ride into Drowned Horse.

While Kettle's gang contained a rogue's gallery, each one meaner than the next, one in particular stood out; a black man the likes of which Will hadn't seen around those parts. Stocky and wearing a stove pipe hat, his ears were pierced with large bones. The man stared into the fire like it contained a whore dancing on a stage. Seeing something he apparently didn't like, he spat into the fire pit, got up, and entered the cave. He didn't reemerge, which gave Will the willies.

Ram exhaled long and hard. "I think that's a black magic man. Like the witch doctors you've read about in those Safari magazines."

"How'd you know that?"

"I'm an undertaker. We know the people in our trade. Voodoo men from Louisiana, like him, specialize in death; creating it, worshiping it, fighting it."

"Fighting it?"

Ram shivered. "It's said they know death's face, and when he comes for you, a voodoo priest can turn him away."

"Why would Kettle have one in his gang?"

"Scare people. Keep his men in line. Who knows? It gives me the creeps, though."

"Me, too. Let's get this over with."

They made their way around the back of Crab Rock and scaled up the side thanks to a series of angled steps. Two guards waited there, looking out at nothing, paying no attention to the lawmen approaching them.

Keeping their hats tilted low, Will and Ram spoke in turn.

"We're here to relieve you."

"Yeah. Boss wants a word."

The guards turned without a concern in the world.

"You're earl—" one started to say, but the sheriff shoved a knife through the bottom of the outlaw's jaw, pinching his mouth shut and driving the tip into his brain.

The second guard, however, was quicker and caught the undertaker's hand before it could plunge in. They grappled, and it soon became evident that he outmatched Ram.

Will moved up fast to wrap an arm around the man's throat, silencing him.

Despite being outnumbered two-to-one, the outlaw held his own. He pushed backwards, dangling Will's feet over the rim. The sheriff looked down briefly at the campfire below him, but God's mercy kept anyone from looking up. Ram pulled them back from the edge. Will tightened his chokehold, but the burly bad guy showed no signs of surrender.

The outlaw twisted the undertaker's knife out his hand. He swung it wildly at Ram, driving him back toward the opposite edge. Suddenly, he turned the knife around and stabbed Will's arm. The lawman let go with a holler and dropped to the ledge. Changing targets, the outlaw looked to send the blade right through Will's heart when a gun went off and a red geyser spurted from the guard's forehead. The sheriff rolled out of the way as the dead man fell forward.

Shouts from below them made it clear everyone had heard the shot.

Moving fast as lightning, Will grabbed a bundle of dynamite from the satchel they'd brought along. Ram did the same with a second bundle. They placed them where Will predicted an explosion could bring a whole cave down.

After lighting the fuses, they hopped down the backside like mountain goats. Kettle's men made it around the bend in time to see the duo reach the trail. Bullets bounced against stone. Will and Ram retreated, doing their best to keep cover between them and their pursuers. They returned fire as often as they could.

The explosion, when it came, took the top off of Crab Rock like a volcano. The lawmen didn't get as far enough away from the blast as they wanted and hit the ground hard. Dirt and gravel sprayed over them. Will came up first, spitting sand from his mouth. Ram rolled on the ground, laughing.

The round-up didn't take long. Most of the Crab Rock Gang had gone inside seeking cover, not expecting the whole entrance would come down around them. According to the surviving crew, Jimmy Kettle, including his voodoo man, had been inside when the explosion sealed the cave. Will would return with the 8th to dig up anybody left alive in a few days.

Will's satisfaction in seeing Forrest's plan though to the end kept a smug grin on his face as they escorted the remaining criminals off to jail.

---

DROWNED HORSE GAVE WILL AND RAM A HERO'S welcome. Music wafted from the Sagebrush for the first time in weeks. Owner made the first round of drinks on him, and both men felt duly bound to imbibe.

Sarah and Sadie, upon hearing of their men's return, came rushing over and lavished both lawmen with a public display of affection. Embarrassed, Will blushed, but Ram jokingly asked Owner if he and his wife could use one of the rooms upstairs.

"You takin' to this deputy stuff, after all?" Will ribbed.

Ram gave his new boss a mischievous grin. "If it's all free beer and taking down men like Kettle, then hell yeah, I'll be your partner." He held up his hand as a warning. "Part time, at least. Still got a business to run and all."

Will handed over a tin star he'd grabbed while at the jail. "Let's make it official, then." He settled the crowd and spoke loudly. "Today, we saw the last day of the Crab Rock Gang and the first day of Deputy Adoniram G. Craddick."

The Sheriff pinned the badge on Ram's pocket, and the crowd whooped and hollered. Sadie gave her man a big kiss. Sarah lifted a sleepy Trina onto her daddy's shoulders.

"Now, take good care of our town while I'm escorting these ne'er-do-wells up to Prescott, tomorrow, 'k, Deputy?"

"Sure thing, Sheriff."

They slapped each other on the back, and all was right with the world.

———

SHERRIFF WILLIAM RAGSDALE RETURNED FROM Prescott two days later to find Ram's body scattered all over the middle of the street.

Blood splattered the area surrounding the body like the pattern on a Navajo blanket. Will scanned the street to find pieces of Ram scattered to and fro; a rib over by the water trough, a foot near the porch to Mrs. Giraud's clothing store. As close as Will could guess, a pack of coyotes had ripped his deputy apart.

He couldn't understand why the body rotted in the center of town. Why nobody had moved it.

Signs of chaos marked every building: overturned chairs, broken windows, loose hanging doors. Something had swept through Drowned Horse, costing his best friend his life.

The town's padre, Pawel Fenski, approached Will with a message that turned the Sheriff's blood to ice.

"He said no one was to touch Ram's body." Fenski shook as if the devil himself had told him that.

"Who? Who said that?"

The pastor held the cross around his neck tightly. "Kettle. Jimmy Kettle."

"No." Will shook his head. "No, it can't be."

Fenski said, "Ask anyone. We're all gathered in the Sagebrush. Ask Owner, if he still lives."

Will ran into the salon. Almost everyone that lived in town were huddled together. Will's sudden arrival caused a panic at first, some sure it was Kettle come back to finish the job he'd started.

On the stage, Doc Rosen ministered to Owner who, while alive, had more damaged than Will after Kettle's gang finished with him.

"He fought hard, but Kettle left him alive for some reason. Said he wasn't the one," Rosen told Will. "When he couldn't find you, Kettle said he knew how to bring you to him."

The sheriff scanned the crowd. "Where's Sarah? Trina?"

The pitying looks told Will all he needed to know. He rushed home to find it ripped asunder. Nothing of their life together remained whole, inside or out. There were no signs of his wife or child. Will expected to find their bodies, but not finding them gave him some hope.

At Ram's funeral parlor, an inconsolable Sadie tore at him as soon as he stepped through the door, alternating between beating Will and trying to gouge his eyes out. Klara Fenski and her teenage daughter, Martha, there to comfort Sadie, grabbed her hands finally, keeping her at bay.

"What happened? Where are Sarah and Trina?"

Sadie composed herself enough to speak.

"This is all your fault! You and Forrest. If you'd done left

Kettle alone, he might've bothered us awhile, and then moved on when he saw there was nothing else for him here. But no! You had to play the hero, and you just *had* to drag Ram along. Wanted to make a big name for yourself, didn't ya? Bigger than Forrest. Bigger than God! Look where it got us!"

Will grabbed her shoulders. "Where. Is. My. Wife?"

"They took her. Kettle's unholy creatures!" Martha shouted, fear cascading as tears over her cheeks.

Klara recited, "'And it is said in the last days, the dead shall rise and walk the earth.'" She pointed at Will. "You've brought on the apocalypse. Kettle has unleashed demons. He is in league with Satan! And it's all because of you!"

Will looked at Sadie. "What is she talking about?"

Sadie wept. "Kettle came back into town. He had men with him. His gang. Some were alive. Others…"

Not understanding, Will asked, "He brought dead bodies with him?"

"Walking corpses," Martha described. "Their souls in hell, but their bodies moved, possessed by demons!"

"That can't…that can't be…"

"Tell that to the dozens who saw them, Sheriff!" Klara said. "Tell that to my husband who soiled his cloth trying to pray them away. Tell that to your friend still lying in the street."

"They came for Ram, and he stood his ground," Sadie interjected. "He kept firing, but they wouldn't go down. Th-they weren't alive. They swarmed him, about six of them. He k-kept fighting as they tore his body apart." She sobbed. "Kettle told us to not touch the body. That it would be a lesson to us all. Not even death would stop him."

Will thought back to what Ram had said about the voodoo man. There had to be a connection. Could he really turn back death?

"Sarah and Trina. What happened?"

Sadie could barely get the words out. "H-he took them.

Left a message for you to come to Crab Rock, alone. Or he'd kill them."

Will turned and double-timed it from the funeral parlor.

Sadie followed him to the porch. "You bring them back! Even if you have to die yourself. Don't come back without them! You hear me, Ragsdale? Don't show your face in this town again if you don't bring them back!"

Sadie's words echoed in Will's ears as he loaded his saddlebags with more weapons than he thought wise to carry. He had no plan for his return to Crab Rock, only a target.

He stormed into the Sagebrush.

"Who's with me?"

No one would meet his eyes.

"They've taken my family. *Your* families will be next." He spoke slowly, but forcefully, "Please. Who is with me?"

Frank Chalker, the town's blacksmith, spoke up, "We've seen what happens when someone rides with you, Sheriff. Best you be off, now. Go."

Pawel said a few un-Christianly words at Will.

Several more got up and drove the sheriff from the saloon, throwing insults, accusations, and threats if he didn't leave well enough alone. Hadn't he already done enough?

"Cowards!" Will spat on the ground. "You let them walk into our town. Steal our women. Kill good men. Take whatever they want, including my child. And you didn't lift a finger to help? You hide, afraid for your lives!" He thought back to Levi's funeral. "Was it all lies, Owner's vow that you swore to uphold?" Will pointed in the direction of Crab Rock. "There's the darkness. Right there! Is no one going to stand beside me and be the light this town needs?"

Chalker retorted, "Kettle's got undead or something riding with him now. We can't fight that!"

No one spoke, nor moved, nor barely breathed.

Disgusted, Will removed his badge and tossed it to the dirt.

"Y'all are dead to me. Dead as those things Kettle calls men."

———

WILL MOVED FORWARD THROUGH THE BRUSH much the same way he and Ram had the other night, painfully putting into perspective why he was back there so soon. The patrols were no longer two men marching side by side, but one living and one undead creature that used to be a member of the Crab Rock Gang.

The resurrected outlaw's eyes never blinked. That was the biggest difference between those two, that and a pallor to the skin that suggested no warmth existed that body. They seemed self-aware, though, as one paused mere feet from where Will hid, questioning, then eventually deciding to move on.

Finally reaching a vantage point, Will spotted the two he and Ram had killed by the flapping neck flesh and then counted six more in various states of damage and dismemberment; from missing arms to crushed skulls. Not all the gang had been killed, several still-living outlaws could be seen. Those among the still living were Kettle's voodoo priest and Kettle himself.

Will watched the walking corpses and deduced they didn't hunt by sight or smell. One of the outlaws teased an undead, taken a step towards it, then stepping back. Step forward. Step back. The creature only reacted when the outlaw got close enough to it. They must have a sense for the living, as if his beating heart drew them. That changed Will's tactics.

Sadie said that guns had little effect, but Will brought Forrest's 4-bore and his own Sharps Big 50. What would the dead do without their heads?

Somebody behind Will kicked a rock, so he rolled and drew. A Wiipukepaya scout held his hands up to show he wasn't armed. Will uncocked his sidearm with a sigh of relief. The scout motioned for Will to follow, and the former lawman figured he had nothing to lose.

---

THE LATE AFTERNOON SUN ALWAYS MADE THE RED rock of the area glow, as if the stone monuments absorbed the heat and then released it back into the world.

William Ragsdale walked right up to Kettle's camp unarmed. He hadn't set two feet into the area before the walking corpses surrounded him. They didn't attack, just subdued him and led him forward. He tested their grip on him. It was as if his arms were in irons. On the smashed rocks that circled the front of the cave, blood and scratches coated many of the largest boulders. The dead must've dug Kettle out.

A devil's laugh bounced off the red sandstone walls of the cave.

"You're late."

Kettle's granite form stepped out from the shadows. Built like a lumberjack, Kettle's muscles appeared ready to burst from the seams of his shirt. He cinched his belt closed as he approached Will. "I've already finished. I expected you to hear her screams when you arrived and you do something stupid." He grabbed Will's chin and tilted it up. "I really wanted you to do something stupid."

Understanding the implications of Kettle's words, Will lurched at the outlaw, pulling with everything he had to break free. His futility brought amusement to Kettle's face. Will cursed and foamed at the mouth. "You cocksucker! You're a dead man! You hear me? If you hurt her in any way, I'll rip your balls off with my bare hands!"

Kettle moved to a chair that sat waiting for him on his imaginary stage. "Oh, she struggled at first, mind you. But I think by the second time, she quite enjoyed it. Turns out she'd only been with boys, not a real man like myself."

"Sarah! Sarah! I'm here! Where is she, you fucking monster?"

The outlaw made a motion, and two of his living gang members went into the cave. Moments later they dragged Sarah Ragsdale's partially conscious body out. Her clothes were torn and, when they laid her out in front of Kettle, Will could see blood on the inside of her leg. She made little choked sobs, and her husband couldn't tell if she knew what was happening anymore.

"Oh, my god! Sarah. Sarah." Tears of futility ran down Will's cheek. He shook them free and glared at Kettle. "You goddamn bastard. Trina, you better not have…"

The voodoo man followed shortly after, pushing Trina forward. He had hands on her shoulder and steered her until they stood beside Kettle. Cheeks stained from crying, Trina held her rag doll tight against her chest, like a cross to ward off evil.

"I haven't done anything to the girl, yet. She's too young. After you're dead, I plan to sell her to a whore house. Once she bleeds, I plan to be the first one to taste her flesh." Kettle gave a pensive look. "I wonder which one will be better: mother or daughter?" He glowered over Will. "I'm sure it'll be your daughter. She'll be fresh, unspoiled. And, after she watches what I do to her mommy and daddy…obedient."

Will gnashed his teeth; rage boiled up from inside. He'd make the deal with any devil, pray to any demon, to get his hands around Kettle's throat.

"When I dropped your broken body off in Drowned Horse, had I'd known then you had such delightful ladies at your disposal, I would've taken them sooner. That sheriff of yours might've come alone, and I wouldn't have needed to have Noqoi's voodoo man here bring so many of my men back to life."

"What?" Will couldn't believe what Kettle had just said. "Noqoi?"

Kettle cackled. "Yes, pup. Your great enemy. The

gambling god himself. I got immortality thanks to his hatred for Forrest. When I gutted your sheriff, I won our bet. Noqoi introduced me to Etienne and showed me what the man could do."

As if to accent the words Kettle spoke, thunder rolled in the distance. A storm rolled through the valley toward them. Everyone alive could taste death in the air. Gang members, licking their dry lips, backed away from their boss, the voodoo man held tighter to his charge, and even the walking dead seemed nervous.

Will's head dropped to his chest and in a voice, barely over a whisper, he pleaded, "What do you want? I'll do anything. Kill me, but just let them go."

Kettle leaned forward. "I'm sorry. What was that?"

"I said, 'You win!' Take the damn town. Take whatever you want. Take me, my life. Just don't hurt them anymore."

The madman stood. "I don't need your permission for that, lawman! I never did. You tried to kill me. Nearly succeeded. What I need now is payback."

"Then take it. Do whatever you want. Beat me senseless. Kill me in the most spiteful way you can imagine. You've already done enough to my wife and daughter. Have mercy."

Kettle stood, grabbed Sarah by the hair, and yanked her head up, causing her to yelp.

"Sarah!"

"No, I don't think I'll let them go. Your wife will recover, and I think I can get some more use out of her before she's unable to walk. And I already told you what I have planned for you little girl." Kettle smacked his lips loudly. "No, I think I will kill you, just as you suggest. Slowly. Painfully. And all the time, you'll know that I have your family from now until I tire of them." He jerked his head toward the cave. "I nearly lost all hope in there, y'know. Luckily, I had my witch doctor with me. He didn't like being trapped any more than I did."

To accentuate the point, the voodoo man slid his hands closer to Trina's neck.

"He brought my dead men back to life. Controls them now, he does. They don't feel pain like we do. Dug us a nice tunnel out."

Will's head, previously hanging low, slowly looked up at Kettle with a strange mix of satisfaction, causing Kettle's brow to furrow.

"So, the voodoo man controls the corpses, huh?"

"What?"

"Your lease's been revoked, Kettle."

Will whistled loudly which was answered by two whooshes as a pair of arrows flew in. One struck the voodoo man in his upper torso. He fell back against the rock, releasing Trina. The stocky man staggered, but kept standing.

Will cursed it wasn't a killing blow, but it was enough that the corpses that held him loosened their grip. Will broke free and ran. The stick of TNT that burned on the second arrow had a short fuse. Kettle and his men scrambled. The explosion blew several of the once-living killers apart.

Kettle grabbed Sarah and dragged her to her feet. He held her like a shield in front of him, one meaty arm wrapped around her waist, his pistol drawn, and poking her in the side.

More explosions followed as the Wiipukepaya took out several more of the walking abominations.

"Call them off, Sheriff! I'll kill her! You know I will!"

Awareness returned to Sarah face. Her eyes darted wildly, finding her husband. Shame, anger, and pain marred the face that once only showed him love and laughter.

Will reached a hand out toward her.

Sarah mouthed, "Save Trina" and then reached behind her to where Kettle's Apache knife pressed against back. She fumbled it free from its sheath and, cocking an arm behind her head, cut Jimmy Kettle from ear to jaw. The outlaw threw Sarah down, holding his free hand to his gushing face. Snarling, he unloaded his pistol into Will's wife.

Noise stopped. Will could no longer hear the cries as *Paya* appeared everywhere to shoot the living and dead members of the Crab Rock Gang. He couldn't hear the moans as the walking corpses attacked, shrugging off damage, and ripping warriors apart.

All Will could hear was the blood pumping through his ears as his wife's arm dropped limp and lay there motionless. Will crawled across the ground to his wife, clinging to the hope that he'd find a spark of life there. Finding none, he pulled her to his chest and cradled her.

Sound returned as Trina called to him.

"DADDY!"

Wildly, he searched. Kettle was gone. The monsters fought the Yavapai warriors, one corpse to five warriors, and the corpses were getting the upper hand. Their number seemed to increase, and Will swore he caught a fallen Paya rising out of the corner of his eye.

The Voodoo man darted into the cave with Trina.

Will found a Colt lying on the ground and set his grief aside to go get his daughter.

---

THE TUNNELS DESCENDED INTO DARKNESS. AN escaping flicker of light below meant Will would also need a torch to follow them. He grabbed a lantern that had busted glass, but still contained oil. He lit it, knowing it'd make him a target.

A dozen feet. Fifty feet. Two hundred feet. He lost track of how far down he went. The path opened up on a cavern easily as big as the Sagebrush. Stalagmites and stalactites made a cobweb of stone throughout. In the center, a locomotive-sized pit yawned.

"Dad—" The word was cut off, but a heavily-accented, "OW!" followed it.

The voodoo priest stepped out from behind a pillar, shaking his hand. Trina looked scared but she smiled when she saw her father. The black man took a knife and pressed it against Trina's collarbone. The wound in his chest still seeped, but he didn't show any signs of slowing or passing out.

"Let her go, and you get to go. Simple as that." Will had the borrowed gun drawn, but both he and the voodoo man knew he wouldn't pull the trigger. So he changed tactics. "What do you want?"

With a Creole accent, he said, "Yore head. You done left me in a hole to die. Now I'm gonna leave you in one to die. I dunna care about da girl. Kettle can have her or da Reds. I jess wanna see you jump in dat hole over dere. Den I let da girl go."

"My life for hers? You swear?"

"I swear."

Will walked over the edge and peered over. It was blacker than a starless night. He kicked a rock and never heard it hit bottom. He turned to say goodbye to his daughter when a large explosion rocked the ceiling above.

The voodoo man smirked. "I lay a spell on the whole area. Any who die around here come back as zhombie. Da Reds be killin' da living, dey come back. The zhombies be killin' da reds, *dey* come back. Hope everyone got enough boom powder."

Another explosion and one of the stalagmites near the black man fell to the ground, forcing him to move Trina and himself closer to the pit.

Will seized the opportunity. He dropped his lantern, extinguishing it, then drew and fired, knocking the torch from voodoo man's hand and down into the abyss.

"And I hope you can see in the dark."

The room went black. Will fired a second shot at the spot where he visualized the wizard to be. The man cried out in pain, but Will didn't hear a follow-up "thump" indicating he'd been killed.

"Trina! Crawl to me, baby!"

The former lawman fired twice more. Once to find the voodoo man in the flash, the second to shoot that direction. He missed, but he caught Trina moving toward him. Will crouched down and crab-walked her way. A clink of metal hitting stone reverberated through the cavern, and Will realized his enemy stabbed the ground in hopes of piercing the girl.

*Two bullets left,* Will thought.

He fired once more, finding the villain poised to bring the knife down on Trina's back.

Will leapt forward, covering his daughter. The knife entered near his left shoulder blade. In agony, he twisted, pulling the voodoo man over him. They wrestled, rolling one way and then the other. The blade tore its way out, causing Will more pain as his flesh shredded.

Will lost track of where the pit was until his leg crossed the rim and hovered over the chasm. A moan reverberated through the cave, and it wasn't one of theirs. The shuffle step of one of the undead told Will the voodoo man had called for reinforcements.

"You heat dat? Dat's death coming for you and yore little girl."

Will got his legs under the larger man and donkey-kicked him up and over his head. The voodoo priest sailed into the pit and Will said, "Not if you die first."

Will had no less than a breath to enjoy his victory before he heard his daughter.

"Daddy! Help!"

"Trina!"

He had no idea where they were. He scrambled around until he found the lantern and relit it. The zhombie held Trina and stood poised in mid-action near the edge, like its last orders were cut off. Terrified, Will cautiously moved closer to his daughter. The zhombie was one of the guards he and Ram bled.

"Easy now, big boy. Don't do anything you'll regret." Not that talking to it would help the situation. To Trina, he said,

"It's okay, sweetie. Just hold your hands out for daddy. I'm coming to get you."

Bravely, she extended her arms, rag doll fisted in one.

"I need both hands, honey. Can you let Miss Molly go for a moment?"

She hesitated, unsure what to do. Slowly, she nodded and released the doll.

Another explosion rocked the surface world above.

The zhombie fell backwards over the edge.

Will dove for Trina, but he wasn't close enough. Their fingers grazed, and she vanished into the black.

Her scream taking his heart along with it.

Will Ragsdale wailed, his anguish magnified by the cave's echo. He rocked back and forth, Trina's rag doll clutched tightly to his chest.

---

THE ZHOMBIES FINALLY STOPPED MOVING UPON the death of their master. The remaining Paya dismembering them with no problems after that. They followed it up with a purification ritual. The smell of burnt carcasses filled the air.

The Paya scout that had fetched Will pushed his shoulder flesh together and stitched it closed. He wrapped a bandage about Will's neck and torso and told him that he needed a doctor to properly mend it.

But Will didn't acknowledge him. He walked to where he'd left his horse and mounted. By the time he'd gotten to Oak Creek, rain fell in sheets. Oblivious to the cold, Will let it numb his body as a partner to his soul.

Kettle had fled this way, up Oak Creek Canyon, thinking only a crazy man would follow him. The trail rose steeply the farther up the trail he rode, becoming increasingly treacherous. Will found spots where Kettle's mount slid in the mud. Within an hour, Will tracked two sets of prints: man and horse. Will dismounted and grabbed his rifle and two pistols. He wacked the horse's butt and sent her back down the way they came. It wasn't five minutes later that the former lawman moved out of the way as a second horse come down the trail.

Kettle was close. Even through the rain, the increasing dark, Will had a sense of him, as if their fates were tied.

A shape moved ahead. A deer, heading up and away from the loosening soil.

The blow from above sent Will to his knees.

Two-fisted.

Hard.

It landed on Will's shoulder—bad one—and he roared. The next strike came from a boot to his back, and Will went all the way to the ground. He felt the stitches in his back pop free. Blood flowed. Will didn't have a lot of time.

He rolled to his right, missing the bullet at his head. Will kicked upwards and knocked the wet gun from Kettle's hand. He kicked again, boots landing on Kettle's gut and forcing him back a couple feet; just enough for Will to get up.

Kettle drew the long Apache blade and squared off with Will. Sarah's wound to his face no longer bled, but it burned red across a wet, angry face.

"Don't 'spose there's much to say at this point, is there?" Kettle asked.

Will drew his Bowie, shorter than the one the outlaw wielded.

"No. I recon there ain't."

They circled each other, gauging their mettle, neither at their best.

Will went low, hoping to gut the larger man. Kettle tucked in, barely avoiding the knife, his own swing taking off Will's hat. Will jumped back as Kettle kicked forward, but he took the boot to his shin. It stung, but not bad.

Kettle bull-rushed Will, slamming into him before he could get his knife positioned. They hit the sidewall together and air escaped Will's lungs.

In retaliation, Will brought up his knee as hard as he could, hitting close enough to Kettle's nutsack that the outlaw retreated. The larger man swung the blade around, Will ducking in the nick of time. Will's blade connected with Kettle's leg, sticking in and coming out bloody. The outlaw grunted, but managed to slice Will's right arm.

They stepped back from each other. Bleeding and woozy, they staggered, trying to stay upright.

Lightning struck a tree a ways from them. Will, facing that direction, was momentarily blinded by the flash. A dark shape moved towards him. Will dropped his knife, using both hands to grab at Kettle's blade arm. The force was too much, and he could feel Kettle's blade pierce his left side down to the bone. The sharp pain instilled inhuman strength. Will rammed his good shoulder into Kettle, taking them both to the ground.

The weight of their bodies caused a chunk of the trail to drop off into the ravine below. Will had Kettle's arm pinned to the ground, but the other was free to land punches to Will's kidney.

The gorge hung next to them, and Will had a momentary flash of Trina as she fell into the darkness. Rage strengthened him, and he twisted the outlaw's arm, forcing him to drop the knife.

Will rained blows on Kettle's face; one after another, after another. Kettle's nose and jaw broke. His teeth cut Ragsdale's hand as he pummeled the defeated man's mouth. Kettle held up his hands to defend himself, but nothing stopped the onslaught.

He pictured his wife's eyes the moment before her death. He recalled the way his heart sank when he found his best friend laying in the street. The fear in Trina's eyes. His own failure to save all of them. Forrest's body.

He didn't notice as he and Kettle slipped closer to the muddy edge.

Kettle got out a garbled, "Stop!" just as they both went over.

They landed on a lower level of the winding trail. The former sheriff propped himself up along the sidewall, forcing himself to his feet. Kettle clawed his way to all fours.

Jimmy Kettle, drawing from reserves no man should have had, lifted himself to kneeling, a hold-out Derringer in his hand.

Ragsdale, the borrowed Colt still on his hip, drew faster.

Thunder muffled the gunshot, but the blossoming bullet wound in Kettle's chest proved Ragsdale the better shot. Kettle wobbled for the moment and then toppled over the edge. The former lawman watched him plummet three-hundred-feet into the raging waters of Oak Creek, swallowed whole and gone.

Will sat down, the deluge doing nothing to fill the well inside him. Nor did Kettle's death seal that hole big as the Arizona territory and as cursed as Noqoi's soul.

---

Three Months Later

FRANK CHALKER POUNDED THE GLOWING-RED horseshoe ten more times before dropping it into the water to cool. It'd been three months since the end of Jimmy Kettle and the Crab Rock Gang, and business had finally picked up again.

Oh, sure, there were still rumors about Drowned Horse being the place where the dead roamed free, but the town had always been the stuff of scuttlebutt and gossip. Sheriff Behran stopped by from time to time, but Owner had not christened a new sheriff yet. After what happened to the last two, there weren't any volunteers.

It was fine, though. Peace reigned over the town—a pleasant change.

"Pa? Mom wants you in for dinner."

"Be right in, Nate," Frank called to his son.

Chalker thought about his boy. The kid hadn't taken to smithing yet, but he had one hell of a dead-eye when it came to hunting. Maybe he could get the boy interested in making rifles instead of railroad spikes, then they could expand the business.

*Chalker and Son Weaponry*, he thought. *Has a nice ring to it.*

The sound of a boot scuffing the dirt came from the entrance to the workshop.

"Almost done—"

When Frank turned, his blood ran cold, the towel he had been cleaning his hands off with floated to the ground.

"Sheriff Ragsdale."

No expression showed on the man's face.

"Not Sheriff anymore. Y'all seen to that."

Frank held up his hands. "Will, listen..."

But the young man didn't seem to be in a listening mood. He drew a pistol and aimed it at the blacksmith's chest. Frank caught a glimpse of something tied to the belt opposite the holster.

A rag doll.

"It wasn't my fault. T'was none of our faults, what happened to your family. Kettle, he had monsters. How did you expect..."

The man cocked the gun.

"Be reasonable, Will. This isn't what your family would have wanted."

"They're dead. So's William Ragsdale. So are you and every man who stood by and let Kettle leave this town alive."

The gunshot drew Nate from the house in a sprint. The man, gun still drawn, reflexively brought it around cocked until he realized it was Chalker's kid.

Nate spotted his father's body and ran to it yelling, "Pa? Pa! Pa!"

The man tracked the boy, deciding whether to cover his

tracks. He'd hoped not to be spotted so quickly. He chose to holster the gun and walk away.

Young Nate Chalker called after him, tears in his voice.

"Why? Why!"

The man stopped. "Revenge. Isn't it always?"

The boy cradled his father's head and between sobs asked, "W-who are you?"

The man peered back over his shoulder.

"Tell everyone a vengeful spirit has returned from his grave. Tell them...

"The Rag Doll Kid's a coming."

# INTERLUDE
## DRAGON DRAW

Spring, 1872

RENOWNED GAMBLER SEBASTIAN MAHER GAVE THE command to his dragon, Caitlyn, to set him down just outside the cave. If he had read the stolen journal correctly, this had to be the place.

He thought it'd be tougher finding the location, but the town of Drowned Horse was a mess. First, their sheriff died, then their undertaker, and finally the deputy, while trying to be a sheriff, went mad and killed a bunch of men in town in revenge. He'd vanished up into the Mogollons, and no one seemed much inclined to find him.

The owner of the Sagebrush Saloon, who'd taken a nasty beating at the hands of some outlaws, barely functioned. Word was that the sheriff was like a father and the deputy like a son. No word on whether the undertaker was like a brother, but clearly, the man had a trunk full of trouble.

That allowed Maher to do what he did best without a watchful eye tracking his movements. He gambled. He lost when he needed to. He bartered for information. He listened to the tales, the legends, until he found what he needed.

With no one really paying attention to the jail and sheriff's office, Maher slipped in and found the journal he'd been told contained all the secrets of the area, especially the person he sought. The pages were unreadable, but tucked between them were notes, loose translations, and suspicions.

He held up one particular sheet and compared it to the cave drawings in front of him. They were a match!

Caitlyn perched on the ledge just outside the cave. He went to her beautiful face and kissed her cheek. "Good work, girl."

The piasa cooed as she did when he showed her affection. Maher had raised her from an egg, given to him by his father just as his father had been given one. Caitlyn and Maher were a team, inseparable. She kept him safe, and he did his best to keep her hidden from the world, except for the times he needed her to keep *him* safe.

It was Maher's sister that'd told him about Drowned Horse, the curse, and the being responsible for it. And with that news, Maher left a lucrative gambling career in the south to come west.

You see, Sebastian Maher considered himself the best gambler on Earth. He needed to know if he was the best in all reality.

Maher went to the crate he had Caitlyn carry up there with them and pried open the side. A table tumbled out with lots of other equipment. He set up the table and placed the items on top.

Decks of cards. A faro board. A tiger box. Chess pieces. Checkers. Twenty other games he arranged on the table. When he finished, he went back to Caitlyn and retrieved two chairs. He set them on either side of the table, and sat in one.

"Ah'm ready," he said to the wind.

Maher blinked. He and Caitlyn were no longer in the cave, but on a high plateau overlooking the Arizona desert.

The gambler drew his gun on reflex, stunned at the change of venue.

Maher blinked several times, checking out his surroundings. When he looked back across the table, an old native sat in the opposite chair. He was like no other Indian he'd ever seen, dressed in poncho, snakeskin boots, turquoise earrings, and a stovepipe hat.

Maher knew immediately he'd found the being he'd hoped to.

"Noqoìlpi, Ah presume?"

Maher holstered his gun knowing it was worthless.

"Indeed." The weathered god smiled wildly. "What shall we play first?"

---

TWELVE HOURS LATER, NOQOI HAD BEAT MAHER AT every challenge. What supernatural tricks he'd employed were beyond the understanding of mortals such as himself. At least the god of gamblers had been kind enough to provide light and food for him. Caitlyn had no trouble securing her own.

Maher lost all the money he'd brought, and he'd brought it all, every bit he'd ever earned as a gambler. He also lost all the jewelry, gold, and artwork he'd "procured" thinking it might tempt the gambling god or at least have him find them amusing.

"Well, Ah believe you plum tapped me out, sir. I have nothing left to bet." Maher held his hands out and flipped them over in the universal sign of being broke.

Noqoi rubbed his chin. "Oh, you still have plenty to bet. Ah must admit, your skill is quite admirable for a human. And especially considering you came to me honestly, not like some of the other humans Ah've played against. No sign you've been blessed by any of my brother or sister gods."

Maher mentally kicked himself that he hadn't even considered that option.

"No, sir. If Ah aim to be the best ever, then Ah couldn't employ tricks of such nature. How would we ever know?"

Noqoi ruminated on that. "Yes, how would we?" The god raised an eyebrow. "You do have one possession you have still not bet yet."

Slowly, Maher followed Noqoi's gaze over to Caitlyn.

"No, sir. No way in hell." He stood up. "Caitlyn is not a possession. She is a partner and Ah would never bet a living being in a game of chance."

But the god continued. "Well, you do have some morals, don't you? Let me dangle a bauble and see if you change your mind."

Over Noqoi's head, a swirling vortex appeared. In it, a vision developed. It was Maher, master of his own casino in Monte-Carlo. Maher strutted around as if he were Prince Charles III.

"You would be." Noqoi stood next to him now. "All the money. All the power. Every player from around the world would come to you to play against the best, which you would be, if you beat me in our final game."

The stuff that dreams were made of. Maher swooned for a moment. Never had he thought, even if he had won, that this could be the outcome.

Caitlyn, studying him, grew concerned and mewed.

That brought Maher back from the illusion. The image shattered, and he stepped away from Noqoi.

"No. It's not going to happen."

The god *tsked*. "But I must insist."

Maher drew not his gun, but his finger as a gun and pointed it at the ancient Indian.

"Do not make me do this, sir. Ah lost, fair and square, and we can walk away from here without further issue. Ah'm content to lick my wounds and strive to get better. But if you think Ah will put Caitlyn in any harm's way…"

Noqoi crossed his arms, smirking. "What do you intend to do with that?"

"This." Maher pulled the trigger and his dragon, Caitlyn, shot up into the sky. She swooped down, red and black-feathered wings flapping fast and hard. Her fire breath scorched the earth where the gambling god stood, leaving nothing but ash.

Yet, Noqoi walked out of the fireball, unscathed, grinning, and clapping his hands slowly.

"Excellent, Mr. Maher. About time. Now, the real games may begin."

Another window, but this one a portal. Through it, a dragon, resplendent with multicolored feathers under its wings, appeared above its master. It was similar to Caitlyn in many ways, but instead of four legs, it only had the two front ones.

Maher swallowed hard. That was a male. He'd been told by his father the last one had died, leaving Caitlyn as the final member of her species. And yet, Noqoi had summoned one with a thought.

"You're not the only one with half of a set." Noqoi raised his hand and pointed his own finger gun at Maher. "Shall we see whose dragon is quicker on the draw?"

The gambler understood that he'd been played from the start.


To Be Continued in…
The Drowned Horse Chronicle
Volume Two – The Lawless Years

# IF YOU LIKE THIS YOU MAY ALSO ENJOY: THE GIDEON THORN SERIES

## THE COMPLETE WEIRD WESTERN SERIES BY MICHAEL NEWTON

**Gideon Thorn: The Complete Weird Western Series**

**Michael Newton's GIDEON THORN is a cross between *The X-Files* and B.N. Rundell's *The Plainsman Western Series*. The series is full of classic western action and adventure, as well as paranormal suspense. Now available as a complete set for the first time.**

Gideon Thorn, survivor at age two of the unknown 'animal' attack that massacred his family in Kansas Territory, roams the West in search of answers to his personal tragedy and other unsolved mysteries of seemingly paranormal origin.

The complete series includes the following titles:

**Skinwalker (Gideon Thorn 1)**

**Leviathan Rising (Gideon Thorn 2)**

**Ghost Town (Gideon Thorn 3)**

**Mountain Devils (Gideon Thorn 4)**

**Soul Slayers (Gideon Thorn 5)**

**Hallowed Ground (Gideon Thorn 6)**

**Night Flyers (Gideon Thorn 7)**

**Empty Graves (Gideon Thorn 8)**

**Rip Tide (Gideon Thorn 9)**

**Warpath: A Weird Western (Gideon Thorn 10)**

**Fans of *The X-Files* and classic western action and adventure will be sure to love the suspenseful, engaging writing of Michael Newton**

*AVAILABLE NOW*

# ABOUT THE AUTHOR

**David Boop** is a Denver-based speculative fiction author & editor. He's also an award-winning essayist, and screenwriter. Before turning to fiction, David worked as a DJ, film critic, journalist, and actor. As Editor-in-Chief at IntraDenver.net, David's team was on the ground at Columbine making them the first internet only newspaper to cover such an event. That year, they won an award for excellence from the Colorado Press Association for their design and coverage.

David's debut novel, the sci-fi/noir She Murdered Me with Science, returned to print in 2017 from WordFire Press. (Simultaneously, he self-published a prequel novella, A Whisper to a Scheme.) His second novel, The Soul Changers, is a serialized Victorian Horror novel set in Pinnacle Entertainment's world of Rippers Resurrected. David edited the bestselling weird western anthology, Straight Outta Tombstone, for Baen, and has followed with Straight Outta Deadwood and Straight Outta Dodge City. David is prolific in short fiction with many short stories and two short films to his credit. Additionally, he does a flash fiction mystery series on Gumshoereview.com called The Trace Walker Temporary Mysteries (the first collection is available now.) He's published across several genres including media tie-ins for Predator (nominated for the 2018 Scribe Award), The Green Hornet, The Black Bat and Veronica Mars.

David works in game design, as well. He's written for the Savage Worlds RPG for their Flash Gordon (nominated for an Origins Award) and Deadlands: Noir titles. He owns

Longshot Productions, a multimedia company specializing in books, games, and short animated videos.

His third go at a "real" degree landed him Summa Cum Laude in the Creative Writing program at UC-Denver. He also is part-time temp worker and believer. His hobbies include film noir, anime, the Blues and Mayan History.